They were caught up in the winds of change . . .
and in the eternal rhythms of the heart

MEDICINE WOLF—From a brave child rescued by wolves to a questing, courageous woman, she was the shining hope of the Cheyenne people—and the cherished love of a forbidden man.

BEAR PAW—One of the plains' fiercest warriors, he was feared and respected by every enemy but one—his own hatred.

WHITE HORSE—A traitor to his people, he had an obsession for Medicine Wolf that would turn him into a twisted, dangerous renegade.

SUMMER MOON—A Cheyenne maiden who had only one weakness: her passion for an unworthy man.

TOM PRESCOTT—A missionary's son, he heard the song of the wolf and secretly loved the woman who taught him its power.

SONG OF THE WOLF

Rosanne Bittner

BANTAM BOOKS

NEW YORK · TORONTO · LONDON · SYDNEY · AUCKLAND

SONG OF THE WOLF
A Bantam Fanfare Book/March 1992

Grateful acknowledgment is made to reprint an excerpt from BLACK ELK SPEAKS, by John G. Neihardt, University of Nebraska Press. Used by permission.

FANFARE *and the portrayal of a boxed ''ff'' are trademarks of Bantam Books, a division of Bantam Doubleday Dell Publishing Group, Inc.*

ISBN 0-553-29014-2

Published simultaneously in the United States and Canada

Bantam Books are published by Bantam Books, a division of Bantam Doubleday Dell Publishing Group, Inc. Its trademark, consisting of the words ''Bantam Books'' and the portrayal of a rooster, is Registered in U.S. Patent and Trademark Office and in other countries. Marca Registrada. Bantam Books, 666 Fifth Avenue, New York, New York 10103.

PRINTED IN THE UNITED STATES OF AMERICA
RAD   0 9 8 7 6 5 4 3 2 1

For my mother, Ethel Ardella (Williams) Reris, whose maternal grandmother was a full-blood Potowatomie Indian. My mother and I both share a deep respect for Native Americans and for a way of life that has vanished . . . or has it? In the hearts of many, the old ways still live.

From the author . . .

The major characters in this novel and their personal life stories are fictitious; however, the historical background on which this story is based is true.

Song of the Wolf is the story of a beautiful People, who were often much more civilized and wiser than the educated Europeans who nearly destroyed them. I have researched the Cheyenne and Sioux for many years, and have strived to show the Indian culture and spirit to the best of my knowledge. I hope I have done justice to the unique spirit, wisdom, and sense of humor of our Native Americans, who over centuries of adversity have managed to keep alive their old customs and language; a People who, in spite of sometimes massive efforts to assimilate them into European society, have clung to their identity and their spiritual beliefs, and who have realized the ultimate triumph over tragedy.

e-maha-nemeneo-o (They are all singing)

Part 1

———————

The nation's hoop is broken and scattered. There is no center any longer, and the sacred tree is dead. . . .

Black Elk
Oglala Sioux
(From *Black Elk Speaks*)

Hear the softly playing flute, if you can.

Set your mind away from today and let it wander to another time, when the air was pure, the sky a deeper blue, a time when the buffalo represented the universe and was treated with reverence and respect, a time when a nation of people walked as one with nature and understood that Grandmother Earth was the giver of life and provided man and animal alike with all that they needed.

Hear the distant drums.

Feel the wind sweeping down from the mountains and smelling of pine.

Hear Grandfather Eagle cry as he glides on gentle winds, looking down upon the dark-skinned children who move across the plains and mountains, following the seasons and the buffalo.

Hear it all. See it all. Perhaps one day life will be like that again. Perhaps the time will come when again we hear the song of the wolf. . . .

———————

Chapter One

1846

Sweet Water could not concentrate on picking the wild berries. She was too excited about being a part of the journey to the north country, where snow remained on the tops of mountains even during the Moon When the Choke-cherries Ripen, one of the hottest months of the year. She was proud to already be six summers in age. Life was becoming an adventure, and as had been done since she was born, her People, the Cheyenne, had come north again the past spring to gather food and hunt buffalo.

The winter had been spent on the open plains to the south, where Sweet Water and her twelve-year-old brother, Runner, and three-year-old sister, Smiling Girl, had shared many days and nights bundled in their family's tipi, sitting around a fire and listening respectfully to their father, Arrow Maker, tell stories about ghost spirits, or about his hunting exploits or how many times he had counted coup against an enemy.

Sweet Water liked to remember those good times, her mother, Star Woman, cooking buffalo meat and turnips preserved from a previous summer of hunting and digging, bellies full, a warm fire. They were good memories, and Sweet Water smiled as she picked off another dark, wild berry and put it into her mouth. She was supposed to be filling her basket, but it was very hard not to want to taste them right away. She let the sweet juice please her tongue and help relieve her thirst, then glanced at her mother, who was picking berries from another bush.

"*Saaa,*" Star Woman scolded teasingly. "We must share these berries with your brother and little sister. If you keep putting them in your own belly, our basket will never be full, and we will never get back to the village."

Sweet Water felt her cheeks grow hot from being caught. She hurriedly began picking more, determined to fill her basket as quickly as possible. She remembered that just this morning her father had warned her and her mother not to take too long picking, and not to stray too far from the village. They were close to where *O-O-O-tan* lived, the Crow Indians, hated enemy of the Cheyenne.

Sweet Water had learned that some humans were natural enemies, like the *ve-ho-e.* For now the strange white men had not given her people much trouble, but some, like her father, believed their presence in the vast domain of the Cheyenne was a bad omen. She remembered the first time she had seen a white man. It was the summer before this one, when her people went to a place on the southern plains called Bent's Fort. She supposed it was because those men looked so different that the memory of them had remained clear in her mind, men with eyes blue as the sky, faces pale, or burned red from the sun; men with hair on their faces. She wondered why the *ve-ho-e* let their face hair grow yet cut the hair on their heads short.

There are many things about the white man that make no sense, her father had told her once. *Only this do I know, that they cannot be trusted. I had a dream once, that many white men came to our country and trampled us into the earth. We must always pay attention to our dreams, Sweet Water. They warn us of the future.*

Arrow Maker had also told her the story of the Cheyenne Savior, Sweet Medicine, and the prophecy He told His People. Strangers called Earth Men would appear, men with light-colored skin and powerful ways, men with short hair who spoke no Indian tongue. *Follow nothing these Earth Men do,* Sweet Medicine had warned His people long ago. The prophet had even said that one day the buffalo would disappear. Sweet Water was sure that could not happen in her own lifetime, for the buffalo were so plentiful that the great herds she remembered seeing on their journey north had seemed to stretch across the plains clear into the horizon.

She did not like to think about Sweet Medicine's dire predictions. Life was too good for now, too exciting. Soon her people would move on to the Black Hills, called *Paha-Sapa* by their Sioux friends. There many Cheyenne would gather to celebrate the Sun Dance. Sweet Water could hardly wait, for it would be a time of dancing and feasting and singing. It was just about all her mother and father and Old Grandmother talked about, and even now many of the men of her own clan were off hunting buffalo to help insure there would be plenty of food for the nearly week-long event. Afterward there would be more hunting, for it was time to store up meat and hides for the winter.

Sweet Water dawdled at a bush, eating another berry, thinking how there would be gifts given at the Sun Dance, and how it was a time for telling stories. Young men would fast for days and sacrifice their flesh in the Sun Dance lodge, offering their blood to *Maheo* so that the Great Spirit might smile upon the People and bring them prosperity.

One of those young men would be Red Beaver, the son of Stands Tall, her father's close friend. Stands Tall was very proud of his son, as was his brother, White Eagle, who, as Red Beaver's uncle, had helped teach the young man the ways of the warrior and hunter. Red Beaver and his father and uncle had sometimes eaten in Sweet Water's tipi as guests of her father, but she had never spoken to Red Beaver. After all, he was eight years older than she, almost a grown man!

After making his sacrifice and fasting, Red Beaver hoped to have a vision, one that would guide him through life. Sweet Water wondered then if young women could also have visions. She wanted to be a soldier girl someday, a young maiden who was special to one of the military societies. Such a girl had to be chaste and honorable. She had to be very spiritual, and many never married. Maybe the soldier girls had visions.

"My child, have you forgotten why we are here?" Star Woman called, her words startling the child.

"Remember that *Maheo* smiles on children who obey and who work hard. Finish picking that bush, and remember to thank the Earth Mother for her gift of food."

"Ai," Sweet Water answered, again embarrassed. She immediately concentrated on picking the berries, telling herself there would be time for dreaming tonight, when all was still and she lay on her bed of robes to sleep.

"There is a stream not far from here," Star Woman said. "We will go and drink. It is a hot day."

Sweet Water followed her mother to the stream, where mountain water splashed white and cold in spite of the hot air. She leaned down beside it, reaching into the foam to rinse berry stains off her hands, then cupped one hand and drank of the refreshing, pure, clear blood of Grandmother Earth. She splashed some of the water on her face, happy to know she carried the name of something that brought refreshment and new life to a hot and thirsty human.

"Maybe the cold water will help you wake up and stop dreaming when you should be working," Star Woman told her.

The woman was smiling, and Sweet Water knew her mother was not really angry. Sweet Water smiled in return and hurried to another berry bush, wondering if she should tell her mother about the recurring dream she had been having. It was something that disturbed her more and more, for the dream seemed to come to her almost every night now. In the dream she was a grown woman, standing on a high mountain, her long dark hair blowing wild in the wind, a white cloud behind her. Behind the cloud the sun glared brightly, its rays spraying out in a spectacular sweep of white and red and gold. She wore a cape made of wolf's skin, and around her wolves had gathered, one howling at the heavens, one resting peacefully beside her, others prowling in a circle around her in that nervous way the wolf has of walking. She was not afraid of them, but rather, they seemed to be protecting her.

She wondered if maybe she should at least tell Old Grandmother about the dream. Old Grandmother seemed to know everything. Old People were very wise that way, and Sweet Water longed for that kind of wisdom.

"We are too far from the village," Star Woman said then, looking worried. "I did not realize how far we had come. You had better hurry and finish filling your basket. We need the berries to make more pemmican so your father will have plenty to take on the hunt."

Sweet Water picked faster, occasionally glancing at her mother, who stood stiffly, watching the deep shadows of a thick grove of pines nearby. Sweet Water's throat began to hurt from fear as she realized her mother sensed something was wrong.

"What we must do now," Star woman told her quietly then, "is go back."

"What is wrong, Mother?"

"Do not look concerned. Smile, Sweet Water. Turn and walk back with me as though nothing is wrong. We have to warn your father and the others. I think an enemy is watching us. If it is *O-O-O-tan*, they probably know about the village and plan to attack it. Follow me, but do not run."

Sweet Water clutched her basket and walked to her mother, trying not to show any fear. *O-O-O-tan!* Were there really Crow Indians somewhere in the trees watching them? She took her mother's hand, and together they headed toward the rise that separated them from the village. Not running was the hardest thing Sweet Water had ever been asked to do, for she had heard many stories about the Crow. Guilt seared in her chest like a burning lance, for she thought that if she had picked faster, she and her mother would already be safely back at the village. If anything happened, it would be all her fault for taking so long.

Her throat felt tight, and her eyes stung with tears as she walked on shaking legs, her soft moccasins making no sound in the soft grass. She clung tightly to her basket of berries, forgetting about her excitement over the Sun

Dance, forgetting about her strange dreams. The village suddenly seemed miles away, and she felt a sickness growing in her stomach, when she heard a rustling somewhere behind her.

Suddenly there came a blood curdling war cry, and goose bumps covered Sweet Water's skin. Her mother quickly swept her up in her arms and began running, screaming the name of the enemy, hoping to alert the village. *"O-O-O-tan! O-O-O-tan!* Help us, Arrow Maker!"

Sweet Water still clung tightly to her basket, and the berries bounced and spilled out of it as her mother ran. She looked over Star Woman's shoulder to see how many berries she was losing, feeling strangely sad that the few she had picked would now be lost. She saw her mother's basket far behind them, where Star Woman had dropped it to pick her up. Beyond that she saw them coming then, Crow warriors charging toward her and her mother, their faces painted a hideous black and white, their eyes looking redder around the rims because of the paint, their lips looking too pink, their bared teeth too white. Sweet Water's eyes widened in terror as the warriors thundered closer. She screamed, *"Na-hko-eehe,"* meaning "Mother." She cringed when she saw the closest warrior raise a club, then tried to protect the back of Star Woman's head with her hand when she realized the Crow devil meant to hit her mother. She felt the blow, screamed with the pain of it as the club landed into her small fingers. Her efforts did little to help her mother, the power of the blow making the woman fall forward.

Sweet Water spilled out of Star Woman's arms. She immediately got up to go back to help her mother, but already the Crow warrior was upon Star Woman, shoving a knee into her back and wrenching her hands behind her. He quickly tied them tightly with a rawhide cord while the rest of the Crow men rode on to the village. Sweet Water ran to the warrior who had attacked Star Woman and began pummeling him with her fists, screaming *"O-O-O-tan,"* ignoring the awful pain in her fingers.

The Crow man turned and grasped Sweet Water's wrists, grinning wickedly. He lifted her with ease and plopped her on his horse. Sweet Water thought about try-

ing to jump down and run for the village, but she knew
her mother was hurt and would need her. She decided she
would stay with the Crow man, even though he terrified
her. She did not want her mother to suffer this alone.

She could hear screaming on the other side of the ridge
now. The rest of the Crow war party was attacking the
village. They would probably try to steal horses, and
maybe more women and children; but Arrow Maker was
there. Her father would protect the others.

She turned tear-filled eyes to see her Crow captor pulling Star Woman to her feet. The woman staggered, looking confused and dizzy. The Crow man looked her over,
grinning as though very pleased, then half dragged her to
his horse, picking her up under the hips and tossing her
over the animal like a sack of turnips. Sweet Water heard
her mother groan, and she wanted to cry; but she was
determined she would not cry in front of the Crow man,
who leapt up onto the horse between her and her mother.
He grabbed Sweet Water's right hand and put it at his
side, indicating to her that she should hold on.

Sweet Water obeyed, wanting only to be with her
mother, no matter what happened. The warrior turned his
horse and rode off as fast as the painted pony could carry
them.

The night was quiet except for the distant cries of the
wolves. Sweet Water had no idea where she was. She knew
only that they were very high in the mountains. She sat
close to her mother, who lay on her side and groaned from
the pain in her head. Sweet Water petted her hair, and
nearby the Crow man sat by a campfire, filling his belly
with deer meat but offering none to his prisoners. He kept
staring at Star Woman, who still lay where he had dumped
her from his horse after riding hard for what seemed hours,
climbing, climbing, going deeper into thick pines. They
had ridden so far that Sweet Water wondered if the Indian's
pony would live through the night. It stood not far away,
its head bent, its breathing still sounding hard.

"You must . . . get away," Star Woman told her

daughter, struggling to find the words, knowing the Crow could not understand the Cheyenne tongue.

"No, *Na-hko-eehe*," Sweet Water answered. "I will stay with you. I am not afraid."

"You must . . . if you get the chance," Star Woman answered her, rolling onto her back and looking at her daughter pleadingly. "If you do not get away, you will be taken far to the north . . . to *O-O-O-tan*, where you will be raised to be one of them."

"I will never be one of them! I am Cheyenne!"

"Then behave as one," her mother answered, her voice firmer. "A Cheyenne warrior does what is right . . . no matter what the cost! You must not allow yourself to be raised as a Crow! You will be . . . used like a slave, taught their ways, forced to marry a Crow man. One day . . . when you are older . . . you will forget the Cheyenne."

"No! Never, *Na-hko-eehe*." Again the tears started to come. "Do not say those things." Sweet Water glanced over at the Crow man, who bit off another piece of meat, all the while his dark eyes watching them.

"I tell you these things . . . because they are true," her mother told her. "Do not think of me now, child. Think of the people. Always we protect the children, for they are our future. Promise me that if you find the chance, you will flee! Your father . . . will come. He will find you. If he must lose me, at least he will not also lose his daughter. His heart . . . will not be quite so broken."

The Crow man startled them then when he loudly barked some kind of order in words Sweet Water and Star Woman did not understand. He threw the meat aside then, rising and walking around the fire and looking down at Star Woman. He grinned as he untied his leggings and threw them aside. Sweet Water's eyes widened when he unwrapped his breechcloth. She did not fully understand the mystery of man and woman, but somehow she needed no explanations to understand what her mother's abductor intended. Surely her mother would never want a Crow man to do such a thing to her! Star Woman belonged to Arrow Maker!

Desperate to stop him, Sweet Water grabbed the Crow man's leg and leaned forward, biting down hard on his calf. The warrior cried out with pain, quickly grasping Sweet Water's hair and jerking back her head. He reached down and grabbed hold of her, flinging her into the shadows like a little stone.

Sweet Water landed hard, a stump cutting into her back, knocking the breath from her. As she lay struggling to find air, she was vaguely aware of a scream, then the sound of weeping in pitiful despair. When she finally found her breath, she stared out from the darkness at the Crow man, who was moving on top of her mother.

She turned away and covered her ears, trying to block out the sounds, trying to think what was the best thing to do. A Cheyenne child's first duty was to obey. Her mother had told her she must try to escape. She thought about killing the Crow man but feared she was too small and weak to do it. She could use a knife, but she might not be strong enough to sink it deep enough to kill him; or he might hear her coming and turn on her, taking the knife from her and using it to slit her own throat and take her scalp, perhaps kill her mother with it.

"Na-hko-eehe," she said softly, more tears spilling from her eyes. She ran off into the darkness, feeling frantic now, stumbling and falling over loose brush and fallen trees hidden by the darkness. Her back hurt terribly, as did her fingers, especially the center two fingers on her right hand. She wondered if they were broken, but there was no time to nurse them. For once she would obey her mother. She would escape the Crow man!

Through tears and darkness and pain Sweet Water felt her way through underbrush, toppling down a little hill and landing near what looked in the moonlight like an old log. Her nostrils caught the scent of moss and wood rot. She was not sure how far she had gone, but she could no longer hear anything. She felt the log and realized she could reach inside it. She drew back her hand. Was there an animal inside that might attack her?

With great trepidation she bravely crawled inside the log. Something skittered out the other end, but she sensed it was something small, probably a rabbit. She liked rabbits. They were soft and quiet, and to the Cheyenne they represented humility. She curled up inside the log, licking at her sore fingers, which she could tell were swelling. Something crawled over her, but nothing bit her. She decided that for tonight the insects would have to be her friends.

She lay waiting, and after a while her thoughts wandered again. She tried to think of things that kept her from being afraid. She remembered Arrow Maker talking about the strange *ve-ho-e*, saying that ever since the *ve-ho-e* had begun crossing Indian land in their "tipis on wheels," game had become more scarce. Once he had mimicked the sound of the white man's rolling tipis. *"Chick-chik-shaile-kikash,"* he had said mockingly, referring to the sound the wagon wheels made when they clattered across the plains. Sweet Water had seen them once, had not forgotten their white tops, or the odd, sad feeling the sight of them had given her.

Terror returned to grab her when she heard a crashing sound outside the hollow log. Was it animal or man? The darkness was frightening. Perhaps a bear or a wildcat would come and eat her! Perhaps *bubo*, the great horned owl who carried the spirit of the dead, would come for her! She heard a man's voice, words she did not understand, but words which she sensed were curses. She recognized the voice of her mother's attacker. She stayed curled up in the log, telling herself to be as quiet as the soft rabbit. Perhaps in the morning the Crow man would give up searching for her and go away. Maybe he would even leave her mother behind.

Finally the footsteps receded, and all was quiet again. She lay shivering, feeling hungry and tired, her hand hurting more. There was nothing to do now but wait, and pray that her mother was still alive.

Sweet Water jumped awake when something bit her cheek. She scratched the bite, then opened her eyes, looking around at the rotted wood of the old log into which she had crawled the night before. Now the sun sent bright shafts of light through the thick Ponderosa pines, and she could see out both ends of the log.

She blinked, confused at first, trying to remember all

that had happened. It was morning, and she was still there, still safe. As the horror of the previous night revisited her, sickening guilt again plagued her. Mother! Was she dead? Had the Crow man ridden off with her? Was this all her fault for dallying while picking the berries yesterday?

She cautiously wiggled toward the other end of the log, then dared to climb out, breathing deeply of the sweet fresh air, wondering how rabbits and other rodents could stand to live beneath the earth. She stood up and carefully studied the shadows of the trees. All was quiet except for the soft wind in the pines. She heard a rustling sound and turned with a start to see that it was only a squirrel skittering about in the leaves.

Something bit her again, and she shook her head, bending over and brushing at her hair and face. She felt bites under her tunic and quickly pulled if off, frantically brushing ants from herself and shaking her hair wildly until she was sure all the ants were off her. She shook out the tunic and checked it over. Seeing no ants, she pulled it back over her head.

The mountain morning was cool, and she shivered. She began walking, hoping she was going in the right direction to find the Crow camp. She had to see if her mother was there and if she was alive, but she couldn't be sure now which way to go. She chose her way carefully, stepping only on soft pine needles so that her footsteps would not be heard, carefully avoiding dry twigs that might snap and reveal her presence. She remembered her father telling her how to walk without making sound, remembered him saying the soft moccasins they wore helped quiet their steps. She strained to hear voices, but there was only the sound of birds singing their morning songs.

She headed up a ridge, and when she reached the top she saw below the remnants of a campfire, a small wisp of smoke still curling from it. There were no humans or horses in sight, just the signs all over the ground that many horses had been there. Others must have come during the night or this morning to meet the Crow warrior. Now they were all gone. *"Na-hko-eehe,"* she said softly. "Where are you?"

She moved closer, her heart pounding. Were they

really gone? Would she find her mother's mutilated, scalped body? Soon she was standing in camp. There was nothing left, and no sign of her mother; nor was there any grave nearby. She was happy that her mother was apparently still alive, but sad that she must have been taken off by the Crow war party. Would they kill her? Make a slave of her?

"*Na-hko-eehe*," she wept. "It is my fault." She wiped her tears, smearing the dirt on her face. She straightened then, her chest jerking in sobs as she tried to determine which would be the best way to go to find her people. The Crow man had ridden far into the mountain before he made camp. Not only was she not sure of the right path, but she wondered how many bears and other wild things might be about that would eat her. And what about her own growling stomach?

You are Cheyenne, Old Grandmother had taught her. *You are strong and blessed by* Maheo. *Like the warrior, Cheyenne women must also be brave. Walk with no fear in your heart, child, not even a fear of death.*

Sweet Water wiped her tears again as she looked around, trying to decide which way to go. She realized she must first find food, and she studied the plants, remembering the many things her mother had taught her, which ones could be eaten. She considered staying where she was and relighting the dying campfire embers with more wood, but she feared that in this high, wooded country, she would never be found. The Cheyenne camp had been in the foothills, somewhere below.

Seeing nothing edible in the immediate area, she moved into a clearing beyond the camp, catching a view of the vast expanse of foothills and flatland far below. Now she could better understand how an eagle must feel, and why the great Grandfather Bird was so powerful and mighty and haughty. Anything that could rule over a place so high that it seemed to touch the heavens was indeed something to be honored and revered. She wished she could spread wings and soar like the Spotted Eagle, fly over all that was below and find her People; find her poor mother.

She pushed her hair back behind her ears and followed a path that looked as though it had been used many times before. If it had, perhaps it was the one by which the Crow man had brought her here, and it would lead her back to her People. If not, it might be a path leading right to the Crow village. She had no way of knowing. She knew only that she would never be found where she was. She started down, feeling as small as a rabbit, fighting the terror of knowing she was totally alone now, lost in this wild land.

Chapter Two

Sweet Water stumbled through a myriad of rocks and trees and wildflowers. Nothing looked familiar. All day she had wandered, hoping to find help. Now it was nearly sunset, and she had found a wide green clearing where an abundance of wildflowers grew including a beautiful white lily that the Cheyenne called the Life Plant. When she started to dig at the plant to find its root, pain tore through her right hand, and she realized she had been so intent on avoiding the Crow and then on finding her way out of the mountains that she had forgotten about her damaged fingers.

She looked down at them, and they were red and swollen. She thought for a moment, trying to remember everything she had been taught about survival. She remembered then how Stalking Bear, the Shaman who lived among her people, healed broken bones by tying them rigidly against a branch or a sturdy stick. She searched for such a stick, finding a piece of flat pine that had somehow become peeled away from a limb, perhaps by a deer. With the thumb and first finger of her right hand, and using her sore but unbroken left hand, she untied a cord from around her neck onto which was tied a turtle shell, a gift from her mother. Perhaps the turtle spirit was helping her now, for she had remembered how to set her fingers, and she had found food.

She untied the turtle shell and pulled open a little pouch she wore on her belt to carry things like pretty stones, and a small comb made of buffalo bone. She slipped the shell into the pouch and pulled shut its string-closed opening. On a rock she laid out the rawhide cord from which she had taken the shell, then laid the piece of thin flat pine over it. She pressed her third and fourth fingers onto the wood, wincing with pain, then brought the cord around, using her teeth and her left hand to tie it tightly so that her fingers were stretched flat against the wood and could not bend. Already they felt a little better.

She studied her handiwork, feeling a sense of pride. She walked back out into the meadow picking up a flat, pointed rock she found along the way. Going back to the Life Plant, she used her left hand to dig with the rock in order to loosen the dirt around the plant. She pulled it then, and it came up suddenly, making her fall back on her rump. She shook dirt from the bulb at the end of the stem, then wiped off more dirt with her tunic before biting into the bland white food. She thought how the bulb would taste better cooked with venison or buffalo meat, but for now she would have to eat it plain.

She finished the small bulb in two bites, realizing she was hungrier than she thought, she dug some more bulbs, caring little that she felt sand in her teeth when she ate them. Among the wildflowers she also found elk thistle. She used the hem of her tunic to break off a few of the spiny stems, the buckskin protecting her skin from the prickly hairs of the plant. With the pointed rock she poked at the stem until she managed to break off the tops of two of the plants, then she carefully peeled off the hairy outer skin of the stems, leaving smooth, chewy stalks. She bit into one, relishing its crispness, taking moisture from the watery shoot.

"Thank you, Grandmother Earth," she said then, grateful for the food. She rose, realizing that the sun was setting behind the western rim of the mountains, which now cast their dark shadow over the meadow. Colorful wildflowers became dancing shadows, and the happy blue sky turned black. The small bit of relief and pride she had realized at setting her own fingers and at finding food all alone was soon replaced with a growing fear. The night before she had gotten through the darkness and danger in the close, safe confines of the hollow log. Now there was no log.

The seriousness of her predicament began to settle in with more reality. She was one small girl alone in a wilderness where grizzlies and bobcats lurked, where the great horned owl carried ghost spirits who liked to snatch away little children. She reminded herself that she was Cheyenne, and like a good warrior she must not be afraid. She looked back at the thick black forest. Now it was dark and menacing. She decided to stay in the open meadow, and she headed toward a rock formation not far away. She peered around the rocks, noticing there was one open area within them where a child her size could fit. She climbed over smaller boulders and huddled down into the opening.

Surrounded by the big boulders, she felt safer again, closed away from the night and its dangers. *Bubo* would not find her here. She wrapped her arms around herself and curled up her knees, leaning back against one of the rocks and looking up at the night sky, searching until she found the Seven Stars that were shaped like the bone ladle her mother used. The sight made her heart ache with memories of her father explaining how they had gotten there. The stars had once been seven Indian brothers who had climbed up a tree to escape an angry buffalo. The tree had stretched and grown into the heavens, where the brothers could not be harmed, and they had turned into stars.

Would she ever hear her father's voice again? What had happened to her mother? And what about her little sister, Smiling Girl, only three? The girl would not understand where her mother had gone. Sweet Water made a vow to herself that she would always look after her little sister if her mother was killed or never found. Her brother was getting big enough to take care of himself. He was being taught by his uncle, Two Moons, her father's brother, how to hunt and how to fight. It was the custom for an uncle to teach a young man, for it was easier for him to be stern than for a father.

There came another howl from a different direction, wolves calling to each other, more active because tonight the clouds had lifted and there was a bright moon. The dry night air was cold, and Sweet Water shivered, closed her eyes, and tried to imagine she was safe and warm in her parents' tipi. The howling of the wolves continued, and some sounded very close, yet somehow she found their cries comforting, rather than frightening.

Finally sleep came to release her from her fears. The howling of the wolves seemed to enter her sleep thoughts, and the dream returned. Again she stood on a mountaintop with wolves all around her, but this time a man stood behind her. Although he was fully grown, his face was that of Red Beaver, the son of her father's friend who had often visited their tipi. He approached her, but a wolf sat crouched between them. The animal rose, looking threateningly at Red Beaver, keeping him at bay; but Red Beaver ignored the animal and daringly moved past it to come to stand behind Sweet Water.

Sweet Water suddenly jumped awake, rubbing her eyes and thinking for a moment about the strange new twist to her dream. She shrugged off the thought, too tired to care about its meaning. Soon she was asleep again, unaware that a pack of wolves had quietly approached the rocks where she lay. They silently sniffed around, then left, all except one white male. The animal sat down nearby, its yellow eyes watching the shadows, its nose twitching quietly as he sniffed the air for predators.

For four days Sweet Water wandered, scratching for food wherever she could find it. Thirst kept her near a stream, and she hoped that as she followed it, the stream would lead her to human life, maybe to her own people. She spotted a rainbow trout in the water, and her growling stomach reminded her that fish was food. She ran along the edge of the stream, grabbing for the trout, laughing when cold water sprayed into her face. Over and over again she failed to catch the colorful, wiggly creature, and she screamed and giggled with each miss, turning the hunt into a game. Having to try to catch the creature with her left hand only made the task harder. She ran and splashed and laughed, nearly falling once into the water. She chased after the fish for several more yards until suddenly she heard a low, menacing growl.

Sweet Water froze in place, raising her eyes to see a huge grizzly on the opposite bank of the stream. The fish swam away and for a tense moment Sweet Water just stared at the bear, having no idea whether it was best to run or stay still. No one had taught her yet about how to face a grizzly. She remembered an uncle who had been attacked by one of these bears, remembered how he had looked when he was brought back to camp, so bloody and torn that it was difficult to tell who he was.

"Please help me, Grandmother Earth," she said in a squeaky voice. The great beast reared onto its hind feet, growling so loudly that it seemed the earth shook with the roar. In Sweet Water's eyes he stood twenty feet tall. He came down on all four legs again, and Sweet Water was sure she would be eaten; thus the bear would consume her spirit as well. The hairs on the grizzly's hump rose in threat, and again the animal reared on its hind legs, pawing at the air in a gesture that warned her to stay away.

Sweet Water slowly backed up. The bear again came down on all four huge paws, its six-inch claws digging into the ground as it charged into the stream, heading straight for Sweet Water. She could not make her legs move. She screamed for her father, but there was no one to come to her aid. She knew she had to run now, but her whole body felt like a heavy rock. Her eyes widened as the beast drew dangerously close, and then, just as she expected to feel her limbs being torn from their sockets and huge teeth sinking into her throat, there came another movement.

Something streaked from behind her, and in the next instant a pack of wolves was charging the bear. The vicious animals growled and barked, baring their teeth, dashing and nipping at the grizzly. The bear looked suddenly confused and defensive. He backed away, and the wolves kept charging at him, forcing him farther and farther away, their jaws dripping saliva, the hair on their backs standing up straight in a defensive reaction.

Sweet Water watched in surprise and awe. One of the wolves got too close, and she gasped when the bear took a swipe at it with one powerful paw, sending the poor wolf flying. It landed hard against a rock. Sweet Water watched in wonder as she realized the wolves were actually protecting her, just like in her dream. They charged the bear over and over until he finally gave up and turned, lumbering away, his thick fur shining in the afternoon sun. Because of his immense size, his giant paws made a thumping sound against the earth.

The wolves trotted about then, some chasing a little farther after the bear. The growling and barking stopped, and suddenly the air hung quiet. The mighty roaring and awful snarling had frightened away the birds and all other living creatures, so that for the moment there was only the sound of the bubbling trout stream.

Sweet Water stood very still as the wolves turned, aiming their attention at her. Their yellow eyes drilled into her, and it seemed to Sweet Water that they were trying to speak. She waited for them to attack, but they made no threatening moves. Three of them trotted over to sniff at the dead wolf, then they all wandered off into the thick pines and disappeared.

Sweet Water looked over at the dead wolf. Blood trickled from its mouth. She walked closer and crouched down to touch it, petting its soft fur for a moment, thanking its spirit for giving its life to protect her. A soft wind moaned through the pines, and a few birds returned to begin singing again. Sweet Water rose and left, feeling dazed and confused. She walked aimlessly, reaching a ledge that dropped down so steeply that it was impossible to go down, so she began climbing again. She moved through more pine forest, came into another clearing, then finally sat down.

She felt like crying, for she was growing more and

more lonely for human companionship, more and more afraid she would never again see her mother and father, or her sister and brother. She knew that somehow she had to find her way off this mountain. The incident with the grizzly and the pain in her empty stomach only made her more aware that she could not survive alone much longer. Without the bits of food Grandmother Earth offered, and without the strange protection of the Wolf Spirit, she would probably already be dead.

She rose and began walking again, deciding she had better again search for shelter. As always, darkness seemed to come too swiftly, aided this time by an approaching storm that she had not known lurked just on the other side of the mountains. She heard the deep rumble of thunder, and she looked up to see churning dark clouds moving rapidly over the peaks above her.

Her heart beat harder with alarm, for storms frightened her. She began a frantic search for a place where she could get out of the rain. The storm moved in with amazing rapidity, rumbling and billowing, the wind getting stronger. Sweet Water screamed when a bright bolt of lightning jolted a tree not far from her, making a popping sound as it split the trunk. The wood sparked and spouted a spiral of heavy smoke, but there was no fire. A great crack of thunder followed the hit, startling Sweet Water so that she screamed again.

She searched the hillside for shelter, but saw nothing. She tripped over a fallen branch and the pain returned to her fingers as she caught herself. The wind ripped at the trees around her, changing them into threatening monsters of death that could fall on her at any moment. The heavens burst open, dumping cold rain in huge drops onto the moutainside, drenching her mercilessly.

Combined with the late hour of the day, the heavy black clouds quickly turned dusk to night, so that it was difficult for Sweet Water to find shelter. Lightning lit up the land like day when it flashed, and Sweet Water used its brightness to try to see where she should go. To her joy, she thought she spotted a cavelike entrance above. Were there animals in it? A bear? A bobcat? A tree came crashing down not far from where she stood, helping her make up her mind. She had to try to get to that cave and take her chances on sharing it with some other living being.

She bolted up the steep hill, slipping and sliding on wet pine needles. All around her, lightning jarred the heavens and thunder shook the earth. The rain came down in a torrent. Sweet Water clawed her way up the bank, keeping an eye on the cave whenever lightning helped her. She finally reached it, breathless, aching, her tunic soaking wet, her hands, knees, and moccasins muddy and sticky from the pine. Just outside the cave entrance the ground flattened out into a kind of ledge. She climbed up onto it, then ducked inside the cave.

She breathed deeply, trying to calm herself. It was quiet inside and for a moment she thought she might be alone. She waited for more lightning to help her, and finally a bright flash lit up the darkened cubicle. Sweet Water's heart seemed to stop beating when she saw what else occupied the cavern.

Today Grandmother Earth seemed intent on pitting her against animals that were not so friendly as the birds and the deer. She waited, wondering if perhaps she had imagined what she saw. Lighting blazed again, the light reflecting on eyes, several pairs of yellow eyes. Instinctively the child realized she had stumbled upon a den of wolves.

She stood very still, every part of her tingling with apprehension and terror, a small voice reminding her of her dreams. Should she fear for her life, or were these wolves her friends? She waited for sharp claws and wicked teeth to sink into her flesh, but she heard not even a growl. Lightning again brought daylight to the cave, and she could see that the wolves were lying about looking as though her intrusion had not disturbed them in the least. One rose, but the cave went dark again.

She shivered, her tunic dripping, water running from her hair down the sides of her face and into her ears. She wanted to wipe it away, but she was afraid to move, still fearing she would be attacked if she made any wrong motions. She shivered when she felt warm breath near her wounded hand, then gasped but remained unmoving when something began licking her sore fingers.

She moved back against a wall. "Please, Grandfather Wolf," she said in a voice high-pitched with fear. "Do not harm me. I am sorry to come into your home, but I have no place else to go."

She let the wolf lick her hand, beginning to realize that when the dogs back at her village licked a person, it was a sign of friendship. The soft massaging of the animal's tongue was soothing to her aching fingers, and she realized that the wolf somehow knew she was injured and was trying to help her.

She heard a yipping, whimpering sound coming from farther back in the den. Pups! Immediately her curiosity made her forget precaution and fear. She moved toward the sound. Oh, how she loved puppies! Her eyes were beginning to adjust to the darkness enough to make out the forms of other wolves. They did not stir or make any threatening gestures. Lightning flashed again, and she saw the mother wolf lying not far away, several pups whimpering and crawling over her, one feeding at her breast. In the brief flash of light, Sweet Water noticed the pups were as fat and furry as dog pups back at her village.

Sweet Water cautiously approached, wanting so badly to touch one of the pups and hold it close to her. Suddenly she had found something alive and warm, something she could hold and love and help remind her that she was not totally alone after all, and it was comforting to her frightened, lonely heart.

There came more lightning, and she saw the female watching her passively. She carefully reached out and picked up one of the pups, smiling, then giggling as she held it close and it licked her neck. Her youthful excitement erased all fear, and she sat down beside the female, laying the pup in her lap and turning it on its back to rub its belly. She gave little thought to the spiritual and prophetic significance of what was happening; she had entered a den of wolves and was sitting among them.

Outside, the storm raged on so violently that even the wolves, who would normally be out on their nightly hunt, would not leave the den. A second female wolf, the one that had licked Sweet Water's fingers, came close again and began licking at the wet fringes of her tunic. The puppy wiggled out of her lap, and when its warmth left her she shivered again. She remembered her mother saying once that staying in wet clothes often meant getting the "lung sickness" that could make a person die. She stood up and pulled off her tunic, looking around in the glow of the lightning to see a rock over which she could lay the tunic to dry. She walked over to the rock, being careful not to step on a paw or a tail. She spread out the tunic, then returned to the mother wolf and her pups.

She pulled off her wet moccasins and set them aside, then grabbed another puppy while one of the others playfully tried to crawl inside one of the moccasins. Sweet Water decided it felt better to be naked than to have a wet tunic stuck to her skin. She sat playing with the pups, and as though their spirits were one, the puppies began clamoring over her. She laughed at the tickly feeling of paws and fur and licks. Was this safe, she wondered. Dangerous? Would she ever be found? Would she grow up with the wolves and forget how it was to be a human being? She decided that for the moment none of those things mattered. She had found comfort and warmth, a place to rest. More than that, she had found companionship.

The pups began to settle down around her, adding their warmth against her skin to ward off the chill of the rain. One of the adult females settled down against her small back, the mother wolf moving to rest her head over the child's lap. Sweet Water's eyes began to droop, and she was soon asleep, a deep sleep brought on by a growing weariness from her struggle to survive.

Fourteen-year-old Red Beaver guided his painted pony on the steep escarpment, urging the sure-footed animal on in spite of loose rock that made the climb dangerous. He had no idea why he had chosen to come in this direction. He knew only that he had been awakened by a dream in the night, a voice from somewhere telling him to come higher into the mountains.

Arrow Maker and the others in the search party did not think the Crow would go so high, and they had gone on through a lower passage. They agreed that if a voice had told Red Beaver to go another way, he should do it. Tomorrow at midday they would all meet in the Valley of Sweet Grass that stretched between the two ranges. There they would decide which way to continue going in their effort to find the hated Crow, who had taken Arrow Maker's wife and daughter. Red Beaver knew that Arrow Maker was hot for revenge. He would find them or die, and Red Beaver wanted to help all he could. He was sure that one day a woman would be just as important to him.

Arrow Maker had openly lamented his wife and daughter's abduction, feeling partly responsible. He had considered forbidding them to go to pick the berries that day, and it was with great reluctance he had finally agreed. When the Crow had attacked, there had been too few men in the village to protect the women and children and old ones, and Arrow Maker had to cover for those he protected until they could scramble to safety. He had been unable to go and help Star Woman and Sweet Water.

After the Crow left, leaving behind burned tipis and the murdered and scalped bodies of three old Cheyenne men and one young woman, Arrow Maker had ridden to the place where his wife and daughter had gone for the berries, but he had found only the baskets they had carried, the berries spilled out of them. He had had to wait two days for the rest of the warriors to come back from the hunt so that he could gather together enough men to ride with him and search for the mother and daughter, and now he was a furious and frustrated man.

The wait had been costly. A vicious storm had brought a torrential rain that had washed away many of the trail markings. Now they hunted almost purely by instinct, Arrow Maker refusing to give up and allow his wife and daughter to be made slaves to some Crow man. Because there was no longer any real trail, Red Beaver had been allowed to follow his dream and take this direction in the hopes it was a sign from *Maheo*. Perhaps some spirit was helping him find the path to Star Woman and the child.

He reached a clearing and halted his pony, turning it in a circle while he scanned the forest and hillsides in every direction. Birds sang, and a soft wind blew down from the western slopes. He dismounted, untying his leggings and throwing them over his horse. The growing heat of the day had already caused him to take off his buckskin shirt. Now he wore only a breechcloth, the rest of his bare skin gleaming dark in the brilliant sun.

Red Beaver knew by the occasional stolen glances from young maidens that he was growing into a handsome young man. He was secretly proud of his lean, muscled body, and his mother never failed to praise his looks, and brag about his prowess on the hunt. She literally boasted to her women friends about the fact that her son would this summer take part in the Sun Dance. Red Beaver knew it would be a painful ordeal, but he was ready and willing to give of his flesh as an offering to the Great Spirit in order that *Maheo* would bless his people with continued life and prosperity, and in order that he would himself be blessed with the vision that would show him the way he must go into manhood. He was anxious to know the spirit that would guide him, to be a full man and be ready to ride with the other warriors.

For now he had no interest in any particular girl, for he was much too young to be thinking of taking a woman. But he had indeed felt the urges that were natural to a man. He had had pleasant dreams in which pretty girls came to him in the night and lay with him the way his mother lay with his father. Someday he would find just the right woman to share his life; but for now his only interest was the Sun Dance, and proving his manhood. He would be greatly honored if he could be the one to find Star Woman and little Sweet Water.

He remounted his horse, sitting straight and proud, letting a cool breeze that came down suddenly off the mountains blow across the sweat of his brow and send his long, dark hair back away from his face. A beaded hairpiece his mother had made for him remained secure. He picked up the reins of his pony and rode toward the mountain, then felt a chill in spite of the heat when he spotted a white wolf standing at the edge of the thick pine forest. He slowed his horse as the wolf began trotting toward him. Red Beaver reached for his bow that hung on his gear, thinking he should be ready in case the wolf decided to attack.

The pony whinnied and skirted backward, afraid of its natural enemy. The wolf stopped, surprising Red Beaver when it wagged its tail. It came forward again, and strangely, Red Beaver sensed that his horse was no longer afraid. The wolf suddenly turned and headed back toward the trees. When Red Beaver did not follow, it stopped and looked at him again, as though to beckon him.

"So, Spirit Wolf, you want me to follow, do you?" He decided that if his dream had told him to come this way, maybe this wolf had been sent to help guide him. He was making little progress on his own, so he decided to follow and see where the wolf led him. Wondering if he was being wise or foolish, he started his horse forward, and the animal followed the wolf willingly into the cooler shadows of the pine forest.

Sweet Water stirred awake, stretching and looking around, confused for a moment. Sunlight shafted into an opening to her right, and she realized she was in a cave. Something licked her, and then she felt the sharp sting of claws on her belly and chest. She turned her head forward to see the muzzle of a yellow-eyed wolf pup looking down at her. The pup whined and wagged its tail as though it wanted to be petted, and Sweet Water smiled, glad to oblige.

She grasped the pup and nuzzled it, then sat up, her smile fading when she realized that her comfortable warmth had come from the fact that wolves lay all around her. Her eyes widened. So, this had not all been some strange dream after all! This was real! This was her own vision come true.

Surely this was a good sign that Grandmother Earth and her creatures were going to guide and protect her! She knew from her teachings that the right thing to do was to sing to Grandmother Earth and to the wolves, to thank them for keeping her safe and warm. She rose, walking to the rock where her tunic lay. She picked it up to see that it was still damp. She carried it outside, where the morning was warm with sunlight. The clouds were gone, the sky a vivid blue.

She laid the tunic over another rock outside in the bright sun. She took a sweeping look at her surroundings, seeing that she stood on a ledge on the side of a mountain, from which she could look out over a sea of forest and grassy valleys below. She could see two lakes, and a whole mountain range across the valley.

It was a magical moment, one she knew she would not forget for the rest of her life; for this, she knew even in her young mind, was her destiny! The Wolf Spirit lived within her! All around her the wolves gathered on the ledge, some stalking nervously, others crouching quietly, two males standing stalwartly, as though guarding her. A soft mountain breeze made her hair blow into wild, tangled wisps. She looked out toward the other mountain range to see one puffy, billowing cloud, behind which the sun shone brightly so that its rays surrounded the cloud in a magnificent sweep of red and gold, just like in her dream; but in the dream that cloud and the sun had been behind her, not in front of her . . . and she had been a woman, not a child.

She felt she must sing to Grandmother Earth. She must thank *Maheo*, and thank the Wolf Spirit for keeping her safe. She raised her arms, standing on the ledge, feeling so much older than her six years, feeling strangely wiser, much braver. She kept her eyes on the lovely cloud, feeling like one tiny speck set against the mighty mountain, the whole world as she knew it stretched out below in a panorama of green and gold and red. She relished the feel of the warm rising sun on her skin as she stood naked before *Maheo* and offered her own prayer song as anyone who had a vision was allowed to do.

Oh, Grandmother Earth, hear me!
Oh, Grandfather Wolf, hear me!
Oh, Great Maheo, hear me!
I sing my thanks to you!
Forever the wolf shall be sacred to me.
Forever the earth shall be sacred to me.
Forever I will please Maheo!
I offer you my life. You protect me.

Oh, Grandmother Earth, hear me!
Oh, Grandfather Wolf, hear me!
Oh, Great Maheo, hear me!

She hoped it was a worthy song. She had never given thought to singing a song of her own before, never thought there would be the need before she was a woman. Her parents and Old Grandmother would be proud to know that she had remembered to do this. Perhaps her vision and knowing she had made up her own special prayer song would help make up for the responsibility she still felt for being the cause of her and her mother's abductions.

Two of the wolf pups began to wrestle, taking her thoughts from serious to playful. The pups began scampering down from the ledge, and Sweet Water ran inside the cave to put on her moccasins, which were not as wet as her tunic. She hurried back outside and made her way down the steep bank leading away from the ledge, clinging to small trees to keep from falling. The rest of the wolf pups followed her, as did some of the adults.

The ground beneath her feet leveled off more as she came to a small grassy clearing where wildflowers grew. She breathed deeply of the sweet, pungent smell of wet pine needles. She looked around at the array of colors and the surrounding mountains, wondering if there could be a more wonderful feeling than the sweet freedom of being one with nature.

The pups yipped and ran, and she began running with them, the grass in the clearing nearly as tall as she. She laughed at the sight of the puppies trying to keep up with her, their little tails standing straight, their ears flopping. She raced and romped with them until she was so weary she fell into the grass, still giggling. The pups crawled over her and she screamed at the feel of it, curling up against the tickly feeling. Soon the pups also grew tired. They stretched out in the warm sun, some beside Sweet Water, one on her chest, one across her legs. Moments later they were all asleep.

Sweet Water dreamed again. This time a big white wolf was talking to her. She couldn't hear a voice, but she could feel the words when she looked into his yellow eyes. He told her she must go back and find the dead wolf that the bear had killed and she must cut off its paws and keep them for her own personal medicine bag. She was to skin the dead wolf and dry its hide, using the fur as a cape that would protect her.

You are blessed with the spirit of the wolf, the animal told her. *When you hear your kindred spirit calling in the night, know that it is our song to you.*

The wolf faded into a cloud, and in her sleep Sweet Water thought she heard a horse whinny, but she could not see it.

Red Beaver slowly dismounted and tied his pony. The animal whinnied and pulled the rope that held it, its eyes wide with fright at the sight of the pack of wolves gathered in the clearing ahead. Red Beaver pulled a knife from its sheath at his side. He began to wonder if the male wolf he had been following had cleverly led him there just to attack him and his horse. Maybe he had done a very foolish thing by coming here.

Feeling led by some strange force, the young man approached the wolves cautiously. To his surprise, none appeared aggressive. There was not even a growl. Most of the wolves seemed to be circling something, as though guarding it. Was it a dead animal? He knew wolves were very protective of their food source.

He moved closer, spotting several puppies. They lay in a sleepy pile. One of them jumped up and yipped, stirring the others awake. It was then that Red Beaver realized it was not a dead animal they were guarding, but a live body; at least he *hoped* she was alive. Her little naked body lay in what appeared a peaceful sleep. ''Sweet Water!'' he gasped.

Chapter Three

Sweet Water awakened to what she thought was a wolf pawing her and she opened her eyes to see Red Beaver. Was she dreaming? She sat up, and he was asking if she was all right. One of the wolf pups scratched her leg as it scrambled across it, and she realized this was not a dream at all. Red Beaver had found her!

She jumped up, then suddenly became acutely aware that she was naked. In spite of the fact that up to now she had often played naked with the other little children of her village and thought nothing of it, she was strangely mortified to have Red Beaver see her this way. This was the young man who had been in one of her dreams! There was something special about him now.

She wiggled away from him, crouching down and wrapping her arms around her knees. Her eyes stung with tears of embarrassment. Why did she feel this way? Something had changed inside. She felt as ashamed as if she were a grown woman caught this way. "My tunic . . . is wet," she told Red Beaver, hanging her head.

Red Beaver wanted to laugh at her, for she was just a small girl with nothing for a man to look at. He thought about teasing her as he walked back to his horse and took out a cotton shirt from his supplies. It was a white man's shirt, of which he had just a few, his father having traded some deerskins for them at Bent's Fort a year before. He approached little Sweet Water, handing out the shirt. "Here," he told her. "You can wear this." She took the shirt gratefully. "Are you hungry?" he asked.

"*Ai*," she replied in her small voice. "I have been eating the Life Plant, but it does not fill the belly so well as meat and turnips." Her lips pouted in a frown. "I do not understand how you close this," she said.

"Do you want me to help you?"

"*Ai*. I cannot do it so well. My fingers are hurt, and I had to wrap them."

Red Beaver smiled at the way the shirt hung on her, nearly to the ground. He knelt in front of her to button it, and Sweet Water held the shirt closed with her left hand. "It looks as though you have been very wise in taking care of yourself. Your father will be proud," Red Beaver told her. He met her eyes, seeing something different there, something that did not belong to a carefree child. He saw a strange wisdom, saw the eyes of a woman. "Where is your mother?" he asked, feeling suddenly stirred and self-conscious, wanting to keep a conversation going. Looking into her eyes had given him a quick sense of desire, which filled him with utter shame, for she was just a child.

"I do not know," she answered, her throat feeling tighter at the memory. "The Crow warriors took her away," she said, struggling not to cry like a baby. She watched the muscles of the young man's strong arms flex slightly as he buttoned the shirt. She felt an odd attraction, and she wondered if she was just feeling strangely drawn to Red Beaver because of her dream. Should she tell him about it? Would he laugh at her?

"How long ago?" he asked, finishing the buttons. He began rolling up the sleeves, and the touch of his strong hands made her tingle. She watched his hands and arms as she answered.

"I am not sure. Maybe four sunrises. It was the next morning after we were captured. I hid in an old hollow log, and the warrior did not find me. The next morning I went to find her, but she was gone."

Her eyes began to tear, and Red Beaver thought how it was not like him to feel this strange, mushy sympathy, but he found himself reaching out and touching the child's shoulder. "We will find her. But first you must eat something. Then we will leave this place. I am to meet your father and the others at the Valley of Sweet Grass tomorrow when the sun is highest in the sky. Then we will find the Crow camp."

His touch was amazingly comforting. Sweet Water felt safe and protected, and she took heart in Red Beaver's words. Maybe her mother *would* be found alive, and they could all rejoin the others and life would be free and happy again. "I must get my tunic," she said. "It is up at the wolf's den. I slept with the wolves last night. They kept me warm."

Red Beaver looked up where she pointed, seeing the cave. Several wolves lay or stood in front of it, watching silently. A chill moved through the young man at the memory of the white wolf leading him to this place. Wolves had been standing all around Sweet Water when he found her, but they had run off as soon as he came close to her, bringing no harm to him. "You slept with wolves?"

Sweet Water nodded. "There was a terrible storm," she told him, suddenly losing her shame and finding it easy to talk to him. "In the lightning I saw the cave, so I climbed up to it to find shelter. When I went inside, the wolves were there. I was afraid at first, but they brought me no harm. I lay down among them, and they lay beside me and over me to keep me warm."

She saw an astonished look come into Red Beaver's eyes, and he looked at her as though she were something to be revered.

"The wolves *protected* you?"

"*Ai*. I will go and get my tunic now, and then I will eat something."

Red Beaver grasped her arm as she turned. "You cannot go up there!"

"It is all right. I told you, they are my friends, Red Beaver. They will not harm me."

Sweet Water hurried to the hillside, then began climbing. Red Beaver followed, pulling out his knife and starting up behind her, ready to do battle with claws and fangs if necessary to save Arrow Maker's daughter. Sweet Water managed to get to the top, the long shirt tripping her at times. She stood on the ledge then, a tiny girl in a too-big shirt, standing among vicious wolves. Several of the wolves that had been lying down got up, and Red Beaver tensed, ready to charge; but they only wagged their tails like friendly dogs, gathering around the child, some licking her.

Sweet Water picked up the tunic, then went inside the cave, coming out with her rawhide belt and her little leather bag of personal items. Red Beaver felt as though none of this was real, as though he were experiencing a vision. Although the wolves did not come to him the way they went to Sweet Water, they made no threatening moves. The mother wolf went to her litter and picked up one of the pups by the scruff of the neck, carrying it over to Sweet Water. It was a white male, and it let out a little whimper. The mother stood looking at Sweet Water, holding the pup as though it were an offering. Red Beaver watched as it seemed Sweet Water and the mother wolf were reading each other's thoughts. Then Sweet Water reached out and took the pup. She turned to Red Beaver with a grin.

"She wants me to keep her son," she told Red Beaver. "He will stay with me and protect me."

Red Beaver watched in awe, feeling blessed at seeing such an astounding event. Surely Sweet Water was one with the wolf. Did the child understand the significance of what had happened to her? He watched the mother wolf carefully as Sweet Water clutched her tunic in one hand and the pup in the other. The mother wolf made no move as Sweet Water took the pup back down the ridge.

Red Beaver followed, feeling the magic of the moment. He watched the white male wolf that had led him there run through the clearing to greet Sweet Water. The animal walked along beside the child, who in turn carried the small pup in her arms. Red Beaver hurried to catch up with her.

"I have to have the paws of the dead wolf," the child called to him.

"What dead wolf, Sweet Water?"

She stopped and looked up at him. "Yesterday. I think it was yesterday. I was playing by a stream, trying to catch a fish. I came upon a grizzly bear. It would have attacked me if not for the wolves. They chased him off, but he killed one of them. Grandfather Wolf has told me in a dream that I must find the dead wolf and cut off its paws for my medicine bag. Then I am to keep its skin for a cape. Will you help me find it, Red Beaver?"

He glanced from the child to the white wolf, which stood beside her. "You dreamed this?"

"*Ai.* The white wolf spoke to me." She felt the heat in her cheeks again. Should she tell Red Beaver he had also been in the dream, and in the vision where the cloud and sun were behind her?

Red Beaver knelt in front of her. "Do you realize what this means, Sweet Water? You have been blessed with a vision, something Indian men long for, something they sacrifice their flesh to find. You have already been shown the animal spirit that will guide and protect you."

Sweet Water watched his dark eyes, thankful that he believed her and had not laughed at her. "You are the only one who knows. I have dreamed about the wolves many times, Red Beaver, but I have never told anyone. Is it right to have a vision without sacrifice?"

Red Beaver wondered at the words coming from someone who should be too young to be worrying about such things. "*Ai*, it is a great gift, Sweet Water. When a vision comes without sacrifice, it has much power. Some will be jealous of this special thing you have found."

Sweet Water watched his long, dark hair blow in wisps across his handsome face, dancing around his wide-set, dark eyes, his full lips and high cheekbones. Why did she feel this strange kinship with him? "Are *you* jealous, Red Beaver?"

He smiled, showing even, white teeth. "No. I only feel honored to be the first to know of your vision." He sobered then. "We are taught that we are not supposed to tell anyone else about our dream visions, Sweet Water, but because you are so small, I suppose it is all right. The wolf spirit would understand why you told me, for you must take the paws and the skin before we leave, and I am the only one who can do that for you. To have such a vision at such a young age is something you must share with Arrow Maker and with the priest, so that they can help you understand it."

Sweet Water swallowed, wanting to tell him there was more reason she should tell him about her dream, for he had been in it.

"Come. I will give you some dried venison," he was telling her, rising. "Before we make camp tonight, I will get you some fresh meat. We must ride for the rest of the day in order to meet your father in time." He put a hand on her shoulder and led her toward his horse. The white wolf followed. Red Beaver stopped, glancing back at it. "What does he want," he asked her. "He will frighten my horse."

Sweet Water stared at the wolf, still holding the pup in her arms. "He is the wolf who spoke to me in my dream," she told Red Beaver. "I think he wishes to lead us to the dead wolf." She looked up at Red Beaver. "Your horse will not be afraid. Its spirit will know the wolf means him no harm."

Red Beaver shook his head in wonder. "We will follow the wolf, then. Come." He led her the rest of the way to his horse, then lifted her up onto the pony with strong arms as easily as if she were a feather. He leapt upon the horse's back behind her in one swift, graceful movement, then reached around the child to pick up the horse's reins. He looked at the white wolf. "Show me where to go, Grandfather Wolf."

They rode off together, and an eagle circled above them.

•   •   •

Sweet Water ate her fill of the fresh rabbit meat. Red Beaver had killed the animal with one shot from his bow and arrow, and Sweet Water thought him a fine hunter. All afternoon and into darkness she had ridden in front of Red Beaver on his fine painted pony, clinging to her wolf pup, pretending to be a warrior's woman. For the first time in days she had felt totally protected as she leaned against Red Beaver's muscled chest and was protected from falling by the strong arm the young man kept circled around her. By now she felt comfortable in his presence, even talkative. Red Beaver did not laugh at her the way some big boys laughed at things little children said.

They had followed the white wolf to where its dead comrade lay, and Red Beaver had cut off the animal's paws for Sweet Water. Together they thanked the wolf's spirit, and Sweet Water had put the paws into the little pouch she still carried on the belt of her tunic. She had tied the belt around the shirt Red Beaver had given her, and it helped make the garment fit her a little better.

Sweet Water had thought it only proper to sing her special prayer song over the dead wolf. Red Beaver agreed, and although she felt bashful about it, she also felt proud at the look of awe in Red Beaver's eyes at the fact that she already had her own prayer song. Red Beaver had skinned the wolf, and quickly scraped the hide and washed it in the nearby stream. He had used his big hunting knife to make up a travois, using young sapling trees for the poles. He tied his supplies onto the travois, then stretched out the wolf hide on it so that it could get air and sun to help dry it faster.

Red Beaver looked around into the shadows beyond the campfire. The white wolf had left them after leading them to the dead wolf. "Is he out there?" he asked.

Sweet Water closed her eyes. "I do not feel him, but he led you to me, and he led us to the dead wolf. Perhaps he will come again and help us find my mother."

Red Beaver leaned closer to her, his dark eyes flashing in the firelight, his features more sharply defined. "It is a great gift you have, Sweet Water," he said reverently. "I wish that I could be so close with an animal spirit."

Sweet Water swallowed, again overwhelmed by the fact that she was talking so intimately with a young man soon to be a warrior. She saw the disappointment in his eyes at not having his own vision yet, and she wanted to erase it. "I . . . I did have a vision about you, Red Beaver," she found herself admitting.

He frowned. "What was it, Sweet Water? What did you see?"

Was it right to tell him? It seemed only right that he should know. Still, the thought of it caused embarrassment to creep under her skin again. Now she had no choice but to finish what she had started to tell him. Would he think she was making fun of him? Would he believe her? Would he think it was bad for a child her age to have a man in her vision?

She looked away, confused by the feelings he gave her. She began petting the wolf pup, which lay by her side. "Many nights I had the same dream," she told him in her small voice. "I was a woman standing in a high place with a cloud behind me, and behind it the sun. Wolves were all around me, protecting me. I did not know until now what it all meant, that the Wolf Spirit would be with me. I was going to tell Old Grandmother about it, or perhaps my father, but I was afraid they would laugh and say children cannot have dreams."

There was a moment of silence, with only the sound of a soft wind in the pines. "I would not laugh, Sweet Water," Red Beaver said softly. "Have I yet laughed at any of the other things you told me?"

She shook her head, swallowing for courage. "The last time I had the dream, you were in it, standing behind me, with the cloud and the sun at your back. You were older, a grown man,—yet I knew it was you. I do not understand why you were there. Perhaps someday the meaning will be revealed to me."

Red Beaver said nothing. Sweet Water felt him move away, and she wanted to dig a hole and crawl into it. Was he angry? Embarrassed? "I have made up a bed for you," he finally told her. "You had better get some rest. We must leave at sunrise."

Tears stung Sweet Water's eyes. She had somehow offended him. Perhaps he was ashamed to be part of a child's vision. Did he think her outrageously bold? Her throat hurt too badly for her to say anything more. She crawled over to her bed and moved under a blanket, pulling the little pup under it with her and holding it close.

In the distance she heard them, wolves, calling to each other, calling to her, singing their special song for their kindred spirit. Their howling made her feel lonely, for it was as though the only living beings that cared about her at the moment were the wolves. She had suddenly lost Red Beaver's confidence and friendship. Oh, how she wished he would say something.

Finally he did speak, almost startling her. "It is indeed a great power you possess, Sweet Water. You think I am angry, but I am not. It gives me a strange, heavy feeling. I want to think that it is just some child's dream, but it cannot be denied you are blessed with the Wolf Spirit. I know you are not making up this story. I will pray to *Maheo* to help me understand this great burden you have placed upon me, for it *is* a burden to be part of another's vision."

He sighed deeply, and there was another moment of silence. A few embers from their fire popped and sparked, creating new little flames that quickly died out again.

"You must tell the priest about your dream," Red Beaver told her. "But now it is our special secret. Sleep well. We must do much traveling tomorrow."

Sweet Water watched his back, feeling a little better. Red Beaver was not angry with her. For the moment that meant more than anything to her. They shared a special secret, and her heart raced with the wonder of all that was happening to her. She turned onto her back, looking up at the seven stars, feeling nothing like the child who had listened to the story about those stars. Something was changed.

Red Beaver and Sweet Water moved through country of astounding beauty, of captivating views of snow-capped peaks and rocky slopes; a land of plunging cliffs choked with loose rock, sage, and yucca plants. They rode past a pristine lake that was so still it perfectly mirrored the blue and gray granite peaks that encircled it. Wildflowers bloomed in every direction, larkspur, paintbrush in its many colors, violets, and columbine. They spotted a herd of elk, but Red Beaver did not stop to kill one. It was important to reach Arrow Maker and the others at the time agreed upon, especially important to tell them he had found Sweet Water.

"For the last two summers I hunted this country with my uncle," Red Beaver was telling her. "That is how we both knew about the Valley of Sweet Grass, where we are to meet. Once we meet him and your father, there will be no time to take you back, Sweet Water. We will have to find the Crow village first, and your mother."

"I will not be afraid, not if I am with you and my father."

Red Beaver felt a surge of manly pride. The white wolf padded along beside them, several yards to their right. Moments later Red Beaver drew his horse to a halt at the top of a high hill. "We are here. Look, down there."

Sweet Water looked down at a broad green valley. She could barely make out a curling wisp of blue smoke from a campfire.

"That will be your father and the others," Red Beaver told her. He headed his horse downward and let out a piercing war whoop, signaling joy and victory. The child had been found! Sweet Water saw a man hurriedly mount a horse and ride at a gallop toward them. She knew it would be her father. The sight of him and the presence of the white wolf who had remained with them gave Sweet Water hope and confidence. Surely now they would find Star Woman! Arrow Maker came closer, and quickly Sweet Water was in his arms, relishing the safety and comfort of his embrace. "My daughter!" he exclaimed. "My prayers are answered." He looked at Red Beaver with tear-filled eyes. "I will pay you many horses for what you have done."

Red Beaver thought about the honor of being part of Sweet Water's vision. "You owe me nothing," he answered. "It is enough to see the joy in your eyes."

•   •   •

"*Ai-ee!* Look where the wolf has led us," Arrow Maker said quietly to the others. "Its power is indeed strong. My daughter surely is a holy child!"

The warriors and Sweet Water all crouched along the ridge of a wooded foothill that overlooked a Crow camp, Sweet Water petting her wolf pup softly so that it would make no noise. Below, a circle of twelve tipis was staked out, and blue smoke curled lazily from a few campfires.

After greeting his daughter with open arms and great rejoicing, Arrow Maker had led the others in a long day's ride, following the white wolf. All of the warriors were impressed by the story of Sweet Water and the wolves, awe-struck by her connection with the Wolf Spirit. The great white wolf had led Red Beaver to the child, and had then led them both to the dead wolf from which Sweet Water had taken the paws, which all were sure must be very strong medicine. They could not help but be victorious now as they rode against the Crow.

They had all ridden into the night, reaching the place of the yellow stones and steaming springs. They had passed by the sacred bubbling mud that was the heart of Grandmother Earth and had moved back into the mountains. They had camped and rested only until the break of day, when they started out again, passing a small herd of moose. Once, somewhere in the rocky hills above them, Sweet Water had heard the roar of a bear. The horses seemed nervous, but soon they calmed.

Since he had been the one to find Sweet Water, and because Arrow Maker had the task of carrying his prayer pipe at all times, Sweet Water remained with Red Beaver on his horse. The wolf had led them through streams and thick forest, descending lower into the foothills at the base of the mountains, north of the place of the yellow stones and steaming ponds. None of the warriors questioned that they were doing the right thing by following the animal. It had led them to this spot just as the sun began to descend toward the western slopes. The wolf then trotted off into the shadows and had not been seen since. Arrow Maker and the others had dismounted and were crouched low, scouting the Crow village in the valley below.

"Do you think this is where Star Woman is being held," Two Moons asked his brother.

Arrow Maker grinned. *"Ai.* Why else would the wolf lead us here? We will get her away from there, and we will get our horses back, as well as take some of their *own* horses! They did not think we would follow them this far, but they do not know we have the power of the Wolf Spirit to help us. They did not think we would find them!"

Sweet Water thought how she would be afraid of her father and the others if she did not know them, for they wore red war stripes on their faces, chests, and arms. Their dark eyes gleamed with a thirst for vengeance, and their nearly naked bodies were taut and ready for a fight. They had stripped off their clothes for battle, as was the custom, so that if they were pierced with a knife or an arrow, no cloth would get into the wound to increase the risk of infection.

"Star Woman will be among the women who do the heavy work," Arrow Maker said quietly. "The women prisoners are always given the heaviest tasks, while the Crow women sit back and give them orders. I am going down closer to those women who are carrying wood. If I see her, I will give her a signal that she will recognize. She will know that she must find a way to walk farther into the woods. Once she is away from the rest of them, I will tell her to run up here, and I will give a war cry and run into the camp to distract the others. When you hear the cry, the rest of you come, and it is each man for himself." He turned to Sweet Water. "When your mother reaches this place, both of you must get on my horse and ride farther back into the hills, following the path by which we came. Hide in that place that I showed you and wait for us. Do not come out unless you hear my voice calling the Wolf Spirit."

Sweet Water nodded. *"Ai, ne-ho-eehe."*

Arrow Maker turned to Red Beaver. "I will go down on foot. Once you hear the signal and the rest of you come down, I will look for your horse. I will ride out with you after I have counted coup and taken a Crow scalp. Put Sweet Water on my horse. She and Star Woman will ride him."

Red Beaver nodded, and Arrow Maker looked at the others. "This will be *our* victory! They will regret what they have done!" The man took his tomahawk from where it rested at his belt and started down the steep hill toward the village.

Another young warrior called White Horse glanced at Sweet Water, envy showing in his eyes. He hoped to one day be a man looked upon with great honor and near worship, the way the others were looking now at Sweet Water. He turned away, thinking that it did not seem right for one small girl to already be blessed by an animal spirit. But one day she would be a woman, and he was already determined he would win her hand and inherit the powerful wolf paws. He already suspected jealously that Red Beaver was thinking the same thing, in spite of Sweet Water's young age. White Horse felt a burning frustration over Red Beaver being the one to find Sweet Water. "We will taste Crow blood this day," he sneered, curling his lips. He looked at Red Beaver haughtily. "Except for you. You are not yet a man."

Red Beaver cast a look of dark pride at White Horse. "We will see who can brag about counting coup at the victory celebration."

White Horse moved his eyes to Sweet Water, then back to Red Beaver, saying nothing more, but looking proud and arrogant. Sweet Water felt a sudden dislike for White Horse, who she knew had a reputation for always challenging someone and wanting to show off his skills. It had never mattered much to her until now. He had insulted Red Beaver, and she wanted to show him that Red Beaver was the better man.

"The white wolf led Red Beaver to me," she said softly. "But it was Red Beaver who noticed the wolf and chose to follow it. That makes him very wise."

White Horse scowled at her, his face growing darker with anger. He moved farther away to wait alone. Red Beaver cast a sidelong glance at Sweet Water, a faint smile turning up the corner of his mouth. There came a soft call then, like that of a dove. Red Beaver turned his attention back to the village below, noticing one woman who had been bent over to collect wood suddenly rise up. She turned her head to listen as the call came again.

"It is she," Red Beaver whispered. "Star Woman!"

Sweet Water's heart rejoiced. Her mother was alive!

"Get ready," Two Moons told the others. "She has moved into the trees."

The warriors quickly mounted their horses, Red Beaver grasping up Sweet Water and setting her on Arrow Maker's mount. He slipped the reins into her hands, then quietly leapt upon his own pony. He had tied some of his supplies onto Arrow Maker's horse. The wolfskin he had saved for Sweet Water had dried, and he had rolled it up with his other things so that he could remove the travois from his pony. The animal had to be free of encumbrances, ready to run hard and fast.

They all waited breathlessly; even the ponies felt the excitement. The next few minutes seemed like hours. Then it came, Arrow Maker's piercing war cry.

"Let's go," Red Foot shouted. *"Hopo! Hopo!"*

Red Beaver turned his pony into a circle, looking once more at Sweet Water. *"Ha-ho,"* he said, thanking her. She knew it was for what she had said to White Horse. He turned and rode off, and Sweet Water watched him, a skillful rider, a young man who she knew would prove himself as good a warrior as any of them.

Sweet Water could hear more war cries now, heard someone cry out as though badly hurt. She hoped it was not any of the Cheyenne. She waited for what seemed an eternity before someone appeared through the trees and ran toward her. She gripped the reins tighter, wondering what she should do if it were a Crow man, for she was supposed to wait for her mother. She saw then that it was a woman, and a smile spread across her face, a face that was growing leaner from losing its baby fat.

"Na-hko-eehe! Hopo! Hopo," she called to her mother.

The woman stopped, then began running toward her, her eyes wide with shock, for she had feared she would never see her little daughter again. How had she survived? *"Na-htona,"* she said, already weeping. "My daughter!"

• • •

The central fire burned brightly against the dark night, casting its flickering glow against the warriors who danced around it. The rhythmic drumming and singing pierced the night air for miles across the vast, open plains. Star Woman and Sweet Water were safe and alive. Horses had been returned, and with them Arrow Maker and the others had brought more horses, stolen from the Crow.

Victory had been sweet in spite of the fact that Arrow Maker had suffered a deep gash on his right thigh and others had been wounded. But there had been no deaths for the Cheyenne, only for the Crow, who had lost four of their finest warriors and many more wounded.

Now it was time to celebrate the return of the woman and child as well as the accomplished revenge. It was a time to be happy, and in spite of her ordeal, even Star Woman was smiling as she watched her husband.

The men danced in near frenzy. Arrow Maker was the proudest of all. Not only did his lance carry the scalp of the Crow man who had taken his wife and child, but his daughter had returned a holy child, blessed by the Wolf Spirit. Some of the women joined in the dancing, giving out their own war cries, pumping up their men's pride with praises and song until the night air came alive, the voices and drumming carrying across a sea of prairie grass in every direction.

Excitement filled the air. The whole village had listened intensely as Arrow Maker and Red Beaver told the story of how the child had been found. Sweet Water herself was asked to tell the story in her own words, and the People had looked upon her reverently. The wolf pup was looked upon as Sweet Water's special guardian; he belonged to the holy child and must never be harmed or even touched. Even the camp dogs stayed away from the small wolf, scouting around it curiously but giving it no challenge.

The dancing, drumming, and singing went on for hours, and the last thing Sweet Water remembered before she drifted off to sleep was the sight of Red Beaver wielding his lance and tomahawk as he crouched and danced before the bright flames, the scar and war paint on his face making him look older than he was, a picture of fierce wildness. His nearly waist-length hair swayed with his movements, his bone hair-pipe breastplate bounced with each step, and he screamed chilling war cries that would surely frighten the bravest enemy.

Sweet Water's head nodded, then her mother's arms came around her and the child slept against the woman's shoulder. The drums and singing penetrated her subconscious, mixing reality with dreams. In her sleep she saw the white wolf beckoning her. She stood beside a stream, and on the other side of the stream stood a man whose face she could not recognize. The man also beckoned her, and she felt a terrible pain in her chest, for the man and the wolf both called to her, but there was only one of her, and she could not go in both directions.

The man began to fade, and she had no choice but to follow the wolf. It led her over a rise, beneath which stretched a sea of white faces, people with blue eyes and short hair, women wearing strange dresses and men with hair on their faces. The wolf told her she must go to them, but Sweet Water was afraid. The wolf assured her she must do this for the People, that if she went to the *ve-ho-e*, she would receive new knowledge, knowledge that would help those she loved.

The sea of white faces turned into one white blur, and the wolf began licking her face. It was then she realized her own wolf pup was licking her. She awoke to realize the drumming and dancing had stopped. Someone had carried her to her own tipi, and all were sleeping peacefully. The child hugged her wolf, wondering what her strange dream about the white people could have meant. And who was the man who beckoned her from across the stream?

Sweet Water felt her blood rushing, her heart pounding with a mixture of dread and anticipation. The priest, Black Buffalo, had summoned her. For one so young to be called before the priest was an honor, but also a frightening experience, for the priest had much power to interpret dreams. He was the one who conducted most of the sacred ceremonies, including the Sun Dance; he was the one who kept the sacred arrows.

Arrow Maker led his daughter to the priest's lodge, a tipi that was bigger than the others. The man rattled the buffalo bones that hung outside the tipi and waited for the priest's wife to open the buffalo-skin flap that covered the entrance.

Sweet Water entered on shaking legs, her sore right hand wrapped around her little medicine bag, her left hand gripping her father's big hand. The wolf pup, which never left her side, trotted in beside her, and Black Buffalo, who sat near a sacred fire, glanced at the wolf. His dark eyes moved to Sweet Water. "It is good medicine you bring inside my lodge," he told her. "Come and sit."

Arrow Maker led his daughter to the place Black Buffalo had indicated. Sweet Water sat down on a blanket made of deer hide, and this morning, for the first time, she wore the sacred wolfskin. It was too warm to wrap it around her shoulders, so she had draped it around her waist and tucked the longer leg skins into her belt to secure it. Now she felt surrounded by the Wolf Spirit, protected. It gave her a little more courage to sit before the priest.

The child found herself almost mezmerized by Black Buffalo's dark eyes, which held her own in a kind of spell. His face bore deep lines from years of exposure to the prairie sun, more age lines than her father. She guessed that some of those lines were put there by the responsibility Black Buffalo had to his people.

Arrow Maker sat down near the tipi entrance to wait. The wolf pup settled down beside the child, and Black Buffalo picked up some sweet grass and laid it on the sacred fire. The smoke it created filled the tipi with a pleasant but pungent smell. Black Buffalo shook a rattle over the fire, then waved some of the smoke over Sweet Water with his hand.

"With this sacred smoke I cleanse you," he told her. "The smoke blesses you and knows that you are pure of heart." He closed his eyes then, and Sweet Water waited for him to speak again.

Black Buffalo was a big man, looking bigger this day because he sat so near and wore a buffalo robe over his shoulders. He also wore a huge headpiece full of eagle feathers and bedecked with a stuffed prairie owl, the only owl the Cheyenne did not fear. The small prairie owl was considered a good-luck charm and was believed to have protective powers. Eagle feathers were tied to the man's wrists and elbows, and his face was painted half white and half blue.

"Last night I prayed." The man finally spoke up again. "The Wolf Spirit spoke to me after I pleaded that it tell me what to do about the holy child, to show me how I might help her." He leaned closer. "It told me this, Sweet Water," he said, his eyes gleaming, his demeanor, to Sweet Water, as threatening as the great grizzly. "It told me that you are to give me, Black Buffalo, the wolf paws." His eyes widened and seemed full of fire. "They are too sacred for one so young. They were given to you only as a messenger, so that you could carry them to me, to the People and their priest." He put out his hand. "Give me the wolf paws."

Sweet Water's heart pounded so hard she thought it might jump out of her chest. She felt perspiration breaking out all over her body, and the tipi seemed much too warm. Her eyes remained glued to the priest, and he literally struck terror in her heart. But for some reason she could not move her hand to take the wolf paws from her medicine bag; nor did she want to do it. She had no idea just what was happening, and she knew it was every good Cheyenne man and woman's duty to obey whatever the priest told them, for everything he did and said was from a sacred vision and must not be disobeyed.

Still, the Wolf Spirit had become special to her. Hadn't the wolf told her the paws would protect her and guide her future? It didn't seem right that she should hand them over to someone else.

"Give me the wolf paws," Black Buffalo repeated, watching the fear and apprehension in her big brown eyes.

Sweet Water began to shake. She squeezed her hand tightly around her medicine bag, a feeling of jealous protectiveness coming over her. She met Black Buffalo's eyes squarely. She wished her father would come to her rescue, but she knew Arrow Maker would not interfere. This was a sacred moment.

"No," she answered, finally finding her voice. She wondered for a moment if the word had really come from her. It came out in more of a squeak than her own voice, and it lacked the firmness she would have preferred.

Black Buffalo sucked in his breath and straightened, pulling back from her as though he had been struck. His hand darted out over the fire, and again he shook the rattle, putting back his head and letting out a startling cry. Sweet Water shook harder, waiting for something terrible to happen to her. One tear slipped down her cheek, and she continued to cling to her medicine bag.

Black Buffalo turned to meet her eyes again, and to her surprise he actually gave her a light smile, reaching out and touching the top of her head. "You are indeed a holy child," he told her. "It took great courage for you to deny a demand from the priest." The man wiped the tears on her soft cheeks with the tips of his fingers. "Do not cry, little one. The Wolf Spirit told me I must test you this way, to see if you were strong enough and worthy enough to hold the sacred paws. He told me I must see if you would protect them with courage and honor. You have done so." The man waved more smoke over her.

"You will no longer be called Sweet Water," he told her. "Your name is Medicine Wolf, and you are holy. The wolf paws you carry possess great protective powers. When dreams come to you, you must tell me so that I can help you understand them, for they will show our People the way to go. Do you understand, Medicine Wolf?"

Sweet Water nodded, trying to imagine answering to a completely new name.

"At the Sun Dance you will become a princess," the man continued. "You will be a soldier girl for the Dog Soldier Society, our bravest men. Anyone you touch with the wolf's paw will be blessed. The man who marries you, if you choose to marry at all, must be a man of great honor and courage, also a man of wealth. He must bring your father no less than fifteen horses stolen from an enemy, as well as a winter's supply of food, four buffalo robes, a

Crow scalp, an eagle feather, and an enemy war shield. He must be a Dog Soldier, and one who has sacrificed his flesh at the Sun Dance. Even then, he must have my blessing as well as your father's. Do you understand all of this?''

Again Sweet Water nodded, not wishing to tell him that she was too overwhelmed at the moment to remember all of this. A soldier girl at such a young age? What were all the gifts her future husband must bring her father? Already she had forgotten some of them.

"The wolf's paws are yours to use however the Wolf Spirit directs you to use them," the priest was saying. "You may give away one, but only to a warrior who has been part of your sacred dreams, and only for something very special, such as the Sun Dance. When you give the gift of the wolf's paw, it must be your secret. No one must know who has it, for it might cause jealousy among the young men. He who owns it will have much power, success, and prosperity." The man leaned closer, his dark eyes holding a look of warning. "Do not take this lightly, Medicine Wolf. It is a great responsibility you carry. You have been chosen, and that cannot be changed."

Sweet Water swallowed, deciding she had better tell Black Buffalo about the dreams she had had the night before, about being torn between following a faceless man and following the white wolf; about how she had chosen the wolf, and he had led her to a place where many *ve-ho-e* waited for her. The wolf told her she must go to them.

Black Buffalo turned to stare at the sacred fire. He told Arrow Maker he must leave, and Arrow Maker quickly obeyed. Black Buffalo breathed deeply of the sweet-smelling smoke, taking several minutes to meditate before answering Sweet Water. "The first part of the dream is something that was also given to me to see," he told her. "The wolf told me that one day you would be challenged again, but in a different way. Someday you will be forced to choose between the wolf paws and someone you love. You will have only one choice, and your heart will be torn. To choose the loved one will be to turn against the Wolf Spirit. This would be a very bad thing to do. You must not tell this to another living soul, not even to the one who challenges you. You must not explain. You must only choose. This is the meaning of the first part of your dream. Do you understand?''

Sweet Water felt like crying. She suddenly wished she were not a holy child at all, wished that the Wolf Spirit had chosen someone else on whom to place this burden. "I understand," she answered in her small voice.

Black Buffalo nodded. "The second part of your dream is very important. You have been chosen to go among the *ve-ho-e* and learn their ways. In this way we can better understand the white eyes, be better prepared to fight them if too many of them come to our land and take our game and hunting grounds. There are not many now, but the spirits have told me the blue-eyed ones are dangerous and many.''

She felt sick inside. How could she ever leave the Cheyenne, leave her mother and father to go and live among the strange, hairy-faced *ve-ho-e*? Oh, why did the Wolf Spirit expect so much of her? She would be terrified to do such a thing! "I—I would not want to go away," she said.

The man's eyes saddened. "This I know. But because of your blessings, you must be very brave, and always obey your dreams. I do not know when this will happen, Medicine Wolf. I know only that it must be so, and you must be ready. You must not cry or refuse to go, for the wolf already told you that you will always return to your people." He touched her shoulder. "Never be afraid, Medicine Wolf. Go now. Remember all that I have told you. Tonight at council meeting I will tell the others that you are now called Medicine Wolf. I will announce the price that will have to be paid to win your hand when you come of age, and that from now on when the Dog Soldier Society holds council, you will be invited to join them as a princess and that you will be allowed to bless them with a touch of the wolf's paw. Think on all that I have told you, and be ready for the time when the things the wolf has told you will come to pass. It is done. You have been chosen.''

The man looked back at the fire, and the child picked up the wolf pup, glad to leave. She stood up, thinking that her legs felt like they were removed from her body. She walked around the fire, remembering it was very bad medicine to walk between a fire and its keeper. She walked out into the bright sunlight, feeling as though she had just awakened from a strange dream. She felt eyes on her again, for many had noticed her go to the priest's lodge. Black Buffalo's words burned into her heart like a hot coal. *Someday you will be forced to choose between the wolf paws and someone you love . . . your heart will be torn.*

She glanced over to where her friends played, little girls carrying their stick dolls, little boys playing war, shooting small, harmless bows and arrows. She felt she didn't belong with them anymore, and it made her sad. She wanted to play, as she did before, but so much was expected of her now. Could she just be a little girl again? What had happened to the Sweet Water who had been taken away by the Crow? She had come back changed. Now even her name had been changed. She was to be called Medicine Wolf.

Part 2

Chapter Four

Medicine Wolf packed her new doll into the little cradleboard she and Old Grandmother had made together from cedar branches and a deerskin Arrow Maker had given them. Medicine Wolf was nine years old now and learning how to do the things expected of a woman. She had sewn and beaded a pair of moccasins, which she now wore, and today she and her friend, Summer Moon, were going out with the other girls to build their own tipis.

For an Indian child, these were good times in spite of the strange events taking place. Medicine Wolf often heard her father and mother talking over the evening fire about how the whites were causing more trouble for the Cheyenne. She did not like to hear talk about white men because it reminded her that she was destined to go and live with them some day. She wondered sometimes if maybe even the Wolf Spirit would forget all that had happened and she would not have to worry about any of Black Buffalo's predictions coming true. Three whole summers had passed since her abduction and her strange experience with the wolves. She still carried the sacred wolf paws in her medicine bag; and the wolf pup she had kept was now a magnificent full-grown white wolf.

In spite of her own importance, Medicine Wolf's greatest pride, although a secret one, was that Red Beaver, now called Bear Paw, was now also a Dog Soldier. He was seventeen, fully a man. Medicine Wolf would never forget witnessing his sacrifice at the Sun Dance. He had been so brave, blowing on his eagle-bone whistle to ease the pain as he had danced around the central pole of the Sun Dance lodge until the skewers that pierced his flesh were torn loose. He had fasted and prayed for many days, asking *Maheo* to bless his people with long life and prosperity. In return for his sacrifice and prayers, he had apparently received a vision that involved the great and sacred bear, for now he had named himself after the beast. As was custom for adult males, Bear Paw had told no one but the priest about his vision.

Medicine Wolf often wondered if Bear Paw remembered all the things she had told him about being a part of her dreams. Did he think now that it was all silly after all? Did he realize how nervous she felt whenever he came with his uncle and father to visit her own father's tipi and take supper with them?

Star Woman tied the small cradleboard to Medicine Wolf's back so that she could pretend she was carrying a real baby. The new doll, stuffed with horse hair, peeked out from the cradleboard like a little papoose. Smiling Girl, now six, watched her sister with a pout, for she wanted to play with her today, but Medicine Wolf would have none of it. Today she was going to build her first tipi. She was doing important "big girl" things.

Smiling Girl held Medicine Wolf's old stick doll. She watched her sister run off happily with Summer Moon. Medicine Wolf took hold of one of her father's horses, which she had packed with hides and poles necessary for building the tipi. The two girls headed for a spot several yards from the main village, where many other young girls had gathered.

Old Grandmother walked with them. She would help teach Medicine Wolf and Summer Moon how to build their tipi. Star Woman knew how much her mother enjoyed helping her grandchildren, so she would stay behind. This was a special moment for Old Grandmother, and Star Woman would not take it from her. Teaching her granddaughter a woman's ways was a pleasure for the old grandmother. Heavy chores were for the young. This was Old Grandmother's time of peace and gentle teaching.

The girls and Old Grandmother reached their building site and unloaded their supplies. Soon the air was filled with laughter and happy voices. This was a time for learning, but also, as with most things an Indian child did, a time for fun. Today Medicine Wolf did not care about the responsibilities of being the keeper of the wolf paws. She did not care about problems with the white men, who were fighting some kind of war of their own far to the south in a place called Mexico. She did not care that the white men were sending many of their own soldiers into Indian lands.

The outside world that was closing in around her seemed unreal to Medicine Wolf. Her life was one of freedom and joy. She migrated north and south along the foothills of the beautiful Rockies and traveled with her People the length and breadth of the great plains and prairies in an endless land that she thought was surely big enough that there should be no problem with the *ve-ho-e*. The men talked about whites killing too many buffalo, but her belly was full, and the warriors still went on the hunt, and the women still were left with many of the great shaggy beasts to skin and dress out, almost more than they could keep up with. Later this summer, when they went north again for another Sun Dance, Medicine Wolf would herself begin learning how to dress out a buffalo. This time they would gather with several different tribes of the Sioux, and her brother, Runner, now fifteen, would participate in the Sun Dance.

In spite of white man's sicknesses that sometimes took many lives among the Cheyenne, no one in her family had suffered or died, and their numbers still seemed strong. She was not concerned that a few of the men of her tribe had taken to drinking something the white men had been selling them, something they called firewater. She supposed it must be a magical, powerful drink, for Indian men who tried it swore that it gave them strength, made them more brave and sometimes caused them to have visions. It did make them act as though they were indeed possessed of a strange spirit. It was so powerful that when a man drank too much of it, he sometimes could barely move the next morning. Her father would not touch the drink, for he had not yet decided if its medicine was bad or good.

There was a white man named Fitzpatrick who sometimes counciled with them now. The Indians called him Broken Hand. He was a scout for white people, and a friend to the Cheyenne. Medicine Wolf was becoming a little more familiar with the *ve-ho-e*, for she had studied them intently every time her tribe traveled south to the place called Bent's Fort, where they visited with their southern relatives and traded buffalo skins to white men for pretty beads and tobacco and other useful things at the fort. She reasoned the *ve-ho-e* could not be all bad, for they sold some wonderful useful instruments to the Cheyenne, like metal pots and beautiful colored cloth and the magical looking glass.

Yes, she decided, things were not so bad; and today she was happy. It was a sunny, pleasant day on the plains. Wolf settled down near her to watch the proceedings. He panted lightly from the warm day, his tongue hanging out, his tail occasionally wagging, appearing as docile as any camp dog.

Old Grandmother seemed proud that she had chosen the best spot for Medicine Wolf's tipi. "Take the skins down from the horse," she told Medicine Wolf with an eager smile. "How to build the tipi is one of the most important things to know," she added. She was proud of Medicine Wolf's importance to the People. The old woman had always felt her granddaughter was meant for great things.

Medicine Wolf's heart beat with excitement. Since there were no trees to which she could tie her father's horse, she bent down and hobbled the animal so that he could not run off. She removed her cradleboard as carefully as she would have had it contained a real baby, and she laid it down in the grass close to her. The horse began grazing calmly as Medicine Wolf and Summer Moon began unloading the hides and poles from his back.

The poles had been cut from young saplings. The two girls had chopped down the young trees themselves with a hatchet, thanking the trees for their offering toward the girls' first tipi. Again it had been Old Grandmother who had shown them the best trees for making the strongest poles. They had been cut over three weeks earlier, from a stand of trees in which they had camped when the Cheyenne had moved north across the Arkansas River.

This time when they visited the fort, she had felt an urgency among her father and the other men, an eagerness to get out of the area. Her father said it was dangerous in the south now; Cheyenne were being blamed for bad things that were happening to white people, things Arrow Maker said were being done by the Comanche and the Apache and some Arapaho, not the Cheyenne.

Medicine Wolf dismissed the thought and laughed when she and Summer Moon made their first attempt at stacking the tipi poles at just the right angle so that they came together at the top and did not fall. With Old Grandmother's help, they finally succeeded.

"You must be patient and learn the right way," the old woman told the children. "Sometimes, when the enemy is coming, you must be able to take down the tipi very quickly and be ready to run. Later today the young boys will come and attack you, and you must be able to take down your tipi before they can kill you."

Medicine Wolf and Summer Moon giggled, excitement building at the thoughts of war games they would play later with the young boys. Medicine Wolf watched her grandmother's thin, bony hands as she helped the girls. She wondered where the old woman got her strength, for she did not look as though she had any muscle left between her skin and her bones. She tried not to think about the fact that Old Grandmother could not keep waking up alive and well every morning for much longer, for she was many summers old, and all old things die.

She paid close attention to everything the old woman

taught her. Later this summer the woman would teach her the art of preparing fresh new buffalo hides. It was a difficult and time-consuming chore, but one that must be done. It was time for Medicine Wolf to learn to help, for one day she would have to do such things for her own family. She had watched it done many times, but had never prepared a hide by herself. She knew the hides had to be soaked until they were soft, then staked out and fleshed, removing all tissue and fat. They had to be washed two or three times with soap made from the yucca plant, then left to dry and bleach in the sun, the bare side painted once it was dry. After that the hair had to be scraped from the other side, the hairs saved for stuffing in pillows and saddles. The hides were softened more by pounding them and rubbing them with buffalo brains and fat. Considering the fact that it took several hides to erect a good-size tipi, preparing enough hides for the structure often took weeks.

The area of tipi building came alive with activity and playful laughter. In the distant village, which was nestled peacefully in a wooded area along the Republican River, women gathered wood, and men smoked their pipes as they rested from another hunt. Everyone was more relaxed now, for they were farther away from the place in the south where there seemed to be so much trouble with the *ve-ho-e*.

Medicine Wolf and Summer Moon worked on their tipi most of the day, putting it up, taking it down, putting it up again. Medicine Wolf wondered if she would ever be able to do this as fast as her mother. She would practice over and over until she had it right. She and Summer Moon worked until the sun began to settle along the tops of the rim of mountains to the west, so far away that they were only a low blue line.

Medicine Wolf thought about those mountains often. Every moment she had spent alone high in the Rockies had remained vivid in her memory. The fourth finger on her right hand remained stiff. It had never healed quite right, and she couldn't bend it at the knuckle, making it difficult for her to do things like sew beads and quills onto moccasins and clothing.

Her father and many of the other warriors had successfully ridden against the Crow several times since her abduction. Bear Paw was one of the more skillful and successful warriors. He had stolen many Crow horses, as well as Pawnee and Shoshoni horses, enough to make any seventeen-year-old very proud, and twenty-year-old White Horse was very jealous. The entire village knew that White Horse was always in competition with Bear Paw. Whatever Bear Paw accomplished, White Horse tried to match it, scalp for scalp, horse for horse, coup for coup.

Medicine Wolf smiled at the thought, for White Horse was having a difficult time keeping up. He would have to try again soon, for the men were planning another raid against the Pawnee, who continued to encroach upon Cheyenne hunting grounds. Years earlier the Pawnee had stolen the Cheyenne sacred arrows. Since then the Cheyenne blamed any misfortune they experienced on the fact that their sacred arrows were in the hands of the Pawnee. Medicine Wolf's blessing of the wolf paws was the most important thing that had happened to the Cheyenne since then, and something that gave them new hope of getting the arrows back from their old enemy.

For the third time Medicine Wolf pounded wooden stakes through the bottom of the tipi skins into the ground to hold them firmly. She stood back with Old Grandmother and Summer Moon to look at the finished project, a dwelling that was twelve feet across on the inside, the skins pulled nice and tight, with a second lining inside for extra warmth and to protect those inside from rain dripping from the support poles. The most important purpose of the inner lining was to keep the tipi fire from casting shadows against the outside wall, shadows that could provide targets for an enemy.

"*Wagh!* It is very good," Old Grandmother told her.

Medicine Wolf and Summer Moon grinned with pride, then grasped hands. "Thank you for helping us," Medicine Wolf told her grandmother.

"Our families will come out later and see," Summer Moon said excitedly, squeezing Medicine Wolf's hand.

"You must also learn how to make backrests and your own parfleches for carrying your things," Old Grandmother told them. "In them you will carry your tools for cleaning hides, your bone needles for sewing skins and decorating them with beads and quills. You will carry soap and perhaps a looking glass. It will be your own parfleche, made with your own hands and decorated with your own sign." Then the old woman gasped, feigning great terror. "Look! The enemy comes!"

She pointed a bony finger toward the village, where a group of boys between the ages of four and twelve were gathering. They straddled horses made from branches, and carried sticks that were supposed to be tomahawks. Some of the older boys carried bows and arrows, which they were learning to use to hunt and sometimes to spear fish, but today they would not use them for any harm.

Medicine Wolf saw her mother and father and brother gather to watch, along with many more from the village. The boys were going to "attack" the girls, and the girls would have to see how quickly they could take down their tipis and flee.

The Cheyenne loved these games. Later the entire village would enjoy a feast of buffalo meat and turnips. But for now there would be entertainment. Medicine Wolf's heart beat harder with excitement as the young boys began calling out war whoops and preparing to attack. All the young girls who had practiced building their tipis began screaming and tearing down the structures as quickly as they could. The boys began running toward them, hanging on to their "horses" and wielding their "hatchets."

Medicine Wolf worked as fast as she could, rolling the hides around and off the poles and throwing them over her father's horse. Wolf stood up, wagging his tail, sensing the excitement, and a little confused over whether he was expected to protect his charge.

"The baby. Do not forget your child," Old Grandmother reminded Medicine Wolf. "Saving the children always comes first."

Medicine Wolf ran to pick up the cradleboard. She quickly tied it to the horse while Summer Moon rolled up another hide. Only the poles were left, but there was no time to gather them. The young boys were upon them. The girls screamed and laughed, picking up sticks of their own that were supposed to be clubs and hatchets. Whoever got touched first went down as though killed. Medicine Wolf managed to touch three boys before one finally touched her arm from behind. She screamed and fell laughing.

All around her the air was filled with giggles and screams. Tipis came down, none quickly enough. The boys jumped up and down as though victorious, and the villagers who watched greatly enjoyed the spectacle. Soon the adults were mixing with the children, talking to the young girls about how much they had learned. Old Grandmother greatly praised Summer Moon and Medicine Wolf. "We will practice again tomorrow," she said. "Perhaps we will build some backrests, as long as we are close to a place where there are trees."

Arrow Maker put a hand on Medicine Wolf's shoulder. "You can make one for your father," he told her. "The one I am using now is getting too old and stretched. It is no longer comfortable."

Medicine Wolf felt a wonderful pride at being asked to build her father a new backrest. Her father was still a strong, honored warrior, a leader among the Dog Soldiers. He helped her gather the skins and poles, and all of them headed back toward the village for a night of feasting and games. Medicine Wolf took the reins of her father's horse and led it, lagging behind the others for a moment, laughing again at the thought of the pretend attack. She felt a presence then, off to her right. She turned to see Bear Paw sitting on a handsome roan gelding, a white bear paw painted on its left shoulder.

Her smile faded. Always there had been the special, secret feeling for Bear Paw, ever since he had found her in the mountains and she had told him about her vision. He rode closer, and again there came the strange rush to her blood, the hot feeling in her cheeks. For the past three years he had hardly spoken to her other than the normal things any young man might say to a little girl when visiting her father's tipi, or the normal respect any Dog Soldier would give a princess of their society whenever she was present at the council meetings.

Today he looked especially grand. It seemed to her he had grown again, that his shoulders were a little broader, his arms a little bigger, his face more manly. Was he really only seventeen? Already his young body bore many scars from the Sun Dance and from battle. She respectfully waited for him to speak first when he drew up his horse near her.

"You did well today," he told her. "I watched you."

Medicine Wolf felt suddenly too warm. "I did not get the tipi down fast enough."

"You will, in time." He gave her a soft smile.

Medicine Wolf was hardly aware that she was literally staring at him. To her Bear Paw was already a great warrior. He made her feel suddenly nervous and undone. This was the first time he had singled her out in the three years since her rescue. He seemed to want to say something more, but the moment was interrupted by White Horse, who rode toward them at a fast gallop. "Come, Bear Paw," he said, a haughty, bossy tone to the words. "You dally here while scouts tell us they have spotted a Pawnee hunting party! We must go and chase them out of Cheyenne country! It is time to take some Pawnee scalps!"

Bear Paw's eyes had been glued to Medicine Wolf— why, she could not imagine. He turned to face White Horse. "I am not dallying, and I do not need you to tell me what to do."

White Horse's dark eyes gleamed with hurt pride. He glanced at Medicine Wolf and her wolf, then looked back at Bear Paw. "She will one day belong to the man who has proved himself the best, the man who brings the most gifts, more than Black Buffalo said would be needed to win her hand."

"She will belong to the man who wins her heart. That is all that will matter," Bear Paw shot back, a fiery determination in his voice.

Medicine Wolf watched in astonishment. She? Were they talking about *her*? She was only nine! Surely Bear Paw was not talking about winning her heart and owning her!

"*Heyoka,*" White Horse snarled, calling Bear Paw a fool. "You know the requirements. Do not think you have an advantage just because you once rescued her! It was only because the wolf led you to her! And for now she is just a child. Did you come here to woo a little girl? You had better turn your eyes to the *women*, Bear Paw. Have you even learned what to do with them yet," he sneered.

Bear Paw only grinned slightly, apparently taking no embarrassment at the words. "A man is not judged by how often he visits the tipis where the Crow and Pawnee women are held," he shot back. "But at least when I *do* visit them, they do not fight me."

To her surprise, Medicine Wolf felt a stabbing jealousy at the words. She became acutely aware of Bear Paw's nearly naked body, his muscled thighs, and flat belly. It almost shocked her to realize she took pleasure in looking at him.

"But that is not how I would be judged," he was telling White Horse. "A man is judged only by his success on the hunt and against the enemy. And maybe you can tell us, White Horse, why *you* are here. I already know the Pawnee are near, and we both know we do not need to ride against them until tomorrow. Could it be that you are jealous that I have come out here to speak to a little girl? If so, then who of us is the real fool?"

More color moved into White Horse's face. Wolf crouched slightly then, growling softly, his yellow eyes set on White Horse. The young man glanced at the animal, trying to hide the fear Wolf put into his heart. He took one more hateful look at Bear Paw, then turned his horse and rode off.

Bear Paw watched after him a moment, then looked back at Medicine Wolf. "Do not listen to the things he says. He does not understand." He moved his horse even closer to the girl. "I understand the vision now, Medicine Wolf. Someday I will explain. Just remember that I was the one in your vision."

He turned his horse and rode off with no further explanation. Medicine Wolf stared after him in wonder. Was he telling her she was meant to be his wife? Was he saying he would wait for her, and that she must choose only him? She was embarrassed that Bear Paw had watched the childish games she had played, carrying a fake papoose, pretending to fight the little boys to protect her own. Had he

seen how clumsily she had erected and torn down the tipi?
Had he laughed at her?

Somehow she knew he had not. On shaking legs she
walked on to catch up with the others, and she had no
desire to play any more games tonight. Again she realized
that in Bear Paw's presence the child in her seemed to
vanish.

Medicine Wolf stood hesitantly outside the entrance to
Black Buffalo's tipi, hoping she was doing the right thing.
The Cheyenne had realized a sweet victory over the Pawnee hunting party that had intruded into Cheyenne hunting
grounds. Many Pawnee had been killed or injured, most
of their horses stolen, their base village destroyed and their
women and children scattered. To the disappointment of
the Cheyenne, the sacred arrows had not been found, but
now at least the Pawnee would stay out of Cheyenne territory for some time to come.

Arrow Maker had suffered no injuries, but a few others
had. Bear Paw was the only one whose injury threatened
his life. He had counted coup several times, but the last
charge had cost him a hatchet wound to his right ribs and
a serious head wound suffered as his head hit a rock when
he fell from his horse. His uncle, White Eagle, had killed
the Pawnee man who had wounded Bear Paw.

The stories had been told over and over the previous
night, each warrior telling of his exploits, showing his
trophies of scalps and stolen Pawnee weapons and horses.
White Eagle, proud of his nephew, had bragged of Bear
Paw's bravery and had shown the Pawnee war shield Bear
Paw had stolen from one of his victims. "If Bear Paw
dies," he had told the others, "we will lay the war shield
on his breast when we place him on the scaffold. He will
be an honored warrior in the Great Beyond, where he will
walk with our loved ones who have gone before us." White
Eagle's eyes had shown tears when he spoke of his beloved
nephew.

Now the celebrations were over. Bear Paw had been
hurt and lay near death, and Medicine Wolf felt as though

her heart would break into a hundred pieces. She had to help him somehow.

She touched the hollow bones outside the tipi to signal her presence. A moment later the priest emerged from the tipi, still looking to Medicine Wolf like a great, giant grizzly because of his size and the shaggy buffalo robe he wore around his shoulders no matter what the weather.

"So," he said. "You have not come to me since first I told you the meaning of your dreams. What brings you here now, Medicine Wolf?" He looked very stern, then softened slightly, as though he had been teasing her. "I think I already know." He stood back and let her inside.

Medicine Wolf sat down at Black Buffalo's ever-burning fire. The tipi was filled with the smell of sage and sweet grass. "You are here because of Bear Paw," Black Buffalo told her.

Medicine Wolf arched her eyebrows in surprise that he already knew. "*Ai.* How did you know?"

The man touched her head. "Because he captured a Pawnee war shield. He risked his life for that shield. Why do you think he did so, child?"

She watched his eyes. "I do not know."

He seemed to want to smile. "Remember the things I told you long ago, Medicine Wolf, that the one who marries you will have to present Arrow Maker with many gifts. Do you remember what they were?"

Medicine Wolf frowned, thinking hard. Fifteen horses, four buffalo robes, a Crow scalp . . . Bear Paw already had a scalp, and several horses. A winter's supply of food, and an enemy war shield!

Black Buffalo saw the surprise in her eyes and nodded. He touched his fingers in some of the cooler ash of the fire, then placed them against Medicine Wolf's forehead and cheeks, streaking them with the holy ashes. "There is much power in being a part of another's vision. Bear Paw knows this, and it was a matter of great concern to him. Already he works at gathering the things that would be necessary to own you. So does another—White Horse. One day, when you are fully a woman, there will be many difficult choices you will have to make; for now, you have a duty to help Bear Paw live. Remember that I told you that you have the right to give one bear paw to a worthy warrior. It will bless him with strength and good fortune. I also told you it should be your secret. No one else should know whom you choose for this special blessing. It will be between you and him.''

Medicine Wolf smiled, knowing now what she must do. "Thank you, Father," she told the man, calling him Father as a sign of honor. She rose. "I must go now.''

Black Buffalo nodded and said nothing more as she left and headed for Stalking Bear's lodge. Stalking Bear was her clan's Shaman, medicine man, who prayed and chanted over Bear Paw.

A warm sunrise took the chill out of the morning, but Medicine Wolf hardly noticed. Without hesitation, she announced her presence, and Stalking Bear's wife folded back the entrance flap of the tipi and let the girl inside. Stalking Bear, kneeling over Bear Paw, raised his head to see Medicine Wolf. He showed a hint of jealousy, for he knew this child might have special healing powers. But he also knew she was someone to be honored, and he allowed her to come closer.

"I . . . I must see Bear Paw alone," Medicine Wolf told the man, again experiencing the sensation of suddenly feeling much older. Where had she found the courage to talk to Stalking Bear with such authority? To her further surprise, the man nodded and rose, taking his wife outside with him. Medicine Wolf felt a strange power move through her blood in a slow, warm flow. She summoned her courage to allow her eyes to look upon Bear Paw, and she sucked in her breath in shock, for in spite of his dark skin, he looked oddly pale, his eyes closed and sunken, dark circles around them.

She went to her knees, gasping his name, but he gave no hint of hearing her. He lay naked, a cloth draped over private parts. His breathing was shallow, and the wound at his side was heavily packed with moss for prevention of infection, and with other healing herbs. It was covered with deerskin that showed bloodstains. Medicine Wolf leaned closer, noticing an odd blue color to the whole right side of Bear Paw's face. She realized it must be from the head wound, but she could not see the wound itself.

Could she really help him? She opened her medicine
bag, still worn on her belt, and she reached inside to take
out one of the paws. She raised it in the air, singing her
personal prayer song. This time, after pleading to Grandmother Earth and Grandfather Wolf and *Maheo*, she asked
that they join in force and use their power to heal Bear
Paw.

> I sing my thanks to you,
> Forever the wolf shall be sacred to me.
> Forever the earth shall be sacred to me.
> Forever I will please Maheo.

"Please, Grandmother Earth," she pleaded quietly.
"Heal this man." She picked up some dirt from the tipi
floor and sprinkled it over Bear Paw's throat. "Please,
Grandfather Wolf, heal this man."

She took the Wolf's paw and touched it to Bear Paw's
wounded side, then moved it to his forehead and touched
him again. "Oh, great *Maheo*, bring life to this man's eyes
again, life to his limbs, a voice to his throat. Take away
his pain, for his pain is my pain."

She had no idea how she knew the right things to say.
She repeated the prayer, touching Bear Paw again, feeling
removed from herself, as though she were watching all of
this from above. The wolf's paw felt warm, as though it
were alive. In moments Bear Paw's eyes fluttered open. A
chill moved through Medicine Wolf as she drew her hand
away and he looked at her as though he recognized her,
although he did not speak.

"I came to help you," she told him. She leaned closer
again, feeling bold but very special, wondering what this
man thought of a child praying over him. "I am giving
you a gift, Bear Paw, but it must be our secret." She took
his hand and pressed the wolf's paw into his palm. She
closed his fingers. "Take the sacred wolf's paw. It is yours.
It will give you strength and protect you from future
harm."

His eyes seemed to tear. "You are giving it . . . to
me?" She nodded, and Bear Paw looked at her almost

lovingly. "Thank you, Medicine Wolf. I stole the shield
. . . for you."

Their eyes held in a new understanding. There was no
need to explain any further. Someday, when she was a
woman . . . She still held his hand and in spite of his
condition, she felt the strength in that hand, took a pleasant comfort of her own in touching it. "This must be our
secret," she cautioned him.

"Our secret," he whispered, searching her eyes. "My
medicine bag. No one must see . . . the paw."

Medicine Wolf's eyes moved down his splendid naked
body, falling on the thin cord tied around his groin area.
A warrior's medicine bag held his most sacred fetishes,
things no one else ever saw. It was worn on his inner
thigh, a personal area no one else ever touched, except,
perhaps, a wife. Even when wounded, a man's medicine
bag was not removed, for it contained magical powers that
could help him heal. Medicine Wolf knew Bear Paw
wanted her to put the wolf's paw into his medicine bag.
To ask her to do it was a great honor.

With shaking hands Medicine Wolf daringly folded
back the deerskin that covered Bear Paw's private area,
thinking that what she was doing took more courage than
facing the grizzly bear when she was six, or walking into
a den of wolves. This was Bear Paw! Never had she been
this close to the most sacred area of a grown man! She
tried not to look too closely at that part of him that both
fascinated and frightened her. With shaking fingers she
hurriedly untied his medicine bag, trying to keep the deerskin over as much of him as possible. For the moment she
was almost glad he was in pain, for he surely could not
be fully aware that a girl was touching his sacred medicine
bag, looking upon him intimately.

. She finally got the bag loose and opened it, surprised
then to realize Bear Paw had raised his hand without help
and opened it to give her the wolf's paw. "Put it . . .
inside," he told her. "Tie it back on me . . . so no one
will know . . . that you touched it."

The child's eyes were wide with amazement at what
she had found the courage to do. She took the wolf's paw
and put it inside his medicine bag, being careful not to

look inside and see anything else it might hold. She drew it shut, then laid it back on his thigh and pulled the cord back through it that held it close to his body. She retied the cord and covered him again with the deerskin.

She could not bring herself to meet his eyes again, until to her surprise she felt his big hand covering her own small one. He squeezed it lightly. "It is . . . a great gift you have given me," he told her.

Never had Medicine Wolf felt more special or more proud. She started to rise, but Bear Paw held her hand with surprising strength, groaning her name. She could not help meeting his eyes. "Touch your cheek . . . to mine," he told her, his voice gruff with pain. "Please."

The almost begging look in his eyes tore at her heart, and embarrassment was replaced with pity . . . and something else. Something she could not quite name. Her whole body felt on fire. More than anything else, she didn't want Bear Paw to die, or to even be in pain. At the moment she would do anything to make him feel better. She leaned closer again, her dark hair falling to shroud his handsome face. She lightly touched her cheek to his own, and a marvelous sensation moved through her, one of comfort and warmth and strength. For this one magical, portentious moment, she was a woman.

"I will live because of you," he told her. "I have the wolf's paw."

Medicine Wolf raised herself up slightly, meeting his eyes again. The tipi seemed misty, and for them both there was momentarily no reality, only this magical, mystical feeling of floating in a vision, of seeing their future in each other's eyes. Medicine Wolf knew then that she did not have to be afraid of allowing herself to be the child that she was, for Bear Paw saw the woman in her and would wait for that woman to blossom.

Chapter Five

"Look!"

Medicine Wolf followed her mother's eyes. Their entire clan had halted on a high Nebraska hill, on their summer migration north to meet with the Sioux. Bear Paw, now healing but still weak, sat on his pony watching with the others. The men had signaled the women and children to come no farther. There was an obstacle in their path, one that was both amazing and unsettling.

Below them stretched an endless line of white-topped wagons. It was a chilling sight, for the *ve-ho-e* paraded their rolling houses right through the Indian lands and hunting grounds. Farther to the east Medicine Wolf could see where a whole stand of trees had been cut down, apparently for several campfires the night before. She was shocked to see that only parts of the trees had been used, many branches and the trunks left untouched. It reminded her of a body lying there dead, its limbs hacked off with no mercy and no honor. Had those *ve-ho-e* thanked the trees for their offering?

She walked closer to her father so that she could hear what he had to say. White Eagle and Stands Tall rode on either side of Arrow Maker, and Bear Paw's horse stood on the other side of his father.

"Ai-ee," Arrow Maker said softly. "At the fort William Bent said the whites in the East were as many as the stars. Do you think it could be so?"

"E-have-se-va," Stands Tall answered, turning to look at his son. "What say you, Bear Paw?"

The young man watched the lumbering procession with its hundreds of oxen and mules, many of the women wearing long skirts and slat bonnets, walking with their children beside the wagons. Behind the wagons more men herded along spare oxen and mules as well as horses.

"All I see are many horses," Bear Paw answered.

"Not for stealing," White Eagle spoke up. "I think perhaps it is best not to anger them. If there are as many as Bent says, we have no hope of defeating them."

"We carry their long guns now," Bear Paw said, his youthful daring bringing forth renewed strength. "With their own weapons we can defeat the *ve-ho-e* as well as the Pawnee and any other enemy." He rested his hand on a new rifle that lay across his lap. He had traded two horses for it back at Bent's Fort several weeks earlier, as many of the other men had traded items for the marvelous new weapons that could kill or injure from a long distance. For now, the Cheyenne warriors had no use for them in fighting, for it was more honorable to fight hand to hand and count coup. Still, the weapons were good for hunting game. Now that the whites were intruding more and more on Indian lands, they were killing off much of the food the Cheyenne and Sioux needed to survive, and scaring off other game so that it was becoming more scarce. With the guns, once the hunters spotted their prey, they could at least kill the animal quickly from hiding, before it had a chance to run away.

I do not know if it is good that we trade for these new weapons, Arrow Maker had complained to Star Woman. *It makes us more dependent on the white man. We need him now, need to trade with him in order to have powder and the little balls that kill. We cannot make these things ourselves. We trade for blankets, cloth, tobacco, metal pots, things that make our lives easier. But what will be the cost in the end? Much more than a few buffalo robes, I am afraid.*

Medicine Wolf had not forgotten the statement, for she had never heard her father say he was afraid of anything. He had ridden against the Shoshoni, the Crow, the Pawnee; he had ridden among a thundering herd of buffalo to make his kill. Now he had said he was afraid of trading with the hairy-faced *ve-ho-e.*

"Those white men also have the long guns," Arrow Maker answered Bear Paw now. "They know how to use them better than we."

"We are learning fast," Bear Paw answered proudly. "One day the *ve-ho-e* will understand that he cannot cut our trees and kill our game without our permission."

Medicine Wolf felt the sick feeling that always came to her stomach when she saw signs of the white man, for she remembered Black Buffalo's prediction that she would have to go with them one day. She could not imagine anything more terrifying and lonely than to be away from Star Woman and Arrow Maker, Old Grandmother, Smiling Girl, and her brother. More than that, she could not imagine being separated from her People, from Bear Paw.

"It is the yellow metal in the land where the sun sets that brings them," Arrow Maker was saying. "Bent says it is considered very valuable to the white man, and he will do almost anything to get it. He said more would come, many more than we can count. All summer they will come."

"Why does he need the yellow metal," Stands Tall wondered. "Look at the riches he already has. He does not even need most of the things he carries or uses. What does a man need besides the land and what she gives him, the animals and trees, the air to breathe? We live just fine, and we have none of this yellow metal."

Arrow Maker's horse shifted nervously. "To the *ve-ho-e* the yellow metal means power. With it he buys all that he needs and more. From those we watched at Bent's

Fort, it seems they are not satisfied just with full bellies. They seem to like to own many things, useless things that one can only look at. But there is one thing that he longs to possess that could mean bad days ahead for us.''

''What is that?'' Stands Tall asked.

Arrow Maker's eyes did not leave the procession of white-topped wagons. ''Land,'' he answered. ''William Bent told me to understand that someday the *ve-ho-e* might want to own some of our hunting grounds.''

Bear Paw snickered. ''Land cannot be owned. Does the white man think he can cut up Grandmother Earth into pieces and say he owns her heart or her hand or a leg? Grandmother Earth is a living being who must be left whole.''

Medicine Wolf dared to raise her eyes to drink in the sight of Bear Paw. He was still too thin, but his muscles were hard and defined. Her heart could not be happier at seeing him riding a horse again. She had not gone back to visit him after the day she had given him the wolf's paw, but she would never forget the moment, the magic of it, the power of it, nor would she forget the odd, possessive feeling she had experienced when she touched his medicine bag and put the paw inside it, as though she had touched and possessed that most private part of him that only a wife would touch.

He belonged to her now. She knew it in the most intimate sense. Without being woman enough to understand the full passion of being united as one, she knew that one day Bear Paw would be her husband. As though to sense her thoughts, the young man suddenly looked her way, and Medicine Wolf felt the heat in her face. Bear Paw gave her a smile in recognition of the secret they shared. Medicine Wolf was embarrassed that he had caught her staring at him, and she lowered her eyes and hurried back to where her mother stood.

Suddenly the men along the front lines began laughing. They rose in their saddles, raising lances and rifles and tomahawks, taunting and hooting, laughing more.

''Look at them run,'' one shouted.

Star Woman and the other women could not help moving closer, and Medicine Wolf followed, to see the wagon train was suddenly moving ahead much faster, men whipping the oxen and mules, dust rolling. High on the ridge the Cheyenne could hear the screams of women and children, muffled by dust and distance.

Bear Paw seemed to laugh the loudest, an air of pride in the sound. "They saw us," he told the women. "They will not stay around long enough even to fight. I think we should chase them and see if they can run as fast as rabbits."

Arrow Maker remained serious while Bear Paw and most of the other warriors continued laughing and making war whoops until the wagon train and its trailing remuda were just a dot in the sunset. The Cheyenne moved forward then, descending the lengthy slope to the river along which the *ve-ho-e* had traveled.

Laughter and smiles turned to sober shock at the filth the white eyes had left behind, pieces of useless furniture, excrement, a dead horse, trees cut down yet only partially used. Trash lay about, broken glass, bent pans, things that could not be used but that also could not waste away into nourishment for Grandmother Earth the way bones and skins and other natural elements would. The trail left by the wagons was making deep ruts in the ground, bringing pain to Grandmother Earth.

Wolf walked beside Medicine Wolf, sniffing at various items, hanging around the dead horse. He remained behind for several minutes while Medicine Wolf and the others moved on. One of the men cried out then, halting his horse and staring at something as though it were the most horrible sight he had ever seen. The others, several hundred strong, gathered around the sight, some of them gasping and even weeping. Before them lay the carcass of a buffalo, part of its shaggy skin removed and a little bit of the meat taken. The rest was left to rot, all the hundreds of parts that the Indian would have used for clothing, nourishment, utensils, medicine, all wasted.

Black Buffalo moved forward, waving a rattle over the dead buffalo, which was gathering flies. "We will burn it and tell the buffalo spirit we are sorry it was treated with no honor," he told the others.

"This is a bad thing," White Eagle muttered.

"Scouts at Bent's Fort told us that the white man, Broken Hand, may try to find us and speak with us when we gather with the Sioux for the Sun Dance," Stands Tall said. "He wishes to speak of a Great Smoke with the white man and many Indians. We will decide where the white man can go and where he cannot. From what I see here, I think it is good to decide, so that we do not have to see such waste and foolishness again."

"I say all white men should stay in the land of the rising sun," Bear Paw said, his face taught with anger.

"And I think we should consider the Great Smoke," Arrow Maker answered. "We must try to remain at peace with the *ve-ho-e*. If he can waste so much this way, then he must have much wealth, much more than we can know, for he throws away good meat and furnishings made of fine wood as though they are nothing."

Medicine Wolf stared in disbelief at the carcass while women hurriedly gathered wood and stacked it around and on top of the dead buffalo. With the magical wooden sticks that made fire, another "white man's" invention purchased at Bent's Fort, Black Buffalo managed to get the wood burning, for the *ve-ho-e* had cut down dead trees as well as good ones. The women had gathered only the drier, dead wood.

"Tonight when we make camp we will offer prayers," Black Buffalo told them. "Then we will hold council and talk about Broken Hand and this Great Smoke, so that when he comes, we will know what to tell him."

They all somberly watched the buffalo begin to burn, and Black Buffalo chanted over the carcass, shaking his rattle, breathing in the foul-smelling smoke to take the buffalo's pain upon himself. For over two hours they all watched and prayed, until two of their scouts approached from the east.

"More come! Many more," one of the scouts shouted.

"We will go now," Arrow Maker told them. Medicine Wolf sensed a quiet panic as everyone gathered their things and hurried away from the site, leaving behind the smoldering carcass of the buffalo, its smoke wafting skyward as though an offering to *Maheo*.

Medicine Wolf felt strangely sad. Until today she had

not given much thought to how the coming of the *ve-ho-e*
might affect her own People. Before this, she had worried
only about the prediction that she might have to live among
the white eyes. Now her concern went beyond her own
self-pity. This was a much bigger thing than she had first
thought. The coming of the white man could have a much
more drastic affect than to disrupt the life of one small
girl. It could disrupt the lives of all her People.

She could feel more change in the wind, could smell
it in the putrid odor of the smoke from the burning buffalo.

1851

It was a chilling sound to the Prescotts, for they did
not fully understand the Indians they had come to "save."
To the Methodist missionary family, the sound of rhythmic
drumming far out on the open plains was just a verification
of the uncivilized state in which the "savages" lived.
Somehow they had to reach them, teach them the "cor-
rect" religion, educate them.

Even now Andrew Prescott knelt in front of the make-
shift altar he had built and brought west with him in a
covered wagon. He was praying for the "poor lost souls"
who danced and chanted somewhere out on the plains,
singing and praying to their heathen gods. The forty-five-
year-old man had given up preaching in the comfortable
confines of a midsize town in New York State to answer
what he considered his calling and truly try to save lost
souls, people who had never heard about his Christ. He
had decided that before he died he would make a personal
sacrifice and give up the luxury of civilization to come
here, to dangerous Indian country, to preach the Word to
the red man.

Prescott was a big man, standing well over six feet,
with a barrel chest and a full beard and mustache. His hair
and beard were blond, with streaks of a darker, dishwater
color; his complexion was fair, now ruddy-red from the
prairie sun.

The preacher and his wife, Marilyn, were camped near
Fort Laramie in eastern Wyoming, the low-lying Laramie
Mountains just west of them. The Bighorn Mountains

painted the horizon to the north; the Rockies towered in
snow-capped peaks west of the Laramie "hills," as some
of the men at the fort called them. Directly to the east the
plains stretched into an endless horizon, and somewhere
on that horizon a huge gathering of Cheyenne and Sioux
were celebrating another Sun Dance, something Prescott
saw as a heathen ritual, one he hoped to eliminate.

Nearby, Fort Laramie was already filling up with soldiers and dignitaries, preparing for the "Great Smoke,"
as the Indians called it, a treaty-signing that would affect
several tribes. Prescott had been reading for nearly two
years about the proposed meeting between Sioux, Cheyenne, Arapaho, and several other tribes. It had taken Congress a long time to smooth out the details and reach an
agreement on what would be offered to the Indians, time
enough for Prescott to sell his home and prepare to come
west. What better place to start saving Indians than at this
great gathering? He was sure he could glean a considerable
amount of information about Indians from the soldiers and
scouts at the fort, learn about their ways before he went
among them to preach the Word.

But tonight . . . tonight it was a little frightening to
think about going near the savages. Tonight things were
relatively quiet at the fort, and the air was still. Everyone
could hear the drumming, and it planted fear in their
hearts. Not only were the Sioux and Cheyenne gathered
in great force, but when they came to Laramie for the "big
talk," they were to be joined by Crow, Arikara, Assini-
boin, Mandan, Gros Ventre, Blackfoot, and possibly even
Shoshoni Indians. Many of those tribes were enemies of
the Sioux and Cheyenne. The soldiers and their commanders at the fort were understandably nervous. There
could be trouble between the Indian tribes, and the whites
present could end up in the middle.

There was also the possibility that a misunderstanding,
a misinterpreted speech, could turn a spark into a blazing
fire, and the Indians could decide to wipe out every white
man in sight. There had been continued trouble along the
Oregon Trail, which was part of the reason Laramie, earlier a trading post, had been manned with soldiers. Something had to be done about the Indians. They had to be

kept away from the major roads west. Often tragedy struck just from misunderstandings. Indians, now beginning to feel hunger because the whites were killing off so much game, often approached wagon trains to beg for food and other items. Someone would misinterpret something an Indian did, the Indians would return an insult, and then there was trouble. If the Indians had been drinking whisky, the trouble was only made worse.

"Things are changing for the Indian," an Indian agent by the name of Thomas "Broken Hand" Fitzpatrick had explained to Reverend Prescott just two nights before. Prescott and Fitzpatrick had been invited to dinner with the fort commander. Fitzpatrick was a true mountain man who preferred buckskins to woolen clothing; but he was amazingly well spoken, and he had a good basic understanding of the Indians. He was the instigator of this great treaty-gathering, and had gone out on his own to visit many of the tribes to try to talk them into coming to Laramie during what the Sioux called the Harvest Moon; the "Moon of Dry Dust Blowing" to the Cheyenne.

"The days of the fur trade are gone, old Bent's Fort burned down," Fitzpatrick had explained. "More and more whites are coming west, killing off the game animals. The biggest loss of the Indians is the buffalo. They need them bad, and they're already getting harder to find. Some of their best hunting grounds are being eliminated, the area they can roam safely is shrinking. They're starting to get scared, Reverend, and I can't blame them. They blame the white man for all the bad things that are happening to them, especially that rage of cholera that swept through the tribes two years ago. Wiped out an awful lot of Pawnee. 'Course, the Cheyenne wouldn't mind that so much, seeing as how they hate the Pawnee; but it also took a lot of Cheyenne lives. Those left want to know what is happening, where they can ride and hunt freely without whites shooting at them like they were nothing but rabbits."

"If they would just hunt, it wouldn't be such a problem," a Lieutenant Webster had put in. "It's when they steal horses and cattle that shooting and bloodshed occurs."

"They steal horses because that's what they've been doing since the beginning of time," Fitzpatrick had answered. "Horses are as precious to the Indian as gold is to the white man. Stealing them is a game with them, something of pride. Any cattle they steal is because they're hungry. You haven't seen much of that yet, but it might get worse. Believe me, an Indian would much rather have buffalo meat than beef. Personally, I would too. At any rate, they don't really want trouble, Lieutenant." Fitzpatrick had looked at the reverend then. "They're a happy, freedom-loving people, Reverend, with no conception of the desire to own land or gold or any of the things we consider important. They just want to be left alone. We're going to try to establish a very big area for them to live in. Trying to pen Indians onto a few thousand acres is like trying to put a grizzly into a small cage. They have a free spirit, and they migrate with the seasons, following the game. To them the land belongs to everyone, to use as needed. The land is alive and has a heart and soul just like a person. It can't be divided into little pieces and owned. I'm not at all sure they'll understand everything we're going to try to tell them at the treaty council. One thing is sure, they had better be treated with respect, and the annuities we've promised them for coming had better show up in time."

Reverend Prescott returned to his praying. The annuities had *not* shown up, and the "Great Smoke" would begin within two weeks.

Outside the tent where his father prayed, twenty-year-old Thomas Prescott stood next to his family's covered wagon, staring into the darkness in the direction from which he heard the drumming. Tom was as fair and nearly as tall as his father, but he did not yet have the fullness of a man, nor did he wear a beard. He had hardly enough hair on his face to shave at all, but it was a handsome face, with full lips and finely chiseled cheekbones and nose, sky-blue eyes outlined with light brown brows and dark lashes.

His mother walked up beside him, her several slips rustling under her gray cotton dress. Marilyn Prescott was a slender woman of little color—light brown eyes, pale skin kept that way by a wide slat bonnet she wore during the day and by the many creams she had brought with her from the East. Her hair was a mousy brown, worn in a tight bun at the base of her neck. Her lips were rather thin, and she wore no makeup, for she considered it sinful.

"Listen to them," she told her son. "How can they live that way?"

Tom sighed, fascinated by the Indians he had already met at the fort, wanting to understand their very different life style. "It's all they've ever known, Mother. They don't think anything about it. Fitzpatrick says they're very happy living the way they do."

"They're destined for hell and damnation if we don't do something to help them," the woman answered. "Imagine! Drumming and dancing and praying to sky spirits and earth spirits! Worst of all is that Sun Dance— men piercing their flesh and hanging from a pole until the skin tears and they fall away, all for some sort of vision! It's one of the most heathen rituals I have ever heard of!"

Tom watched the darkness. "Maybe there are things about it we just don't understand. Maybe it's not as heathen as we think."

"Thomas Prescott! How can you even *think* such a thing?"

Tom shrugged, wondering why he had bothered to make the remark. His mother was a rigid woman, unbending in her beliefs, cold, stern, determined. "I don't know," he answered. "I just remember some of the things Fitzpatrick told us—like about the Cheyenne girl called Medicine Wolf. Do you really think it's true about how she slept with the wolves and is protected by the Wolf Spirit?"

"Of course it isn't true! The Indians see everything as some kind of omen or something spiritual. Our dog led us to you that time you were lost when you were little, remember? That doesn't mean you and the dog shared the same spirit. And it didn't make you holy. That's *heathen* thinking! Besides, I think the Indians make up half these stories."

"But Fitzpatrick said she actually has a pet wolf, and she carries wolf's paws in something called a medicine bag, and they have a special magic. He says she even healed a young warrior once with them.''

"If he was healed, it was because God *wanted* him healed, and that's all there is to it. You would do best to stop listening to that old mountain man so much and get back to your Bible reading. If you're going to start thinking like the Indian, how will you ever be able to help us save them? Maybe I should have your father send you back east.''

Tom frowned, burying his anger. "Don't worry, Mother. I'm just saying we can't help them if we don't understand them.''

"I understand enough to know that they need the word of God drilled into them. They need to be shown the true path.'' The woman sniffed. "You had better get some sleep. It makes no sense to stand out here all night listening to those drums.'' She left, and went inside the tent. Thomas, as he had been doing, would sleep in the wagon.

The drumming stopped for a moment, then started up again. Occasionally, when the wind was just right, Tom caught the sound of voices, faint yipping sounds, chanting, a high-pitched sound that resembled a whistle. He wondered about the girl called Medicine Wolf. Was she out there? Would she come to the treaty council? He wanted to see her for himself. He wanted to know just how much power there was in the Indian spirits. One thing was certain, it was going to be one of the most exciting events of his life. He was not about to let his father send him back east. This was something he was not going to miss!

The "Great Smoke" would forever be a vivid memory for eleven-year-old Medicine Wolf. She wondered if there would ever be another such gathering, at least ten thousand Indians of many tribes. It was a time of excitement and tension, for the Crow and Shoshoni were present. The presence of the Shoshoni was especially irritating to the Sioux and Cheyenne, for the Mountain Indians were not only an enemy, but they sported new rifles, one to nearly every man, something the Sioux and Cheyenne suspected came from cooperating too easily with the whites. The guns were gifts from the mountain man Jim Bridger. The Sioux and Cheyenne, on the other hand, owned very few rifles, and Arrow Maker already spoke of making new rifles part of their bargaining agreement.

Peace among the various tribes was kept under precarious control. Most of the Indians were more concerned with impressing the white chiefs who were present than with making trouble for their enemies. But time was passing. Medicine Wolf and her clan had been in the Laramie area now for close to two months. Promised annuities had not arrived, and the talks could not begin until the *ve-ho-e* had in their hands the many presents promised to the Indians.

Some of the young warriors continued to find ways to stay active while they waited. Medicine Wolf's seventeen-year-old brother Runner, now called Swift Fox since his Sun Dance vision, rode often with Bear Paw, and together they and others showed the visiting white men and women some of their skills. There were bow and arrow contests and wrestling matches. There were many horse races, and much betting took place. Young warriors rode back and forth on their swift ponies in front of the tents of the visiting whites, performing riding tricks that made the whites gasp and clap. Bear Paw was especially adept at the riding tricks, and it warmed Medicine Wolf's heart to see that he was well and strong again, now even more filled out, his muscles and frame that of a man.

More Indians had poured into the Laramie area for the Great Smoke, and the gathering had become so large that there was no game left in the immediate area of the fort. Thousands of grazing horses had consumed all the grass for miles around. It had been decided that the meeting place should be moved several miles to the south, to a place called Horse Creek, where new grasslands could feed the horses and game could be found to feed hungry bellies.

This was a pretty place, and a time of great pageantry, pipe-smoking, and gift-giving. White chiefs were finally beginning to arrive, and one man ran around with some kind of pad in his hand and a writing instrument. He talked

with Indians, using interpreters, and he wrote things down
on the pad, using strange signs. He had noticed Medicine
Wolf watching him, and he had shown her the writing,
saying something to her she did not understand. Maybe
this man would take her away, for always she feared Black
Buffalo's prediction that one day she must go with the white
eyes. She had run off, and was glad now that she had not
seen the man since.

Still, tonight was not a time to worry about those *ve-
ho-e*, nor about how soon gifts would arrive and the great
council would begin. Tonight she was as beautiful as she
could possibly be, wearing a bleached tunic her mother
had made for her, one Medicine Wolf had beaded herself,
a beautiful star pattern on the front and an eagle on the
back. Beads and bells were tied into the fringes so that
she made pretty music when she moved, and tonight she
would dance better than she had ever danced, for she would
join the women and eligible young girls in the blanket
dance.

Her heart pounded with joy and anticipation. Bear Paw
was there, watching. Did he expect or even want her to
share her blanket with him? Was she pretty enough? She
had brushed her hair a hundred times over, and her mother
had brushed her cheeks with red powder made from clay
and berries. She wore the lovely white tunic, but she still
had no shape to her to fill it out the way some of the older
girls did. The drumming had begun, as well as the happy
singing, and a crowd of white visitors had gathered to
watch.

On shaking legs Medicine Wolf joined in the dancing,
holding her arms out so that her blanket was open and her
white dress showed in the firelight. She moved in a circle,
turning, singing, moving her arms, her heart pounding
with fear that when it came time to throw her blanket,
Bear Paw would already be sitting under one with some
other girl.

The central fire burned brightly, and the night air was
filled with singing. Medicine Wolf's heart soared. Summer
Moon, now twelve, also danced. She had had her flowing
time and was a woman now, but still not old enough to
marry. Summer Moon was fond of White Horse, in spite

of his haughty ways. Medicine Wolf hoped her good friend could snare White Horse, for the young warrior continued to bother Medicine Wolf at times, staring at her, showing off in front of her. He seemed to always be challenging Bear Paw, and for several months after Bear Paw had been wounded by the Pawnee man, White Horse had taunted him, saying he was not much of a warrior, even though Bear Paw had suffered the wound because he had so bravely counted coup on several Pawnee warriors.

Medicine Wolf wanted nothing to do with White Horse. She hoped that the advances of Summer Moon would draw his attention away from her. Now a few of the young girls were leaving the circle, swaying in front of their favorite warriors, throwing their blankets over their heads so that they could talk alone in good-humored fun and flirtation. Medicine Wolf noticed White Horse watching her with great hope in his eyes. For a moment she almost felt sorry for him, but she reminded herself he was a man of too much puffed-up pride. And besides, her best friend loved him. If he would just notice!

A few older women threw their blankets over their husbands. Medicine Wolf began to get nervous. Did Bear Paw really expect her to pick him out? Would he be embarrassed to have a girl of only eleven, and who had not yet even had her flowing time, choose him? She drew near to where he sat, and she saw an older girl swaying seductively in front of him. Her heart sank with dread, for it was Silver Moon, a pretty girl of sixteen. She wanted to cry, and prayed that as the drumming and singing continued, Silver Moon would go around the circle once more.

Finally the girl moved on, and the thought of how Bear Paw had watched her made Medicine Wolf's heart hot with jealousy. Silver Moon was a woman, with a woman's seductive fullness, all the right curves. Medicine Wolf decided that it was now or never. She came closer, and Bear Paw smiled at her. She felt almost faint. Surely that smile meant he wanted her to throw her blanket.

She moved closer, raising her blanket and summoning her courage. She approached him and circled her blanket over their heads, sitting down beside him. She was at once

oblivious to the laughter and jokes around them, an effort
by the older ones to embarrass them.

"What are you doing under there?" some asked.

"The child chooses a man," said another.

Beneath the blanket Medicine Wolf was closer to Bear
Paw than she had been since touching his cheek when he
was sick. Now he was well and strong, a man fully aware
of his senses. "I was afraid another would choose me
before you reached me again," he told her.

Medicine Wolf was literally shaking with excitement.
"You do not mind, then?"

She felt a big hand touch her face. "You know that I
do not," Bear Paw answered softly. "You are not a woman
yet, but already my heart is full of you, Medicine Wolf."

Everything tingled, and it seemed terribly warm under
the blanket. Bear Paw! He was such a strong, beautiful
man! To think that he would say such a thing to her at her
age . . . All reality left her. There was no world beyond
the blanket, no drumming and singing, no great gathering
of Indians and whites. There was only Bear Paw.

"I wish that I *was* already a woman," she said boldly.

He took her hand, squeezing it. "As do I. But even
though you are not, you are still a thing of great beauty.
The woman you become will bring pride and joy to her
man's heart."

Her eyes teared at the words, and her heart was so full
of love she thought that it might burst. "It is true, then?
You still want to wait for me?"

He kept hold of her hand. "You know that is how it
must be. You gave me the greatest honor a man can know
when you gave me the wolf's paw. Our visions are as one.
One day *we* must be as one."

The meaning of the words made her tremble. She was
glad it was dark under the blanket so that he could not see
her embarrassment. He leaned forward, brushing her
cheek with his own, turning his face to lightly lick her soft
skin. Outside, those around them made crude remarks and
laughter, but neither Bear Paw nor Medicine Wolf heard
them. Medicine Wolf shivered with the ecstasy of his
touch.

"Thank you for choosing me, Medicine Wolf," he

said softly. "We dare not stay under here any longer, or your father will say I have insulted you. I will go now. But remember that when I sleep, you are with me."

He threw off the blanket and rose, shaking his head and waving off those around him who teased him mercilessly, unaware of the white missionaries who were watching.

Marilyn Prescott shook her head in disgust. "Would you look at that sinful dance, and that mere *child* was sitting under a blanket with a grown man," the woman fumed. "It's a disgrace!"

Tom watched Medicine Wolf in fascination. "She's the one, Mother, the girl called Medicine Wolf. I saw her earlier, and a reporter told me who she was."

"What a challenge she would be," the Reverend muttered, stroking his beard. "If we could win over one like that, take the Indian out of her, make a Christian of her, it would be proof that they can all be tamed eventually. It's the young ones we have to start with. The older ones are too set in their ways."

Marilyn frowned. "What are you talking about, Andrew?"

"I'm saying that somehow I'd like a chance to get that child away from those savages. Apparently her people think she has special spiritual gifts. If we could convert her, teach her, we could show the rest of them the error of their ways, show them that she is just a child who needs to be steered in the right direction."

"And how do you propose to convert her? After the treaty talks she will leave with the rest of them, and we will have a fine time locating them, let alone convincing them to come to church or school."

"I don't know yet," the preacher replied. "I'll talk to that Fitzpatrick. Maybe there is a way we can convince her people to let her stay with us a while."

Medicine Wolf did not notice she was being so closely scrutinized. She wrapped her blanket around herself, thinking how this would forever be her favorite blanket, for she had shared it with Bear Paw. He had said she was beautiful! He had said he would wait for her! She touched her cheek where his lips had brushed against it. The memory of the flick of his tongue against her cheek made her shiver with wonderful new feelings. A thousand questions and curiosities about man and woman raced through her mind, and her heart ached with what she was sure now was love.

She rose, ready to run to Summer Moon and tell her what had happened, but for the moment Summer Moon shared her blanket with White Horse. Medicine Wolf wondered if White Horse would give poor lovesick Summer Moon the kind of hope Bear Paw had given her.

She turned, and it was then she noticed them, a small group of white people staring at her. Her momentary joy left her, for there was a cold, derisive look in the white woman's eyes, a pompous look in the man's. He was a very big man with a hairy face. She did not like the way any of them looked at her, as though they were singling her out deliberately.

She thought of Black Buffalo's prediction again, that one day she must go with white people. Surely this was not the time! She would never leave her People. Never! More than that, she could never leave Bear Paw. Not now!

She turned away, hurrying back to her own tipi, always feeling safer inside the shelter with Old Grandmother. She could almost feel hands grabbing her, could feel those *ve-ho-e* eyes drilling into her. She ducked inside to see her Grandmother repairing a pair of Star Woman's moccasins by the light of a fire. The old woman looked up.

"So, already you are back. Did you throw your blanket?"

Medicine Wolf moved to sit down near the fire, grateful the horrid disease the white man called cholera had not hurt the old woman. *"Ai,"* she answered.

The air hung silent for a moment, and when Medicine Wolf met her grandmother's eyes, the old woman was smiling a nearly toothless grin and watching her. "Well?" the woman asked expectantly.

Medicine Wolf felt herself blushing. "I threw it over Bear Paw," she told her grandmother.

"Saaaa, aren't you the daring one!"

Medicine Wolf giggled. She wrapped her blanket closer, almost lovingly. "He said he would wait for me,

Grandmother. He said our visions were as one, and that one day *we* would be as one. He touched my cheek.''

The old woman nodded. ''My holy granddaughter *should* have the best.''

Medicine Wolf smiled, moving her eyes to watch the flames, seeing in them Bear Paw's handsome face, his fine body, his brilliant smile. Old Grandmother understood how she felt. The woman would not laugh or make teasing remarks.

Outside, the drumming and dancing continued. The Prescotts turned away in disgust, Andrew Prescott leaving his wife and son to go to find Agent Fitzpatrick. Maybe the man could convince Medicine Wolf's people that it would be a sign of their sincerity in keeping the treaty promises if they left their holy child with a ''holy'' white man to learn new ways.

Besides, he thought, what would it matter to the Indians? They surely didn't have the same feelings as white people. They were too uncivilized to understand love. Leaving one young girl behind probably wouldn't make much difference to them.

Chapter Six

Because she was a soldier girl and a holy child, Medicine Wolf was allowed to sit near the great council when the Cheyenne and Sioux smoked the pipe with the white "chief" called Mitchell. He was a representative of the Great Father of the *ve-ho-e* and was called a commissioner. Mitchell promised many things, namely that if the Indians allowed soldiers to come into Indian country and build forts, it would not be just to protect the white travelers from Indians, but to protect the Indians from "bad white men" who make trouble for them. Hundreds of thousands of acres were designated as land on which the Cheyenne and Arapaho could live, with no mention made that they could not go beyond the boundaries to hunt if necessary. The Sioux were offered most of the land in the Black Hills and the Dakotas. The Cheyenne land included an area that began nearly as far south as the site of old Bent's Fort, north to the North Platte, west to the Rockies, back south to the Arkansas River and back east to Bent's

Fort. It was an enormous amount of land, and the Cheyenne were promised no whites would settle on it. A few of the Cheyenne men agreed to cease making war against enemy tribes, for often in such wars whites ended up getting hurt. Medicine Wolf wondered if the commissioner understood that a few Indians could not speak for all. The interpreter seemed to be very eagerly telling Mitchell the Cheyenne had agreed, and Mitchell looked pleased. The honored chief of another Cheyenne band, Yellow Wolf, was doing most of the talking, and the commissioner seemed to think that the man represented all the Cheyenne. If she could speak English, Medicine Wolf would tell the white men that Indian men act individually and do not have any one leader. She highly doubted that all Cheyenne would refrain from making war against their enemies.

Arrow Maker shared a peace pipe with Yellow Wolf, Arapaho leaders, and the white leaders, signifying the Indians' desire to have peace with the white man. Arrow Maker complained that the whites who traveled through their land left filth and destruction behind and killed off too much game. Commissioner Mitchell promised that the Indians would be compensated. A wagon train full of gifts and supplies was "on its way," but Medicine Wolf had to wonder if it would ever really arrive, as it had been "on its way" for months now. Mitchell promised that every year new supplies would be brought, according to what was needed each time, to ensure that bellies would always be full and blankets provided. The Cheyenne would even be provided with more rifles and ammunition, but the Cheyenne must promise to keep their part of the treaty.

This new treaty seemed to Medicine Wolf to be ideal. Her People could hunt both the northern lands and the lands south of the Platte River that had been awarded to the Southern Cheyenne. They would have the best of both worlds. For the winter, they would go south to the *Hinta-Nagi*, the Ghost Timbers, an area along the Arkansas River on the southern Colorado plains near the ruins of Bent's Fort. It was warmer there in winter. It was in this area that the Cheyenne were to meet every year to collect the annuities promised them by the Great Father in Washington.

Clothing and blankets were handed out to the Indians, including soldier uniforms and striped flags that they were told were the sacred sign of the Great Father, like the animals and designs that the Indians considered their personal signs. Copies of the treaty were given to Arrow Maker, Yellow Wolf, and others, rolled-up pieces of paper tied with scarlet ribbons, promises written in words the Indians could not read. Designated representatives were picked from among the Cheyenne nation to travel to see the Great Father in the place in the East called Washington. Those going would be Little Chief, White Antelope, and Alights-on-the-Cloud. Medicine Wolf envied them, for they would see the mysterious world from which the whites came, although she was sure she would be too afraid to go there herself. She would never want to be so far from her People.

That night a great feast was held to celebrate the new friendship between Indian and white. Medicine Wolf joined in the festivities, again wearing her white tunic. She made a point to wander near the area where Bear Paw sat around a campfire with several other young warriors and she heard them arguing over whether or not they could trust the white leaders to keep their promises.

"We will go wherever we choose," Bear Paw said firmly. "Grandmother Earth welcomes us wherever we go."

The others agreed and there was a restlessness in the air. The presence of a few Pawnee, who now scouted for the white soldiers, did not help matters. The younger warriors were itching to get back on their horses and go on one more hunt before winter set in. It was already the month of the Drying Grass Moon, and the leaves were turning. There were not many warm days left. It was time to be heading south.

Bear Paw and White Horse both caught Medicine Wolf watching them. When they noticed her, the girl darted away. Bear Paw grinned, feeling an ache deep inside for the woman she would become. White Horse puffed haugh-

tily on the small pipe a white soldier had given him and
watched Medicine Wolf until she was out of sight.

"She will go to the highest bidder," he said then,
moving his dark eyes to Bear Paw.

Bear Paw met his challenging gaze without a flinch.
"She is already taken," he said firmly.

White Horse snickered. "Just because she threw a
blanket over you? She is not even yet a woman. She does
not know her mind, or her heart. Wait until she thinks and
feels as a woman before you become so sure of her future."

"I already know. Nothing can change what must be,"
Bear Paw told him.

A look of hatred came into White Horse's eyes. "Any
man will be free to court her," he sneered.

"That is true. Every eligible man who wishes may
court her, but all his efforts will be to no avail. She will
go to only one, and that one has already been chosen by
Maheo, and by the Wolf Spirit."

"You take much for granted, Bear Paw. We shall see
who wins in the end."

"Summer Moon has made it known her feelings for
you," Bear Paw reminded White Horse.

White Horse smiled derisively. "Summer Moon is not
the keeper of powerful charms like the wolf paws. She is
not a soldier girl, or one blessed by sacred spirits."

Bear Paw rose. "It is not Medicine Wolf that you want.
It is the wolf paws, and the *powers* that she holds. You
think you can steal them through marriage. But they will
never belong to anyone but Medicine Wolf!"

White Horse also rose, his body tense. "And *you* don't
want to own them?"

Bear Paw hesitated. He could tell White Horse that he
already did own one of the wolf paws. But Medicine Wolf
had told him it must be a secret. If anyone was to know,
it was Medicine Wolf who must tell them. He drew in his
breath, putting on a defensive stance as though ready to
fight. "I want only to own the woman, whether or not she
possesses the wolf paws. That is where we are different,
White Horse."

White Horse grinned. "So you say."

"Bear Paw!" The young man turned to see his uncle watching him. "We are all eager to leave this place. A young man is easily bored and restless. Do not let such things make you do something foolish. Come now. You, too, White Horse. The Dog Soldier Society must meet with Black Buffalo and Arrow Maker. The white holy people have requested a meeting with us. They want us to leave Medicine Wolf behind with them when we go from here. Come."

White Eagle turned and walked toward another campfire, where others of the Dog Soldier Society were waiting. Bear Paw and White Horse looked at each other in disbelief, and White Horse stormed off, cursing. Bear Paw was too stunned to say a word. Leave Medicine Wolf behind? With strange white people? Why? For how long? Who would watch after her? What was this crazy thing his people were thinking of doing?

He hurried to the meeting site. Medicine Wolf was already there, looking frightened and heartbroken. Bear Paw reasoned she must have just been told about this, for only minutes earlier she had looked happy and teasing when he had caught her watching him. Now there was no happiness in those pretty, dark eyes, only fear.

Agent Fitzpatrick was also present. Many other Cheyenne had gathered, and drumming and dancing ceased as the rumor quickly spread that white people had come to their camp and had dared to ask to be allowed to keep the holy child. A white man and woman stood near Broken Hand. The man was tall and bearded. He wore a dark suit and carried the "magic book" Indians had been told about, a book that told all about the white man's God. The woman had a stern look about her, and Bear Paw could not help wondering if her thin lips ever curved into a smile. A younger man stood next to the woman, and from the resemblance, Bear Paw supposed the younger man was a son.

Broken Hand stepped up to Arrow Maker, giving him the sign of peace. "Arrow Maker, the man and woman who have come with me tonight are missionaries," he told Medicine Wolf's father in a mixture of Cheyenne tongue and sign language. "They have come here to teach the

Indians about their God, the only true God, they believe. They gave up much to come here, made a big sacrifice, so you know that they are sincere. They are not here to steal land or buffalo from the Indian. They want only to win your hearts, to teach you white-man ways and white-man beliefs.''

Arrow Maker moved dark eyes to the missionaries. The younger man nodded and smiled, the older man managed a pleasant look; but the woman watched them as though she considered them beneath her. He looked back at Fitzpatrick. ''We have our own ways and beliefs. We want nothing from the white man's world. That is why we have signed the treaty, so that we can go our way and they can go theirs.''

''I understand that,'' Broken Hand answered. ''But whether you like it or not, the white man is going to become more and more a part of *your* world. If you want any hope of always keeping the treaty and living in peace, you must learn more about the white man. The Reverend and Mrs. Prescott over there, they feel that the best way is to teach your young ones. They know you aren't going to be ready to send all your children to their schools and places of worship right off, so they wanted to try a little experiment. They are very interested in the fact that you consider Medicine Wolf a holy child. They feel their way is the only right way, and they think that if Medicine Wolf could stay with them awhile, she would begin to see that the white man's way is better. They feel that if they can bring Medicine Wolf into their world, teach her their way of worship, their way of dressing and living, teach her white man's writing and reading, she will understand that this would be good for *all* Indian children. They feel that because Medicine Wolf is a holy child, if they can win her over, it will be more proof to the rest of you that the white man's way is the best way. They want your permission to keep Medicine Wolf for two summers. They will take good care of her, and they would not take her away from here.''

Medicine Wolf's chest hurt so bad that she wondered if she would be able to continue breathing. Two summers! She could not help looking over at Bear Paw. She saw his own devastation and fear. Surely he wondered that if she stayed behind, would she ever come back to him? Two summers away from Bear Paw, away from Arrow Maker and Star Woman and her friend Summer Moon, away from old Grandmother and her brother and little sister!

"Two summers is a long time," Arrow Maker answered. "My daughter will be afraid, a young child among strange white men. Who will protect her? Who will care about her?"

Broken Hand interpreted to the Prescotts. Reverend Prescott answered, and Fitzpatrick explained to Arrow Maker. "The reverend says to tell you that according to his religion, his God commands that he love all people, for all are God's children and special to Him. He says to tell you that if you really believe that Medicine Wolf is a holy child, and that she is protected by the wolf's paws, you should not be afraid to let her stay. He says it would be a good test of which is stronger, the Wolf Spirit within Medicine Wolf, or the white man's God. If the white man's God is stronger, Medicine Wolf will one day give up her wolf's paws and her Indian ways and will grow to understand that the white man's God is the only true God, and the white man's ways are best. After two summers she can choose. But they would want your promise that you and the rest of her family will not come back here to try to influence her during that two years. She must not see any Cheyenne that she knows."

Medicine Wolf struggled frantically against tears. Her throat ached and her head felt swollen and on fire. Not see anyone she knows? Her parents and Old Grandmother could not even visit her? And did she have no say in this?

Arrow Maker turned his eyes to Black Buffalo. "What do you say to all of this? You are the one with whom my daughter shares her visions. What does the Wolf Spirit wish her to do?"

Black Buffalo sat straighter, calling Medicine Wolf forward. On shaking legs she walked toward the man, feeling a thousand eyes on her. Oh, what a burden the Wolf Spirit had placed upon her! She knew without asking that this was the fulfillment of her vision about being among whites. Not only that, but this was a test of her own courage, and her devotion to the Wolf Spirit. She remembered Black

Buffalo's warning that one day she would have to choose. Here, then, was her first challenge. Black Buffalo had been right. To choose the Wolf Spirit meant to turn away from loved ones and to have her heart broken in many pieces.

"You have heard," Black Buffalo told her. "You know the things about which we spoke. You know what you must do." The man rose, speaking louder then the rest of his people. "This can be only Medicine Wolf's decision," he told them. "Because she is a holy child and has had a vision about this day, we cannot council and make the decision for her. Not even her father can have the last say."

Fitzpatrick was rapidly interpreting for the Prescotts, who looked bewildered. They had thought it was the parents' permission they needed, not the child's. It was obvious these Cheyenne set great store by the "magic" wolf's paws the girl possessed, enough that they were literally letting the "Wolf Spirit" decide what the child should do. All eyes were on Medicine Wolf. Wolf stayed close to her, occasionally licking her hand.

Marilyn Prescott felt a shiver at the sight. The white wolf looked dangerous. How could Medicine Wolf's parents let such a fierce-looking beast stay so near the girl? Didn't they know the wolf could rip her to pieces if he so chose?

Black Buffalo was still talking. "Medicine Wolf has had a vision that one day she must go among the whites," he told the others.

There was a general murmur among the Cheyenne. Bear Paw watched Medicine Wolf sadly. He had not known of her vision about the whites.

"It is up to her now to decide if this is the time of her vision," Black Buffalo continued. "I say it is a good thing. We must not look upon it with fear. Broken Hand is right that we should better understand the white man's ways. Let Medicine Wolf go with the holy man. They think they will make her like a white girl, make her forget her people. I say it cannot be done. They think they can change her, change us. But we will always be Cheyenne, and we will always worship Grandmother Earth and Grandfather Eagle, the four directions and the animal spirits, for they all come from *Maheo*, and who is to say *Maheo* is not the same God the white man worships, or who is to say it is not *our* God who is the one true God?''

People nodded and agreed, and a look of disdain came into the reverend's eyes when the words were interpreted to him.

"I say there is only one reason to learn the white man's ways," Black Buffalo continued, "and that is to understand him so that we know how to deal with him in the future, as we live our way and he lives his. I say we must learn only to keep the peace and to understand these treaties. I say the Wolf Spirit means for Medicine Wolf to go with these people because the Wolf Spirit knows that to not understand could mean we will lose much of our freedom, perhaps our lives."

"How can that happen," Bear Paw put in. "This is a big land. We have signed a treaty giving us rights to hunt it as we always have, a treaty that is to keep the white man from *ever* settling near us!"

Black Buffalo turned to meet his eyes. "Some of us have already seen that the white man does not always keep his promises," he told Bear Paw. "*Maheo* has shown me in my dreams that there will be many more treaties, that the Great Father in Washington is sincere, but that his people are not. More will come, Bear Paw. We must be ready. We must understand. If Medicine Wolf goes with these people now, she can learn much, and she can in turn teach us. Remember the power of the Wolf Spirit, Bear Paw. Do not be afraid of this. Medicine Wolf's power is much stronger than the white man. She will learn from them, and she will come back to us."

Bear Paw moved his eyes to Medicine Wolf again, his anger and frustration evident. He seemed to be pleading with her not to agree to stay. Black Buffalo stepped in front of her then. "It is your choice," he told her.

Choice? Did she really have one? The only courage she mustered came from the fact that Bear Paw had also been part of a vision, and that he had promised he would wait for her. If she could survive the next two years, surely she would find her way back to the Cheyenne, and to Bear Paw. She knew she could not ignore the edicts of a vision.

She met Black Buffalo's eyes, her own watery, but she refused to break into babyish sobbing in front of the gathering. She was Medicine Wolf, the holy child. Her People must have confidence in what she was doing. They must feel good about it and not be afraid. The Wolf Spirit expected her to be strong and brave.

"In two days, when my family and the rest of the Cheyenne leave this place to go south for the winter, I will stay behind with the holy man. I will learn the ways of the white man, for this is what the Wolf Spirit wishes me to do." Medicine Wolf was not sure how she had managed to get the words out without breaking down. Grandmother, Mother, Bear Paw, and the others. How she would miss them! She looked over to where Bear Paw had been standing. He was gone.

Medicine Wolf wept until there were no tears left. Her eyes were swollen and red, and she felt weary. The woman in her wanted to be brave, to accept this challenge without question. In some ways she was even curious and eager to learn about the strange white world. But none of those things could outweigh her love for her family and for Bear Paw. Two summers! It seemed a lifetime.

She had left the Indian encampment around Horse Creek to come out onto the plains alone to pray. She had begged Grandfather Wolf and *Maheo* to show her a sign that would mean she did not have to do this. But there was no sign. Shivering from another sob, she turned to Wolf, squeezing her hands into his thick white fur, burying her head against his neck. "You will stay with me, won't you, Wolf?" The animal let out a little whimper and licked her face. Yes, she had Wolf. There was a comfort in animals. Medicine Wolf's only bit of joy was to know Wolf could stay with her when her family left.

She wondered how she could bear staying in one place like this. It was time to migrate south. She was supposed to help Old Grandmother smoke and dry meat to be stored for the winter. This year she was supposed to be the one to make the pemmican. She had planned to work all winter on the large, beautiful buffalo skin Arrow Maker had given her, a start on a collection of skins that she would use one day for her own tipi.

Now all those things would have to wait. She let go of Wolf, as she sniffed and wiped her eyes. The sun was setting. Tomorrow the Cheyenne would leave her behind with the preacher family. How would she talk with them? She didn't know their language, and they didn't know hers. She got to her feet. There was nothing more to say or do. She had a duty, an obligation to the Wolf Spirit and to the People. She knew already that it would always be this way.

Tonight there would be a feast in her honor. The pipe would be smoked with Arrow Maker, the Reverend Prescott, Broken Hand Fitzpatrick, and a leader from Fort Laramie, sealing the agreement involving her fate. Her heart heavy, she started back to camp, but waited when she saw a rider coming toward her. She recognized Bear Paw's roan gelding. She could easily tell who it was. She knew how he sat a horse, so straight and handsome! A tight feeling came to her chest, and she wondered how she looked. She smoothed back her hair with her hands, sure her eyes must look terrible from so much crying.

What did he want? He was doing a daring thing to come out here alone when he knew she was also alone. Since he walked away last night after she said she would stay with the Prescotts, she had seen nothing of him. Was he angry with her? He came closer, halting his horse, sitting proudly, watching her in silence, for a moment. "You have been crying," he finally said.

She swallowed before answering. "I do not want to stay behind, but I have no choice, Bear Paw. It is expected of me."

Bear Paw swung his leg around in front of him and slid off his mount, coming to stand near her. He wore no shirt, and his hard-muscled arms glistened with sweat from a hard ride. His presence produced an aura of virility and strength. Wolf made no move to keep Bear Paw away. The young man held Medicine Wolf's eyes, and she wondered where she would find her next breath. He looked splendid, wearing only a breechcloth and no weapons. He wore no paint, but only a beaded hairpiece tied at one side into his long black hair. At nineteen, he was every bit a man,

muscular, lean, handsome, and already showing battle
scars from acts of bravery.

"I know you do not want to go," he told her. "When
first you said you would, I was angry, not with you, but
with the others for letting this happen to you. But I understand now that it must be so. I know that you must
follow your visions, even if it hurts us. I just wanted to
tell you that you must not cry or be afraid, because I know
you are coming back to us, Medicine Wolf. I know it
because—" He reached out and took her hand. "Because
just as I was a part of your vision, so were you a part of
mine. We share something special, Medicine Wolf, and
because of that I think it is right to tell you of my vision."

Medicine Wolf stood mesmerized by his presence, a
pride filing her heart at the fact that this young, honored
warrior would share his vision with her. A vision was as
sacred as *Maheo*.

"In my vision I was a bear," he told her. "I was hurt,
and a wolf came and licked my wounds and healed me,
just like when you came to heal me after I was hurt in the
raid against the Pawnee. I knew that in the vision the wolf
was you. But in the vision it did not happen just once,
Medicine Wolf. It happened twice. The second time I was
not a bear, but a man; and the wolf was a woman." He
squeezed her hand. "That means you will help me again,
Medicine Wolf, and you cannot do that unless you are
with me. That means you must return. Just as you saw us
as man and woman in your vision, I saw the same."

He let go of her hand, but she could not tear her eyes
from his own dark, hypnotic gaze, nor could he in turn
stop thinking how pretty she was, what a beautiful woman
she would be one day. "Go to the missionaries, Medicine
Wolf," he told her. "Obey what must be. Learn from
them and bring that knowledge back to our People. But
do not let them steal your spirit, your heart. Your spirit
belongs to the Cheyenne, and your heart belongs to me."

A light breeze blew her hair back from her face, and
for that moment Medicine Wolf felt almost sick with love.
"Nothing they do or say can make me turn away from the
Cheyenne, Bear Paw, or from you. But it hurts." Her eyes
teared again.

"I know." He drew in his breath, as though taking a deep breath for courage. "I want to hold you, Medicine Wolf, just for a moment. I want you to remember me."

She felt faint with a mixture of sorrow and love and ecstasy. "How can you think I would ever forget you," she answered, tears slipping down her cheeks.

He reached out hesitantly, pulling her close, wrapping strong arms around her. Never in her young life had Medicine Wolf experienced anything quite so wonderful. In his arms she felt no fear of tomorrow, because *this* was tomorrow. This was her future, and the white preacher could not change it no matter how hard he tried.

She let her head rest against his chest for several long, wonderful seconds. He drew back then, touching her cheek with his fingers and wiping away her tears. *"Ho-shuh,"* he said softly. "Do not be afraid. No matter how far the distance between us, we will be together." He put a fist against his chest. "Here. We share a vision. It cannot be changed." He stepped back, his eyes moving over her in a way that made her shiver. *"Ne-mehotatse."* He turned and swung himself up on his horse, looking at her once more. "I am to scout ahead for our journey south. I leave today, Medicine Wolf. I will not see you again until two summers."

Medicine Wolf was shocked to see that his eyes looked teared. He turned his horse and headed south. She watched after him, her own tears vanishing. *"Ne-mehotatse,"* he had told her. "I love you." Could such a splendid warrior feel that way about an eleven-year-old girl? Or was it the woman-to-be to whom he had spoken? She looked at Wolf, who got up on all fours and trotted closer. "It is time," she told the animal. "I'm not afraid any more, Wolf."

She walked back to the village, wishing she could have ridden back with Bear Paw; but she knew that although he had done nothing wrong in coming out to see her alone, he was being careful that nothing be misinterpreted. Someone like White Horse might try to make trouble over this.

Her heart soared with love and happiness. She came in sight of the village to see women packing parfleches and supplies onto various travois, making ready to leave at sunrise. She raised her chin proudly. If she was indeed to be Bear Paw's woman one day, it was time to start behaving like the strong, brave woman she would have to be if she was to belong to such a man.

She spotted Old Grandmother then. The woman gave her a familiar toothless grin, and Medicine Wolf ran to her open arms. This was the hardest part. Bear Paw, even her parents, were young enough that two summers was not so long after all. But Old Grandmother . . . for such an old woman, two summers was a very, very long time.

"Ho-shuh, Nexahe," the old woman told Medicine Wolf. *"E-peva-e."*

"Be still, my granddaughter," Old Grandmother had told her. "It is good. It is right that you do this."

She drew back from Old Grandmother and studied the woman's hollow, aging eyes. It struck her again how things are always changing, but this time she felt the change in the air was something frightening, something she could not name . . . a way of life perhaps.

She met her grandmother's eyes again, and she held her chin proudly. "I am not afraid, Grandmother," she told the woman. "I am Medicine Wolf, and I am Cheyenne. The white missionaries cannot change me. They can make me dress like them and can teach me their talk and their writing, but they cannot change my heart."

The old woman nodded, looking proud. A tear slipped down her cheek, and she quickly wiped it away. "Come, *Nexahe*. We will pack your things."

Chapter Seven

The historic Laramie Treaty signing ended. The "Great Smoke" was finished and a new pact was struck between Indian and white leaders. Still, many Sioux and Cheyenne were wary of the white man's promises, and those who had disagreed with the treaty had already determined they did not have to abide by any white man's rules.

For the moment the treaty meant nothing to Medicine Wolf. She felt sick as she watched her family leave Horse Creek. Her sister, Smiling Girl, had cried, as had her good friend Summer Moon. Star Woman had looked back once with tears on her face. Old Grandmother had not wept, and Medicine Wolf knew it was only because the old woman was trying to be strong for her. Arrow Maker and Swift Fox had refused to look back, afraid they might show tears in front of the other warriors.

Medicine Wolf's throat ached fiercely now from trying not to cry. She watched until she could no longer see any of her family. They melted into the southern horizon, and the worst loneliness Medicine Wolf had ever suffered stabbed at her like a knife. Now she would be surrounded by the strange *ve-ho-e*. She was not free to run with the wind; she would not be able to tell Old Grandmother her secrets, or be able to help her mother make the pemmican, or to clean hides and build tipis and she could not dance for Bear Paw.

Someone touched her shoulder, and she looked up at the Reverend Prescott. Fear filled her at the sight of him because of his size and his hairy face. "We must go now, child," he told her. She didn't understand what he said, but she reasoned he wanted her to come with him. She turned and hugged and petted Wolf, then picked up her parfleche full of clothing and supplies. She turned to follow the holy man, hoping she would not be sick in front of him, for her stomach felt on fire from fear and loneliness.

She watched the holy man's wife and son, who were waiting beside a covered wagon. The son smiled warmly, but his mother watched her sternly, her thin lips pressed tightly. The woman's gray eyes moved to Wolf as they came closer, and she said something to her husband, appearing irritated. They seemed to be disagreeing about something, and Medicine Wolf had a feeling it involved Wolf. She moved closer to him, petting his head and waiting. The woman finally threw up her hands and climbed up onto the wagon. The reverend took Medicine Wolf's parfleche and placed it inside the wagon, then lifted her into it. The son climbed in after her and the reverend got into the seat and picked up the reigns, whipping into motion the four horses that pulled the wagon.

The wagon clattered away, heading for Fort Laramie. A few soldiers accompanied the procession. Medicine Wolf sat at the back of the wagon, where she could keep an eye on Wolf, who followed behind. She wished he could ride with her in the wagon, but apparently the holy man did not want the animal inside. She glanced at the soldiers and saw how they watched Wolf, looking as though they would like to shoot him. One of them had a great deal of trouble with his horse because it was afraid of the wolf, and he had to drop back. Some of the other soldiers exchanged angry words.

The sick feeling in Medicine Wolf's stomach grew worse. She knew without understanding a word of English that the white soldiers did not like Wolf, nor did the holy man's wife. Would one of those soldiers harm her beloved pet? She was already aware of how little respect these *ve-ho-e* had for animals. She was in their world now. They surely had no idea how important Wolf was to her, not just as a pet, but as the Wolf Spirit in the flesh, a part of her very being.

Her worry over Wolf only added to her stomach woes, and the rocking of the wagon made her feel even worse. She had never ridden in such a contraption before, and they had not gone a mile before she could no longer control the physical reaction to her fear and loneliness. She leaned over the wagon gate and vomited, unable to control herself, wanting to die then of shame and embarrassment. The preacher's wife yelled something to her husband, and he stopped the wagon.

"Lord help us," the woman gasped. Medicine Wolf wished she knew what was being said, but at the least, she noticed the woman's eyes showed a hint of concern. The woman handed her a cloth to wipe her mouth. "All we need is for her to get sick and die on us."

Medicine Wolf realized she was talking to her son.

"I think she's just nervous, Mother. She's been taken from her family, you know. I imagine that's as frightening for her as it would be for a white child to suddenly be forced to live among Indians."

"For heaven's sake, Tom, it's not the same at all! She'll live a much better life with us than if it were the other way around! Give her some of that peppermint I gave you this morning. Do you still have some? Maybe it will make her stomach feel better."

Medicine Wolf sat shivering and embarrassed, feeling better only when the young man reached into his pocket and handed something out to her. "Try it," he said. She glanced at his hand, seeing two small round objects with pretty colors in them. She hesitated, not sure what he wanted her to do. He took one and put it into his own mouth, rubbing his stomach. "Mmmm," he told her. "It's good. Try some." Again he put out his hand.

"Take the candy, child," Mrs. Prescott told her. She pointed to her mouth, then to the little object. Medicine Wolf glanced at the young man once more, thinking that so far he had not died from putting the object into his mouth. She cautiously took the object and tasted it. To her pleasant surprise, it had a marvelously sweet flavor that took away the sour taste of vomit and even soothed her stomach.

The young man who had offered it smiled, and Medicine Wolf managed a slight smile in return, thanking him in her own tongue. She looked at the woman then, deciding she did not like this wagon. She was not used to traveling this way.

"I wish to walk," she told the woman in her own tongue. She saw the frown on the woman's face, so she repeated the words, pointing outside the wagon to the ground. She waited as the woman climbed out of the wagon herself and called out to someone. A bearded, buckskin-clad white man rode up to the woman on his horse, and Medicine Wolf recognized him as a scout who had been at the treaty gathering. He had served as an interpreter, and he understood the Indian tongue. He was one of those white men who used to hunt beaver in the mountains and trade with the Indians.

The scout approached the wagon after conversing with the white woman, and he asked Medicine Wolf what she was trying to say. She repeated her request to be allowed to walk, and the man told Mrs. Prescott, who appeared irritated. She indicated that Medicine Wolf could get out, which the girl gladly did. Once her feet were on Grandmother Earth, she felt much better. The preacher's son climbed out to walk beside her, and the little procession was off again.

Medicine Wolf reached down to pet Wolf, wanting to show the soldiers and the preacher's son that the animal was tame and would not harm them. She indicated to the son that he could pet him too. The young man walked around to the other side of Wolf and cautiously reached out, touching his head. When Wolf made no threatening moves or sounds, the young man grinned, looking excited.

Medicine Wolf nodded and smiled to him, and he pet the animal more, looking almost grateful. He pointed to himself then. "Tom," he said. "Tom."

She looked him over. He was not as muscular as Bear Paw, but he looked about the same age. He was tall and rather lanky, but pleasant-looking, rather fascinating to her because of his blue eyes and hair the color of straw. She wondered if this Tom knew anything about hunting, if he had ever counted coup. There was something in his eyes that made her feel more comfortable, and she smiled, repeating his name. She pointed to herself then, speaking her name in the Cheyenne tongue.

Tom shook his head. He touched her shoulder. "Medicine Wolf," he said in English.

Medicine Wolf frowned. Was that her name in the *ve-ho-e* tongue? He repeated it, and she said the name slowly. "Me . . . da . . . sin . . . wolf."

Tom smiled and nodded. "Medicine Wolf," he repeated. He pointed to Wolf and said "Wolf."

Medicine Wolf frowned. *"Ho-nehe,"* she told him.

He shook his head. "Wolf," he repeated. He pointed to her. "Medicine Wolf." Then to himself "Tom." He pointed to the wagon and told her what it was called. He pointed upward. "Sky." He walked closer to one of the soldiers and patted the rump of the man's horse. "Horse."

Medicine Wolf frowned. Horse? That was *mo-ehe-no-ha*. She realized it was not going to be easy to learn the white man's words, but concentrating on learning them would help keep her from thinking about Bear Paw and Old Grandmother. If this was what was expected of her, she would concentrate and do her best, especially if it might someday help her people.

She repeated all the words Tom had given her, pointing to the objects as she did so. Tom seemed delighted. Medicine Wolf felt a little better. She still did not like or trust the holy man or his wife, or any of the soldiers; but Tom made her feel more welcome. He held out another piece of the hard delight he had given her after she vomited.

"Candy," he told her. "Peppermint."

She smiled, taking it from him and putting the sweet morsel in her mouth. "Candy," she repeated.

Tom nodded, reaching out and patting her shoulder as though to tell her not to be afraid. Everything would be all right. The wagon and soldiers headed north, toward a strange new world for Medicine Wolf. She touched her little medicine bag, feeling the wolf paws and reminding herself that this was all just a part of her vision and she must accept it as best she could.

"She cannot sleep next to that dirty animal," Marilyn Prescott insisted. She made motions to Medicine Wolf, indicating the wolf must be left outside the tent. Medicine Wolf, unsure what the woman wanted, knelt beside Wolf and put her arms around him protectively. Did the woman want her to send Wolf away? How could she do that? Wolf had slept at her side ever since she had brought him home as a pup.

The woman approached, apparently to try to make the wolf go outside, but Wolf growled at her. The look of fright in Mrs. Prescott's eyes almost made Medicine Wolf laugh, and she would have if she were not so afraid for Wolf. These white people all seemed afraid of him. She feared for his life. She was more sure than ever now that she did not like this Prescott woman, for Wolf also disliked her.

The woman hurried out of the tent, and young Tom looked at Medicine Wolf. "You can't keep the wolf in here," he tried to explain. "Mother thinks he's dangerous and that animals are dirty." His eyes looked apologetic, but Medicine Wolf could not understand a word he said. Moments later Mrs. Prescott returned with the same scout who had accompanied them to Fort Laramie. He knelt in front of Medicine Wolf and explained that Wolf would have to sleep outside.

"But he always sleeps with me," she tried to explain. "He is like part of me."

The bearded man sighed, the Reverend Prescott and his wife and son looking on. "I'm told you're here to learn the way of the white man," the scout told her in her own tongue. "It is not their way to let animals sleep with them, especially wild animals like a wolf. In their minds it's dangerous and unclean. Now, I tend to think like you do, and personally, there's a lot of animals I'd rather sleep with than some people. But Mrs. Prescott here, she wants to teach you how the more educated, proper white women conduct themselves, so you ought to do what she tells you." He nodded toward Wolf. "He's got to be tied, Medicine Wolf, outside of the tent."

"No!" she objected.

"There no getting around it. And the thing is, this here pet of yours, he isn't going to let just anybody drag him out and tie him up. You'll have to do it yourself. That's the only way he'll cooperate, I expect. It's best you do what the lady wants, Medicine Wolf, because some of the soldiers, they don't trust Wolf either. If you tie him, he can't be blamed if a chicken gets eaten during the night or a young calf is attacked. You don't want one of the soldiers to shoot Wolf, do you?"

Her eyes widened in shock and fear. Shoot Wolf? She shook her head.

"Then you've got to tie him at night," the scout told her. "I know where there's some old meat I can bring over for him to eat. And we'll set out a pan of water for him."

Again the sick feeling came to Medicine Wolf's stomach. Her eyes teared, and she looked up at Mrs. Prescott, who showed no sympathy. She looked at Wolf. Would he understand? How could she tie such a wild, beautiful thing? Animals should not be tied. It was cruel. Mrs. Prescott handed out a rope, and Medicine Wolf realized that if she was to bear her stay here, she would have to cooperate with the woman or constantly face her consternation. She reasoned that if she did not tie Wolf, something bad might happen to him, like the bearded scout told her. The scout had honest eyes, and she knew he was telling her true.

She rose, commanding Wolf in the Cheyenne tongue to follow her. She took the rope from Mrs. Prescott, giving her a look of mutual disdain, and led Wolf outside. It seemed more reasonable to her to let the animal sleep with her. As long as he was at her side, what harm could he do?

Through tears she tried to explain to Wolf. He sat still while she tied the rope around his neck, then tied the other end to a nearby cottonwood tree. It nearly broke her heart to see him sitting there looking so bewildered. She waited until the scout brought the meat, and Tom brought out some water. Tom took her arm then and urged her to come back inside the tent to sleep. He said something to the scout.

"Tom here says to tell you that soon his father will have a cabin finished where all of you will live," the scout told Medicine Wolf.

Medicine Wolf hung her head, glancing back at Wolf once more before following Tom inside the tent. How could she explain that she hoped the reverend never got a cabin built? She would much rather sleep in this thing called a tent, which was more like her own People's tipis. She had no desire to live in a white man's house, with its hard floors and hard walls and with a roof overhead so that one could not see the stars. It frightened her to think of living in such an enclosed area, to not feel Mother Earth beneath her when she slept.

She went back inside and lay down on a bedroll that had been prepared for her, refusing to look at Mrs. Prescott. The reverend knelt before a tablelike structure on which sat something metal that was shaped in a cross. Medicine Wolf studied it a moment, wondering if the cross represented the four directions to which the Cheyenne prayed. It was obvious the reverend was praying now. Maybe their religions were not so different after all.

She pulled a blanket over herself, turning her back to the rest of them, wondering how she was going to sleep through the night without Wolf close by. Outside, she could hear him whining. She knew it would be a long night for him also. The reverend continued praying in words Medicine Wolf could not understand. Finally he stopped. He and his wife and Tom all talked together in a little group for a while, then they retired to their own bedrolls, Tom going outside to the wagon.

Medicine Wolf waited until she heard the soft rhythmic

breathing of people in deep sleep. She sat up then, looking over at the Prescotts, thinking it odd that husband and wife shared separate bedrolls, which were laid out several feet apart. Her own parents always slept beside each other. She watched a moment longer, able to see them clearly because of a lantern the reverend had left lit. She wanted to be sure they were sleeping hard. Finally, she picked up her blankets and quietly exited the tipi, laying the blankets out beside Wolf, who wagged his tail eagerly and licked her.

She lay down, and Wolf stretched out beside her.

"My heavens!"

Medicine Wolf awoke to the sound of Mrs. Prescott's screech. She looked up at the woman, whose eyes showed anger and horror. The reverend came hurrying out of the tent, hastily tying a robe.

"Would you look at this, Andrew!" Mrs. Prescott gasped.

Medicine Wolf's heart pounded at the woman's hysteria, wishing she knew what was being said. Tom stuck his head out of the wagon, disturbed by his mother's carrying on.

"Dear, oh, dear, oh, dear!" The woman stood with folded arms speaking to her husband. "We certainly have our work cut out for us! Maybe it would help to get rid of the wolf completely and to make her give up those heathen wolf paws she carries."

"We'd better wait a while on that," Prescott warned his wife. "It's too soon. Give her a little more time. She's still afraid."

"Perhaps," the woman answered. "But eventually the wolf's paws have to go."

Medicine Wolf watched them apprehensively. What were they talking about? She understood the word "wolf" now. Had she done something terribly wrong that meant something would happen to Wolf? What was the problem? She had kept the animal out of the tent as Mrs. Prescott had requested. Was it so wrong to come out here and sleep with him?

She moved her arms around Wolf protectively, and

Mrs. Prescott shook her head again. "This is going to be more of a project than first we thought," the woman lamented. "She must be punished for this. Not severely, at least not this first time. These savages *must* learn discipline! That is the first order of business!"

The reverend rubbed his beard. "I agree. The child must learn more respect for authority."

"She doesn't know what she's doing," Tom put in. "She's just scared. She probably figures if we won't let the wolf sleep in the tent, then she'll just sleep out here with the wolf."

"Well, she will learn she can*not* sleep outside with the wolf," Mrs. Prescott said. "Her ridiculous attachment to the animal must be broken. Find the interpreter. The wolf must be turned loose outside the fort grounds. I want her told that if she cannot make the wolf stay away from the fort, then it will be shot. A small whipping will set her straight. Get my switch, Tom."

Medicine Wolf watched in wonder, still clinging to Wolf. Tom had a pleading look on his face and seemed to be almost arguing with his mother about something. The woman barked an order then, and Tom turned back inside the wagon. It seemed strange to Medicine Wolf that a young man who must be nineteen or twenty years old should so easily be ordered around by his mother. At his age a young Cheyenne man was free, his own man. He had much respect for his mother, but was not expected to be ordered around by her. In fact, she had never seen a Cheyenne mother talk to any of her children, no matter what the age, the way Mrs. Prescott talked to her son, always a scolding look on her face.

Tom reappeared with something Medicine Wolf had never seen before, but it resembled the small quirts Cheyenne men carried to spur their horses to run faster, sometimes used with much more force on an enemy. To her horror the preacher's wife took hold of the little whip and raised it as though to hit her with it.

Hit a child? No Cheyenne, man or woman, ever hit a child! She had never seen it happen, nor had she ever been hit herself. The whip came down across her legs before she could jump out of the way, bringing an awful sting that made her cry out. In the next moment Wolf leapt into action, clamping his teeth around the whip and growling furiously, tugging it away from Mrs. Prescott. The woman screamed as though she were being horribly beaten, turning and running as fast as she could run. She tripped over her long skirt and fell forward into soft mud left from where a horse had just urinated. She screamed again, breaking into angry tears and running on into the fort, shouting something about the wolf.

Medicine Wolf's eyes teared as she rubbed the red welt that appeared across her lower calves. Her hand shook as she looked up at Tom, seeing a sympathetic look on his face. He climbed down from the wagon and reached out cautiously, indicating that Medicine Wolf should get the whip away from Wolf and hand it to him.

Sniffing back tears, Medicine Wolf spoke softly to Wolf, and he gave up the ugly instrument of discipline. Tom took hold of the whip and turned to his father. "If Mother ever uses this on that girl again, I'll personally ride into Indian country and take her back to her People, Father! I mean it! She had no right doing that!"

Prescott stiffened, eyeing his boy sternly. "You should not interfere in this, son. You haven't lived long enough to know what is best in these cases."

"I mean it, Father!"

"And soldiers would catch up with you in no time. You won't do any such thing, and you know it! Now, you calm down. I'll not have a son of mine talking to me this way. We'll get an interpreter and we'll try to reason with the child. No more whippings, unless after a while she continues to be disobedient. That much I promise."

Medicine Wolf's heart pounded with fear and dread as in the distance she saw Mrs. Prescott returning with some soldiers. It was obvious young Tom had tried to defend her, but it was equally obvious that he had little say in anything his parents decided to do. Mrs. Prescott was in a rage; her plain gray dress was covered with mud and her hair fell out of its neat bun. Medicine Wolf wrapped her arms around Wolf and held him close. The interpreter accompanied the little group, and she knew this would have something to do with Wolf.

While Mrs. Prescott watched with folded arms and a scolding look, the interpreter explained to Medicine Wolf that Wolf must be kept away from fort grounds. The words were like a stabbing sword, and the sick feeling returned to her stomach. She knew by the looks on everyone's faces that she must do what they asked or risk Wolf's life. She hugged the animal closer, unable to keep the tears from coming. They wanted her to be separated from Wolf! It would be like pulling out her heart and laying it someplace else!

Tom cast a dark, angry look at his mother, then turned and walked away. Medicine Wolf finally managed to control her tears. She stood up, untying the rope from the tree and keeping hold of it. She looked up at the scout.

"Tell them I will take him out alone," she sniffed. "I do not want that bad woman with me!"

The scout nodded, saying something to Mrs. Prescott. Medicine Wolf wondered if he would tell her she had called her bad, but from the woman's reaction, she supposed he had not. Mrs. Prescott simply nodded, a victorious look on her thin face. She said something to the scout, and the man told Medicine Wolf that he was to go with her to make sure she didn't try to run away.

Medicine Wolf walked off with Wolf, heading toward the hills outside the fort. How she wished she could just keep going and never return! But she had made a promise, and her People expected her to keep it. This was part of her vision, and she could not change it. Still, the Prescotts had told her People that she could keep Wolf with her. They had not mentioned he would have to stay completely off fort grounds. These *ve-ho-e* did not seem to be very honest.

Days turned into weeks and into months, long, lonely months for Medicine Wolf. Her only solace was when she was allowed to walk daily beyond the fort to see Wolf. She had hoped that the scout who had interpreted for her when she first stayed here would always be around, for he seemed to understand her, and he helped her communicate with the Prescotts. But he left within the first month, and

Medicine Wolf was on her own in this strange world, among a people who understood nothing about her language or needs.

Being separated from Wolf was agony, but the animal seemed to understand. Sometimes, when she looked into his all-knowing yellow eyes, she thought he might speak as he had spoken to her in her dreams. The animal seemed to sense the danger that lay in being caught inside fort grounds and he stayed away, waiting every day at the same time on a rise west of the fort, where Medicine Wolf came out to see him.

It had not been easy getting permission for these daily visits. When first she insisted on going out every afternoon to talk to and feed her pet, Medicine Wolf suffered repeated scoldings, sometimes being refused supper, sometimes receiving a painful whipping on her legs, but only when Tom was not present. Finally, when she realized that nothing was going to deter Medicine Wolf from seeing her sacred pet, Mrs. Prescott had given up her efforts at keeping the two of them apart. It had become obvious that Medicine Wolf had made up her mind that the woman could beat her to death if she wished. She would not miss one day of going out to Wolf to assure him that she still loved him. Medicine Wolf could only hope that Wolf understood that being separated was not her choice.

"One day, when all this is over, and we are back with the People, we will be together again," she assured him many times over, hugging him and petting him.

On every daily visit Tom was instructed to go with her to be sure she did not try to run away. Medicine Wolf understood the white man's language well enough by now to realize why he had to come, but she couldn't speak it well enough to fully explain why it was not necessary for him to be there. She had agreed to stay for two years and she would not shame her people and herself by breaking that promise.

She had already learned a great deal, and she had even won praise from Mrs. Prescott for her ability to learn quickly. She knew now what "very bright" meant, but she could not understand why the woman always added "for an Indian," as though she didn't think Indians could learn anything.

There were many things about the woman and her ways that Medicine Wolf did not understand. Why did speaking her own tongue mean getting rapped on the knuckles or switched across the shoulders? Why did she have to wear the hot, rough, binding clothing that white women wore, and why did they dress this way in the first place? She was learning enough of the language now that soon she intended to try to talk more with Tom, for he seemed genuinely friendly and accepting. Maybe Tom could answer many of her questions, and would answer them honestly.

For now she remained almost silent, speaking only when she had to repeat words for Mrs. Prescott. She did not like being whipped and would never understand why anything she did was so terrible that she should be so severely punished. No Cheyenne child was ever treated this way. If she did not sit just so in a chair, she was whipped. If she did not eat properly, which included the confusing way the whites had of using certain dishes or certain forks for certain foods, holding a teacup a particular way, she was whipped, but always only when Tom was not around. She was warned not to complain to Tom, or she would only be whipped again, and Tom would be sent away. She did not want Tom to leave, for he had become her only friend.

She shivered, for now it was winter, and even the thick woolen clothes she was forced to wear did not always keep her warm when she went out on the open plains to see Wolf. A cold wind blasted her face, the fine sleet it carried stinging her skin. Mrs. Prescott had tried to discourage her from going out, but she would have none of it. She would not let Wolf think she had deserted him. She gave him the meat she had secretly saved from her own meal, as she did every day. She knew Wolf was probably doing just fine finding his own food, but she wanted to be sure he did not go hungry.

It was not hard to give some of her own food to Wolf, for ever since that first awful experience with Mrs. Prescott over her pet, a day did not go by that her stomach did not hurt her. She hated it here among the *ve-ho-e*, hated the way soldiers stared and pointed at her, hated being away from Wolf, from her family, from Bear Paw.

She gave wolf a hug and kissed his head, tears welling up in her eyes. The animal licked one tear that slipped down her cheek and she kissed him once more before rising. She turned to Tom, who smiled and handed out another piece of meat. "I saved mine too, this time," he told her. "Just don't tell Mother."

She understood enough of the words to feel at least a little relief from her loneliness. "Thank you," she told him in English, turning and handing the meat to Wolf.

Tom shivered, turning up the collar of his wool coat. "We'd better get back."

Medicine Wolf pulled the hood of her cape over her head. Tom touched her arm as she started away. Met his gaze. "Maybe sometime, when we come out here, you can tell me about some of your ways, tell me about the wolf's paws, how you got them, what they mean to you," he told her.

She was surprised that a white man cared. She nodded. "When I . . . speak good," she answered.

"You're doing real good right now. But it's too cold today. Maybe someday when it's warmer." He sobered. "I'm sorry, Medicine Wolf, I mean, Martha," he added, using the white woman's name his mother had given Medicine Wolf. "Sorry my mother and father don't try harder to understand." He searched her eyes. "*I* want to understand," he said. "I don't think Indians and whites will ever really get along the way they should until we *both* try. I've told Mother it isn't right that it should be all our way, but she won't listen."

Medicine Wolf was not certain of everything he had said, but she picked up enough to know he was not like either of his parents. Tom was wiser. He realized there could be more than one way of living and believing. When she was taking lessons from Mrs. Prescott, or praying and listening to Bible readings from the reverend, she only listened and obeyed. She knew they both thought they were changing her, making her see their way of life was best; but they had done nothing to take her heart from the People or her own beliefs. She had simply decided it was not worth the whippings for her to object to anything they taught her or to try to make them see her point of view on anything.

She longed to talk to someone about Old Grandmother, about the wolf's paws and the Sun Dance, about the buffalo hunt, the first time she built a tipi, and all the things she missed and loved. Maybe Tom would listen. Maybe with him for a friend she could survive the next year and a half without wanting to die.

She smiled for Tom in spite of the painful cramps she was feeling deep in her belly. The pains had started before they left from visiting Wolf and were growing worse. She had never felt such pain before, and was not sure of the cause. She turned away, suddenly wanting very much to get out of the cold. She wondered if she was getting some horrible white man's disease. Would she die and never see her parents or Bear Paw again?

She reminded herself of her vision. She could not die. She must return to the Cheyenne. It was written in the wind. She walked back toward the fort, struggling not to show her pain. Before entering the parade grounds she turned once more to look back at Wolf. He sat in the same place, looking lonely and forlorn, hardly visible against the white snow that was beginning to build on the ground as sleet turned to fat flakes.

"Looks like quite a storm coming," Tom told her, taking her arm. "We'd better get back to the cabin."

Medicine Wolf did not argue. It was difficult for her to stand up straight as they hurried to the warmth of the Prescott cabin, where she fell to the floor in front of the stove and curled up with the pain. She could not imagine what was happening to her, but she was sure it was something horrible, for the pain had become deep and stabbing.

The reverend picked her up and carried her to her bed, he and his wife both appearing to be genuinely concerned. Medicine Wolf huddled into the blankets, frightened, lonely, praying to *Maheo* that he would not let her die.

Chapter Eight

Medicine Wolf was beside herself with anxiety, trying to make Mrs. Prescott understand that she had to get out of the house. To her horror and humiliation, the woman had sent for a white soldier doctor when she fell "ill," and the man had discovered the cause of her terrible stomach cramps. She was having her first flowing. She was a woman!

Normally this would have been cause for celebration among her People. Once her time of month was ended, there would have been a special ritual and blessing for her coming into womanhood. It was a great honor. The ability of women to have babies was something of wonder and mystery to the Cheyenne. It gave her great powers, so much power, in fact, that during her time of month a woman was expected to go to a tipi somewhat removed from the village. It was not good for a warrior or a holy man to be near a menstruating woman, or he might lose his spiritual strength. Men were not even supposed to bathe downstream from a menstruating woman. In her case, Medicine Wolf supposed her coming into womanhood would be an even greater cause for celebration because of her special spiritual gifts.

Oh, how she longed for Old Grandmother and Star Woman! They would know what to do. They would happily take her to the menstrual tipi and talk to her about a woman's ways, explain what was happening to her. Old Grandmother would make an herbal drink for her that would take away the cramps. Arrow Maker and Black Buffalo would prepare for the ritual of her becoming a woman, and there would be great feasting and celebrating. And Bear Paw . . . Bear Paw would look at her very differently.

Mrs. Prescott took away all her joy at this wonderful new thing that was happening to her. The woman would not let her leave the cabin. Didn't she understand that her husband and son could be affected by being near her? The woman insisted she stay piled up in the soft bed, which she hated. Mrs. Prescott fussed and fumed, and for some reason she seemed ashamed and embarrassed by the situation, which to Medicine Wolf was perfectly natural. She wondered if the white doctor, after being so close to her, had now lost his power to heal. She hoped he never came back. She did not like a strange white man looking at her.

Outside, the wind howled, and she worried about Wolf. In other winters he had been allowed to stay inside her tipi next to a warm fire. Now he was out on the prairie alone in a fierce snowstorm. The thought of it made her cry. In fact, it seemed that suddenly every little thought made her cry. Did it have something to do with this new thing that was happening to her? Was it only because of the painful cramps? If only they would go away.

Mrs. Prescott came into the small room where Medicine Wolf lay curled up, and the reverend came in behind her. Medicine Wolf's eyes widened in surprise. He should not be here! It was bad medicine for him!

"My husband wants to pray for you, Martha," Mrs. Prescott told her. "He wants to pray for your chastity, pray that you will not do the foolish thing so many other young Indian girls do and marry at an age far too young. Such a thing is wrong and sinful, Martha, and it is even more sinful for a man to have more than one wife. What you are experiencing is something God meant as a punishment for women because of the past sins of other women who have married too young or who have slept with more than one man.''

The woman took her hand, and Medicine Wolf thought how cold was her touch. "We know how your people are when it comes to, well, to lovemaking,'' the woman continued. "They are much too free and easy about it, and your people marry without proper ceremonies to make it legal. I don't doubt that young girls like yourself are allowed to run and romp with as many young men as they wish until they are married, and I'm told that even after marriage they can leave their husbands anytime they want to go and sleep with another man. We will pray that you do not fall into such sinful ways.''

Medicine Wolf pulled her hand away. "It is not that way,'' she tried to explain. How dare this woman sit in judgment over something she knew nothing about! "Cheyenne girls—very good. Cannot see young men alone. Mother always with them,'' she tried to explain. "And we *do* have marriage ceremony.''

"A pagan one,'' the woman answered, patting her shoulder. "We're only trying to help you, Martha. If a marriage is not a Christian one, then it is not a real marriage. Haven't you listened to anything we've taught you so far?''

Medicine Wolf moved farther back in the bed, pressing her back against the wall. "You do not know about Cheyenne,'' she told the woman. "How can you help Medicine Wolf if you do not understand?'' She looked at the reverend. "Make him go. It is bad medicine for holy men near me at flowing time. He not touch or look at me.''

Mrs. Prescott was both shocked and disgusted. Her shock came from hearing the girl say so much at once. Medicine Wolf had been nearly silent during the past five months of intensive schooling, speaking only during lessons and even then only repeating words as they were given to her. After repeated whippings and raps on her knuckles during lessons, she had finally learned not to speak in her own tongue, but the woman did not realize until now just how much English the girl had learned. Her intelligence in that respect had surprised her, yet she was disgusted and amazed that in spite of all the lessons and the Bible reading and the praying, Medicine Wolf continued to think like a savage. Here was another ridiculous superstition that she obviously sincerely believed.

"Being around you is not going to hurt Mr. Prescott," she told Medicine Wolf. "That is just another foolish superstition, Martha. You must stop thinking this way. How can we help you if you don't give up these heathen beliefs?" The woman glanced at the iron railing at the head of Medicine Wolf's bed, where she had tied her medicine bag that held the wolf paws. "I will prove to you that none of your superstitions mean a thing." Before Medicine Wolf could stop her, the woman had yanked the medicine bag from the railing. "This silly bag has no power, Martha. Your power comes from inside yourself, and from God. I'll never cure you of your heathen ways if we don't get rid of this."

Medicine Wolf's eyes widened in horror. "Give it to me," she said, sitting up and ignoring the cramps. "It is mine!"

"It means nothing, child. You have to learn this." The woman turned and marched out of the room.

"No!" Medicine Wolf tried to rise and go after her, but Reverend Prescott grasped her arms and held her down in the bed.

"It's for your own good, child," he told her. The man was far too big and strong for Medicine Wolf to overcome him. Medicine Wolf heard the squeak of the door to the wood stove in the main room. A second later it slammed shut.

"Noooo," she screamed again. "They are mine! Mine! I must have the wolf's paws!"

Mrs. Prescott marched back into the room, looking down haughtily at her while the reverend continued to hold her long enough that there could be no hope of saving the paws. "Now you will see that they mean nothing," the woman told her. She knelt down beside her husband. "Let us pray for her soul, Andrew."

The reverend let go of Medicine Wolf and knelt beside

his wife. Both began praying in earnest. Medicine Wolf shook with horror and hatred. How could they do this! She turned away from them, curling up and weeping, hearing none of their prayers.

The winter storm raged outside, and the groaning wind seemed only to accent the aching loneliness in Medicine Wolf's heart. Not only was her medicine bag with its wolf paws gone, but the storm outside was so fierce that she was not allowed to go to find Wolf.

"It's for your own good," Mrs. Prescott had told her. How many times had the woman said that to her? Everything they did for her or to her was "for her own good." This time she realized the woman truly did seem concerned, for anyone could easily be lost in such a storm. Medicine Wolf wondered if the woman truly cared what happened to her, or if she was just worried about how Arrow Maker and the other Cheyenne would react if they came to get her, only to find she had died.

She wondered how she could bear another year and a half with Marilyn Prescott and her domineering, condescending husband. Tom was her only relief, but she did not get to be alone with him often. Without the wolf paws she felt vulnerable, powerless. Maybe now none of her visions would be fulfilled. Maybe now she would not have a future with Bear Paw after all. Maybe something had happened to Wolf when the sacred paws were destroyed. Was he dead? Could he have survived the awful storm?

By the time her menstrual period was over, so was the storm. In its wake there came sunshine and blue skies. The wind died down, and the plains around Fort Laramie were a sea of blinding white. After much begging, and a promise to say extra prayers that night, Medicine Wolf was allowed to venture out to try to find Wolf. The wheelwright at the fort had fashioned a sleigh from a light wagon in which to haul supplies while the snow was deep; Medicine Wolf and Tom were allowed to use it to go and find Wolf, since the snow was too deep to walk through for any distance.

For Medicine Wolf, getting out of the cabin was like

being released from a prison. Outside, the air smelled sweet, even though it was so cold that it made her nostrils feel like they were sticking together. She and Tom both wore black netting over their faces to guard their eyes against the glare of the snow.

Oh, how good it felt to get out and away! And how happy she was that it was Tom who was taking her, for she had not had a chance to talk to him alone since that last time they went out to meet Wolf. Both had brought food they had saved for the poor animal, realizing that in this weather it was very hard to find food, especially for Wolf, because he refused to wander very far from the fort area.

"Do you think he'll be there?" Tom asked.

"He has to be," she answered, her throat aching with dread.

Tom headed horses and sleigh toward the spot where they always met the animal this time of day. Under her wool coat Medicine Wolf had put on her wolfskin for good luck. She had kept it packed with her other things, and she was glad now that Mrs. Prescott never knew about the skin, or she might have burned that too. She wondered sometimes how such a woman could have mothered a son as nice as Tom. How many whippings had he received over the years?

Her heartbeat quickened when she saw him then. Wolf! "There," she said excitedly, pointing. Tom drove the horses toward the spot, and before he even halted the sleigh, Medicine Wolf had jumped off. She trudged through thigh-deep snow, and Wolf bounded toward her, looking more like a great, moving snowball than an animal, for his coat seemed whiter than ever. In seconds he had leapt into Medicine Wolf's arms and she fell backward, hugging the animal while he licked her face. Medicine Wolf laughed and cried, so happy to see that he seemed all right.

"I wanted to come," she told him in the Cheyenne tongue, digging her fingers deep into his thick fur. "But the white woman would not let me. You knew, didn't you, Wolf?"

The animal whined, his tail wagging in sheer ecstasy.

Tom jumped down from the wagon and carried over the food, dumping it from a gunnysack. Wolf jumped off Medicine Wolf and immediately attacked the tasty morsels of stale bread and spoiling meat, and both Medicine Wolf and Tom laughed, watching him. Medicine Wolf met Tom's blue eyes, realizing she was growing to love him as a dear friend, her only friend here in this strange white world. Their eyes held for a moment, and he sobered, taking the netting away from his face and reaching into his wool jacket. "I have something for you," he told her.

"For me?" Medicine Wolf removed her own netting and stepped closer, her smile fading in reaction to her shock and immense gratitude when he held out his hand. In it was her medicine bag, slightly scorched but still intact. Medicine Wolf gasped in surprise, and her eyes teared.

"As soon as Mother went back into your room that night, I opened the door to the stove and grabbed it out," he told her. "It wasn't easy. I burned the ends of my fingers."

She looked up at him. "I remember! You tell your mother you burn them when you put in wood."

He grinned. "Well, what she doesn't know won't hurt her, will it?"

Medicine Wolf smiled in return. "You are good, good man, Tom Prescott.' "

He reddened slightly, pulling the medicine bag away when she reached for it. "You can have it only if you promise to tell me all about it, why it's magic. I want to know, Medicine Wolf, about the Cheyenne, about how you live. I want to learn some of your words."

She nodded. "I tell you, as good as I can say in English." She sat down in the snow, and Tom sat down beside her, finally handing her the medicine bag. She took it gradually, squeezing her hands around it, her eyes tearing again. Wolf came over to her then and lay down over her lap.

The sun shone brightly, and without any wind, it was actually warm sitting there against the side of a hill. Medicine Wolf carefully opened the little leather bag, making sure the wolf paws were inside but not showing them to Tom. "You did not look in the bag?"

Tom shook his head. "No. I wanted to, but for some reason I couldn't. I felt like the paws were too special to you, and I got the strangest feeling, like they were too sacred or something.

"They *are* sacred. They are for my eyes only, to be taken out of medicine bag only for sacred ceremonies," she told him. "I was six summers when the Wolf Spirit chose me."

In her own stumbling English she told Tom about the Crow attack and how she was left with the one stiff finger on her right hand. She told how she came to be alone, how she slept among the wild wolves, how the white wolf spoke to her in a dream. She clutched the medicine bag to her heart as she spoke, and Tom listened with the attention of a young child. She told him about Bear Paw—how he found her, what he had already accomplished as a hunter and a warrior.

"Bear Paw soon be twenty summers," she said. "But he not marry. He waits for me."

"For you! You'll only be twelve this spring," Tom exclaimed. "How can you know you're supposed to marry Bear Paw? You won't marry him as soon as you leave us, will you?"

She shook he head. "No. But I know I must be his wife someday. I cannot tell you how I know, for it is a part of my vision, and of his. We cannot speak of these things to others. I know only it must be."

Tom shook his head in wonder, feeling a secret envy of the warrior called Bear Paw, sometimes dreaming of that kind of life, wild and free, proving his manhood. "It's hard for me to understand these things," he said. "I've been brought up so differently. I find it so fascinating that your people can live out there on the open plains with none of the conveniences we have, and still survive."

Medicine Wolf petted Wolf, running her hand from his head down his back. The animal's eyes drooped shut. "We need only the things Grandmother Earth provides for us with her plants. We eat some of them, use others for medicine. Most of all, we survive because of the sacred buffalo. We get everything from him—clothing, shelter, the things we use for cooking and for grooming, weapons and shields, water bags, fat to make pemmican.''

''Pemmican? What is that?''

''Pemmican is a mixture of meat fat and berries and meat. It is pounded together and dried, makes good food for warriors to take on hunt, lasts very long time.''

She explained how Old Grandmother had been teaching her how to make the pemmican, explained how buffalo meat was the basic essential to their diet. ''That is why we are afraid when white man kills so many buffalo for themselves. It is very bad that they sometimes leave much of the meat and take only the hide, or they cut out only what meat they can carry and leave the rest to become bad. It is sad for us when we see this. It also hurts us to see trees cut down. Trees have feelings. It hurts them to be cut down and cut apart when they are still green and alive. The Indian takes only dead wood.''

Tom grinned at her simplistic attitude. ''I never thought of it that way.''

''Your people have no spirit. They say their God made Grandmother Earth and the animals, yet they have no respect for either. For the Cheyenne, God *is* the earth. He *is* the animals. He is everywhere. All that we have is his gift to us. When we kill animal for food, we thank his spirit for offering itself to us. Even our clothes make us feel close to the animals. We wear their skins, their furs.'' She met his eyes. ''Why do your people dress this way, in clothes that are stiff and hot, clothes that hurt? I do not like these hard shoes and this stiff thing your mother makes me wear beneath my dress. Indian women do not wear such things.''

Tom reddened slightly, realizing she thought nothing of discussing a corset. His mother would be mortified to speak of such a thing. ''I don't know,'' he said, reaching over to pet Wolf. ''A lot of what you say makes sense to me, but I wouldn't dare tell my mother that.'' He sobered. ''I'm sorry for the way she treats you, Medicine Wolf.''

''Is not your doing. I think she is not happy woman. She has no spirit. She does not try to see another way. There is only her way.'' She sighed. ''I ask her why I must learn numbers and letters. Why does this mean so much to the ve-ho-e. She has no answer. She tells me every child must know these things and must not question them. For a long time back, my People have lived without knowing these things. I do not see why learning numbers and letters makes a person happier. I would be happiest being free with my People. Knowing all your words and numbers and reading your holy book cannot change how I feel inside." She put a hand to her heart. "Or change what I am. I am Cheyenne. My *heart* is Cheyenne."

Tom studied her, thinking how pretty she was, and how mature in her thinking for an eleven-year-old. His mother thought Medicine Wolf's beliefs were ignorant and savage, but Tom did not see her that way at all. Sometimes she made a lot of sense. "Thank you for telling me these things," he said to her. "I feel very honored that you shared them with me, and I understand some of your thinking." He sighed deeply. "I hate to say it, but we had better get back now."

Medicine Wolf leaned down and kissed Wolf's head. "I do not want to go."

"I know. But we have to, Medicine Wolf." He knew she hated being called Martha.

Medicine Wolf looked at him. "What about my medicine bag? What if your mother finds it again? She will be angry with you, and she might truly destroy it."

Tom looked around, spotting a large rock below a drift against the hillside. Around the rock the snow had blown in such a way that the ground was left bare. "We'll hide it," he told her. "Every time you come out here you can look and see that it's all right. Come on." He walked toward the rock, and Medicine Wolf stood up and followed "I bet the ground is still soft under this rock," he told her. "The rock might have insulated it."

She frowned. "In . . . soo . . . late?"

"Protected the ground from frost. Here. I'll raise it up and you see if you can dig a hole deep enough to bury the medicine bag. The leather should protect the paws inside."

With much grunting and straining, Tom managed to raise the rock enough for Medicine Wolf to dig underneath. His face reddened from the effort, and Medicine Wolf dug vigorously to hurriedly bury the medicine bag before he might drop the rock. "You are right," she told him, shoving the precious medicine bag into the hole. "I *can* dig the earth here. The ground is not frozen." She covered the hole and closed her eyes. "Thank you, Grandmother Earth," she said aloud. "Again you have helped me. Keep the wolf's paws for me. Protect them until I can come for them again."

She moved back, and Tom let go of the rock, perspiring in spite of the cold. "Maybe we *won't* dig it up every time," he told her with a grin, his breath coming in pants. "That wasn't easy."

"I am grateful," she told him. "You do not have to raise the rock each time. I will leave the paws buried here until my People come for me. The Wolf Spirit smiles kindly on you, Tom Prescott."

"He does, does he? Well, I don't know how much I believe in your Wolf Spirits. I didn't do that so much to save your "great medicine" as I did to pull a good one on my mother."

"Pull a good one? What does this mean?"

He leaned closer, his handsome blue eyes sparkling with humor. "It means we've fooled her. She thinks the wolf's paws burned up, but we know better, don't we? We have a secret, Medicine Wolf."

She smiled more, then covered her mouth and giggled. "It is a fine joke on her."

"Yes, it is."

Their eyes held for a moment, and in Tom's eyes Medicine Wolf saw a hint of the same emotion she had often seen in Bear Paw's eyes. Her smile faded and she lowered her eyes, turning to go back to Wolf. "Among my People, now that I am considered a woman, we would not be allowed to be alone this way together."

Tom laughed lightly. "Well, don't worry about it. Among *my* people you're a long way from being a woman. There is nothing wrong with me coming out here with you. If you were sixteen or seventeen, then my mother might think twice about it, but not eleven or twelve."

She shook her head, petting Wolf once more, a sad

inflection to her voice. "It is not as your mother said, Tom. Young Cheyenne girls are very . . . very . . . what is the word?"

"Chaste? Unspoiled?"

"*Ai.* I mean, yes. Once we are old enough to wed, we go no place without our mothers or grandmothers beside us. Often if a young woman and young man are caught alone, they must marry. It is considered an insult to the woman's family if they do not. Only under a blanket can a man and woman talk alone, and even then they must be in the presence of others. We are not bad like your mother says."

Tom leaned against the sleigh. "Why do some Indian men take more than one wife?'"

She turned to look at him. "Sometimes it must be so. An Indian man is responsible for his brother's wife if his brother should die. When Cheyenne woman loses husband, she needs a man to protect her and her children, and to feed them. Many times when Cheyenne man takes another wife into his tipi, they do not . . ." She felt her cheeks growing hot. "She is not always a wife in every way." She looked away. "Sometimes Cheyenne man takes a second wife to make less work for his first wife if she has many children to care for and many chores to do. In our world it often takes more than one woman in family to finish all the hard work of carrying wood and cooking and cleaning skins. Our women make all the clothes, make many weapons, make pemmican. On the hunt they spend long hours skinning and cutting up the buffalo, preserving the meat, cleaning and drying skins. They are the tipi builders, and often they must stop to nurse babies. Two or three women in one tipi can make the work much easier."

She turned to him again, hoping to make him understand. "Sometimes Cheyenne men take a second wife if the first wife cannot give him children. Children are most important. They are our life. Sometimes many of our people die quickly, like when we are attacked by other tribes, or when white man's diseases come upon us. It is important to have many children so that our people do not die completely away. Children very precious to the Cheyenne."

Tom nodded, smiling softly. "I think I understand." A sad look came into his eyes. "Do your People ever take a whip to their children like my mother does?"

Her eyes turned colder. "Never! Cheyenne child learns by his own mistakes. Early in life he learns that shame is much worse punishment than to be hit. Always doing what is right is first thing we are taught. If we disobey, the elders look at us as though they are ashamed of us and sad for us. It hurts our hearts and makes us want to be better. But no matter how bad we are, we are always easily forgiven."

Tom snickered almost sarcastically. "Well, try to explain *that* one to my mother. She talks about Christ and his forgiveness, but she doesn't know the meaning of the word." He turned and climbed into the sleigh. "Come on. Let's get back before Mother sends a regiment of soldiers after us."

Medicine Wolf turned and petted Wolf once more, promising him she would come back again tomorrow. Her heart felt much lighter now that she had her medicine bag back again, and knew that Wolf was all right. She turned and climbed up into the sleigh. "Thank you, Tom," she said, putting his black netting back over her face. "It is a fine thing you did, saving my medicine bag. I will tell my People there *are* some white people who have good hearts and who want to know our ways." She faced him as he snapped the reins and got the horses into motion. "I will tell them about Tom Prescott."

Tom grinned bashfully. "I take that as a compliment." He looked ahead, watching the snow fly as the horses trudged through it. "I just wish—" He halted the sleigh for a moment, looking out at the vast expanse of snow-covered plains before them, Fort Laramie lying spread out like a town. "I wish your people and mine could always get along. I'm afraid for the future. The Cheyenne, the Sioux, they all live so differently from us, and I'm afraid my people have little tolerance for the way others live. They think everybody should live just like we do."

Medicine Wolf frowned. "I cannot understand this thinking. My People do not try to make others be like us. We live the way we choose and let others do the same."

She breathed deeply of the fresh air, hating the thought of going back to the confining, stuffy cabin. "We should not have to listen so much to the *ve-ho-e*. The Great Father of your people has agreed to let us live free on much land. I think not so many more of your people will come here. They have promised not to settle on the land we are told is ours. Even your white soldiers are to help keep white people from living on Indian land." She sighed. "What I do not understand is this thinking your people have about saying any man can live only on this piece of land or that one. Grandmother Earth belongs to all of us. She cannot be divided and owned by one person."

Tom looked at her, smiling sadly. He said nothing, realizing it would do no good. She still had no real conception of the white way of looking at such things. He was well aware that most eastern tribes had already completely disappeared. He supposed they had thought the same way Medicine Wolf was thinking now, that this country was big enough for both races; but already thousands of whites had trekked their way through Indian country to California to dig gold. Who was to say there wasn't gold in the Rockies, or in the Bighorn Mountains or in the Black Hills? If there was, he knew that there was not a treaty promise strong enough, or an army big enough, to keep out white men who would kill for a handful of nuggets. What would the Sioux and Cheyenne do then? Was this country really big enough for both races?

He decided not to worry Medicine Wolf right now with his thoughts. Maybe it was best to let her learn these things as they happened, to let her go back to her People and live her own way for as long as it might be allowed.

Medicine Wolf saw Old Grandmother walking toward her, the old woman's arms outstretched. She smiled her toothless smile, and Medicine Wolf came closer, taking the old woman in her arms.

"Medicine Wolf," the woman told her. "I have missed you, *nexahe*."

"I am so happy to see you again, *Ne-ske-eehe*."

"Do not desert your People," the old woman told her.

"You are the holy child, and you will be long remembered among both the *ve-ho-e* and the Cheyenne. Be faithful to the Wolf Spirit, *nexahe*. And be faithful to your own heart."

The woman suddenly became very light, then turned to a crumbling dust in Medicine Wolf's arms. Medicine Wolf gasped and cried out for her, sitting up in bed, realizing it had been a dream. It was then she heard the mournful howling in the distant hills. She knew it was Wolf. She got up, pulling a blanket around her because of the cold room. The fire in the wood stove in the main room was nearly out, but that was of no concern to her now. She knew how important dreams were, knew with the sick feeling of sorrow what this dream had meant.

She went to a window to look out. A bright full moon lit up the snowy plains almost like early morning light. Wolf howled again, a mournful wail that seemed only to exemplify what she was feeling in her own heart. Did Wolf know too? Old Grandmother was dead! She did not need to have anyone find out for her. She knew it in her heart.

There it came again, the awful howl that stabbed at her heart. She went to her knees, a similar wail coming from her own throat in the mournful keening that was the way of a Cheyenne woman when she lost a loved one. Tears spilled down her face as she cried out in a strange chant that awoke the rest of the household. All three Prescotts hurried into her small room to find her on her knees, rocking, her head flung back as she sang the strange chant. The accompaniment of the howling in the distant hills made the sight only more eerie and chilling.

"What on earth?" Mrs. Prescott walked around the foot of the bed. "Martha, what is wrong? Stop carrying on so!"

Tom walked around his mother and knelt beside Medicine Wolf. He touched her arm gently. "Medicine Wolf, what's happened? Are you in pain? Are you sick?"

She stopped rocking long enough to look at the only person she knew would understand. "Old Grandmother," she sobbed. "She is dead."

Tom frowned. "How do you know?"

Again came a long, sorrowful howl in the distant hills.

"I dreamed about her. She came to me and embraced me and then she turned to dust." She looked toward the window. "He knows. Wolf knows." She choked in a sob. "Go away, Tom. Make them go away. I have to be alone. I have to sing my prayer song." She returned to the strange chant, and Tom rose to face his mother.

"She's got to stop this barbaric nonsense," the woman insisted.

"Her grandmother is dead. The old woman meant everything to her. She's in mourning, Mother."

"That's ridiculous! How would she know the woman is dead?"

"She knows, Mother. Leave her alone."

"What!"

"You can't talk to your mother that way, Tom," the reverend told the young man.

"I'll soon be twenty-two years old," Tom answered, moving his eyes to his mother. "I'm too big to whip and too old to be ordered around! Medicine Wolf has cooperated in every way possible, but she's still an Indian, and this is something personal that you can't take away from her. For just this once let her *be* Indian! You have nearly a year and a half to try to change her. One night isn't going to make any difference!" He stormed past them, then turned. "Personally, I don't think you're *going* to change her."

He walked out, heading back to his room. The reverend and his wife looked at each other, then at Medicine Wolf, who continued her crying and rocking as though they were not there.

"You've placed a great burden on me, Andrew, taking this barbaric child into our household and expecting me to be able to do anything with her. Look at her, after all my work, chanting away in her own tongue! They're hopeless, Andrew! Ignorant and hopeless!"

"They're God's children, Marilyn. It's our duty to show them the way." The man sighed. "But for the moment I don't think there is anything we can do about this. She believes her grandmother is dead, so let her mourn." The man touched his wife's shoulder and urged her out of the room, closing the door.

Medicine Wolf was practically oblivious of anything that had been said. She was aware of one thing only—that Old Grandmother had died, and she had not been with her. But then, maybe she had. Old Grandmother had come to her in the dream, and she had embraced Medicine Wolf, had spoken to her. Surely the old woman had known in her heart that Medicine Wolf loved her and missed her and was always with her in thought and prayer.

"Ne-mehotatse, Ne-ske-eehe," she cried. "I will always love you, my grandmother."

Wolf howled again, and Medicine Wolf wondered if people ever died from grief. She put a hand to her aching heart, and she could not stop her tears.

Chapter Nine

The months passed in a monotonous schedule. Marilyn Prescott insisted on doing everything by the clock, an instrument which made no sense to Medicine Wolf. She knew how to read it, but she could not figure out why anyone would want to use one. All a person had to do was get up with the sun, then go about whatever needed doing; eat when he was hungry, not because the clock said it was time to eat; sleep when he was tired, not because the clock said it was time to go to sleep.

Most of the day was spent in lessons. Medicine Wolf learned more words, bigger words. She learned how to use verbs correctly, how to multiply, subtract, divide. She practiced writing, copying things from books. She read aloud. Lunch was always promptly at twelve o'clock, after which the afternoons were spent reading the Bible and listening to Andrew Prescott interpret what she had just read.

In Medicine Wolf's mind this white man's God was a

strange sort, for he was supposed to love everyone as His children, yet He did not seem very forgiving, at least not according to the reverend and Mrs. Prescott. So many things were wrong in this God's eyes that Medicine Wolf wondered if a person could ever please Him. He supposedly created the heavens and the earth, yet according to the Prescotts, the same God demanded of his followers to overcome and destroy the wilderness in order to build white man's homes and farms and "prosper."

Prosper and *progress* were two words both the Prescotts used often. They believed that it was man's responsibility to conquer the wilderness areas and "bring the light" to the ignorant, unsaved "savages" who lived in these new lands. Time and again Mrs. Prescott had tried to teach Medicine Wolf about owning land. Land was everything to the whites. It seemed to represent power. Medicine Wolf understood the theory of having rights to certain land, as her own people should have rights to the plains and mountains so that they could hunt and survive. But she did not understand "owning" little pieces of land. What good did it do to "own" little plots on which sat a hard-walled house? Could that little piece of land provide food and enough animals on which to survive? Of course not! Whoever lived there still had to go out onto other land and hunt, or to work at a white man's job in order to have the things he needed.

Even more confusing was the fact that the white man "needed" so many things, and he was willing to live a miserable life in order to have them. The way Mrs. Prescott explained it, the average white man in that strange land in the East believed in getting up "by the clock," going away from the home to work hard all day at farming or in things called factories or stores to make what was called money. They used the money to buy things, nor just food and clothing, but "things," unnecessary things like little figurines and pictures, heavy furniture and fancy buggies. Mrs. Prescott herself had a special cloth on her table that had to be removed every time they ate so that it did not get soiled. Meals were served on special dishes, a different dish for the main meal, the dessert, the bread, the soup; different utensils for meat, salad, soup, potatoes. Everything was served in different sizes of bowls.

It was amazing and to Medicine Wolf ridiculous. What was wrong with drinking soup from a bowl and eating meat with fingers and teeth? Her people did not need all these "things" just to eat! And why have a table at all, let alone the special cloth that Mrs. Prescott carefully draped over it after every meal? Why have pretty little figurines sitting around on shelves that were only for looking at but served no purpose? And why must everything be just so, creating even more work to keep them that way? A woman's work was hard enough without all these extra particulars.

Most confusing of all was trying to understand why on earth a man should work all day to have things he did not need or use, or to earn money to buy food, when Grandmother Earth provided everything he needed. Her people had no money, but they ate just fine; they had no pictures or fancy dishes or heavy furniture or oil-burning stoves for cooking. But they didn't need those things. Everything they owned or ate came from Grandmother Earth and from the animals. Why should a man own more than he could carry on a couple of horses? The white man seemed to have a way of making everything more complicated and difficult than it needed to be.

All these things passed through her mind as she prepared herself for another Sunday worship service inside the fort. Reverend Prescott preached to the soldiers every Sunday, another thing done according to "schedule." Medicine Wolf was always expected to be there. She could not understand how God could be worshipped by sitting on a hard bench inside closed walls, where the spirit of the land and the sky could not reach them. She hated the reverend's sermons, for they always made her feel like some kind of ignorant fool who was lucky God would even consider "saving" her. She was not at all sure what it meant to be saved. The only thing she needed saving from was these white people who worked so hard to destroy her special spirit.

She had already decided that the white man's God was probably the same as the Cheyenne God, but that the white man, in his inability to understand anything spiritual, and in his misguided ideas that man must "conquer and own," had surely misinterpreted the holy book and was using it strictly to his own advantage. Many things about the white man's story of creation resembled the Cheyenne version. The Cheyenne even believed that at one time there had been a great flood. The white man's Christ was born of a virgin, just like the Cheyenne prophet, Sweet Medicine. He told of the future, just like Sweet Medicine. Perhaps this Christ *was* Sweet Medicine, and he had visited the white people just like he visited the Cheyenne. If so, it was possible the white man simply did not correctly understand what this Christ taught them, because a white man's heart is not open to things that are of the spirit world.

She buttoned the top button of her dress, remembering how difficult it had been to learn to use buttons when Mrs. Prescott first made her put on these awful clothes. She looked at herself in a mirror, wondering what Bear Paw would think if he saw her in this white woman's dress. She turned sideways, studying her form. It had been a year and a half since the Cheyenne had left her here. Since then she had become a woman, and she was developing curves, the kind of curves that made a young man turn his head.

Would Bear Paw be pleased with what he saw? Tom had told her she was pretty, and in the mirror she saw a delicate face and wide-set dark eyes. Her lips were full, her complexion smooth. She decided Bear Paw would not like her hair this way, all wrapped up in a tight bun, but she wore it like that because Mrs. Prescott had said that for a woman to let her hair hang long and loose was another one of those "sins" that the white man's God would not allow.

She would be thirteen summers this year, in the Moon of the Thunderstorms, when wildflowers bloomed all over the prairie and the grass began to grow lush and green again. Thirteen summers! Only five more months, and Star Woman and Arrow Maker would come for her! She could go back to wearing her tunic and her wolfskin. She could live the free life again, without clocks and schedules and lessons. She could straddle a horse and sleep with Wolf on a buffalo skin that lay against Grandmother Earth.

She shivered at the ecstasy of the thought. She would be with her People again, out on the open plains, migrating with the seasons and the buffalo . . . and she would see Bear Paw. Had he waited as he had promised? He would be twenty-one summers now, fully a man.

She was suddenly more aware of him as a man and the womanly instincts he created in her. Perhaps this awareness came from having her time of month and developing breasts. The woman in her was telling her that someday she would need a man at her side, making her want babies. Being around Tom had made her think more about Bear Paw lately, for they were close in age.

Tom had remained a good friend. He had a job at the fort so that he could earn some of that money his people seemed to think was so important. His parents received money from some church far in the East. They had stayed on at Fort Laramie, building their little chapel and the cabin, now trying to "save" the Indians who were beginning to hang around the fort. They were mostly Shoshoni and Pawnee, and the soldiers called them "Laramie loafers." Medicine Wolf avoided them as much as possible, for they were enemy to the Cheyenne, and some now worked for the soldiers as scouts. Whenever she saw them near she refused to look directly at them.

Sometimes some Sioux and Cheyenne would show up at the fort, wanting to trade hides for tobacco. Those who did come, sometimes camping outside the fort, were not part of any of the Indians she knew well, and she knew also that her own People would not come, for they were of their word, and they had promised to stay away. Still, it would not have mattered if those who came *had* been Indians she knew, for whenever any Sioux or Cheyenne came near the fort, Medicine Wolf was locked in her room, the shutters on her window closed. She had gotten used to her near imprisonment, telling herself it would not be long now before she would be free of Marilyn Prescott and her strange ideas.

Tom knocked at her door then and ask if she was ready. She walked around to open the heavy pine door. Tom stood there in a three-piece wool suit, dressed in that uncomfortable way all white men insisted on dressing. She wondered if the white scouts and mountain men were the only ones with any sense when it came to dressing comfortably.

"Mother and Father have already left," he told her. His eyes moved over her in a way they never had before, a look in them that reminded her of the way Bear Paw sometimes looked at her. It surprised Medicine Wolf, for she had never thought about Tom as anything but her dear friend with whom she had had many long talks. He was secretly learning her language and customs, for he had said that someday he, too, would teach the Indians; but not in the condescending way his parents tried to teach them. He wanted to understand them, to work with them, not against them.

"You look prettier than ever today," he told her, smiling a handsome smile. He was filling out more now, and Medicine Wolf thought that for a white man he was handsome, although he could never be as handsome as Bear Paw, nor was he a man in the sense of proving himself as a warrior and a hunter. Still, that was simply not his way. Perhaps if it was, Tom would have been a good fighter and skilled hunter.

"Thank you," she told him, feeling oddly uncomfortable around him for the first time. It seemed strange to have Tom look at her the way a man looked at a woman he cared about. She was aware that many white hunters and trappers had come to this land and married Indian woman. Was Tom having such thoughts about her? It made her feel embarrassed but flattered, even though she could never have those thoughts for him. Her heart belonged to Bear Paw, and she could think of nothing now but the fact that soon she would be with her people again, near Bear Paw again. "I will get my shawl," she told him.

She started to turn, but Tom grasped her arm. "Medicine Wolf," he said, using her Indian name as he always did when his parents were not around, "I need to ask you—" He hesitated, swallowing. "Is there any chance that when your People come . . . any chance that you will decide to stay with us?"

Her eyes widened in surprise. "You know that all I live for is to go back to the Cheyenne," she told him.

His eyes looked watery. "I'll miss you. I miss you already, and you aren't even gone yet." He smiled as though somewhat embarrassed. "I just—I wanted you to know that."

She moved her arm and took hold of his hand. "I will miss you too. But I cannot stay here, Tom."

He squeezed her hand. "I hate to see you go, but one thing about it makes me happy. My mother was so sure she could change your heart and your beliefs. I have to tell you I'm glad she didn't. She's so sure you won't go, and I look forward to the day she has to watch you walk away. I want to see the look on her face."

Medicine Wolf smiled sadly. She also had no liking for Marilyn Prescott, but it was not the same for Tom. The woman was his mother. "You should not want your own mother to feel bad," she told him.

He shrugged. "Why not? She's made me feel bad most of my life. First there were the whippings when I was little, then the verbal reprimands, terrible scoldings with her eyes and her mouth about things I did that just come naturally to young boys. I've never been a 'good enough' Christian in her eyes, which means I've disappointed her as a son."

Medicine Wolf shook her head, watching him sympathetically. "If you were my son, I would be very proud. You have stood up to her many times, and you had the right. You are a good man. The things you are doing, learning my language and my ways, it is right. I can tell you that the only way to reach my People is to understand them. I think your mother and father are wrong about your God. I think He is the same as mine, and that He wants people like you to teach about Him, not people like your mother and father."

He squeezed her hand again. "Thank you, Medicine Wolf. In everything I do, I'll always remember you and think about what you would have to say about it." Before she realized his intentions, he leaned down and kissed her lightly on the lips. Medicine Wolf stared at him in near shock when he straightened.

"You told me to be my own man, and I'm doing it," he told her, his face reddening slightly. "I won't kiss you again, Medicine Wolf. I just wanted you to know I have a deep affection for you. If you decided to stay, I would wait for you, just like Bear Paw is waiting. My mother would probably have a heart attack and die if she knew how I felt, or if you stayed and I made you my wife one day. But if you would have me, I would never let her or my father stop me." He let go of her hand and turned away. "I'll be waiting outside to walk you over to the chapel."

Medicine Wolf watched after him, stunned. Tom had kissed her! A *white* man had kissed her, and he had said that if she wanted him, he would marry her when she was old enough! She had no idea he had been having such thoughts! What did he expect of her now? She wrapped he shawl around herself with shaking hands and went outside, unable to look at him as she began walking toward the chapel. Tom hurried up beside her.

"Don't be mad at me, Medicine Wolf."

"I am not angry. I am confused. I do not know what you want of me."

He sighed deeply. "I don't want anything from you, and I'm sorry if I offended you. I just—I know I had no right kissing you like that. I just wanted you to know how I feel, how much I think of you. I didn't mean that kiss like a man kissing a woman. I meant it, I don't know, just as a sign of affection. Please don't feel embarrassed. I know you're still just a kid, and I know how you feel about Bear Paw." He turned up his collar against a cold March wind. "I envy him, not just because someday you'll be his wife, but I envy the way he lives." They neared the chapel, and he took hold of her arm, turning her. "I'll worry about you after you go. I'll always wonder if you're all right. And I don't want you to leave with hard feelings. I want to continue our talks, continue to be friends."

She watched his eyes, seeing that he was sincere. "I am honored that you think so highly of me. Because of you I know that there is good in some white men, that some of them can respect the land and the Indian way. But you should not worry about me. The Wolf Spirit will be with me. I do not have bad feelings, Tom. You make me feel very special, and I do want to always be friends. I think I understand how you feel.''

He smiled. "You understand because you have an ability to understand things far beyond most girls your age. You seem older than you really are, Medicine Wolf."

She turned away. "Many times I *have* felt older. It is because of the Wolf Spirit. To receive a vision and be blessed by an animal spirit at such a young age makes someone change. It makes you feel different. You see things with the eyes of someone much older."

"Tom! Where have the two of you been!" Mrs. Prescott appeared at the doorway to the small chapel. "Your father is about to begin prayers. Hurry and come inside." The woman turned away, and Tom and Medicine Wolf looked at each other. He leaned close to her. "I meant what I said about wanting to see the look on my mother's face, even if it means having to say good-bye to you," he told her. His eyes looked sad and misty, but he smiled.

"*Saaa*, Tom," she answered chidingly. "Such a bad thought for one with such a good heart." She smiled, and he knew she was teasing him. He laughed lightly and followed her into the chapel.

Inside, Medicine Wolf felt the soldiers all staring at her as she sat down. She never felt comfortable at Sunday services. The rest of the week she could avoid the *ve-ho-e* soldiers by staying in the cabin or going for long walks outside the fort; but at these services the soldiers always gave her a strange feeling. Some looked at her with unexplained malice, others were indifferent toward her, as though she were nonexistent, as unimportant as a fly. Whenever very many Indians would come to the fort at one time, the soldiers always seemed tense, clinging to their rifles as though ready to use them. There were giant guns at the fort called cannon, and she supposed such a contraption could do much harm to a people armed with only bows and arrows and old rifles.

Reverend Prescott began his prayers, but Medicine Wolf did not hear him. She silently spoke her own prayer, a prayer to the Wolf Spirit and to Grandmother Earth that the time until her People came for her would pass quickly;

she prayed that both Indian and white would be able to keep to the treaty agreement, and that the bluecoat soldiers would never use those big guns against her people . . . against Bear Paw and Arrow Maker. It was one thing to make war against another Indian tribe; to make war against these whites who were so afraid, so ready to use their big guns, was another matter. The longer she was with the Prescotts, the more she could see how different were the two races, and how difficult it was going to be to keep to the treaty promises, difficult not for the Cheyenne, but for the *ve-ho-e*.

Two full moons! Two full moons and her people would come for her! Medicine Wolf could barely sleep. Finally, the long wait was nearly over. She was anxious now, for she was beginning to feel a danger. It was not that she thought anyone at the fort would hurt her directly. It was an abstract sort of danger, something in the wind, something in the eyes of the soldiers and the sneering Pawnee scouts.

Just today Tom had told her there had been more trouble, both in the South along the Santa Fe Trail, and here in the North along the Great Medicine Road that the whites called the Oregon-California Trail. Indians were being accused of riding beyond their treaty boundaries and sometimes harassing white travelers; white travelers were letting their fears get the better of them and were shooting at Indians without reason. Tom told her that various Indian agents, white men representing the Great Father who were appointed to keep the peace with the Indians, were being kept busy on all fronts. The problem was, many of them didn't really understand the Indians' problems, and already there was talk around the fort about the "damn Cheyenne and Sioux" not keeping their end of the bargain.

Medicine Wolf knew there was more to it than she was being told, that there was some reason her people were breaking the treaty, if indeed they really were. She was eager to be with them, hoped she could help them with what she knew now about the *ve-ho-e*.

Mostly she was afraid for Wolf. A calf from among the herd of cattle kept near the fort for meat for the soldiers had been found killed and half-eaten several mornings before. Some chickens had also been killed. Wolf had immediately been blamed, even though there were plenty of other wolves in the area, for they could be heard howling at night. All the time she had been at the fort, she had felt the resentment on the part of the soldiers that she should have a wolf for a pet, and that she could consider the animal sacred.

Tonight she could hear wolves howling again. Because of their closeness, and stories from emigrants about trouble with Indians, there was a tension among the soldiers that worried Medicine Wolf and made her feel unwelcome. Now that she had filled out more and looked older than she was, some of the soldiers looked at her with hungry eyes, the way the Crow man had looked at her mother all those years ago before he raped her. She stayed in or near the Prescott cabin most of the time, finding Marilyn Prescott's cold demeanor more bearable than the derisive looks she got from most of the soldiers. Whenever she did leave the cabin, it was usually only to go to chapel with the reverend, or to the supply store with Mrs. Prescott, or to take her walks with Tom to find Wolf. She always felt safest with Tom.

There came one long, lonely howl then. She knew in her heart that one was Wolf calling to her, reminding her he still waited faithfully. Did he know that it would not be long before they could be together again? Yes, he surely sensed it. She closed her eyes, smiling at the thought, she and Wolf walking out to greet Arrow Maker and Star Woman. Wolf howled again, and then came a sound that almost made her heart stop beating. A gunshot suddenly pierced the crisp night air.

Medicine Wolf waited, barely breathing. Wolf did not howl again. ''No,'' she whispered. She sat up, reaching for her robe and pulling it on. She tied it, then slipped her feet into her old moccasins, which she still sometimes wore around the cabin in the evenings. They were much easier to get on quickly than the ugly, uncomfortable high-button shoes Mrs. Prescott made her wear during the day.

A horrible fear engulfed her, choked her. Wolf! Something was terribly wrong! She opened her door and went into the main room of the cabin, where she saw Tom hurriedly buttoning the pants he had just slipped on. He looked at her, and by the light of a dimly lit oil lamp she saw it in his eyes. "You heard it too?" she asked.

He nodded. "Let me go, Medicine Wolf." He pulled his suspenders over his shoulders, then began putting on a shirt he had brought from his bedroom.

Medicine Wolf shook her head. "I have to see for myself. Some wolves look alike. I will know if—if it is my Wolf."

Another door opened, and a robed Reverend Prescott stepped into the main room. "What is going on? What are you two doing up?"

Medicine Wolf hurriedly ran out the door, afraid the big man would catch hold of her and try to stop her. She was not going to wait for Tom to explain. She heard Tom call for her to wait, but she kept running. Wolf might need her!

Medicine Wolf picked up her gown and robe so that they would not get in her way as she tried to run fast as a deer. Someone else called out to her. "Halt! Who goes there?" She did not stop to answer. The sprawling fort was not surrounded by gates, so she had no barriers to stop her. She darted into shadows to help hide herself, in case someone might be chasing her, then finally emerged from fort grounds and ran out onto the open prairie.

The land was well lit by a full moon. She ran so hard that her heart pounded wildly and her lungs hurt her. In spite of the cool night air, she began to perspire. Wolf! She still had not heard another sound from him. Her chest hurt so bad that she felt as though the gunshot she heard had hit her square in the heart. In spite of the darkness she knew where to go. She had taken this path every day in the nearly two years that she had been there so that she could be with Wolf. The only thing that had stopped her had been that time of her first flowing, and a couple of blizzards that made it too dangerous. But always Wolf had been there when she was finally able to come to him.

Always he had been there . . . always. Since she was

six years old he had been at her side, loving her, sleeping with her, protecting her, guiding her. He was a part of her. To lose him would be to cut away a piece of her heart. By the time she reached the place where he usually waited for her, her breathing came in great gasps. She stopped to catch her breath, her dark eyes studying the moonlit landscape intensely.

Finally she saw it, a light-colored form against the darker prairie grass. She stood frozen for a moment. "Wolf," she called. The form did not move. She finally made her legs move to carry her closer. She gasped. There lay a white wolf, and in the moonlight she could see dark stain on his fur, near his shoulder. It was exactly where Cheyenne hunters aimed for an animal when they wanted to hit the heart so that it would die instantly.

She fell to her knees, bending over to touch him. "Wolf," she groaned. She knew in that touch that he had no life in him. She gathered him into her arms, sitting down and holding him close, caring little that she got his blood on her robe. He had died alone, calling for her. She was convinced one of the soldiers on night guard had done this, but she was equally sure that none of them would admit to being the culprit. White men had a way of blaming others for their wrongdoing. There was no reason to shoot Wolf way out here. There were no cattle in the area. It was obvious he was doing no harm. He had just been howling at the big moon, calling to his owner because he was lonely.

She buried her face in his fur and wept, hardly aware of the clatter of the wagon that approached, paying no attention to the carryings-on of Marilyn Prescott, who, surprisingly, was furious over the killing. Her anger was not out of concern for Wolf or even Medicine Wolf's feelings, but because she feared the incident would ruin all her efforts at winning over Medicine Wolf. "She'll blame us," the woman lamented. "This will set us back almost to where we started! Andrew, I want you to find out who did this! He should be reprimanded!"

"They'll just say he had cause," the reverend said sadly. "It's a fact that wolves have been making trouble around here lately. Who is to say this wolf wasn't one of the culprits."

"Well, she can't stay out here. Make her come home. Tomorrow we can come out and bury the thing."

The reverend approached Medicine Wolf, but she jerked away when he touched her arm. "No," she said, a vicious tone to her voice. "Tonight I stay here with Wolf! Tonight he will sleep with me, as you should have let him do from the beginning!"

"You can't stay out here, child," the reverend tried to explain.

Medicine Wolf carefully laid Wolf aside, then rose, facing them. "I am not going back. If you make me go back, I will *kill* myself! I will stay with Wolf, and in the morning Tom will bring me a shovel, and I will bury him and say my own prayers over him!" She turned her eyes to Tom. "Do not let them take me back!"

Tom sighed, going to the wagon and taking out two blankets he had thrown in without his parents' knowledge. "She stays," he told them, "and I'm staying with her."

"What!" His mother gasped in indignation. "I'll not have either one of you—"

"You have no choice in the matter, Mother. I'm staying. That wolf was like a part of her." Tom moved his eyes to his father. "Don't try to stop me. I don't want to have to fight my own father."

Prescott sighed. "I think it's time to send you east to school, son. I can see that this girl has had a bad influence on you."

"A *bad* influence? I have learned more from her in these two short years than in all my life before that. Please leave now. Let her be alone with Wolf."

The reverend took his wife's arm. "Let's go, Marilyn."

The woman glared at her son. "May God forgive you for your disobedience, and for accepting this child's pagan beliefs!" She turned and climbed up into the wagon with the reverend, and the two of them drove off. Tom turned, the blankets still in his hands. Medicine Wolf had sat back down again and was holding Wolf. Tom draped one of the blankets around her shoulders.

"I'm so sorry, Medicine Wolf. I don't know what else to say."

"It was not your doing." She dug her fingers into Wolf's thick fur, her grief so deep that for the moment she could not even cry. It did not seem real that she could be sitting holding a dead Wolf. "I should have been with him," she told Tom, her voice stony and cold. Tom sat down across from her and wrapped a blanket around himself. She met his eyes. "Never again will I leave those that I love. When my People come for me, I will never leave them again. This happened because we were apart, and because I did not carry the wolf paws close to me. Dig them up for me, Tom. I must have them when I offer my prayers to the spirits to protect Wolf for me so that when I walk *Ekutsihimmiyo* to the Great Beyond, he will be waiting for me with Old Grandmother."

Tom nodded, unable to answer verbally for fear of breaking down. He had grown to love Wolf nearly as much as Medicine Wolf had. Someone would pay for this. He had never felt animosity and a need to use his fists before. For the first time he hated, truly hated. He left to dig up her medicine bag.

Medicine Wolf lay down in the soft prairie grass, holding Wolf close and pulling the blanket over them. Tonight they would sleep together. He would not be alone.

Chapter Ten

Tom finished digging the hole. The morning had turned warm, and he wiped sweat from his forehead with the sleeve of his shirt. He stabbed the shovel into the ground and looked at Medicine Wolf, who still lay holding Wolf close to her. "It's ready," he told her.

Medicine Wolf sat up, and Tom almost gasped at the haunted look in her eyes. She didn't seem like Medicine Wolf at all, but rather a sort of abstract figure, an apparition possessed by something nonhuman. "I need a knife," she told him, her voice flat and hard.

"A knife? For what?"

"Wolf wants me to have his fur. He told me so as I slept. I am to keep even the head."

Tom frowned. "Do you know how hard it is to skin an animal that well?"

"I can do it. I have seen it done many times. Bear Paw skinned the other wolf for me, the one that saved me from the grizzly." She looked down at Wolf. "I need the knife."

Tom sighed deeply. "All right. I'll go and get one."

He left to get the knife, returning to find Medicine Wolf chanting over Wolf in her Cheyenne tongue. He recognized the song as the one she had taught him, her prayer song.

> Oh, Grandmother Earth, hear me!
> Oh, Grandfather Wolf, hear me!
> Oh, Great Maheo, hear me!
> I sing my thanks to you!
> Forever the wolf shall be sacred to me.
> Forever the earth shall be sacred to me.
> Forever I will please Maheo.

She continued with words about being one in spirit with the white wolf, thanking it for offering its sacred coat of fur, singing something about always being together. Tom watched, mesmerized. He knew he was seeing something close to the heart of the Cheyenne, something sacred. A chill moved through him at the realization that Medicine Wolf truly did seem to have a mystical aura about her. Did she truly share the wolf spirit? Was such a thing possible? He had never thought of animals as being sacred and having spirits, until he met Medicine Wolf.

With a strange, sad feeling he realized that even if he waited for her to mature, and she was willing to marry him, it could never work. He had never been more aware of how different their worlds were. He could understand her world, but he could never be a part of it, no more than she could spend the rest of her life being part of his. She was not just Cheyenne; she was a part of the spirit world. She would become a woman of strength and power.

Black clouds began to billow toward them from the western horizon, moving down off the mountains and churning across the prairie. Medicine Wolf stopped singing and turned to him, reaching out for the knife. After she took it, she held up her arms and said another prayer. Tom expected her to begin cutting into the wolf, but to his shock she suddenly slashed open her left arm. He shivered, a chill moving up his spine. He wondered if he could believe his eyes. A great clap of thunder seemed only to accent the mystical moment, as Medicine Wolf hung her head and let the blood from her arm drip onto Wolf.

Tom watched in wonder. She had told him once that her People sometimes made a blood sacrifice to express their sorrow when a loved one died. Her tears came then, in great, moaning torrents. Tom stood speechless, amazed by what he had seen. Thunder shook heaven and earth, and the dark clouds moved closer. Medicine Wolf seemed unconcerned that a storm was coming, and he wondered if she was even aware of it. She seemed lost in a world of her own. He slowly approached her, kneeling down near her and touching her shoulder lightly. "Storm's coming," he told her.

She sat up straighter, looking up to the heavens. "It is only *Maheo* showing his anger at what has happened to Wolf." Her voice seemed deeper, more womanly. She turned Wolf over, preparing to cut open the skin over his belly, when Tom grasped her wrist.

"I loved him too," he told her. Medicine Wolf watched in surprise as he rolled up a sleeve. He held out his arm, imagining the look on his mother's face if she saw him doing such a thing. "I hurt too, Medicine Wolf. I want to make a blood sacrifice in mourning."

She looked at him, her eyes red and swollen, her face stained with tears. A few raindrops began to fall. "You are sure?" she asked.

Tom nodded. The rain began to fall harder as Medicine Wolf grasped his wrist and quickly cut a long gash on his left arm. He made no sound. He leaned over and let some of the blood drip onto Wolf, and Medicine Wolf saw tears in his eyes. She took his arm again and pressed her own wound to his.

"Now our blood is mixed," she told him. "You are my brother, Tom Prescott. Forever you will be able to walk among my people and fear no harm. The blood of the Cheyenne runs in your veins."

She took her arm away, and Tom could not find his voice for the lump in his throat. Medicine Wolf opened her robe and tore off the bottom ruffle of the flannel gown she still wore from the night before. With the knife she cut it in half, using one half then to wrap around Tom's cut. She tied it off. "Now when you roll down your shirt-sleeve, your mother will not know what you did," she told him. "It is our secret." She picked up the other half and handed it to him, then held out her own bleeding arm.

With shaking hands Tom wrapped it and tied it off. "Thank you," he told her, finally able to speak. He cleared his throat and sniffed. "Thanks for letting me be a part of this. I feel honored."

She lowered her eyes. The rain began to pour even harder as she pulled the sleeve of her robe over the bandaged arm. She began cutting into Wolf.

"Shouldn't we wait until the rain is over," Tom asked.

"This cannot wait. The body will quickly turn bad in this warm weather."

Tom winced at the sight, but she worked quickly and expediently. He began helping her, pulling at the skin while she worked the knife under it to gently peel it away. "Once it is all off, I will scrape it clean," she told him, "then wash it and stake it out to dry and bleach in the sun. It will be beautiful. I will wear it, with Wolf's head draped over my shoulder so that he is always close to me. He will always be with me in spirit. He will protect me."

Rain soaked them, but she kept working until the skin was finally clear of the rest of the animal. She cut under the tail in such a way that it was left intact. She saved the jaw and teeth, cleaned the brains from the skull. She smiled then, gently caressing the fur. "It is so beautiful." She carefully laid it aside, her hair dripping now from the rain, the wolf's fur soaked too.

"Everything else must be buried so that no other animals can get to it," she said. She seemed to think nothing of picking up the raw muscle and bones with her bare hands. She dropped what was left into the hole he had dug, then came back to carefully scoop the brains into her hands and put them also into the hole. It rained even harder, and she held out her hands, letting the rain wash blood and flesh from them into the burial hole. Tom did the same, his own hands bloody from helping with the skinning. They each rubbed their hands together, and Tom wiped at the blood that was on his pants. He grasped the shovel then and began filling in the hole.

"I would rather put him up high on a scaffold," she told him. "But this is not a sacred burial ground, and I am afraid the soldiers would knock it down and let the other animals devour what is left." She held out the front of her robe and gown to let the rain wash away some of the blood.

Tom began to realize how much a part of life blood and pain were to the Indian. There could be no sacrifice without pain. It struck him how the pain a warrior suffered during the Sun Dance, offering flesh and blood to the spirits in order that the People would be blessed, resembled Christ's sacrifice on the cross. Before Christ, the Jews used to sacrifice young animals. Was their religion really so different? Were the Cheyenne just as close, if not closer, to God than people like himself who called themselves Christian and studied the Bible daily? There was something deeply spiritual about the Indian, something he supposed was almost inborn, as though their blood were part human and part animal. He wished someone could help him understand all of this better, decide whether or not the way Medicine Wolf's People lived was really wrong. His father certainly could not help him, and his mother would think he had lost his mind. All he could do was keep praying in his own feeble way for God to help him understand these things.

Thunder rumbled to the east as the storm began to move away from them across the open prairie land. Tom packed down the dirt over the grave, then turned to Medicine Wolf. "We really should go back now, or we'll both have pneumonia. You don't want to get sick and die now, do you, when the time for your People to come is so close?"

She leaned down and touched the grave, then walked over to pick up the wolfskin. She looked over at him. "Thank you for understanding."

He smiled sadly. "Thank *you*, for making me your brother." He thought how he might have wanted to be more than that someday, but he also knew such a thing was impossible. He clutched the knife in one hand and stooped to pick up the shovel. "And thank you for letting me be a part of this. I'm sorry, Medicine Wolf, for all you've suffered since you've been here."

She blinked as rain hit her eyes. "It had to be. It was part of my destiny, part of my vision. Now I have seen the good in your people, through you." She looked at Wolf's grave. "And I have seen the evil." She clutched the wolfskin and turned away, heading back to the fort, her robe hanging limp from the rain, the front of it filthy with dirt and blood. One last clap of thunder made the ground seem to shake, and Tom wondered if it really was *Maheo* expressing his anger. The rain continued to fall, tapering off to a steady, quiet flow, mixing in the earth with Medicine Wolf's tears.

This was a new dream, a new warning. Medicine Wolf could see it coming, a black monster belching smoke. It came from the East, making a terrible roaring sound, then a long, wailing sound, similar to a wolf's howl but much louder. It seemed to be announcing that it was coming, screaming to the animals in its path that they had better move out of the way. Buffalo scattered, people ran. As it came closer, there seemed to be a fire in its belly. There came the mournful scream again. Black smoke poured from the top of its head. It thundered closer, as though it meant to gobble her up.

Medicine Wolf jumped out of the way at the last minute, and in doing so she awoke with a start. She gasped, sitting up in bed, her body drenched in perspiration. It was then she realized Marilyn Prescott was in the room, holding a dimly lit lantern. She was standing near the chair where Medicine Wolf had draped the wolfskin so that it would begin to dry out. Earlier she had spent hours on her knees on the front porch of the cabin scraping away more flesh from the underside of the skin. Because it continued to rain, she had brought the skin inside to begin drying more quickly.

Mrs. Prescott turned and looked at Medicine Wolf with a start, looking strangely guilty.

"What do you want?" Medicine Wolf asked her.

For the first time since Medicine Wolf had known the woman, Mrs. Prescott actually looked afraid of her. "You can't keep this thing in your room, Martha. It smells. It's unsanitary." She reached for it again.

"Do not touch it!" The words came out of Medicine Wolf's mouth with a deep and vicious tone. Mrs. Prescott hesitated. "It is only until the rain stops," Medicine Wolf told the woman. "Then I will wash it and stake it outside to dry in the sun."

Mrs. Prescott sighed. "I see no reason why you can't leave it outside now, Martha."

Fresh grief caused Medicine Wolf to be unconcerned about what was right and wrong, made her forget being obedient. She threw back her covers and got out of bed. "I do not want you touching it, *ever*! It is too *sacred* for the likes of you! And I will not put it outside where animals might come and tear it up!"

Mrs. Prescott drew in her breath, looking both shocked and hurt. "I just don't think it's healthy for you, Martha."

"Do not call me Martha! I am *Medicine Wolf*! I am not white, and I do not want a white woman's name! And do not worry about what is healthy for me. My People have been cleaning skins since the beginning of time. When I am through, that skin will be soft and bleached and as clean as any of your cloth." She approached the woman with a threatening look in her eyes, and Mrs. Prescott actually backed away. "You were going to sneak in here and take it without my knowledge. You have no right!"

"I simply thought it might be for your own good."

"You know *nothing* about what is good for me. You cannot begin to understand. You do not even *try*."

Mrs. Prescott's eyes moved to the medicine bag Medicine Wolf wore around her neck. She had hidden it under a loose floorboard in her room when she first got back, then had taken it out and hung it around her neck when she went to bed so that it would be close to her as she slept. Mrs. Prescott's eyes widened. "Where did you get that!"

Medicine Wolf's hand moved to touch the precious bag. She did not want Tom to get into trouble. "I told you it was magic. I looked into the stove later, after you threw it in to burn. It did not burn as you thought it would.''

The woman let out a little gasp. ''That's impossible! It's Tom, isn't it? My own son saved that heathen thing for you!''

Medicine Wolf shook her head. ''No,'' she answered, telling a lie for the first time in her life. ''It simply did not burn. It has great power. You just refuse to believe it is true. It is as I said. I looked in the stove, and it was burned only a little.'' She moved her hand to show the woman the scorch marks.

Mrs. Prescott's eyes narrowed. ''Give it to me,'' she said coldly. ''Give it to me, and I'll throw it in my cooking fire in the morning! We'll just see how much power it holds!''

''No! You will never touch my medicine bag again!''

''We'll see about that!'' The woman whirled and left, and Medicine Wolf quickly removed the medicine bag and put it in its new hiding place. She ran over to her parfleche and took out her own knife that she had kept with her when first she was left at the fort. She gripped the knife, moving closer to the chair where Wolf's fur was draped. She knew Mrs. Prescott would return with her husband, and moments later both of them came storming into her room. Mrs. Prescott's eyes widened when she saw that the medicine bag was gone.

''What did you do with it?''

''I will not tell you. Search my things if you wish, but you will not find it!'' Tom walked in behind his parents, his eyes widening at the wild, vicious look on Medicine Wolf's face. Her hair hung long and loose, and her eyes, although not yellow like Wolf's, looked as cunning and threatening. She held out the knife in a threatening pose. ''If you do find it and try to take it, or to take my wolfskin, I will *kill* you,'' she seethed.

''Dear God,'' Mrs. Prescott gasped.

''Medicine Wolf,'' the reverend said sadly. ''Have you learned nothing in all the time you have been with us?''

''I have learned much,'' she sneered. ''I have learned your writing and your numbers, but they are of no use to me. I have learned how you live by meaningless schedules, how you wear clothes that do not let the skin breathe. I have learned about a God who loves and forgives, but that those who worship this God know *nothing* of love and forgiveness! I have learned how your God made the universe and all that is in it, yet He allows his worshippers to destroy it all! I have learned that your people have no respect for Grandmother Earth and the animals, no respect for the way others might choose to live! I have learned that my People are fools to think that the *ve-ho-e* will ever keep the promises they give us in the treaties! What the white man has gained will not be enough, will it? He will want more, and more and more, and he will not be happy until my People are either all dead, or until those left live according to your ways, warriors turned to *farmers*, Indian women wearing stiff dresses and living in hard houses surrounded by useless things, our People sitting in your churches worshipping a God who surely cannot even hear them because they are closed away from the earth and the sky and the animals! There is nothing more you can teach me!"

Mrs. Prescott shook her head, actually looking ready to cry. "After all of this, we have failed to take the savageness out of her," she lamented.

"It's inborn," the reverend answered, the two of them talking as though she were not there.

"She isn't savage at all." Tom spoke up, surprising them. "Sometimes I think *we're* the savages! Right now she's only protecting what is dear to her. How would the two of you feel if it were the other way around? What if the Indians overcame us and tried to force you to change your customs and faith? What if they insisted you deny Christ and the cross? You'd react the same way Medicine Wolf is reacting! For God's sake, put yourselves in her shoes for once!"

"You!" Mrs. Prescott glared at her son. "You've let her influence you, haven't you? You were supposed to be helping us teach her the right way to go. Instead, *she* has been teaching you *her* ways! I never should have let you have any part in this! I should have sent you back east to finish Seminary! I thought this experience would be good for you!"

"It *has* been good for me, Mother! I've learned what I need to know in order to be able to come back here someday and help these people the *right* way! You can't do it by condemning what is personal and sacred to them, by trying to erase in a few months what has been in their blood and hearts for centuries! It doesn't work that way, Mother!"

The woman sucked in her breath, her thin lips pressed tight for a moment, her blue eyes blazing. Wisps of her graying hair had fallen out of her bun in sleep and hung about her face. "You're *weak*, Tom," she almost sneered. "You had better pray to God to give you more strength and wisdom!"

Medicine Wolf saw Tom flinch at the words. She knew that deep inside it had always hurt him that his mother never quite approved of anything he did. He shook his head. "I'm not weak, Mother. I'm a lot stronger than you think. I'm strong enough to do what I know in my heart is right. I'll go back and finish Seminary when I'm good and ready. And I'll come back out here and teach the Indians *my* way! And *you're* the one who had better pray for more wisdom. Read the Bible again, Mother! Think about what Christ's teachings *really* mean!"

As usual in these situations, the reverend seemed disinclined to come between mother and son. Medicine Wolf suspected he sometimes sided with Tom, but that he was actually afraid of his wife's wrath if he spoke in his son's defense. "We're all tired," he put in. "You're all saying things you don't really mean."

"For God's sake, Father, why don't you ever say what *you* really mean?" Tom turned and stormed out of the room.

The reverend looked at Medicine Wolf. "Put the knife away, child. No one is going to take your medicine bag or your wolfskin." He sighed deeply, touching his wife's arm. "We have obviously failed miserably. We should have taken a younger child like Fitzpatrick warned us. I'm beginning to think some of the things he told us about Martha were true. There is something about her we can't touch. Soon her People will come for her. You did your best, Marilyn."

The woman actually shivered with anger and disappointment. She glared at Medicine Wolf, her eyes tearing. "No matter what you think of me," she said, "all these months I have truly had your best interest in mind. I thought I was doing what was right."

Medicine Wolf lowered the knife, seeing for the first time in nearly two years a hint of sincere emotion in the woman's eyes.

"If your people will not listen to us and learn our ways, Martha," the woman warned, still using her white name, "they will someday be destroyed. Things are going to change, and there won't be anything they can do about it! They will either have to change, or die! It's that simple!" The woman turned and walked out, and after a long look of derision, the reverend also left the room.

Medicine Wolf stared after them, blinking back tears. She was sorry she had spoken such ugly words and had threatened them with the knife, but she was so full of sorrow for Wolf that she knew she would have used the knife if Mrs. Prescott had come one step closer. She felt suddenly weak and spent, and she laid the knife on the seat of the chair near which she stood. She walked to her window, unlatching it and pushing open both sides.

She breathed deeply of the cool night air. The sky was a mass of stars, and she realized the rain had finally ended sometime during the night. The prairie smelled fresh and clean.

Her heart ached fiercely. Was Mrs. Prescott right? Would her People die if they did not learn the white man's way? Why was the white man so concerned about how her People lived? What difference did it make to them? This was such a big land. There was plenty of room for all.

She left the window and lay back down in bed, remembering again the dream about the black monster that belched smoke. What had it meant? Was it something from the white man's world? Was it one of the things that would cause her People to die? She decided that since she could not tell Black Buffalo about the dream, she would tell Tom. He was a blood brother now, and he knew about things from the white man's world in the East. Maybe he would know what the black monster was. Then she could tell her People about it.

She wondered if Mrs. Prescott would bother giving her any more lessons. What was the point now? All she cared about was the fact that her People would come for her in only two more moons. The only sad part about it was she would have to say good-bye to Tom, maybe forever.

Medicine Wolf approached the tent, calling out for Tom. She had not had a chance to talk to him that morning as she had planned, for as soon as he got up he had packed his things and moved out of the cabin, telling his parents he could no longer abide living with them. He would set up the tent and live in it, staying around only until Medicine Wolf was gone. Then he was going back east, perhaps to school, perhaps to work. He was not sure.

"Come on in," Tom answered her.

Medicine Wolf hesitantly ducked inside. She wore her tunic and moccasins now, her hair brushed out long and loose. To Tom she looked more like sixteen than thirteen, and he could imagine how exquisitely beautiful she was going to be when she really was sixteen, for already her beauty was striking and rare.

"Welcome to my new home," he told her with a grin, noticing she wore her medicine bag around her neck. "You should like it. It's a lot closer to the way you like to live than the cabin." He patted his hand on the blanket beside him. "Have a seat. I was just doing some reading. Shakespeare. Did Mother teach you anything about old Bill?"

Medicine Wolf frowned. "Bill?"

"Shakespeare. William Shakespeare."

She smiled then. "We studied his writing a little. His words are very confusing to me."

"Well, join the crowd." He set the book aside, concern showing in his eyes. "They treating you all right? I see you're wearing your tunic. What did Mother have to say about that?"

Medicine Wolf shrugged. "Nothing. She has not spoken to me since last night. I think she has decided I will do what I will do, and she cannot stop me. She did not even scold me about the cut on my arm. She put a fresh bandage on it and just gave me that chiding look of hers.''

"Ah, yes, I know it well. Took her long enough to give up, didn't it?"

She studied his eyes, the sadness behind them. "I am sorry, Tom. It is my fault you had to move out. I think your mother feels bad about it."

He sobered, his blue eyes looking colder. "My mother hasn't had any kind of feelings for years. And don't think for a minute that any of it is your fault. It's no one's fault but her own. My father didn't help the matter any. Is *he* speaking to you?"

She looked down. "He told me this morning that I am still welcome to come to church services, that I can still be saved if I want it. He said he feels sorry that I am still what he calls a heathen." She raised her eyes again. "Do you think I am bad, Tom?"

He let out a little gasp of disgust. "Of course you aren't bad. They just don't understand, and they don't *want* to understand."

"I should not have pulled the knife, but I was afraid."

"Fear makes a lot of people do strange things." He drew up his knees and wrapped his arms around them. "Trouble is, something like that could happen on a larger scale. My people might try to force your people into living the way they want, try to force them to give up their beliefs, push them onto less land. If that happens, your people are going to react just like you did last night. They're going to fight back, with knives and guns. It's already happened a few times."

Medicine Wolf felt an ache in her throat. "Will they die, like your mother said?"

Tom looked at her with pity. "All I can tell you is that the same thing happened to a lot of Indians back east, and now many of the eastern tribes don't exist anymore. The rest live on a few little reservations, some of them clear up in Canada. Most of them were herded out here to land set aside for them. A lot of them died."

She traced her finger over a design on the blanket. "But that cannot happen here. It is such a big country, and there are not so many *ve-ho-e* here."

"I hate to tell you, Medicine Wolf," Tom answered with a sigh, "but more will come. Someday they won't just pass through your land. They'll find some reason to want to settle it."

She faced him, holding her chin proudly. "Then we will fight them! They will quickly learn that it is not healthy to try to take our land and the game we need for food! They will not stay long!"

Tom watched her, unable to keep from smiling at her pride and innocence. He could just imagine her warrior father and the one called Bear Paw riding down on some wagon train or some farmhouse, determined to keep the *ve-ho-e* away. He had no doubt they would be successful at first.

How could he make her understand? Maybe it was best not to try. Why should she live her life full of fear and dread for her own future? And maybe she was right. Maybe the land *was* big enough for all of them. *And maybe you're a damn fool,* he told himself.

"Well, I hope you're right, Medicine Wolf. God knows you have a right to this land. But I'm afraid most of my people don't think like I do. All I can say is I'll do my best to *make* them understand." He leaned back, resting on one elbow, his tall, now-muscular figure stretched out on the blanket. "In fact, I've been thinking. I'm going back east to finish some schooling as soon as you're gone. But I'm coming back, and when I do, it won't be as a preacher, like my parents always had planned for me. It will be as a teacher, and I also intend to do some reporting, send some articles back east for their newspapers, telling people about Indians, helping them understand your ways. What do you think of that? Mother explained to you about newspapers, didn't she? You've read some of those we have shipped out here."

She nodded. "I have seen them. They tell stories about your people. My people talk to each other through the drums, and tell stories over campfires. I think it would be good for you to do this. You will tell the truth. Many do not."

"Well, it's one small way of maybe avoiding more trouble."

Medicine Wolf also leaned back to rest on an elbow. She faced Tom, her eyes showing deep concern. "I had a dream, Tom. You say you think more whites will come west. I am wondering if you can tell me the meaning of the dream. A great, black monster was coming toward me, screaming and wailing a lonely call like many wolves howling at once. Fire burned in its belly, and black smoke came from its top. It moved very fast, and it made so much noise that it frightened away the animals. What do you think it was?"

Tom watched her, astounded. This girl could not possibly have ever seen a train or a steam locomotive, yet she had just described one. "My God," he muttered after a moment of silence. "You truly *are* prophetic! You really *are* blessed with spiritual powers, Medicine Wolf!" He sat up, and Medicine Wolf watched him curiously. Why was he so surprised? She had told him all along that dreams were important. Seeing the future was commonplace to many of her people. It frightened her a little to see the look on Tom's face, for surely the dream did mean something bad.

"Is the black monster going to come here and eat us?" she asked.

He leaned closer. "My mother must have shown you pictures of—" He hesitated. "No. We don't have any pictures of trains. She at least must have told you about them. That would explain the dream." He ran a hand through his hair. "Still, to dream about it that way, thundering across the plains, frightening the animals . . . it's truly prophetic."

Medicine Wolf sat up straighter. "Trains? I think your mother did speak of one once, but I have never seen a picture."

"Trains are what they use back east to haul freight and passengers. They're being used more and more all the time, and they've been creeping farther west out of Chicago. What you described sounds like a train. The engines that pull the cars are big and black. They burn wood to make the steam that makes the wheels turn. The smoke from the fire comes out of a stack at the top of the train, and a train whistle *does* kind of sound like a lot of wolves howling at once. They move on tracks, iron rails that are laid down for them."

Medicine Wolf thought for a moment. "Does my dream mean these trains will come to our land?"

Tom shook his head. "I can't imagine they would ever come this far west, but then, my people have a way of doing a lot of things in the name of progress. I suppose it's possible."

Medicine Wolf frowned. "I would not want these monsters to come here and frighten away the animals. And if they are so loud, they will take away the peace of our land. We will not hear the birds. I do not understand why your people think these things are so important, why they make things like these trains."

Tom thought how lovely and innocent she was, sitting there in a simple tunic, worried about animals and birds. "Well, maybe you shouldn't bother trying to understand," he told her. "Maybe you should just go back to your people and live the way you want to live and hope the trains and more of the *ve-ho-e* never come out here."

She turned away. "But they *will* come, won't they?"

"I'm afraid they will." Tom reached out and touched her hair. "God, I'm going to miss you, Medicine Wolf. I'll always remember you and think about you, until I'm a very old man."

His touch gave her a strange feeling, made her realize that if she were white like him, she could have fond thoughts for him like she had for Bear Paw. They had shared some special moments together.

"And I will think of you," she answered, meeting his eyes again, "until I am a very old woman. Do you think I will live to be old, Tom?"

He smiled. "Sure you will." He looked toward the entrance to the tent. "You'd better not stay too long. If anybody saw you come in here, they might get the wrong idea."

"The wrong idea?" She thought for a moment, then blushed and jumped up. "I will go!"

Tom laughed. "I didn't mean you had to flee like a sacred rabbit." He also rose, coming to stand close to her, towering over her with his father's height. He touched her shoulders. "I'm your brother, remember? Don't ever be afraid to come and see me, especially now, when there is so little time left. I just know how some of those soldiers out there think about Indian women. I don't ever want anyone thinking anything bad about you. From now on we'll meet and talk in the open." He held out his left arm and pushed up the sleeve. "Brother and sister. Right?"

She touched the bandages. "You never told your mother?"

"You said it should be our secret."

She smiled. "I am glad."

She could see by his eyes that he was not thinking of her like a sister. She realized it was best that she would be going back to her People soon, for even if she could love him as a husband, she could never truly share his world, and he could never live in hers. And there was Bear Paw. Always there was Bear Paw. Her heart rushed at the thought of it. She had left a child and would return a woman.

She turned away and exited the tent, heading away from the fort toward the hill where Wolf was buried. She wanted to check the grave, and she needed to think about the things Tom had told her about whites coming, and about trains. Was her dream prophetic, as Tom had said? The thought frightened her. Her mind swirled with all the things she had to think about now, and with the strange emotions she felt for Tom. It was not the same feeling she had for Bear Paw. Tom did not make her heart pound and her knees feel weak. She supposed she loved him in a special way, more than like a brother yet less than she would love a man who would be her husband. Perhaps he only represented things that might have been.

She did not notice a rider coming toward the fort from the south, a nearly-naked Indian riding a painted pony. She knelt beside Wolf's grave to pray, to ask *Maheo* to help her use what she had learned, to talk to Wolf, whose skin was pegged out behind the cabin to dry in the sun. For several minutes she meditated, relishing the comfort of wearing her own tunic again, her feet enjoying the soft moccasins. She was not aware that Tom was running toward her until he had nearly reached her. She turned then to see a look of excitement on his face.

"I came to tell you," he said, panting slightly from running. "One of your runners just came into the fort to tell the commander that your People are coming for you sooner than you think! They are hunting along the Republican. They will be here in less than a month!"

Joy filled Medicine Wolf's heart. She jumped up and hugged Tom without realizing what she was doing, and having no conception of how it felt to him to hold her. "I must go and talk to him," she said then. "Maybe it is someone I know! Oh, how I long to see someone from my own village! I must ask him about my parents!"

She ran off before Tom could say another word. He watched her sadly. "Good-bye, Medicine Wolf," he muttered. *"Ne-mehotatse."*

Chapter Eleven

Medicine Wolf waited, wearing her best tunic, the one bleached white and beautifully beaded by Old Grandmother. She had not worn it since the blanket dance during the treaty-signing, when she wore it for Bear Paw. She was well aware that she filled it out much better now. In fact, it would soon be too small for her. She was not the same child who had sat under the blanket with Bear Paw. She was more a woman physically; but she was proud that she had also grown mentally and emotionally. She had learned much about being strong and independent.

Another messenger had come just last night to tell her that her People would arrive early this morning. Her heart was filled with joy at discovering they were on their way north to join the Sioux for the summer Sun Dance. Not only would she be with her family again, but she would enjoy the summer celebrations.

She gave no thought to whether or not heading into Sioux country went against the new treaty. To the Chey-

enne, who were friendly with the Sioux, there could be
nothing wrong with going into the Black Hills. Not many
of her People cared to stay in the country in the south
when the hot summer months came upon them. Maybe
they would even go into the mountains again.

Tom watched Medicine Wolf study the horizon. He
realized for the moment that she gave him no thought.
He stood several feet behind her, thinking how lovely she
looked, her young form a fetching sight beneath the utterly
beautiful tunic. The long fringes at the bottom of the tunic
danced across her beaded moccasins. She wore the white
wolfskin draped over her shoulder, her medicine bag
around her neck. Her hair hung long and shining, blowing
in the gentle wind. She was the picture of Indian beauty
and elegance.

Tom was curious now to meet Bear Paw, not even sure
what he looked like. He had seen him only once, the night
of the agreement between his father and Medicine Wolf's
people; but it had been dark, and Bear Paw had quickly
left.

"They are coming," Medicine Wolf called out excitedly. She stood at the southern fringe of the fort grounds,
shading her eyes. The Prescotts stood behind her with
Tom, the fort commander, and a grizzly Indian scout also
waiting with them. Tom stepped farther away, glancing
back at his parents to see the stern but disappointed looks
on their faces. He was aware that his mother had tried to
convince Medicine Wolf that she should wear white wom-
en's clothing today, to accent how much she had learned
about the white man's world, but Medicine Wolf would
have none of it. If Bear Paw was with those who came for
her, she wanted to be wearing her best tunic.

There had been a few lessons over the past month,
once Marilyn Prescott managed to force herself to start
speaking to Medicine Wolf again. The woman had never
quite forgiven the girl for pulling a knife on her, but Tom
realized his mother was trying to salvage what little she
could from all her efforts over the past two years.

As horses began to appear on the horizon, Medicine
Wolf ran farther ahead in her excitement; Tom saw the
look of wounded pride in his mother's eyes. The woman's

disappointment did not give him the full satisfaction he thought it might, for to his amazement she looked ready to cry. He realized she truly must have cared about "saving" Medicine Wolf, but he could not abide her tactics, and he was still convinced there had to be a better way.

He turned his attention to the horizon, and what he saw stirred a hint of fear in him as well as deep admiration, and a longing to live that free, simple life that Medicine Wolf's People lived. It was not just Medicine Wolf's family coming, but what seemed to be a full tribe, perhaps two hundred strong. The warriors appeared first, spread out side by side in a straight line and moving toward the fort. Tom realized how important this occasion was to them, for they were dressed out in full regalia, ponies and faces painted, feathered war lances held upright, barechested warriors wearing beaded necklaces and bone breastplates. The dark, oiled skin of their muscled bodies shone in the morning sun.

When they finally reached fort grounds, Medicine Wolf cried out to one of them. A handsome older man swung his right leg over the front of his saddle and slid off his horse, grabbing a blanket from it. He opened the blanket and wrapped Medicine Wolf into it as a sign of affection. A woman came running toward them then, breaking away from the other women and children who followed behind the warriors, some of the women riding horses, others walking. The woman cried out something in the Cheyenne tongue and the man opened his blanket so that she could also embrace Medicine Wolf. He folded the blanket around both of them.

So, Mother, Tom thought. *Take a look. You think these people have no feelings. Look at the father embrace the wife and daughter.*

Several soldiers stood watch, prepared for trouble, for there were many Pawnee scouts also standing about, and all were well aware of the hatred between the two tribes. Tom decided it could only get worse as more and more Pawnee began hanging around the forts, offering their services as scouts against other tribes. Besides that, these Cheyenne were not supposed to be heading into Sioux country, but the army was not yet willing or prepared to try to force the Indians to adhere to every treaty rule, not as long as there was no trouble from them. Washington had not yet said exactly what should be done if the treaty were broken. Still, his own government had already broken the treaty by being late with supplies and money promised the Cheyenne. He had heard that the original treaty, signed nearly two years earlier by the Indians, still had not been ratified by Congress! And if they made any drastic changes, these Indians were not going to understand. They would consider any changes made after the fact as nothing more than broken promises.

He watched Medicine Wolf's welcome patiently, unable to hear what was being said. He moved cautiously closer, his eyes scanning the rest of the warriors, wondering which one was Bear Paw. One young man in particular watched Medicine Wolf intently, a look in his eyes that said he was surprised at how beautiful and changed she was.

So, you're the one, Tom thought. He was a magnificent young man, looking a little taller than the average Cheyenne man, his muscles hard and defined. Tom had already decided that Cheyenne men seemed more handsome than the men of most other tribes, but this one went beyond that. His finely chiseled face seemed perfectly formed, his nose straight, his chin square, his lips full. A white scar ran down the left side of his face, put there, Medicine Wolf had told him, by a Crow warrior. Tom shivered slightly, realizing that even if he had decided to try for Medicine Wolf's hand, he might have quickly given up if it meant having to go up against the young warrior who was watching her now.

As though to read his thoughts, the young man suddenly turned to look at Tom. Tom nodded and smiled slightly, feeling foolish and awkward, not sure what he should do. The warrior did not smile. He only studied Tom intently, dark eyes drilling into him with a look of sly contempt. Tom could almost feel a knife in his gut.

Medicine Wolf finally pulled away from her parents, wiping tears of joy at knowing they were all right. She looked at her mother. "Old Grandmother?" she asked in the Cheyenne tongue.

Her mother's eyes saddened. "She has walked the white road of the stars to the Great Beyond," her mother answered. "It was that first winter. She got sick, and she never got well again."

Medicine Wolf looked down, the pain returning to her heart. "I knew it. She spoke to me."

Star Woman touched her hair. "A day did not go by that my mother did not talk about her favorite granddaughter and pray for her. She understood, Medicine Wolf. She would want you to be happy for her, happy that she is free of the pains of old age. She waits for you in the Great Beyond, where you will be together again. She was buried on sacred grounds at *Hinta-nagi*. We will visit her when we return south."

Medicine Wolf swallowed back the tears, looking then for her little sister. Her gaze happened upon Bear Paw, who was watching her intently. She knew by his eyes that he was pleased with what he saw, and he in turn looked magnificent! She had almost forgotten just how handsome he was. The realization that she was surely to one day be his wife made her cheeks burn, and she quickly looked away. Her breasts tingled, and strange urgings pulled at her insides.

Had he waited for her as promised? She felt his eyes on her, felt suddenly naked before him. This was not the boy who had rescued her in the mountains, or even the young man with whom she had shared a blanket, the young man who had tasted the skin of her face. This was a full man, a magnificent warrior who she would one day have to please as a wife, the way her mother pleased her father. She kept her eyes averted.

"Saaa," Star Woman said. "You are a woman now, I see, for you cannot look at Bear Paw." She put her arm around Medicine Wolf. "We will have a celebration of womanhood for you when we meet with the Sioux. This is a time of great joy for us all, Medicine Wolf, for we have our holy child back with us." She grasped Medicine Wolf's shoulders. "Or have you decided to stay with the *ve-ho-e*?"

Medicine Wolf's eyes widened. "Never! My heart has never turned from my people. The *ve-ho-e* have no feelings for the land and the animals, and they hit their children.''

''Hit them!'' Arrow Maker frowned, handing his blanket to Star Woman.

''Did they strike you?'' Bear Paw spoke up, his anger instantly aroused. His horse turned in a quick circle, seeming to sense its master's fury. Tom watched from where he stood, fear gripping him at the obvious fact that the Cheyenne men were alarmed about something.

Medicine Wolf had no choice but to look up at Bear Paw. As long as she was with her mother, it was allowed, but it was difficult for her, for she felt a rush of excitement and embarrassment when their eyes met. ''I will not talk about it now, Bear Paw. I do not want trouble. There are many soldiers here, and they will use their guns. I do not want my return to end in bloodshed.''

''It will not be *our* blood that gets shed,'' Bear Paw fumed. ''It will be the blood of the *ve-ho-e*, and the stinking Pawnee who quickly forget their own and lick the white man's hands!'' He raised his lance and shouted a Cheyenne obscenity at two Pawnee scouts who stood in the distance. Several other Cheyenne warriors joined him, a mixture of name-calling and war whoops that made the soldiers uneasy and made Tom break out in a sweat. He was not certain just what was happening, what had suddenly riled the Cheyenne.

Medicine Wolf looked pleadingly at her father. ''I do not want trouble, Father. When we are away from here, then I will tell all of you what I have learned. It is dangerous to make trouble here with so many soldiers.''

Arrow Maker shouted at the young warriors to stay calm. Bear Paw lowered his lance. ''The Pawnee killed one of my finest horses, stole many more, burned our tipis,'' he growled.

Medicine Wolf listened in confusion. Had her people had another major conflict with the Pawnee?

''They will be repaid,'' Arrow Maker told Bear Paw. ''But when we are stronger. First we will celebrate the Sun Dance, make new sacrifices, and now we will again receive the blessing of the wolf paws. *Then* we will join the Arapaho in the South and we will teach the Pawnee to never again strike against our people! For now it is a time to celebrate. My daughter is with us again.''

The Pawnee scouts shouted back a few words of derision, but Bear Paw backed his horse into place again, proud that he had earned a position next to Arrow Maker so that he could be close to Medicine Wolf when they came for her. He looked over at White Horse, who was watching him challengingly. Bear Paw knew that White Horse was thinking the same as he, that Medicine Wolf had become much more beautiful than either of them had expected. It was amazing how two years could change a girl that age. She was becoming a most fetching young woman.

''Only two moons ago a war party of Pawnee attacked a large village we shared with the Cheyenne who stay to the South,'' Arrow Maker was telling Medicine Wolf. ''Things are bad for the Southern Cheyenne, and the Pawnee try to make it worse, try to make us break the treaty by forcing us to make war against our enemy. But we cannot let this go. It was a surprise attack. We lost many horses, and some of our people were killed. Summer Moon lost her mother.'' Medicine Wolf felt a sadness in her heart for her good friend. ''We plan an attack of our own,'' Arrow Maker continued, ''but not until we offer many prayers and sacrifices. And we were waiting for our holy child so that she can give us the blessing of the wolf's paws.'' The man touched her hair lovingly. ''My daughter has grown very beautiful. My heart is glad that she is still Cheyenne.''

The man turned and called to Swift Fox and Smiling Girl to come and greet their sister. Smiling Girl, now ten, had been waiting eagerly with the other women and children who walked behind the warriors. Swift Fox, nineteen, had remained proudly in the line of warriors. He rode forward, and Medicine Wolf felt a great pride at the sight of her brother, who was much more a man now, obviously a respected warrior in his own right.

Smiling Girl came running, hugging Medicine Wolf. She was bigger-boned than Medicine Wolf, and was a little heavier set, but she had a pretty face. Medicine Wolf hugged her, enjoying the ecstasy of again being with her loved ones. Swift Fox dismounted, throwing a blanket around Medicine Wolf for a brief embrace, then stepping away as though embarrassed to be showing emotion. Medicine Wolf knew by his eyes how happy he was to see her, knew that once they were in the confines of their parents' tipi, more emotion could be shown.

She called to Tom then, who looked surprised. She saw the fear and apprehension in his eyes as he approached. The air was heavy with tension, for there was still some name-calling going on between the Cheyenne and the Pawnee scouts. Bear Paw's stare as he came closer did not help erase Tom's fears. Their eyes held briefly, and Tom did not mistake the warning look in Bear Paw's dark eyes. Bear Paw moved his horse forward and followed close behind Tom, and a chill moved up Tom's back as he imagined how it might feel to have a knife stuck in one's spine. He decided not to turn to look at Bear Paw, for fear the young man would think the look was some kind of challenge. He walked closer to Medicine Wolf, who moved to his side and faced her people.

"I can tell you there are some *ve-ho-e* who have good hearts, who want to understand our ways and who love the land and the animals," she said in her own tongue.

The Prescotts watched, both of them surprised and disappointed that it was Tom whom Medicine Wolf introduced to her people first instead of them. Still, they were worried about their son, for one warrior kept prancing his horse near Tom as though to challenge him. Surely Medicine Wolf was saying only good things about Tom, since they seemed to be such good friends. "This is Tom Prescott," Medicine Wolf told her father. "He has a true heart. He is my friend, and my blood brother. Because he is my blood brother, I can look into his eyes and speak to him without the presence of my mother. I have not done wrong in being friends with him."

Bear Paw watched with great interest, studying the blue-eyed, light-haired Tom, who was quite tall, although, Bear Paw surmised, not very strong. He could not help thinking how easily he could whip the *ve-ho-e*. Perhaps he was a blood brother to Medicine Wolf, but Bear Paw could tell by his eyes that the young man had perhaps wanted to be more than a brother. It rankled him to realize this young man had spent the last two years with Medicine Wolf and had apparently became quite close to her. The only thing that controlled Bear Paw's jealousy was his respect for Medicine Wolf and anything that was important to her. She would not have made this young man a blood brother without a very good reason, and because of that alone, Bear Paw knew he must allow nothing but honorable feelings for this Tom Prescott.

"How is it you have made this *ve-ho-e* a blood brother?" Arrow Maker asked.

"Tom has a good heart. He has patiently allowed me to teach him about my People, our beliefs and customs, and he has listened with an open heart and an open mind. I understand this with great clarity after Wolf was shot by a white soldier."

Star Woman gasped, and Bear Paw spit out a word that Tom figured must be another Cheyenne cuss word. He wasn't sure just what Medicine Wolf was saying, but he trusted her to keep Bear Paw from sinking a lance into his back.

"Wolf, shot?" Arrow Maker reached out and touched the head of Wolf's skin, which hung near Medicine Wolf's shoulder. "When I saw this, I did not want to ask about it right away, for I knew that to lose Wolf would be a moment of very great sorrow. I thought perhaps he had died the natural way. When did this happen! And why would anyone shoot Wolf!"

"It happened one moon past. Young calves were being killed. I was not allowed to keep Wolf with me, so he always waited for me in the hills. He was blamed for killing the young calves. One night a soldier shot him. None of them has admitted to the killing. I think whoever did it is afraid."

"As well he *should* be," Arrow Maker growled. He looked around. "This is a bad place, Medicine Wolf. Children hit, sacred wolves shot! We should not have left you here!"

"It was good that you did, Father, for I learned many things. I have told you about the wolf only to help you understand about Tom." She touched the wolfskin fondly.

"I kept the skin because Wolf told me in a dream that I should. You should know that Tom also grieved his death. He helped me cut away the skin and bury Wolf. Wolf meant much to him. He used to walk with me every day to come and see him. We would feed him, and we would talk. Tom wanted to know about the Cheyenne, and he has deep feelings for our People. When I cut my arm in grief over Wolf, Tom asked me to cut his also, for he wanted to express his sorrow in the Cheyenne way. It was then that we mixed our blood." She looked up at Bear Paw. "Forever Tom will be a good friend of the Cheyenne. Once his mother tried to destroy the sacred wolf paws, but Tom saved them. If he should ever ride into our village to greet us, he must never be harmed. He is a good white man. He is my friend. He has a Cheyenne heart."

Tom stood waiting, unsure what was expected of him. He almost jumped with fright when Bear Paw suddenly touched his shoulder with his lance. *"I-tat-ane,"* he told Tom, moving his horse around to face him.

"He called you brother," Medicine Wolf explained to Tom. "He is Bear Paw, the young man I told you about."

Tom looked up at Bear Paw. *"I-tat-ane,"* he repeated, wondering if he had said the right thing. To his relief Bear Paw gave him a look of respect, although there was still a hint of warning in his eyes.

Arrow Maker grasped Tom's shoulders and said something to him with a look of friendly gratitude.

"He says he is happy that I had a friend here," Medicine Wolf told Tom. "He says you are a rare white man, one with a good heart, one who understands the sacredness of the animals. You will forever be our brother."

Tom felt a keen temptation to ride off with these people when they left, but common sense told him he would never survive living their life. He nodded and smiled to Arrow Maker, putting out his hand. They grasped wrists, and Tom's parents watched in amazement. Tom turned to Medicine Wolf. "What was all the yelling about a minute ago?"

Medicine Wolf held her chin proudly, turning and casting a defiant look to the Pawnee scouts. "It is the Pawnee," she told Tom. "There has been much trouble. Soon my people will ride against them in revenge for an attack on our People. It is hard for our warriors to sit here and look at those Pawnee without attacking them.''

Tom looked around, sighing deeply. "Well, maybe it's best you all get going then, before something happens to get a lot of people hurt.'' His eyes moved over her. "It is against the treaty to war with other tribes, Medicine Wolf. Don't they understand that?''

The look of a warrior came into her eyes. "Tell that to the Pawnee.''

Deep concern moved into Tom's eyes. "Will you be all right? Will you be in danger when your people attack the Pawnee?''

Her eyes warmed again. "For my people there is always danger. But I have the wolf's paws.'' She touched the medicine bag. "For this I will ever be grateful to you. Do not fear for me, Tom. You must go on with your own life, as I will go on with mine.'' She touched his arm. "Come, we will go and speak with your parents before I go.'' She turned to Arrow Maker and Star Woman. "I will go and speak with the woman who has been teaching me.'' She left them, going with Tom to the Prescotts.

Bear Paw watched, his thoughts confused between jealousy and respect for Tom Prescott. He was glad Medicine Wolf was leaving the young man for good. Soon, perhaps two more summers, he would make her his first wife. For years he had waited for the child to become a woman. She was thirteen summers now, and her hips and breasts were developing an enticing roundness that stirred manly desires.

Still, it was more than her utter beauty and the thought of touching her secret places that made him want her with this aching desire. She was Medicine Wolf, the woman of his vision; and he had been a part of her own vision. He knew already that he loved her, loved everything about her—her magic, her wisdom, her power, her innocence. He had seen in her eyes that her own feelings had not changed.

Medicine Wolf and Tom approached Tom's mother, who stood stiffly, trying to show no emotion. "I know that you tried in your way to teach me that the way you live is the only right way," Medicine Wolf told the woman, eyeing her boldly. "But this is not so. I am sad that you waited until now to show that deep inside you truly cared. I know now that you did, and I am sorry for the things I said and did that hurt you. But no matter how you had acted toward me, you could not have taken me from the Cheyenne, or convinced me to abandon my beliefs." She turned her attention to Tom's father. "You must understand that I have been blessed by the Wolf Spirit," she told the man. She lovingly touched the wolf's head that graced her shoulder. "What has happened to me is sacred and holy. It could not be changed, no more than anyone could have convinced your Christ to abandon Jehovah. He died because it was expected of him by Jehovah. He died for his people. Whatever the Wolf Spirit expects of me, I will also do. It is the same. And if I must die for my People, I will do it."

Mrs. Prescott blinked back tears. "I truly am sorry about the wolf," she told Medicine Wolf. She handed out a Bible. "Will you please take this and study it more? Will you do that much?"

Medicine Wolf took the Bible, holding it close. "I will keep it, as a reminder of what I have learned, and because much of it is very much like what my own people believe. That is the other thing you never understood."

"Think about the things I have told you, Martha," Mrs. Prescott told her, refusing to use her Indian name. "Someday, when you see the end is near for your people, you will understand that I was right. You will know that your people must learn our ways or die. You will tell your children to come to our schools and learn the white man's way."

"I cannot say that such a thing will not happen. But our way of life, our beliefs, are precious to us. We will live our way as long as we can. We cannot abandon what has been in our hearts and our blood since our people were first created and visited by the prophet Sweet Medicine. You do not realize that we are already aware of what might happen, for I never told you that our own prophet told us that one day our ways would have to change. He predicted long ago that one day we would not remember our old ways, that we will leave our religion for something new. We will quarrel among ourselves and forget the good things about the way we lived.''

Mrs. Prescott looked surprised at the words. ''Then why have you fought me so strongly?''

Medicine Wolf's eyes teared. ''How would you feel if the same were told to you?'' Medicine Wolf saw a hint of understanding in the woman's eyes. ''My people do not want to believe this could happen,'' she told Mrs. Prescott, speaking with a wisdom far beyond her years. ''We all hope that such a thing is many years in the future. We know that if it *is* to happen, we must make sure it is not during our own lifetime. We know what is good and right, what is the best way to live and believe, and for now we will fight to keep this life, fight to keep the prophecy of Sweet Medicine from coming to be. Even if this should happen, Sweet Medicine did not say it would be because a new way is the right way. It will happen only because another people have come along who are much stronger than we. We believe deep in our hearts that if we must change because of outside forces, it will not erase the old ways, or mean that our God never existed. He will not change. He will only wait. We believe the day will come, Mrs. Prescott, when the white man will no longer walk this earth. We will again ride free wherever we choose, and there will be much game. Our ancestors will rise from the earth and be with us again.'' She smiled, petting the wolf's head. ''Old Grandmother will be with me again, and so will Wolf.''

Mrs. Prescott shook her head. ''You are a strange young woman,'' she told Medicine Wolf. ''I wish you had told me some of this earlier.''

''I wanted you to understand from your own heart, your own desire. And I knew you would not listen, not until you finally realized that nothing you could do would change me.''

Medicine Wolf clutched the Bible, turning to Tom. ''For the rest of my life there will be a special place in my heart for you, *I-tat-ane*. If I should never see you again, I will still feel you with me, and you will know that I am with you. Life will be good for both of us, but each of us will know that we have a friend in that other world that we cannot share.''

Tom's eyes teared, and his jaw flexed in a struggle not to break down. "I will never forget you, Medicine Wolf. Never." He leaned down and embraced her, touching his cheek to her own. His parents watched with mixed emotions, wishing they could have influenced Medicine Wolf more, now glad to see her go, for instead she had influenced their own son to the point where he had turned away from them.

Bear Paw watched from a distance, a stabbing jealousy gripping his heart when Tom embraced Medicine Wolf. Had he not been the one to embrace her when he told her good-bye two years before? Did she take the same comfort in Tom's embrace that she had taken in his? Was the embrace truly like that of brother and sister? He decided he would quickly begin doing everything possible to erase from her mind and heart this blue-eyed white man called Tom Prescott!

"Good-bye, Medicine Wolf. I pray we will meet again, and that . . ." Tom smiled sadly. "That my God will watch over you."

"And I will pray that *my* God will watch over *you*. Just remember that He is all things, in the earth upon which you walk, in the animals, in the wind. My spirit is also in those things, so that everywhere you go, in everything you touch, you will feel me with you." She turned away, walking over to pick up her personal belongings, placing the Bible in her parfleche. She carried her things back to her People.

Her mother embraced her again, then took her parfleche and walked back to the other women and children, tying Medicine Wolf's belongings to a horse-drawn travois. Swift Fox brought Medicine Wolf a magnificent Appaloosa mare. Tom thought she must feel very proud being given a horse to ride, for it not only meant that her father and brother were wealthy because they had many horses, it also meant she was greatly honored to be given a horse of her own at her young age. Arrow Maker helped her mount the horse, and she seemed to feel no shame in the fact that her legs showed when she straddled the animal in what his mother would consider a very unladylike position. Tom did not see it that way at all. He saw only a beautiful, proud young woman doing what came naturally.

She sat straight and almost queenly on the horse. She looked back at Tom and waved, and he waved in return, his throat aching. He thought how lonely and boring it was going to be without her, and he supposed it was time to go back east and finish his schooling.

Medicine Wolf and the rest of her people rode off toward the northwest. Bear Paw broke rank as they moved over a rise. He rode back through the following women and children and remained perched on the rise, watching Tom until all others were well on their way.

Tom wondered for a moment if the young man meant to come back and kill him, but finally Bear Paw only raised a lance and gave out a chilling cry. He turned and rode off, and Tom was left wondering if the gesture had been in honor, or if it was a deadly warning. He breathed a deep sigh of relief, but he also felt a great sorrow that Medicine Wolf was gone. He did not think he would ever see her again.

Part 3

Chapter Twelve

Medicine Wolf had never felt quite so important and honored as she did this night. She and her tribe had joined the Sioux in a massive gathering, celebrating the Sun Dance as well as holding a feast and special ceremony to welcome Medicine Wolf and several other young women into womanhood.

Medicine Wolf enjoyed a new prominence among her people because of her stay with the *ve-ho-e*, and after the special ceremonies she had been brought before her tribe, the men sitting in a great circle around her, women and children gathering behind them. Medicine Wolf was asked to tell them about the *ve-ho-e*, and she was both proud and nervous, feeling shy about having to speak before all these older, much wiser people who had gathered around a central ceremonial fire.

The flames glowed against Medicine Wolf's white tunic, and she proudly wore Wolf's skin around her shoulders. Black Buffalo had called the council, and on his left sat Arrow Maker and Medicine Wolf's fraternal uncle, Two Moons; next to him was her maternal uncle, Red Foot. On Black Buffalo's right sat Bear Paw, and his father and uncle, Stands Tall and White Eagle; beside them sat White Horse, and Medicine Wolf's brother, Swift Fox.

It was a gathering of the best Dog Soldiers, as well as other respected men among Medicine Wolf's tribe, including the Shaman Stalking Bear, and a highly respected warrior named Old Whirlwind. Some Sioux who wanted to hear from Medicine Wolf about her stay with the Prescotts had joined the gathering of Cheyenne men. A prayer pipe was passed among all the men before Medicine Wolf would be allowed to speak, and the women and children waited, watching Medicine Wolf with great respect and attention. It was the highest moment Medicine Wolf had so far experienced in her young life.

Bear Paw watched with a secret pride the beauty of the young woman he had sworn would belong to him one day. She had grown taller, and this night he could easily see the more mature woman she would soon become. No warrior could ask for a more beautiful, honorable, or highly respected female than Medicine Wolf. Already he ached for her.

Finally Black Buffalo rose, taking the last draw from the prayer pipe and blowing the smoke over Medicine Wolf as a blessing. "We thank *Maheo* for giving this woman back to us," he told the others. Medicine Wolf's breathing quickened with surprise and pride that he had called her a woman. "Soon the Cheyenne will join the Kiowa-Apache and the Arapaho in the South and ride against the Pawnee," Black Buffalo added. "Because Medicine Wolf is with us again, and can offer the blessing of the wolf's paws, I know that we will be victorious!"

The men broke out into war whoops, raising fists and weapons, the women joining them so that the noise was almost deafening, and Black Buffalo had to raise his hands to quiet them.

"We know that soon our war will not be just with the Pawnee and other eastern tribes who are friendly with the *ve-ho-e*, but with the *ve-ho-e* himself! For this we will need more rifles. We will trade for them, steal them in

raids, get them however we can. But we also must understand the white man, decide if his promises are true, or if
they are lies. This is why we offered our own honored
holy child to live among them for two summers. Now she
will speak to us, and we will ask her what we want to
know." Black Buffalo turned to Medicine Wolf. "Tell us
what you have learned, Medicine Wolf." He sat down,
and Medicine Wolf felt damp with nervous perspiration.
She swallowed and took a deep breath.

"I think that the white man's promises are lies," she
told her people in the Cheyenne tongue.

A wave of gasps and ooohs and *saaas* moved through
the crowd of painted warriors and their women.

"The white man seems confused," Medicine Wolf
continued gaining more courage when she saw how eager
all were to hear. "They say one thing and do another.
They worship a God who is called Jehovah, and his son,
who is called Christ. They say this God created Grandmother Earth and all her living beings, yet they in turn
have no respect for the land or its animals. They do not
understand their own God, who I feel in my heart is the
same as our *Maheo.* The son called Christ is our Sweet
Medicine. I believe this because many of his teachings are
the same as the teachings of Sweet Medicine."

She held up her Bible, which she had brought along to
show them. "This is the white man's holy book. Its teachings are good, but the white man does not truly follow
them. He turns the words around to suit him. He says his
God wants the white man to rule the earth over all other
races. He believes that his God means for the white man
to own land, each man having a little piece. He believes
it is his duty to conquer the wilderness, to chop down
trees, to dig his plows into Grandmother Earth and tear
her skin. It is his duty to make all Indians abandon their
beliefs and customs and live like the white man. He builds
things called factories. I have seen drawings of these factories, and they are big and ugly. Every day many whites
in the East go to these factories, where they work all day
at making things, never seeing the sun, never riding free.
They work to earn money. With this money they buy
things, silly things that they do not need. They seem to

think they must have many things, and much money. Gold is most important of all to them. Gold and land.''

The crowd muttered, talking among themselves for a moment.

"If the *ve-ho-e* can twist the words of his own holy book, can he not twist the words and promises of the treaties he makes with us?" Medicine Wolf asked them.

More murmurs moved among the others, heads nodding.

"The white eyes do not honor the sacred animals," she continued. "They do not thank an animal's spirit when it is killed to fill their bellies. Some of the soldiers at the fort killed buffalo just for sport, or would take only the best meat and leave everything else to rot. When Wolf was shot, it was for no good reason except that some cowardly soldier feared him. When the commander of the fort questioned his men, none of the soldiers would admit to killing him. It was not a very brave man who did this thing."

Heads nodded, and a few braves uttered curse words.

"The white man wants us to live like him," Medicine Wolf continued. "But I saw nothing about the way he lives that would make me want to stop being Cheyenne. He does everything by a schedule, using something he calls a clock. It is an object that comes in many shapes and sizes, with numbers all around and little markers that move, pointing to different numbers. The numbers represent the time of day, and always the white man is looking at this clock. He rises by the clock, eats by the clock, works by the clock, worships by the clock, and goes to bed by the clock. Always, it seems, he is looking at this clock to see if it is time to do this or that. Even if he is not hungry, he eats at a certain time every day. And if he *is* hungry, but the clock says it is not time to eat, then he does not eat. When he does eat, he uses many plates for all different foods. He must sit at a table and use utensils called knives and forks. He is forbidden to eat with his fingers, and sometimes he does not even finish what is on his plate."

Some of the women voiced their astonishment. No Cheyenne took more than he could eat. And it was an insult to the woman who cooked the food not to finish what he had been given.

"The white man's clothing is unsanitary," Medicine Wolf told them. She was surprised at how easily the words came now. Fear left her, replaced by an eagerness to share what she knew with these people she loved. Surely the Wolf Spirit was helping her, speaking through her, for she was talking like an older, much wiser woman "Their clothing does not let the skin breathe. It is hot and binding and scratches. Their shoes are hard and pinch the toes, and they offer no warmth in winter. I think it is this painful clothing that makes the white man so impatient and often angry. They cannot be comfortable, and this makes them irritable.

"They have no patience for the ways of another. They truly believe there is only one right way, and they are not willing to listen to anything different. Many times I tried to explain to the white preacher's woman that our religion is not really so different from theirs, but she calls us heathens and thinks we are bad. I told her our women are chaste, but she would not believe me. She is a woman always angry and scowling, not happy and free like the Cheyenne. It seems most of them are that way. They have no spirit, no connection to the animals and Grandmother Earth. They do not often laugh. Even when they worship, they are scowling and sober instead of happy, as they should be when they talk to the Gods. They sing songs, but still they do not have happy faces. They seem to be afraid of their God. When they worship him, they sit on hard benches inside a building, away from the sun and the sky and the earth. And they are always so angry and worried, and so anxious that their children do things just so, that they hit their children."

Whispers moved through the crowd. "Hit a child!" one woman gasped.

"Once I saw a white woman who was part of a wagon train coming through the fort. This woman had a baby, about one year old. Every time the baby cried, she hit it, and then it would cry harder. She punished the baby just for crying, when it was probably only hungry or wet, or perhaps it sensed that it was not loved. I myself was whipped many times by the white woman for wanting to be with Wolf, or for speaking wrongly or eating wrongly. It seemed I could do nothing right in her eyes."

Women looked at each other, near horror in their eyes, and Medicine Wolf saw Arrow Maker and Star Woman stiffen with anger at the thought of their precious daughter being struck.

"The white man seems to think that learning numbers and letters and earning money and owning land are more important than freedom and happiness," Medicine Wolf continued, "more important than sharing and being close to the spirit world. His children are expected to sit in buildings called schools and read and do numbers all day, instead of being free and happy and learning to ride horses and playing with one another.

"Men and boys are expected to wear their hair very short, and women must keep their hair tightly bound. If a woman wears her hair long and loose, and does not wear the tight, hot underclothing of the white woman; if she does not keep her arms and neck covered, she is considered a bad woman. Their men cannot wear just a breechcloth like our men. They must always wear shirts and long pants and hard boots. A nearly naked man or woman is very shocking to the *ve-ho-e*, and that is part of what they consider bad about the Indian. They think the Indian is what they call savage and heathen, simply because he dresses, lives, and worships differently from the white man. *Savage* and *heathen* are words the white man uses for someone he thinks is bad."

Again the crowd muttered and whispered. "Are there no good *ve-ho-e*?" Swift Fox asked her. "None who have the spirit, who understand our ways?"

"For many years now we have traded with the longhair trappers," Arrow Maker put in. "And with the Bent brothers. They have been good to us. The trappers have even lived as we live. They have never been a danger to us. Are these new white people from the East so different, then?"

It seemed strange to Medicine Wolf to be answering a question from her own wise father. Always before it was she who asked the questions.

"They are very different, my father. There are not so

many trappers left, and most of them have turned to scouting for other whites, these new *ve-ho-e*, a people who are nothing like the hunters and trappers who came before them. These newcomers want nothing of our life, and there are many more of them than there are trappers and traders who came here before them. The son of the holy man told me there are many, many more of these new *ve-ho-e* in the East, as many as the stars.''

It hurt Medicine Wolf to have to tell her people these things and see the worried looks on their faces. But they must know the truth and decide accordingly. Still, maybe there were more good-hearted white men in the East than it seemed. She thought of Tom Prescott, feeling a gentle ache in her heart. He was probably already on his way back east to one of those schools she had just talked about. She would miss him very much, miss their talks.

"Some of these new *ve-ho-e* do have good hearts," she told them then, wanting to give them at least some hope. "The son of the preacher that I spoke of, Tom Prescott, he had a good heart. He wanted to know about the Cheyenne. His heart was true. He defended me when his mother wanted to destroy my wolfskin and my medicine bag because she thought they kept me from turning to the white man's religion. Tom understood that they were important to me. He helped me bury my medicine bag to hide it. When Wolf was shot, he helped me take the skin, and when we buried what was left, Tom wept. He let me cut his arm as a sign of mourning, and we mixed our blood so that he became a brother.''

Bear Paw straightened at the words, as though something had pricked him. He did not like hearing the story again, did not like hearing Medicine Wolf speak of Tom Prescott.

"Tom truly wanted to be one of us," Medicine Wolf continued, "and some white scouts also are like us and are our friends; but most now turn back to their own kind, helping soldiers, leading more whites into our land. And the new whites they bring do not seem to be willing to continue to allow us our land and our freedom. I fear for our future. The whites who came through Fort Laramie in their covered houses on wheels looked at me as though I were beneath them. Few had kind eyes for me. It was the same with the soldiers at the fort. And there are big guns at the fort that Tom told me can kill many men at once. If they do not intend to use these guns against their own kind, then who are they for but the Indian?''

Many murmured their agreement.

"We must be very cautious when dealing with the white man, for Tom told me that in the East there once were many Indians, but now most have completely died away. They have no land left. That is why many of those remaining have come into our lands. I see far in the future a time when all Indians will have to work together to save themselves; even enemy tribes will join us in this fight.''

Many gasped. "Never," one warrior growled.

Medicine Wolf hoped she had not offended them. "I tell you only what I fear lies far in the future, or perhaps in our own lifetime. We must remember Sweet Medicine's warning about forgetting our ways and taking on a new religion and new way of living. We must not let this happen, and if it *must* happen, we must find a way to preserve all that is Cheyenne—our religion, our language, our possessions. We must make sure our children and their children remember."

Star Woman watched with deep pride. What had happened to this daughter of hers, the little girl who used to daydream and sometimes be so disobedient and absentminded? She was not watching a child. She was watching a woman, one of amazing wisdom for her age, one of strength and composure and courage. She felt greatly blessed to be the mother of such a daughter.

"We must be ready for the day when the white man breaks the treaty," Medicine Wolf told them. "We must pray much, seek visions, be strong. We must be ready to defend our lands and our way of life. Remember that the white man loves land and gold. These two things might mean much trouble for us in the days to come. Already you have seen how many thousands of white men traveled through our land to reach the gold fields in the land of the setting sun. You have seen the path of destruction they left behind. If gold should ever be discovered on our own lands, then bad days lie ahead for us. And there is something else we must watch for. I had a dream not long ago, about a great, black monster with fire in its belly and smoke belching from its head. It moved across the plains and prairies, howling like many wolves, making much noise, frightening away the buffalo and the birds. I told Tom about this dream because I thought this monster came from the land in the East. Tom told me what I described was what the white man calls a train. It is a great iron thing that travels on roads of rails, and is used in the East to haul supplies and people. Tom said it is possible these trains will come into our land. If they do, they will frighten away the buffalo and other animals, fill our skies with smoke, and chase away our peace with its howling cry. Worse than that, it will bring people, more *ve-ho-e* from the lands in the East. Tom feels that these white men will someday want to settle on Indian lands, lands promised to us in the treaty. The white man will try to twist the words of the treaty, or make new treaties with us that will erase the promises in the old ones. We must not let them do this. The treaty promises us these lands, and we must fight to keep them!''

Another round of war cries filled the night air, and Medicine Wolf began to realize the power she possessed because of her special gifts, and because she had lived among the *ve-ho-e*. This night had been a strangely exhilarating yet humbling experience.

Black Buffalo rose, quieting the excited warriors. "Medicine Wolf has given us much to think about," he told them. "If there are truly so many whites in the land of the rising sun, then we must do what we can to remain at peace with them, but we will not let them insult us or force their ways upon us. We will not abide their breaking of the treaty promises." He raised the prayer pipe again and moved it over Medicine Wolf's head. "The holy woman has spoken. Let us remember what she has told us. Let us not allow the *ve-ho-e* to destroy what belongs to the Cheyenne!"

The priest raised his fist, and the warriors joined in again, raising a cry for freedom and power. A few had been drinking whiskey, and they began singing their war songs and dancing around the fire. Others joined them, and drummers spurred them on with rhythmic pounding accompanying chanted songs and war cries. They had already been heated up with plans to ride against the Pawnee in retaliation for the Pawnee attack against the Cheyenne nation a few weeks earlier. Now they were incensed over the attitude of the *ve-ho-e*, and their dancing and songs included outcries against the white man and how they would not let him destroy the Cheyenne.

Arrow Maker grasped Medicine Wolf's shoulders. "It is a fine talk you gave," he told her. "My heart is full of pride for my daughter, who is no longer a child. This has been the greatest moment of my life."

Medicine Wolf doubted she would ever know more joy and pride herself than at this moment. "Thank you, *Ne-ho-eehe*," she answered. "My own pride comes from saying that Arrow Maker is my father."

Arrow Maker squeezed her shoulders, tears of pride in his eyes. He touched her cheek, then left her to join the men in their dancing. Medicine Wolf turned to go to her mother, but was startled when a warrior screamed an extra-loud war whoop deliberately near her, making her jump and turn. She looked into the eyes of White Horse. He had painted white circles around his eyes and red lines across his cheeks. He grinned, but it was a wicked rather than a warm smile. "You are mine," he told her, coming close. "One day you will know it!" He moved away, joining the dancers.

Medicine Wolf felt a chill until she turned to see Bear Paw watching her quietly. She felt suddenly warm and protected. She hurried off to find her mother, afraid to be caught staring at the young man, but Bear Paw's one look had erased the odd fear White Horse had planted in her heart.

She reached her mother, and the woman hugged her, telling her how proud she was of her. "I must tell you that someone spoke with me earlier," she told Medicine Wolf. "If a young man throws his blanket around you later, do not fear that it is wrong. He has our permission."

Medicine Wolf's heart pounded. It was accepted custom for a young man interested in courting a young woman to wait outside her tipi and throw his blanket over her when she came out so that they could talk for a while. The young woman's mother had to approve, and had to be nearby to make sure nothing improper happened. What had Medicine Wolf wondering was who the young man might be. White Horse had said she would be his someday. The last thing she wanted was to share a blanket with White Horse!

Some of the joy went out of her. She did not ask her mother who the young man was, because it was to be a surprise. With a worried heart she watched the men dance, some of them, including White Horse, drinking the white man's firewater that they felt gave them visions. Her mother finally left to take Smiling Girl to the tipi, for she was very tired. Medicine Wolf followed, glad to leave White Horse to the dancing. Maybe he would dance all night and finally pass out from too much firewater.

She moved inside the tipi and stirred the fire, adding some wood to it, for the nights had turned suddenly cool for this time of year. Her mother sat down next to Smiling Girl and began talking to her about one of Arrow Maker's great conquests, always telling Medicine Wolf's younger sister some kind of story before she fell asleep. Within minutes someone rattled the buffalo bones over the tipi entrance to announce his presence.

"Come out," a man called in a hoarse whisper. Medicine Wolf could not tell for certain who it was. She looked over at her mother, who only grinned and nodded, indicating her permission. Feeling sick at who she feared it was, she exited the tipi. Someone threw a blanket over her and drew her to the ground to sit beside him.

"So, finally I can touch you again," he said softly.

It was Bear Paw! Medicine Wolf could hardly find her voice for her relief and ecstasy. "I missed you so," she told him quietly, relishing the feel of his strong arm around her. In spite of her own new importance and the fact that her People practically worshipped her, she was in awe of the man sitting next to her.

"And I missed you." Medicine Wolf felt a big hand at the side of her face, and Bear Paw leaned close to touch her cheek. She breathed in his manly scent, felt his power, felt weak with the thought of being a woman to him. "I waited for you, as I promised," he told her, his lips close to her ear. He moved his mouth to her neck, licking her skin, sending shivers through her and making her think forbidden thoughts. His hand dropped down to brush against her breast. "And now you are a woman," he added. "I am pleased with what I see. I have never seen one quite so beautiful, and after tonight I am honored to share a blanket with you."

"It is I who am honored," she answered, her voice squeaking from nervousness.

His lips and tongue caressed her neck again, and his hand lightly squeezed her breast. "Tell me that Tom Prescott meant nothing to you."

She shivered at his touch. "He was only a friend, a brother," she answered. "He could never mean to me what Bear Paw means to me, and now he is gone from my life. He is from a world I could never share."

He took hold of her hand then, pressing it against his powerful chest, which was wrapped tightly with bandages, for he had participated in the Sun Dance for the second time in his life, something few men did more than once. His wounds were still fresh. "When we raid the Pawnee," he told her, "I will capture many horses. Already I own a Pawnee war shield, a Crow scalp, and three Pawnee scalps. Tomorrow I leave here to go to the mountains to capture an eagle so that I can own its feathers. I will collect all the things Black Buffalo says are required to marry you, those things and more. Do not let your father give you to anyone else."

"I can never belong to anyone but you, Bear Paw," she answered. "Surely you already know this."

"I know it, yet I need to hear it from your own lips." She realized then that he was also shivering. "Give me your mouth, Medicine Wolf, quickly, before I must leave you. If we stay here too long, it will bring you dishonor."

His face was so close. She touched her cheek to his, then turned so that their mouths touched. His tongue slaked between her lips, and she touched it with her own tongue, a sign of deep affection, an intimate moment, perhaps too intimate for a first meeting, yet it seemed so right. Bear

Paw took a quick deep breath, suddenly drawing away, shuddering.

"I leave you now," he told her. "I only wanted to welcome you back, to tell you that I have waited and that my heart still longs for you alone. I will begin bringing gifts to your father, and I will play my flute for you. Listen for my song."

He took the blanket away and rose, quickly leaving her. Medicine Wolf remained sitting on the ground for a moment, too shaken to rise and walk. She moved her tongue between her lips, savoring the taste of him.

Bear Paw waited patiently, trying to ignore the gnawing feeling in his stomach. He was tempted to eat the raw rabbit meat that rested above him, but that was for the eagle; not only that, but if he ate it, he would break his four-day fast. He had already suffered too much to get this far. He was not about to break the spell now.

He reminded himself that this was for Medicine Wolf. One of the required presents to her father was an eagle feather. He intended to give the man an entire eagle! He had not come to this high place above the Black Hills just to look around an eagle's nest for feathers that had been shed. That was the coward's way! He would capture one of the mighty Gods of the sky and take it to Arrow Maker and let the man decide whether to just pluck a few feathers and let the bird go, or to kill it and keep it as a magnificent present and good-luck charm from Bear Paw.

He had prayed long and hard for this, and to bring him success, he had endured the Sun Dance for a second time. He had wanted to be sure Arrow Maker realized what a brave man he was, and how much he loved his People. Again he had shed blood in an offering to *Maheo* to prove his sincerity when he prayed for the prosperity of the Cheyenne. Again he had suffered and had not cried out, but there had been another reason for the sacrifice. He had wanted to show Medicine Wolf again how brave he was. The first time he had participated in the Sun Dance, she had been just a child and had not fully appreciated the magnitude of his sacrifice. Now she was a woman, and she looked upon him differently.

Even White Horse had not been willing to go through the sacrifice a second time. Bear Paw smiled at the thought of it. He knew that White Horse had last summer gone to the big mountains to find eagle feathers. How jealous he would be when Bear Paw arrived with an entire eagle! But he had to capture it soon, for the Cheyenne were preparing to go back south to meet with the Kiowa-Apache and the Arapaho, after which they would all but destroy the Pawnee!

Again hunger and pain stabbed at him, for his wounds from the Sun Dance were still not healed. He had eaten only a little in the first few days after the celebration, then had gone to the high country, again fasting, singing his prayer song for three nights in a row over a campfire. Surely Grandfather Eagle would understand his needs and would bring one of his own to Bear Paw as an offering. Grandfather Eagle understood how important this was to him, for he must be the one to possess Medicine Wolf, the one who held her and made a woman of her in every sense.

He licked his lips in thirst. It was hot and stuffy in this hole, but he would sit it out. He had heard of a few men who had done this, knew how dangerous it was. His uncle, White Eagle, had done it as a younger man, and he still carried an ugly scar next to his eye where the live eagle had nearly plucked it out, as well as deep white scars on both hands and arms from the mighty eagle's great claws.

He had done everything as White Eagle had told him, searching the high hills for a place where it was obvious eagles nested. He had managed to find a spot of soft ground, where he had dug a hole big enough for him to sit inside it. He had fashioned a large, flat bed of woven branches and leaves, then killed a rabbit with his bow and arrow, not using a gun for fear of scaring off any eagles that might be close by. He had laid the rabbit on the bed of branches, cutting it open so the eagle could readily pick up its scent. He had then climbed into his hole and positioned the bed of branches above him so that he could not be seen. The raw rabbit meat lay on top, a tempting mor-

sel for a hungry eagle. It was tied down so that the eagle
could not come and grab it up and fly off with it. The bird
would have to sit on the bed of branches and try to get the
meat loose, or it would just have to stay there and eat it.

That was when Bear Paw would grab the bird. He had
known he might sit there for two days before one of the
great birds came along, for it would take at least that long
for the smell of the dead meat to overpower his human
smell. This was already the second day, and he was getting
weaker. During the Sun Dance sacrifice the Bear Spirit
had told him he must fast and pray for many days before
trying to capture the eagle, and he had obeyed what he
had been told. Now his body was suffering the effects of
his sacrifice and starvation.

The sun began to set, and finally he heard an eagle's
cry. All senses came alert, and he sat up straighter, waiting. Finally he heard the rush of wind, the sound of the
wings of a huge bird. It sounded close. His heart pounded
wildly then when he saw huge claws gripping the bed of
branches! He could tell by the way the branches moved
that the eagle was tugging at the raw meat. He knew this
was no time to lose courage. It was now or never.

He shoved his right hand through the branches to grab
hold of the eagle's legs, and the battle was on. The bird
was much heavier and stronger than Bear Paw had imagined it would be, and he was himself weak from fasting.
He hung on for dear life, pushing his way out of the hole,
the bed of branches caught around his wrist while his hand
held the eagle's legs. He climbed out of the hole and
grabbed up a large leather bag with his left hand, crying
out when the eagle, in fear and defense, began craning its
neck to bite at him.

Its strong beak began taking off pieces of flesh, but
Bear Paw would not let go. It bit at the sores left from the
Sun Dance, and Bear Paw screamed, but still he hung on.
With great effort he struggled to get the leather bag over
the eagle's head. The bird began chewing at his left arm
and hand, and Bear Paw realized that there suddenly
seemed to be blood everywhere. He knew it was his own.

Finally he managed to get the sack over the bird's head,
which made it calm down somewhat. He wrapped the end

of it around the bird's legs, holding them with his left hand while he let go with his right so that he could pull his hand out of the bed of branches and untangle the eagle's claws from it. When he finally managed to get the bird loose, he grabbed the claws, grimacing as they dug into his right hand. He shoved hard, pushing the feet inside the sack, then quickly drew it closed with a leather cord.

He collapsed to the ground then, panting, bleeding profusely. He watched the movement in the sack and smiled. He had done it! Arrow Maker would be greatly pleased and highly impressed, as would Medicine Wolf. For years to come he would have a wonderful story to tell of how he captured a live eagle! He would have the scars to prove it!

He grabbed the sack and stood up, laughing. He raised it, blood streaming down his arm when he did so. He let out a long, piercing war whoop, feeling invincible, victorious. He had not just captured an eagle. He had come one step closer to making sure Medicine Wolf shared no one's bed but his own! He would do anything for her, capture ten more eagles, if that was what Arrow Maker and Black Buffalo asked. He loved her, he wanted her, and she was the most beautiful creature who ever walked among the Cheyenne!

He cried out to the heavens, thanking Grandfather Eagle for offering one of his own. He thanked the spirit of the eagle that clawed around inside the bag. Never had he been more proud. He would take the eagle to Arrow Maker, and watch the pleased and proud look on Medicine Wolf's face. Then he would ride against the Pawnee and capture more enemy weapons and horses, and take more scalps!

He began his descent from the mountaintop, letting the blood flow from his wounds. He would not wash it away. He would leave it there to dry, to show everyone what he had suffered in order to capture the powerful Grandfather Eagle. He had managed the ultimate conquest, and no one could doubt his worth as a warrior, or as a man who should stand at Medicine Wolf's side!

Chapter Thirteen

Medicine Wolf visited Old Grandmother's burial site at *Hinta-Nagi*. Her clan migrated farther south then, past the burned-out ruins of old Bent's fort, visiting the new stone fort William Bent had built on the Arkansas River, where they traded buffalo and deerskins for more guns and tobacco. They had to be careful how many skins they traded away, for all along their journey they noticed that the buffalo herds were becoming ever smaller and harder to find.

Tempers were not good, for everywhere game was becoming more scarce because of the thousands of travelers from the East. Medicine Wolf's sadness over the signs of destruction was soothed only by the thought of the day Bear Paw had returned with the eagle for Arrow Maker. What a glorious day that had been! Other warriors and women had gathered around him, exclaiming over his brave catch, studying the bloody wounds he had suffered

. . . suffered gladly, just to make an impression on her father.

It had been a moment of great honor for Bear Paw, and great pride for Medicine Wolf. White Horse had watched with jealous eyes, embarrassed that he had already given Arrow Maker a handful of eagle feathers that he had stolen from an eagle's nest, not from a live bird. He had stalked away.

Arrow Maker and Bear Paw's father and uncle had joined Bear Paw in holding down the bird while Arrow Maker took a few of its finest feathers, thanking the bird's spirit and offering a prayer that the missing feathers would grow back soon. They then released the bird, and the missing feathers did not seem to alter its ability to fly. It ascended high into the blue sky, screeching a farewell to them, its great wings casting a shadow on the earth as it passed between them and the sun.

Now Bear Paw rode at Arrow Maker's side, a young man already holding an honored position. Out of respect, he had not mentioned that catching the eagle had anything to do with winning Medicine Wolf's hand. It was simply understood. She was too young for marriage, so it was not discussed, but Arrow Maker was well aware of Bear Paw's intentions. Star Woman found it a source of great amusement and pride every time Bear Paw sat outside their tipi and played his own special love song for Medicine Wolf, using a flute made from a leg bone of a deer.

Medicine Wolf knew the tune well by now, and she hummed it as she walked beside her mother. She could have ridden her horse, the spotted Appaloosa given to her by her brother, but she preferred walking and being near her mother. It was a beautiful day, the kind of day when one could convince oneself that all was right with the world and the future held only wonderful things. Sometimes she wished she could again be the little girl who had picked berries with Star Woman, the little girl who was completely oblivious of the outside world; the little girl who knew nothing of visions and wolf spirits and special gifts, who had no knowledge of white man's ways.

Her thoughts were interrupted when she spotted Summer Moon walking ahead of her. So much had happened since she first returned to her People that she had not had a chance to talk to her good friend. Summer Moon had been with her family visiting a Sioux family during the Sun Dance. Her sister had married a Sioux man, and they had been celebrating. They had left the North later than Medicine Wolf's clan, and had only two days earlier caught up with them. Even so, it seemed to Medicine Wolf that Summer Moon had been avoiding her.

She called out to the girl, but Summer Moon only glanced back at her and kept walking. Medicine Wolf felt a strange alarm. She hurried up beside Summer Moon, leading her horse along. "Summer Moon, did you not hear me? I have hardly seen you since I returned. It is so good to see my good friend again. We will have to build a tipi together again and—"

Summer Moon shot her a dark look that startled Medicine Wolf. "I do not wish to be your good friend any longer. They all think you are so special now. *You* think you are special."

Medicine Wolf was shocked at the words, and she felt a stabbing pain at her heart. "That is not so, Summer Moon," she answered. "You know me better. I cannot help being chosen by the Wolf Spirit. Many times I wish it had happened to someone else, for it is a great burden, and often I feel very lonely. It was terrible for me with the *ve-ho-e*, so terrible that sometimes I cried and was sick to my stomach. I have never known such loneliness. All that saved me was knowing I would one day return to my People, and to my good friend."

Summer Moon scowled, glancing at her again, her eyes moving over her with a hint of jealousy. "I would not mind so much that you are considered sacred, and wise for your age. I would not mind that you are so beautiful, that you are a soldier girl, or that you have lived among the white man and know their language and can write it. Our friendship could be as it always was, if not for White Horse."

"White Horse! What has *he* to do with our friendship?"

Summer Moon tossed her long hair. "Do not pretend such innocence," she told Medicine Wolf. "From the day you left he has hardly looked at me. Even before you left, I saw how he looked at you, saw his eager eyes the night of the blanket dance. I did not care so much then because I was too young to understand. But now I am old enough to care about White Horse as a woman cares for a man. I saw how he watched you when you returned, saw the hunger in his eyes. I saw him speak to you that night after you spoke before the council about the white world. And I saw his jealous eyes when Bear Paw brought the eagle. I know that he also brought eagle feathers to Arrow Maker, and I know why."

The girl's eyes teared, and Medicine Wolf felt embarrassed and frustrated. "But I have no interest in White Horse. Surely you know that."

Summer Moon flashed her an angry look. "Are you saying he is not worthy of you, that he is not a fine warrior?"

Medicine Wolf felt the deep hurt at the look in her friend's eyes. Such hatred! "Of *course* he is a fine warrior," she replied. "Any Cheyenne woman would be proud to be courted by him. But there are things you do not know, Summer Moon. The only one who can own my heart is Bear Paw. Even if White Horse were the most honored warrior among all the Cheyenne, I would still have to go to Bear Paw. It is written in the wind. I cannot tell you how I know this, for it is forbidden. I can tell you only that I have eyes for no other man."

Summer Moon stared straight ahead. "White Horse does not want to believe that. He will keep trying for your hand. And while he does, he hardly knows that I exist. I have loved him for many moons, but he does not bring eagle feathers to my father or look at me the way he looks at you."

A tear ran down Summer Moon's cheek, and there was a terrible hurt in her voice. They both walked on in silence for several minutes, while Medicine Wolf struggled to find her own voice again. "I am sorry, Summer Moon, but it is not my doing. I would like nothing more than to know that White Horse is courting you. But do not hate me for something I have not done. I have missed you. Most of the others avoid me because they seem to think I am too

sacred or special to be their common friend. Old Grandmother is dead, and my Wolf is dead. I had one friend
among the *ve-ho-e*, and now I will never see him again. I
am very lonely sometimes, except for my mother and my
sister. I would like very much to have Summer Moon back
as my good friend.''

The girl sniffed and shook her head. ''No. It would
only be worse. I would know every time White Horse
comes around you and tries to court you. Go away from
me, Medicine Wolf.''

Medicine Wolf felt as though someone was squeezing
her heart with strong hands. She held back as Summer
Moon moved on, and her tears spilled silently down her
cheeks. She remembered Black Buffalo saying something
about her being lonely, remembered him saying she would
have to choose between a loved one and the wolf's paws.
Was this what he had talked about? If she just gave the
wolf paws to White Horse, he would probably be satisfied
and stop trying to win her. But she knew that bad things
could happen to her and to her People if she gave away
what the sacred wolf had entrusted to her. It was very bad
medicine to turn from a spirit gift.

She petted her horse's neck, realizing with even greater
clarity how lonely life was going to be as long as she
possessed the wolf paws and the special powers they
brought. She watched Summer Moon move away from her,
feeling as though she were watching her childhood leave
her forever. Sometimes it was hard to imagine she had
ever been a child at all.

The Cheyenne moved on to Fort St. Vrain, where the
Great Father in Washington had told them to gather for
their annual rations. They had been patient, accepting the
fact that the year before the supplies had been fewer than
promised, and had arrived late. Now their patience was
running out, for again the annuities promised by the Laramie Treaty of '51 were late. Finally Broken Hand Fitzpatrick arrived with the wagon train of supplies, including
more badly needed rifles, and some notes that the Indians
were to use at trading posts to buy things. The notes, so

the Indians understood, could be used by the post suppliers to turn in to the government for money.

Medicine Wolf was told by her father to speak with Agent Fitzpatrick and make sure all promised supplies had arrived. Medicine Wolf had by now resigned herself to being the spokeswoman for her clan when dealing with white traders and government representatives. It was one more burden to the young woman who would rather live the carefree life of her peers, but she knew by now that she would forever hold a certain position among her people, and that position would bring her a loneliness no one else could ever understand. She told herself this was for her people, that she had a responsibility from which she could not turn away.

As usual in such moments, that responsibility caused her to carry out her task in a manner of pride and eloquence. She was learning not to be afraid and shy, learning her people respected her position and her knowledge. And she decided that if she was going to hold such an honorable position, she would do her best and show her people she was worthy of that honor. That meant making sure they were not cheated by the Great Father in Washington, who had ways of easily fooling those who did not understand his language and thinking.

Medicine Wolf studied the monetary notes that were to be exchanged for needed goods. She asked Agent Fitzpatrick why the government did not just give real money directly to the Indians, and Fitzpatrick, surprised by the girl's knowledge of the English language, told her the Great Father was afraid the Indians would not understand its value and might throw it away or lose it.

"You are right that we do not understand its value," Medicine Wolf answered him, "but it is not because we are ignorant, Agent Fitzpatrick." She held the man's eyes squarely, astounding him and the other white traders present with her almost regal presence and her intelligence. "It is because it makes no sense that a small piece of paper can be traded for such valuable things as guns and tobacco. We find it strange what the white man considers of value—gold and paper money, which has no use for eating or wearing or riding; land, which no one can really own. It can only be borrowed for a while."

Medicine Wolf carefully counted out the notes then, making sure everyone got their fair share, but she soon realized that the amount offered was not the same as promised in the treaty. Fitzpatrick explained that the dollar amount promised included paying for the supplies brought out—guns, blankets, flour, tobacco, and such. Whatever was left over was given out equally among the Cheyenne. Medicine Wolf had shopped often enough with Marilyn Prescott to know that what was left would not buy much. She explained the same to Fitzpatrick, as well as explaining that game was becoming more scarce.

"We will need more than this," she told the man, who appeared nervous and irritated at her knowledge. "I learned that every year the American money buys less, that it will take more and more of the paper notes to buy things as the years go by. In the fifty years this money and these supplies have been promised us, the money will be worth nothing, and if our people grow in numbers, the supplies will also not be enough."

Fitzpatrick told her that the White Father's government in the place called Washington had only recently finally ratified the treaty, and that they had changed a few things. The treaty no longer was good for fifty years. Now the White Father's government said the treaty would be good for only ten years, and two of those years had already gone by since the original signing at which the Indians had agreed to fifty years. Fitzpatrick explained that the men in Washington who had changed the treaty wording wanted it re-signed by the Cheyenne.

Medicine Wolf felt disappointment at realizing she had been more right than she had imagined in her prediction that the white men would find a way to twist the words of the treaty. She explained to Arrow Maker what was happening, that Fitzpatrick wanted to read to them a new treaty and wanted the Cheyenne leaders to sign it.

"How can this be?" Arrow Maker asked in surprise. "We already made the agreement! It has been two summers since we had the Great Smoke. All of our people are not even represented this time! We cannot sign now to new promises without all being present, and there should *be* no new agreement! We signed according to what the Great Father promised us in the first treaty. *That* one carries our signatures! We do not need to sign another!''

He turned and explained to the others what had happened, and a restless anger seemed to fill the air. Medicine Wolf told Fitzpatrick to read her the changes in the new treaty, which included sending fewer supplies than promised, as well as changing the years from fifty to ten. The Cheyenne were shocked and angry at the changes, which to them amounted to nothing more than broken promises.

Besides the changes, *all* Cheyenne were expected to meet here, far in the South, every year to collect their supplies, which was quickly becoming an inconvenience for the Northern Cheyenne, who did not like to even be in this part of the southern plains in summer. They were there only to meet with the Arapaho and Kiowa-Apache. They wanted their share of the supplies to be delivered farther north.

Fitzpatrick shook his head. ''Can't be done,'' he told Medicine Wolf. ''The government promise is for only those Cheyenne who agree to stay on the land laid out in the treaty. That means those of you who go north with the Sioux are breaking the treaty and are not allowed these annuities. And you had better know that you'll be in a lot more trouble if the rumor we hear that you're preparing to attack the Pawnee is true. Fighting other Indians is against the treaty.''

Medicine Wolf explained to her father, who went into a rage. ''He speaks of *us* breaking the treaty,'' the man fumed. ''His people have *already* broken it, by changing its words and not giving us what we signed for! For us there *is* no longer a treaty! The Pawnee struck against us first, and they used rifles given to them by the whites! They work for the white soldiers, yet they break the treaty in the worst way! We will not let it go, nor will we abide by a treaty that the white man feels he can change any way he chooses! From now on I will hunt where I choose, make war when I choose, and *live* where I choose! If other of our leaders wish to sign this new treaty and remain here in the South, where it is hot and dry, it is their choice!''

The man stormed away, and other warriors joined in defiant war whoops. They were thirsty for Pawnee blood, and no treaty, whose words meant so little, was going to stop them. White traders backed off in fright as the Cheyenne began rummaging through the meager supplies, taking what they needed.

Medicine Wolf explained to Fitzpatrick how her people felt, and the man just shook his head. "I'm sorry, Medicine Wolf. I'm as angry about this as your father and the others. But I can't do any thing about it, and making more trouble won't help matters any."

"The *white* men have made the trouble," she answered. She turned away. A few of the leaders of the more entrenched Southern Cheyenne approached the agent to sign the new treaty, and Medicine Wolf felt sick inside. Already, as Sweet Medicine had prophecied, her people were becoming divided. She rejoined her own clan, her heart heavy. They divided up their supplies, more warriors now possessing new rifles that they would use against the Pawnee. She knew deep inside that it would not be long before they would use those same guns against the whites, and she could not help thinking about the big guns at Fort Laramie.

They all left, seeing no more reason to talk with Agent Fitzpatrick. They headed west for a meeting with the Kiowa-Apache and Arapaho. It was time to make war against the hated Pawnee! There was no longer any treaty to stop them. The white man had been the first to break his promise. Now the Cheyenne were free to do as they wished.

Medicine Wolf watched anxiously as the warriors rode back into the village after being gone for nearly three weeks. They were returning from the raid against the Pawnee, and many sported bandaged wounds as well as fresh scalps hanging from their lances. Arrow Maker stopped long enough to look down proudly at Star Woman, who touched him and wept with relief to see him back safe. He looked over at Medicine Wolf, handing out a feathered Pawnee tomahawk.

"For you," he told her. "Because of your blessing of the wolf paws upon us before we left, we were victorious!"

Medicine Wolf walked up to him, afraid to ask about Bear Paw for fear it would sound as though she were more concerned about his well-being than about the fact that her father had given her a token of their great victory. She took the tomahawk. "Thank you, my father."

Arrow Maker met Star Woman's eyes again, and Medicine Wolf knew by the way he looked at her that he would carry her off tonight to renew their love. She wondered what such a homecoming would be like for her and Bear Paw, once they were married, if he was indeed still alive. Smiling Girl ran over to her father and hugged his leg.

"Swift Fox brings the horses," Arrow Maker told Star Woman. "We captured many!" He gently moved his horse away from Smiling Girl and rode off to join the rest of the shouting warriors. They rode proudly through the village, enjoying the praise of their women and old ones. Dust rolled from the many horses, and there was an air of general pandemonium throughout the village.

Several families of Kiowa-Apache and Arapaho, who were camped with the Cheyenne, joined in the celebrating. Hot dust filled the air, along with an electrifying excitement. A successful raid against the hated Pawnee was always reason for great joy. Medicine Wolf clung to the tomahawk as her uncles, Two Moons and Red Foot, rode past, then White Horse, who watched Medicine Wolf with a haughty air, hoping she was happy to see him return. He was leading three horses by his own rope, an indication he had managed to steal them from the Pawnee. His father rode beside him, leading four more horses that already belonged to himself and White Horse.

Medicine Wolf met White Horse's eyes defiantly, trying to tell him by her look that he might as well give up on trying to impress her. "I see only three Pawnee horses," she called out haughtily. She knew that White Horse had challenged Bear Paw that he would bring back more stolen horses than Bear Paw would. She prayed that Bear Paw had won the bet, and by the way White Horse's smile faded at her remark, she took hope. She wanted to feel bad about the look of near hurt in White Horse's eyes, sorry for her cutting remark, but when she thought about how Summer Moon felt about White Horse and how he ignored her, she could not feel too much pity for him.

She anxiously watched for Bear Paw. Surely he was all right, for White Horse did not seem very happy. He was followed by White Eagle and Stands Tall, and behind them came Swift Fox, leading four Pawnee horses with ropes. Beside him rode Little Bear, Two Moons' twelve-year-old son, who was a companion to Swift Fox and was learning the warrior way. He had gone along on the raid to accompany his cousin and help tend his war ponies. Now he led Swift Fox's two extra war ponies as well as three more Pawnee horses.

Behind them approached a whole herd of horses, which Medicine Wolf surmised belonged to several different warriors. More young boys helped herd them, along with other older warriors, some Cheyenne, some Kiowa-Apache. Behind them, at last, Bear Paw appeared, white cloth wrapped around his middle. As he approached, Medicine Wolf could see many scalps tied to his lance. He held ropes that led five horses, and his aide, White Otter, a boy of thirteen who all but worshipped Bear Paw, led another six horses.

Medicine Wolf knew by the way Bear Paw led the horses on his own ropes that they were all his, stolen from the Pawnee! He had taken only two of his own war ponies, the one he rode, and the one White Otter rode, boasting that they were all he would need, once he stole many more from the Pawnee. He had been true to his word, but he had also been hurt. Medicine Wolf hoped his wound was not dangerous. She knew by the fact that he had been injured, and the fact that he carried so many scalps and led several stolen horses, that he had counted many coup and had more than outdone White Horse.

Bear Paw rode toward Medicine Wolf, who stood beside her mother. "Look at the many horses he brings," Star Woman told her daughter with an excited smile. "I think he will give some to Arrow Maker. This Bear Paw is becoming a wealthy man, Medicine Wolf. He takes many risks to gain the eagle feathers and more scalps and horses. Why do you suppose he does this," she teased.

Medicine Wolf reddened at the remark, glancing up at

Bear Paw. He gave her a hint of a smile, and she knew he was wishing that tonight he could celebrate with a wife the way the others would celebrate with theirs. The thought of it made her cheeks feel hot, and she looked down until Bear Paw came close to her, handing her a rope.

In surprise, Medicine Wolf looked up to see that at the end of the rope was tied a beautiful black gelded stallion. "It is taken from a Pawnee who was highly respected as a warrior," Bear Paw told her. "Now he is dead, and his horse is mine. I give it to you as a gift."

Medicine Wolf did not feel worthy of such a handsome present. Surely Bear Paw had fought bravely for it, risked his life for it. She could not turn it down, for it would be a great insult to Bear Paw. With a shaking hand she took the rope from him, shivering when their hands touched.

"I . . . thank you, Bear Paw," she told him, keeping her eyes cast down.

"It is in return for the gift you gave me, the gift only you and I know about. I have been looking for something fine enough to give in return. Now I have found it. He is a good, fast horse, but he obeys well."

Her eyes teared and she hardly knew what else to say. "I am deeply honored," she told him.

He turned and rode off, and Star Woman let out a long sigh of exclamation. "Such a gift," she carried on, gently touching the horse as though it were sacred. "It is a fine, strong horse, Medicine Wolf. As fine as any owned by the warriors. Such gifts Bear Paw brings, and it is almost two summers before he could ever take you for a wife. By then your father will be a rich man!"

Medicine Wolf's heart swelled with love. She petted the animal's neck, wondering just how rich *she* would be by then! She already had the Pawnee tomahawk her father had given her, the holy book from the *ve-ho-e*, the sacred wolf paws. She had the Appaloosa her brother had given her, two eagle feathers from her father, which in turn had come from the eagle Bear Paw had caught. She had two wolfskins, and the white beaded tunic Old Grandmother had made for her. She was collecting buffalo skins for her own tipi, and now she had this beautiful black gelding!

What a rich woman she was! Nothing from among the many things the Prescotts owned could match this wealth!

She squinted her eyes against dust as she watched after Bear Paw. This was a good day. This was the way they should live. It had been only three months since she left the Prescotts, but it was as though she had never lived with them. The only memory that she cared to cling to was her friendship with Tom. She was back where she belonged, and it was right. They would winter here, at *Hinta-Nagi*, and then they would go back north and join the Sioux. She breathed a little easier in that there had been no particular trouble over their migration or over their war with the Pawnee.

"I will call him *Nahkohe*," she told her mother, hugging the black gelding around the neck. "He is a gift from Bear Paw, so he will be called Bear."

The horse nuzzled at her neck as though he realized he belonged to her now. He and the Appaloosa mare helped ease the hurt of losing Wolf, although it was not quite the same. Wolf's loss had left an empty place in her heart that could never be filled. She led the horse to the grazing area, where the Appaloosa was tethered. She tied one foot to a stake, using a long rope so that he could graze in a wide circle. She stood back then, admiring her two horses, great wealth for a thirteen-year-old female!

She watched the celebrating from the distance, eager for the scalp dance that was sure to be held later that night. These were good times. As her memory of things Tom had told her began to fade slightly, and as she was more and more removed from that world, she began to believe that maybe the bad things she feared the white man would create would not come to be after all. She watched Bear Paw in the middle of the yipping and shouting warriors. He kept turning his horse in a circle, waving his blanket in a victorious manner.

None of them knew that several hundred miles to the east, in the place the white man called Kansas, and farther north in the place they called Nebraska, railroad surveyors were slowly making their way into Indian country, mapping out the best routes for rails west.

Chapter Fourteen

1854

Medicine Wolf awoke with a start, only vaguely remembering her dream. Big guns, like those she had seen at Fort Laramie, had exploded all around her. White faces had fallen on her, trying to smother her, but then they turned red with blood.

She got up from her mat, walked over to a wooden bowl of water to splash her face, for the dream had left her in a sweat. She was afraid to think of what it might mean. She glanced over at her parents, brother, and sister, who all slept soundly. She pulled on her moccasins and went out, then walked to a stand of trees, where she relieved herself, cleaning herself with fresh leaves.

She walked back toward the village, the dream still haunting her. It was a beautiful summer morning, the air hanging still and a little damp, the day so young that not even the birds were awake yet. She watched the village, thinking how peaceful it looked. The air smelled sweet, and a rising sun lit the sky red and cast a beautiful glow upon the painted tipis. A large herd of horses grazed in the distance, and she felt an eerie feeling that this was a rare sight . . . that peaceful camps and full bellies and this feeling of security would not last.

They were camped only about two miles from a village of mostly Brule Sioux, a few Minneconjous among them. There had been a little trouble lately, started last year when a Minneconju Sioux, who Medicine Wolf decided must have been drunk from firewater, shot at a soldier. Soldiers had come to arrest the man, and some gunfire had been exchanged.

The entire matter had finally been settled, but it had plagued Medicine Wolf ever since, for the soldiers had seemed very eager to charge upon the Indians. The strangest part was, it seemed that if one Indian did something wrong, all the rest of them were blamed and were hunted as a whole. Did the soldiers actually think that a single act by one drunken Indian meant the whole tribe was declaring war?

Because of her knowledge of the white man's way of thinking, she had felt a kind of secret dread ever since the incident. Only a few weeks earlier some of the younger, prouder warriors, Bear Paw and Swift Fox included, had deliberately run off several horses belonging to the white interpreter at Bordeaux's Trading Post, near Fort Laramie. They had not intended to actually steal the horses. They were simply angry with the interpreter, who Medicine Wolf had caught twisting the words of her Father and others when interpreting for soldiers and agents at the trading Post. He had made the Cheyenne men appear ignorant and untrustworthy.

After the incident over the interpreter's horses, several white citizens who lived around the post had formed a war party of their own and had come after the Cheyenne; but when the young warriors took a stand to fight, the frightened citizens backed off. This had fed the ego of the Cheyenne warriors, who had felt quite victorious and figured they had taught the interpreter and the people who were, in their eyes, illegally settled around the post, a good lesson. They were cockier now, sure that most people, and probably even the soldiers, were afraid to go up against Cheyenne Dog Soldiers, or Cheyenne men of any other warrior society.

Medicine Wolf was not so sure. She walked toward the horse herd to check on *Nahkohe* and her Appaloosa, whom she called *Nonoma-e*, which meant Thunder. She would not feel so much alarm over the matter of the mis- understanding over the interpreter's horses if it were not for the presence at Fort Laramie of a new soldier leader called Lieutenant Grattan. Grattan seemed possessed of a strange hatred for her People, and he often threatened them, shaking his fist at them and telling them they had better be careful or he would come after them. He often boasted about how powerful the army was, and he had even said to Arrow Maker once that with only ten men he could defeat the entire Cheyenne nation.

Arrow Maker had only smiled, wise enough to realize that Grattan was obviously very stupid, and quite puffed up because of his uniform. "Perhaps one day he will get the chance to try to prove what he said," he had told Medicine Wolf and Star Woman later that night.

Medicine Wolf had no doubt that Grattan would not need much of an excuse to use the big guns that were kept at the fort. She had half hoped that Tom would be at Fort Laramie when she and her People arrived there, so that she could ask him his opinion of this redheaded soldier who seemed to be much more eager to make trouble than were the Indians. But according to a post trader, Tom Prescott had gone back to the East, and his mother had gone home also for a rest. Reverend Prescott had re- mained behind and continued trying to urge more Indians to come to church and learn the new religion, but he was having little success. Medicine Wolf had not bothered to find the man and talk to him. She had nothing to say to the reverend, and the sight of him brought back too many bad memories. She was glad to be away from the fort again.

A few birds began to sing, and again Medicine Wolf felt it was almost too peaceful. What could all the bloody white faces and the exploding guns of her dream have meant if not some kind of battle? Was it possible there would be trouble over a more recent incident in which a Minniconjou Sioux had killed an old, worn-out, abandoned cow that had belonged to a Mormon emigrant? The man had needed the hide, and the cow seemed of no use to anyone, yet later the cow's owner had complained to the soldiers at Fort Laramie. The Sioux had offered to pay for the cow, but the owner had demanded far more than it had been worth, and the Sioux refused to pay. A Brule chief, Bear That Scatters, had told the soldiers that if the guilty Indian must be arrested that he would be given over to the soldiers if it meant keeping the peace.

Bear That Scatters was a fine Sioux chief who always cooperated fully with the white traders and soldiers, so much so that some of the other Indians, Sioux and Cheyenne alike, sometimes felt he tried too hard to please people they considered lying and treacherous. Ever since the Laramie Treaty had been broken, few Indians had bowed to every order given them by the *ve-ho-e*. After all, it was the white man and his leaders who had broken the treaty, and they were not on this land just because of words on a piece of paper. This was their land, treaty or no treaty, and the whites who were here were lucky they had been allowed to stay!

Medicine Wolf returned to her tipi, rekindling the fire and adding some water and turnips to the pot of leftover buffalo stew that had simmered there all night.

At age fourteen, she had begun helping her mother more and more. Arrow Maker awoke and looked at her. "You are up early, my daughter."

Medicine Wolf continued stirring. "I had a dream." She looked over at her father. "I think there will be trouble between the soldiers and the Sioux because of the settler's cow. I think many soldiers will die."

Arrow Maker rose and pulled on his leggings. "Good."

Medicine Wolf could not help the sick dread that ate at her. "It is not good, Father. If many soldiers die, many more will come to avenge them."

"I am not afraid of any white-eyed soldier."

"I know that you are not. But to kill many of them

might be bad medicine. Do not forget how many more of them there are in the land in the East.''

"I think they exaggerate.''

"Tom Prescott would not lie.'' She sighed, casting a pleading look toward her father. "Father, please promise me that you will not involve our People in a matter between the Sioux and the soldiers. Our own time is coming, and we will need to be strong.''

He met her gaze in mutual understanding. "My daughter is wise and blessed. This morning we will move farther south, try to find the trail of the buffalo. We need more meat. Half the meat we get from the post trader is rotten. If we leave today for the buffalo hunt, we will be far from the fort and the soldiers.'' He pulled on a deerskin skirt. "But do not think I run from them. I know you are right when you say our time is coming. I do not like to think of it, but when I see men like that Lieutenant Grattan, I know that it will not be long before we, too, have problems with them. But let them come to us so that all will know they started the trouble and not us.''

Medicine Wolf nodded, feeling at least a little relieved. She believed as strongly as any warrior that if threatened, they must fight, but she also believed that the white man would actually be glad if the Cheyenne were to start the trouble, so that they could say it was all right to make war against them. The ve-ho-e seemed to have two forms of justice, one for themselves, one for the Indian.

She tasted the stew while back at Fort Laramie an insanely excited Lieutenant Grattan rounded up thirty men and two howitzers, all to march into the Brule Sioux camp and arrest one man who had shot a half-dead cow.

Medicine Wolf worked long, hard hours, but she did not mind, for her people were rich in a new supply of meat and hides. The hunters had found a large herd of buffalo, much bigger than any they had seen in many months. For days the men hunted, risking their lives riding their hunting ponies into the herd as they followed its daily migration, their sure-footed, well-trained mounts managing to avoid prairie-dog holes and buffalo wallows while the men trained guns and arrows at the great, shaggy beasts.

Sometimes it took several lead balls or several arrows to bring down just one cow or bull, and one warrior had lost his life when his pony stumbled and fell. What was left of him after several buffalo trampled over him remained a chilling memory in Medicine Wolf's mind, and she hoped such a terrible thing never happened to her father or brother, or to Bear Paw.

Still, this was the risk that had to be taken to keep children fed and clothed. Now the men rested while the women were faced with the task of cleaning and dividing up the several buffalo that had been killed. No woman complained. This was a time for celebration. All winter, bellies would be full because of this wonderful find! The women went to work in unison, no one trying to claim more than another. It did not matter which warrior had killed the most buffalo, or that some had not managed to kill any at all. The spoils of the hunt were divided equally among everyone, and everyone shared in the work.

Hides were stripped, bones saved, brains scraped, blood drained and cooked, meat divided up, some smoked, some dried, some eaten right away in grand nightly feasts. Bellies would be full now; there would be new hides for tipis, clothing, moccasins, war shields, blankets; bones for glue, for making utensils. Some of the meat would be mixed with berries and herbs and made into pemmican, which would last for months. Bladders made good water bags, teeth made fine jewelry, and tails made fine switches to keep flies away. Not one part of the beasts that Grandmother Earth had seen fit to offer them in such abundance would be wasted. Even the feces would be saved and dried, for it made excellent fuel for hot, nearly smokeless fires. Such fuel was important when living out on the open plains with few trees in sight.

To Medicine Wolf this was true wealth, much more valuable to the Indian than the paper notes the white man's government handed out. This was all they needed, the buffalo, to live in peace on the land they had roamed for centuries. They had left Sioux country, and here along the Smoky Hill there was not a white man in sight. It gave all of them new hope that perhaps the coming of many whites was not so imminent after all. Maybe here they could live more like they had always lived, forget about treaties and handouts, forget about soldiers like Lieutenant Grattan.

Over the next several peaceful days the men smoked their pipes and cleaned weapons, made new war shields, fashioned new arrows. The women cooked, prepared pemmican, cleaned and dried hides, stripped meat to dry, made utensils. It was a happy time. This was the closest Medicine Wolf had felt in a long time to the way she had lived as a little girl, the closest to living as a free Cheyenne in a world where no whites existed.

Tonight the warriors retold their stories about the hunt, its dangers, the trophies they had taken. They all sat around a huge campfire, everyone so full from buffalo meat that they could hardly move, but not too full to boast. The men loved to brag, although it was expected of them never to lie. When Medicine Wolf had told Tom about this ritual storytelling, he had called it "stretching the truth." She had to smile when she thought of it, especially now, as one older warrior carried on about one particularly ornery bull that he claimed had turned on him.

"He wanted to kill me," the man said. "I think he even wanted to eat me and my horse."

The children gasped, their eyes wide with fascination. Medicine Wolf shyly glanced over at Bear Paw, who had told his story straight and true. He had killed five buffalo, a fine accomplishment. She knew that later he would come to her tipi and sit outside, again playing his love song on the flute.

With the hides he had collected from the hunt, and the extra meat he would offer from his own family's share, Bear Paw would have fulfilled every marriage requirement except the fifteen horses. But Medicine Wolf knew that he already owned at least eighteen mounts. By the next summer he would have more. Medicine Wolf knew he was saving the horses for last; he would offer them at a time when he felt Arrow Maker might agree that she was old enough to finally marry.

Medicine Wolf feared that White Horse would spoil her dreams of being with Bear Paw. He had already given

Arrow Maker five horses, and he had killed three buffalo. One more kill, and he would have the required number of robes. He had even begun playing his flute for Medicine Wolf, sometimes coming and playing at the same time Bear Paw played, so that Arrow Maker had to shout at both of them to stop and leave because he could not sleep.

It would have been almost humorous, if not for the fact that Medicine Wolf had lost her best friend over White Horse's attentions. It was even less humorous when at times bad words were exchanged between White Horse and Bear Paw. One night White Horse had even threatened to kill Bear Paw, but when Bear Paw stood his ground in a challenge, White Horse had backed off. Tonight he sat drinking the firewater, something he had begun doing more and more. Medicine Wolf did not like the way he looked at her when he drank the white man's whiskey. She moved to a place behind her mother, where White Horse could not look directly at her.

White Horse lowered his whiskey bottle and watched Medicine Wolf, sometimes hating her, always wanting her, thinking how good it would feel to kill Bear Paw. So far Bear Paw had outdone him in everything. He did not like the thought that the young man might also outdo him in winning the beautiful, powerful Medicine Wolf. He was beginning to feel desperate, beginning to study the ways he could make sure the holy woman and her wolf's paws belonged to him.

If he could get Medicine Wolf alone, he thought, perhaps he could get her to drink some of the whiskey. Whiskey made a person have nice visions. She might let him mate with her, and then she would be his. If she refused, he could easily subdue her and put his life into her, and she would still be required to marry him or face the shame of it. But it was still too soon. He would have to wait until Medicine Wolf was a little more a woman, so all would believe she had taken him willingly.

He rose and stumbled off toward the tipi of Clay Woman, who was shunned by the other women and even her own family because she liked all the men. Various young men brought her meat and hides in return for her favors, and tonight White Horse needed a favor very badly.

Clay Women always welcomed him, and someday, he determined, Medicine Wolf would also be eager for him. He would get rid of all her fancy thoughts about Bear Paw!

The news passed through the Cheyenne camp with such alarm that near silence hung heavy among them. A runner came from a village of Brule Sioux to tell of the terrible events. Lieutenant Grattan had come to arrest the Sioux man who had shot the settler's cow. The Sioux had wanted to wait for the Indian agent to resolve the matter, but Grattan would not listen. The Indians had even tried to offer a mule in payment for the cow, but no matter how hard they tried to reason with Grattan, the officer had become only more belligerent.

He had arrived with at least thirty men and his big guns, which had frightened the Sioux. Finally the soldiers had raised their rifles as though to fire them at the Indians. One of them shot, and the Sioux Chief who had always tried to keep things peaceful, Bear That Scatters, was wounded in three places. The Sioux fired back in self-defense, and Grattan started to retreat when he was attacked from the other direction by a village of Oglala Sioux. A sick feeling came into Medicine Wolf's stomach when the messenger told them that Grattan and every one of his men had been killed!

This was very bad medicine! She felt a mixture of satisfaction that the hot-tempered, hateful Grattan was dead, and dread at what the white man's government might do in retaliation. Surely this would wipe out any remaining ideas that the whites might have that the Laramie Treaty was still valid. Already more whites were beginning to settle on Indian lands. This would only give them more excuses to accuse the Indians of breaking the treaty and saying they could settle anyplace they pleased.

Many Cheyenne braves raised their fists, saying that if this meant war, they were ready. Medicine Wolf knew that many whites thought of her people the way Mrs. Prescott did, that the Cheyenne were bloodthirsty savages. She remembered overhearing one soldier telling another that they should just ''shoot all the Indians and get rid of them the same way they clear out prairie dogs." Now she knew the meaning of her dream. The white faces that had all turned bloody belonged to Lieutenant Grattan and his men.

As though to read her mind, her father moved closer to her. "So, Soldier Girl, your dreams continue to have importance. We must talk to Black Buffalo about this and hold council. We now live closely with the Sioux much of the time. Whatever happens to them because of this massacre could also be visited upon us."

A restless mumbling moved through the village, and the joyous atmosphere they had shared over the past several weeks because of the successful hunt was now tempered by this news. The messenger was offered food and rest, and a council meeting was called to discuss the matter. It was decided that they must continue to try to keep the peace, unless they were attacked and forced to fight. They would go and live among the Southern Cheyenne for the winter, but they would return to the North. Perhaps by then the soldiers would have calmed down. If not, and there was trouble for the Sioux, they would stand and fight beside them. They would spend the winter praying for wisdom and strength.

To the shock and increased worry of the men in council, the runner had even more bad news. "On my way to your village," the man told them, "I came upon an encampment of white men, who offered me food and tobacco. These men did not seem to know about the massacre, for they were friendly toward me. They had with them many strange instruments, which stood on tall legs and through which they looked out across the prairie. A scout who could speak our language a little, and who knew sign language, was with them. He told me that the white men are called surveyors. They were making a picture on paper, deciding the best path for something called a railroad. I saw a picture of this thing. It is like a great iron horse, and is called a locomotive. It pulls a long train of cars full of people and supplies from one place to another. I did not like to see this great iron monster."

Arrow Maker and others turned their eyes to Medicine Wolf. Some whispered among themselves.

"It is as my daughter told us." Arrow Maker spoke

up. "We must continue to listen to her dreams, for she saw the iron horse in a vision. She also dreamed of the killing of Lieutenant Grattan and his men. These are bad times. We must pray constantly, fast, and seek visions. We must stay strong and not cower under the white man."

Medicine Wolf turned away, her heart heavy. How many more dreams would she have, and what terrible things would they show her? She was afraid to dream again for fear of what she might see next.

Black Buffalo called for a smoking of the prayer pipe, and Arrow Maker announced that tonight there would be a meeting of the Dog Soldiers for which Medicine Wolf should be present. There was much to discuss and decide, and her presence always brought them strength and courage and good luck.

The men gathered, a somber silence in the air. The prayer pipe was lit, and the men began passing it around, offering its holy smoke to the four directions, to Grandmother Earth, and to *Heammaihio*, God of the Sky. The days were coming when they would need much strength and wisdom.

Tom Prescott put down his pen again, unable to concentrate on the thesis he was writing about the American Indian, particularly the Sioux and Cheyenne. The newspaper headlines about the Grattan massacre had thrown a new light on things.

"They all ought to be lined up and shot," one student had commented in one of his classes earlier in the day. "Hell, they're just Indians, no different from rabbits and skunks. They've got no feelings."

Tom still felt a stabbing pain at the words. He touched his arm where he had let Medicine Wolf cut it so that he could mourn with her over Wolf. He remembered how she had wept over Old Grandmother, how her family had greeted her when they returned for her.

"In some ways they have more feelings than most of us," he muttered absently. The room was empty and quiet, and he tried to imagine the battle between Grattan's men and the Sioux. He knew by letters from his father that Bear

That Scatters was a peace chief. Surely he would not have deliberately made trouble. Now he was being called a renegade and a liar. The papers were saying the Sioux had deliberately attacked Grattan and his men and viciously murdered all of them for no reason.

No reason? Tom could not believe it. But with no one to speak in their defense, how could the Sioux tell their side of the story? No one wanted to hear it. Already the War Department was trying to decide how the Sioux should be punished for their dastardly deed.

Tom's biggest worry was Medicine Wolf. Was she all right? According to his father, her people seemed to be mixing more and more with the Sioux, joining in their battles, living among them.

He sighed with frustration, eager for the day when he would be finished with his schooling and he could return to the land he had learned to love. He knew it was not just the land that he loved, but one young woman in particular who he did not doubt would be utterly beautiful when fully mature. But his love for her would have to remain his own painful secret, for she was someone who could never share his world. The best he could do was to go out there and help her People the best way he knew how, to do all he could to help bring about some kind of peace that would avoid more senseless death. And for now, all he could do was pray that Medicine Wolf would remain safe, if indeed she was even still alive.

Chapter Fifteen

After the Grattan affair, it seemed to Medicine Wolf that wherever her People went, there was trouble. They continued a policy of not starting battles with the soldiers, and often, even when attacked, they retreated, struggling to continue to show that it was the soldiers and white settlers who started every incident. Their original decision to fight back aggressively in retaliation for every insult from the whites had been tempered by the soldier attack on a peaceful camp of Brule Sioux at Blue Water Creek in the fall of 1855. It was assumed this was in retaliation to the Grattan killings of the year before. This time the big guns had been used. The attack had been vicious, a running battle in which many women and children were killed, and nearly seventy women taken captive. The Sioux village's huge store of food and supplies for the winter was taken by the soldiers, much of it deliberately destroyed.

The fight at Blue Water Creek had shocked the entire Cheyenne nation. Medicine Wolf was astonished to realize the whites were capable of murdering women and little babies, and this was the first time the white man's army had come after Indians with so much deliberate aggression. The whites seemed to almost *want* a fight, and what gave Medicine Wolf and her People the most concern was that it seemed to be the white man's policy that entire villages filled with innocent people should suffer for every minor act against a settler or traveler.

The days of peace and happiness and full bellies were fast dying. Railroad builders were beginning to advance across Indian lands, both in the North along the Platte and in the South along the Smoky Hill. Medicine Wolf and her People had yet to see one of the dreaded iron horses, but the warriors were growing restless and wary, and already they talked of attacking any railroad builders who came into their prize hunting grounds.

It seemed that everywhere they went now they had to be very careful to avoid settlers and soldiers. It was hard to say just how and when things had so quickly turned from the peaceful agreements made in 1851 to these constant skirmishes only five years later; nor was Medicine Wolf quite sure when so many of the young warriors had begun heavily consuming the white man's firewater, drinking it in order to seek visions and to feel even more courageous. They claimed that when they drank the whiskey, their wounds did not hurt so much. Medicine Wolf decided there was something evil about the whiskey, and when she sat in on council meetings of the Dog Soldiers, she advised the warriors not to drink the evil brew.

Some of the young men had scoffed at her, which only made her more sure the whiskey was a bad thing, for these same men had previously always honored everything she told them. The whiskey made them foolish and careless, and during the buffalo hunt in the summer of 1856 four young men lost their lives because they were full of whiskey.

With an aching heart Medicine Wolf was beginning to see a drastic change to the way her People had to live, and in their own attitude. She was only sixteen, and it worried her to think what might lie ahead for her and her children. Good times of peace and prosperity seemed to be quickly disappearing, and her only comfort was that Bear Paw had not yet been badly hurt, nor did he drink the firewater.

Now the hunts took more and more time because of the continuing scarcity of game. When the men were in camp, they were always holding council meetings to decide what to do about this skirmish or that. The women were busier than ever, for the Cheyenne were constantly on the move because of trouble.

Medicine Wolf faced the additional worry of problems with White Horse, who had presented her father with every gift needed to win her hand. When she was fifteen, both he and Bear Paw had openly expressed their desire to marry her, and Medicine Wolf thought that Black Buffalo would finally give permission for her to choose; but the priest had said she was not ready. He had declared there must be one more test to prove which man should claim her, Bear Paw or White Horse.

Medicine Wolf could still feel the terrible disappointment of that day. She most certainly *was* ready to marry! How could Black Buffalo bring her such heartache, after waiting so many years for Bear Paw? And what was the test he spoke of? She had begged Black Buffalo to give Bear Paw permission to marry her, but the man insisted it was not the right time. Now she was sixteen summers, and still she waited for the sign.

"There must be a final reckoning between White Horse and Bear Paw," the priest had told her. "Only in this way will all the others know that Bear Paw is the right one. It will not be just my decision. It will be the decision of all. It must be this way, Medicine Wolf, because you are so highly honored by the People."

He would tell her nothing more, and when Bear Paw and White Horse both began pursuing her with even more intensity, she refused to accept gifts from either one, refused to sit under a blanket with them. She wanted nothing at all to do with White Horse, who was drunk more than he was sober, and who frightened her. And to sit under a blanket with Bear Paw and be allowed only to talk a little, touch a little, was too painful. Because of her refusal, and because of more and more trouble with the whites, she saw less now of Bear Paw than ever, and she worried that maybe he would give up on her. At twenty-four summers, perhaps he would take a different wife, one who did not require so much work and sacrifice to claim.

It was these thoughts that plagued her when she walked to a little creek that meandered south from the Republican River. Her people were camped in one of the few areas where whites were seldom seen. It was becoming more difficult to find such places, and now she realized that this land was not so big after all, for the whites in the East were indeed many. Rivers of them never ceased to flow across the Indian lands. But here along the Republican it was still relatively peaceful and safe, although this place was not a part of the lands supposedly given the Cheyenne in the Laramie Treaty.

She sat down near the creek, unaware that she had been followed by White Horse who ducked behind some shrubs, watching her. She took an eagle feather from her belt, one of those her father had plucked from the eagle Bear Paw had brought him. Her heart was heavy, for she still loved Bear Paw, and she could not endure this distance between them. She was fully a woman now, and womanly desires for the handsome Bear Paw brought near pain to her insides. She studied the sacred feather, remembering the day Bear Paw had brought the eagle, how he was covered with blood. He had suffered greatly just to outdo White Horse and bring a finer gift to Arrow Maker.

She lay the feather aside and stood up, removing her medicine bag and her tunic belt. It was hot, and a swim in the creek would feel good. The brush was thick there, and no one was about; her parents knew she had come here to be alone, so no one would bother her. She unlaced the shoulders of her tunic to let it drop and walked into the cool water.

The creek was wide and deep from a recent rain. She crouched down and shivered as the cold water bathed her. She dunked her head, wetting her hair and cooling her scalp. She smiled and splashed, enjoying the sound of the water, the singing of birds nearby. Finally she left the water, walking to pick up her tunic.

Nearby a drunken White Horse hungrily ogled her naked splendor, the whiskey in his blood making him want her with a violent passion. He studied her slender form, her full, virgin breasts, the patch of hair between her lovely thighs. She turned around, and her hips were round and firm and enticing. While her back was to him, White Horse took advantage of the moment, having already stripped away his weapons and breechcloth while she bathed. On bare feet he walked across the quiet earth.

Medicine Wolf bent down to pick up her tunic. She was stunned then by the tackle, a heavy weight upon her, a strong hand clasped painfully over her mouth. Someone turned her, pressing her back against the grass. A stick poked painfully at her shoulder. Her attacker's weight was instantly upon her so that she could not move. She looked up into the eyes of White Horse, and she knew by the feel of him against her that he was naked!

She began clawing at him, and he grimaced, making a fist and slamming it into her jaw to stun and silence her, giving him time to roll her over and to grasp her wrists and quickly tie them tightly behind her back with a piece of rawhide he had kept between his teeth for just this purpose. Medicine Wolf realized through a daze that he must have been watching her all this time, his eyes seeing her nakedness, the man in him lusting after her.

She gasped when he rolled her onto her back once more and clamped a strong hand around her throat so tightly that she could barely breathe, let alone cry out. His eyes were wild, his smile vicious. "For years I have dreamed of this," he sneered, his face bleeding from her scratches. "After today you will be mine, Medicine Wolf, and so will the wolf paws and the power that comes with them! Black Buffalo has said it will be me or Bear Paw who claims you, that there will be a test. *This* is the test! I will plant myself inside of you, Medicine Wolf, and then you will have no choice but to marry me or face the shame of it and be shunned by your own People! After today Bear Paw will no longer want you, but *I* will! I will *always* want you!"

He maneuvered himself between her legs so that they were spread apart, making it impossible to use them to fight him. She felt his hardness pressing against her, felt the terror of what it might be like to lose her virginity, the horror of being taken by a man she did not want. This could not happen! She belonged to Bear Paw! She wanted desperately to scream, but the blow to her face and his fierce choking left her breathless. It seemed as though her windpipe were crushed, and she thought she might die if he did not release his hand from her throat.

White Horse fumbled at her privates, and she waited for the horror of the inevitable, wondering how she would explain this had been against her will, for everyone knew White Horse had courted her. She had come here alone. He would tell everyone she had tempted him, had bathed in front of him. They would know she had not screamed.

Her eyes were wide with terror, reminding White Horse of a frightened deer. He rose on his knees, showing himself to her. "Now you see a *real* man," he said with a grin. He reached over and grasped the wolf's paws. "I will take you, and I will take *these*!" He tossed them aside and grasped her hips, preparing to shove himself into her, but suddenly a body appeared, seemingly from nowhere, and slammed into White Horse, sending him sprawling.

Medicine Wolf gasped and quickly scrambled farther away, drawing up her knees. Bear Paw had come to her rescue! How much had he seen? She wanted to die of shame! She could not even get to her tunic, for it lay where Bear Paw and White Horse wrestled wildly. Even if she could grab it, her hands were tied behind her back, and she could not possibly get the tunic on. In spite of pain and dizziness, she finally found her breath and managed to get to her knees, then to her feet, stumbling to a stand of brush behind which she could at least hide her nakedness.

She choked and gasped for breath while through the brush she watched the fight. Bear Paw and White Horse rolled and scratched and punched, and finally Bear Paw got to his feet, taking out his knife. He stood in a crouched position, murder in his eyes.

"Rapist," he growled. "Put on your breechcloth and take up your weapon! Today you will *die*!"

White Horse stood naked and panting, his body filthy, his cheeks and eyes still bleeding from Medicine Wolf's scratches. She realized with at least a little relief that the scratches would be proof to the others that she had not willingly submitted to White Horse. She thanked the Wolf Spirit that Bear Paw had come along when he did, for in only another moment White Horse would have taken what she wanted to give only to Bear Paw, except that now White Horse had made it ugly and terrifying.

White Horse, his eyes gleaming with hatred, edged his way over to the shrubbery where he had left his clothes. He tied on his breechcloth, then took his knife from his weapons and faced Bear Paw. Medicine Wolf shivered from her damp, naked condition, but more from fear for Bear Paw. What if White Horse won this fight? Would that mean she belonged to him? Was this the test Black Buffalo had spoken of?

The two men circled each other, gauging, testing, each taking a slice, the other ducking back so that the knife missed. Medicine Wolf gasped when finally White Horse's knife cut a deep gash across Bear Paw's belly. White Horse grinned with deep satisfaction. "She belongs to me, and you know it," he told Bear Paw. "This is the test! When I win this, I will take Medicine Wolf, and that will be the *end* of it! You will be dead, and Medicine Wolf will share my bed."

"*Never!*" Bear Paw growled. He lunged, and the two of them locked wrists, each struggling to hold the other's knife hand away from himself. They seemed almost evenly matched in size. They pushed and strained and sweat, and Medicine Wolf feared Bear Paw would be the worse off because of his wound. He was bleeding badly, and she knew each drop of blood would make him weaker.

Finally Bear Paw managed to push White Horse away, and they circled again, crouching, each man bearing the look of a snarling bobcat ready for the kill. This time White Horse lunged, and when he did, Bear Paw drew his blade across the young man's right arm. White Horse grunted and jumped back, looking at the arm, which began bleeding heavily. With wild eyes and a growl he lunged again, and this time they again locked wrists, pushing, growling, falling to the ground and rolling, White Horse on top of Bear Paw, then Bear Paw on top of White Horse.

Bear Paw strained to make his knife come down into

White Horse's throat, but White Horse managed to keep it inches away from himself while Bear Paw in turn held back White Horse's knife hand. They lay almost immobile for a moment, until White Horse managed to bring his legs up and force Bear Paw over his head in a wrestling maneuver. Bear Paw landed on his back, and in an instant White Horse was on his feet. He landed his knife into Bear Paw's right forearm, pinning it to the earth.

Bear Paw cried out, and Medicine Wolf felt sick. He would surely be killed! White Horse quickly jerked Bear Paw's knife out of his hand and tossed it aside, then pulled his own knife out of Bear Paw's arm. He stood back.

"Now, Bear Paw, you can fight with no weapon," he sneered. "Prepare to die!"

Bear Paw rolled to his knees, grasping his forearm as he got to his feet. Medicine Wolf wanted to weep for him, but for the moment she was too frightened. Both his wounds were bleeding badly, but so was White Horse's arm. They circled again. White Horse slashed at Bear Paw, who kept stepping back, watching White Horse's every move, looking for an opportune moment, his senses ever more alert because he was defenseless.

White Horse lunged then, bringing his knife down and in toward Bear Paw's belly. Bear Paw managed to grab the man's arm just before the blade could be buried in his insides. Medicine Wolf could see fiery determination in Bear Paw's eyes as he jerked White Horse's arm upward, quickly turning the man so that his back was to him, then bringing White Horse's arm around White Horse's own throat, so that it was bent around himself. He managed to shove White Horse's face down into the grass, keeping the arm bent around his throat.

White Horse began screaming as Bear Paw kept pulling and bending until an ugly popping sound came from White Horse's elbow. Medicine Wolf shivered. White Horse dropped his knife, and Bear Paw picked it up, preparing to lunge it into White Horse's back.

"No, Bear Paw," Medicine Wolf called from the bushes. "It is bad medicine to kill one of our own!"

Bear Paw hesitated, blood streaming down his arm and down the front of him. "He *deserves* to die!"

"Not by your hand," Medicine Wolf pleaded. "You will be banished from the tribe and we could never be married! Let *him* be banished for what he has done! The shame of it will be worse than dying."

Bear Paw remained poised over White Horse, considering what Medicine Wolf told him. White Horse was groaning, almost weeping. Bear Paw finally tossed the knife aside and got off White Horse's back: White Horse lay prostrate in agony.

Bear Paw stumbled over to where Medicine Wolf's tunic lay, picked it up, and brought it over to where she hid behind the shrubbery. She sat crouched. "My . . . hands are tied," she told him in a shaking voice.

Bear Paw had already seen enough to feel crazy with the want of her, but he knew that for the moment her shame was great. He walked back to pick up his knife, then came back to her and quickly cut the cords at her wrists. "I saw him follow you, so *I* followed *him*," he told her, his breath coming in pants, his body covered in blood. "I had no bad intentions, Medicine Wolf. I meant only to protect you. I . . . I had to wait until he went far enough that I could prove he meant to bring you great shame. He violated something very sacred by trying to force himself on a holy woman. He will be punished."

He stood up then and handed her the tunic. "Put this on. We will take White Horse before Black Buffalo and tell him what happened." He saw tears forming in Medicine Wolf's eyes. "You did nothing wrong," he assured her, turning away. "And White Horse did not . . . he did not have a chance to take what belongs to me. Already I have forgotten what I saw, for I was too full of hatred for White Horse and a need to help you, to remember. When next I look upon you, as my wife, it will be as though it is the first time my eyes have beheld you."

She pressed the tunic against herself, a tear falling down her cheek. She quickly slipped on the tunic. "You would still want me?" she asked.

She heard a deep sigh. "You are too wise to ask such a question. I have never wanted you more, and I believe this was the test of which Black Buffalo spoke. I fought

for you and I have won." He turned back to face her.
"Enough of talk for now. I am bleeding badly."

She raised her eyes, feeling foolish for hesitating when
he was so badly hurt. "I am sorry, Bear Paw. I did not
think. We must hurry and tell Black Buffalo and get help
for you."

He turned to walk over to White Horse, kicking his
body over onto its back. White Horse screamed with pain
as his arm flopped away from him, his forearm completely
separated from his upper arm, except for the skin and ten-
dons. Bear Paw only grinned at the man's obvious hideous
pain. In spite of his dark skin, White Horse looked pale.

Medicine Wolf emerged from behind the shrubbery.
Bear Paw looked over at her, and their eyes held for a
moment, saying all that needed to be said. "Go and get
the Shaman," he told her, "and Black Buffalo. I do not
think White Horse can walk just yet. The Shaman can tend
to all of our wounds, and Black Buffalo can decide what
should be done about this."

Medicine Wolf lowered her eyes and headed toward
the village. Bear Paw called out to her, and she turned.
"Remember that you did nothing wrong," he told her.
"You are going to be my wife, Medicine Wolf. I will wait
no longer. And when Black Buffalo comes here and others
follow, I do not want to see shame in your eyes. Hold your
head proudly and tell the truth. Only White Horse should
suffer any shame. My woman is wise and proud and
strong."

Their eyes held and she nodded, feeling a sweet rush
of excitement at him referring to her as his woman. *"Ai,"*
she answered. She turned and ran toward the village.

They stood before the council—Medicine Wolf, her jaw
showing a bruise and swelling, her chin held proudly as
Bear Paw had asked; White Horse, his right arm heavily
bandaged and tied to his side so that it would remain immobile while his elbow healed, his face bearing scratches
from Medicine Wolf's fingernails; and Bear Paw, his belly
and his own right arm bandaged.

Black Kettle had called a meeting of the elders and

most prominent warriors. The pipe had been passed, and it was time to decide what to do with White Horse. Medicine Wolf was required to tell her story, and although it was difficult to tell the details, she did so, for she knew the council must know everything that White Horse did. Her eyes stung with tears, but she did not hang her head.

The men in council vented grunts and remarks of disgust. Arrow Maker looked ready to kill.

Bear Paw was called upon to give his version, to be sure it coincided with Medicine Wolf's story. It was important that the stories all matched, important to be sure that Medicine Wolf had not deliberately tempted White Horse. White Horse also spoke, and because of the scratches on his face, he had little choices but to tell the truth. He tried to blame it on the whiskey he had drunk, saying the spirit inside that particular bottle must have been an evil one.

Medicine Wolf faced him defiantly. "It was not the whiskey," she said boldly. "It only gave more courage to be a coward!" He flinched at the insult. "You have thought about this for a long time, White Horse! Many times you have threatened me, warned me that I would never belong to Bear Paw!"

Summer Moon watched with mixed emotions. She still loved White Horse, and it hurt to know he had lusted after Medicine Wolf; but it was obvious Medicine Wolf had fought him, and she realized then that Medicine Wolf had truly never wanted any man but Bear Paw. She was sorry and ashamed that White Horse had attacked her, yet she also felt sorry for White Horse, who she was sure had been tricked by the evil spirits in the firewater. She wanted to go to him, to comfort him.

Black Buffalo rose, walking around the inner circle. "I spoke of a test," he told them. "I knew that it would come to this, and that Bear Paw and White Horse would have to fight for Medicine Wolf's hand. It is good that Bear Paw did not kill White Horse, for that would have been bad medicine. Now that the final test is completed, I can tell all of you that Medicine Wolf could never have taken any other man for her own. Long ago, when she was only six summers, she saw Bear Paw in a dream. He was a man and she was a woman. I knew then that this meant Bear Paw was to one day walk beside her.''

Everyone murmured and stared at Medicine Wolf and Bear Paw, and White Horse's eyes grew narrow with anger.

"Likewise, Bear Paw had a dream about Medicine Wolf. He was an injured bear, and a wolf came to lick his wounds. I knew that the wolf was Medicine Wolf.''

"Why was I not told of this?'' White Horse seethed. He glared at Bear Paw. "You let me make a fool of myself! If I had known of this vision, I would not have brought gifts to Arrow Maker and risked my life many times to obtain the things that were required!''

"You know neither a man nor a woman is allowed to speak of such a vision,'' Black Buffalo told him. "If a vision is one that is a warning, something to guide the People, it must be told. But if it is personal, such as the visions the warriors have from suffering the Sun Dance, or one that tells of a man's personal future, it is not to be told, except to me. The only way to be sure of the true meaning of Medicine Wolf's vision was to let you and Bear Paw, and any other warrior who chose, court her. That is why when Bear Paw came to me for my approval, I turned him away and said there must be another test. Now that the test is over, now that Bear Paw has proven his worth, and you have proven your shame, the vision can be revealed.''

White Horse whirled to face Arrow Maker. "I wish to take back my wasted gifts! I gave you scalps and horses and eagle feathers!''

Arrow Maker, his heart full of hatred for what the young man had tried to do to his daughter, rose, an imposing figure compared to White Horse, for Arrow Maker was still strong, and much more filled out and brawny. He was a weathered, tested warrior, and few cared to challenge him.

"I give you nothing,'' he growled. "Your gifts were given in good faith, and accepted as any father would accept things given in courtship of his daughter! If you had been an honorable man, White Horse, I would consider returning some of the things, but even then I would consider it an insult! You should be ashamed to ask for them!''

"I think he should *die*," Swift Fox put in, furious at what White Horse had tried to do to his innocent sister.

White Horse moved his eyes to scan the circle of warriors, feeling helpless. He knew he had done something as shameful as any Dog Soldier could do. He looked at Medicine Wolf, remembering how she had looked, wishing now more than ever that he had been successful in planting himself inside her and claiming her! If he had done so, and then learned of this secret vision, he would have cast her out and let her live a life of shame, labeled a bad woman by her own People. Their eyes held, and it irritated him that she showed no shame, or even fear. He stepped closer to her, and Bear Paw moved to stand beside her defensively.

"One day," White Horse told them both, "you will both pay for your treachery. It is *I* who have been shamed this day!''

"You shamed yourself," Bear Paw sneered. "We bring our own troubles upon ourselves when we do not obey the spirits and the laws of our People.''

"I say White Horse should be banished from our village," Arrow Maker said. "I say he should also be banished from any other Cheyenne village, north or south. He should not even be allowed to live among the Sioux or the Arapaho!''

"There is no other tribe who would take me," White Horse argued. "I would be an outcast, a man without a home!''

Arrow Maker only smiled wryly. "A just punishment." The man turned. "I ask all who agree with me to rise.''

All, including White Horse's own father, rose to express their agreement. White Horse's jaws flexed in anger, and his eyes seemed to tear. Arrow Maker turned to face him. "It has been decided. We will send runners to the other villages and to the Sioux and Arapaho so that they will know you are not honorable enough to be welcomed into their villages.''

Summer Moon felt like crying. To her, the punishment was too severe.

"You will leave us yet tonight," Black Buffalo put in. "Gather your things, White Horse."

"But I am injured! I need time to heal!"

Black Buffalo stepped closer, his eyes narrow slits. "You have heard the punishment. Leave tonight, or I cannot be responsible for what Arrow Maker and Swift Fox might decide to do to you."

White Horse moved his eyes to Arrow Maker, then to Medicine Wolf's brother. He knew his life was in danger if he stayed much longer. He turned to face Bear Paw once more. "We will meet again, Bear Paw. Perhaps it will not be until far in the future, but we will meet again, and then I will prove who is the better man!"

"That has already been proven," Bear Paw answered haughtily.

White Horse whirled and stormed away. Black Buffalo turned to the rest of the warriors then, raising his arms and looking at the heavens for a moment, then looking at Arrow Maker. "I now give my approval of Bear Paw as a husband to Medicine Wolf. The final decision belongs to you and your daughter. Bear Paw has brought all the required gifts and more. Only your permission is left, and we shall have a marriage ceremony. It must be done according to the law, for Medicine Wolf is holy, a Soldier Girl with special gifts. This is an honorable and sacred union. It will take much preparation."

Arrow Maker rose, facing Medicine Wolf. "Do you wish to take Bear Paw for your husband?"

Her eyes teared, and her blood rushed with anticipation and apprehension. She felt her cheeks growing hot, felt Bear Paw's eyes upon her. If she said yes, the ceremonies would begin the next day, and by tomorrow night she would belong to Bear Paw. The thought of what that meant brought a nervous excitement, and pleasant urges deep inside. How could it seem so horrible with White Horse, and in the next moment be thought of as something of ecstasy with Bear Paw? She knew instinctively Bear Paw would be loving and gentle and patient with her.

"Ai," she answered. "I wish to be the wife of Bear Paw." She heard Bear Paw breathe deeply from delight.

"Then so be it," Arrow Maker answered. "I declare you of age, and I give my permission." He raised his fist and let out a war whoop of celebration, and others joined in. Medicine Wolf could not bring herself to meet Bear Paw's eyes, but he moved a big hand to wrap around her small one, and he squeezed it lightly.

At his own tipi White Horse angrily flung some things together and stuffed them into his parfleche. His mother, ashamed, refused to look at him. Her heart was full of pain, and silent tears slipped down her face. This was her beloved son, but he had brought shame to himself and his family. Even so, she would always love him. He dragged his parfleche and bedroll outside, awkwardly trying to prepare his horse for his departure. With one arm it was difficult, but he knew no one would help him. Then he noticed someone watching him, and he turned to see Summer Moon standing a few feet away.

"Take me with you," she asked. "You need help, White Horse." She was nervous and embarrassed, and she knew that to run away with White Horse was a shameful thing, and would mean she would be a woman without a home, but she could not bear the thought of him going away without her. "For many summers I have loved you," she told him boldly. "I will be a companion to you in every way. I can cook for you, prepare your pony, help herd your other horses, pack your things, clean your weapons, carry wood for you . . . be your . . . lover. Why did you spend so much time on one you could never have, when here is one who would have come to you whenever you asked?"

White Horse looked her over, thinking how plain she looked compared to Medicine Wolf. And she had no special powers. Still, he needed the help, and she was a woman. Any woman could satisfy a man's sexual needs, and this one would do whatever he told her. If she displeased him, he could vent his anger on her and the foolish thing would probably come right back and share his bed.

"Go and get your things," he told her coldly. "Then come here and help me finish loading my own. Do not expect too much from me, Summer Moon. I have no love for you."

"I do not expect it. After a while you will forget Medicine Wolf and learn to love me, for I love you more than she ever would have."

White Horse felt a hint of pity for her, yet her simpering willingness annoyed him. "I will expect you not to speak unless spoken to."

"I understand."

"I will bed you whenever I wish. I will expect you to cook for me when I am hungry, build a tipi for us when we are in one place for more than a day, tend to my horses, carry the wood, keep my clothes repaired and make new ones for me, clean my weapons. I do not want arguments from you, especially when I wish to drink the firewater. Some women object to this. I will not be without the firewater."

She nodded. "I will do all the things you ask of me."

He looked her over, thinking what a weak, foolish woman she was, little realizing the amazing strength she truly possessed. "Then you are my woman. Hurry and prepare yourself. I must leave soon."

Summer Moon hurried away, her heart racing with anticipation. She would take White Horse on any terms, for in spite of what he had done, he was a handsome, accomplished warrior. If he had no home with his People, they would make a new home together, and he would know that he was loved.

Chapter Sixteen

Medicine Wolf clung to her father's arm as he walked her to the edge of the village, where Bear Paw waited. Bear Paw would take her to the wedding tipi Medicine Wolf and her mother had erected out of sight of the village, along the river, a peaceful, pretty place, where they could be alone. It was nearly dark, and at last she would sleep the night in Bear Paw's arms! The thought brought a mixture of anticipation and apprehension. The splendid Bear Paw would be her husband!

They came closer, and Bear Paw stood next to the white stallion he had recently captured from a herd of wild horses. It was a magnificent animal, fitting for this grand occasion. Medicine Wolf was sure he had never looked more handsome. He wore bleached buckskins, the leggings and fringed shirt beaded by his own proud mother, Little Bird. His long black hair was tied at the side of his head, beads woven into it. A bone hairpipe necklace accented the muscles of his neck. Such a magnificent war-

rior he was! Medicine Wolf could hardly believe that after
this day she would truly belong to him, having the honored
place of a first wife. She wanted to shout and sing. Could
any woman on earth be as happy as she was today?

She watched his eyes fill with pleasure as he looked
upon her. Yes, today she was a woman. She wore a new
white tunic her mother had made for her, for she had out-
grown the one Old Grandmother had made so many years
before. Her wedding tunic was covered with circular designs of colorful beads, little bells tied into the long fringe
at the sleeves and hem. Star Woman had worked on the
dress for many months, in anticipation of her daughter's
marriage. The dress represented her mother's love, for to
get deerskins so white and soft was not an easy thing, and
the beadwork was the result of many, many hours of in-
tricate labor.

Medicine Wolf's hair hung long and straight, a bright,
beaded headpiece tied into one side. On the belt of her
dress she wore her little medicine bag containing the wolf
paws, but she would not need their magic this night to
keep her happy. There was only one tiny bit of sadness to
this day, and that came from thinking how Summer Moon
had run away with White Horse. She suspected White
Horse would not be kind to her friend. And then there was
the sad fact that Old Grandmother could not be here for
this splendid occasion.

Black Buffalo stood beside Bear Paw. When Arrow
Maker came close and held out his daughter's hand to her
chosen husband, Black Buffalo chanted a prayer to *Maheo*
to bless the marriage with much love and happiness. Bear
Paw took Medicine Wolf's hand and could feel her trembling. He squeezed her hand more firmly, giving her a
smile that told her never to fear him.

Black Buffalo finished, and Bear Paw captured Medicine Wolf's gaze as he spoke his vows.

"Forever I will love you," he told her. "I will provide
for you and protect you. Your vision has been mine, and
mine, yours. We have been one in heart and spirit for
many years. Now we will be one in body."

The words made Medicine Wolf feel hot all over, and
she struggled to find her own voice. "And forever I will

love you," she repeated. "I have loved you since I was but a child and you were part of my vision. I will keep your tipi warm and provide you with many sons who will one day become great warriors like their father."

"It is done," Black Buffalo told them. "Medicine Wolf now belongs to Bear Paw." He gave out a piercing cry, signaling the village.

Medicine Wolf and Bear Paw both smiled as those in the village whooped and shouted in return, expressing their joy. Black Buffalo and Arrow Maker left them. There would be much feasting and celebrating in the village this night, but the newlyweds would not be there. Already they could hear drumming as Bear Paw took hold of Medicine Wolf and lifted her with ease onto the back of his horse. He mounted up behind her, putting strong arms around her and riding off into a thick grove of trees, toward the wedding tipi.

Finally, after all these years and all their dreams, they belonged to each other. They reached the secret place that belonged only to them, and Bear Paw lifted her down. Everything they needed was here—food, extra clothing, all was prepared. Bear Paw took his straw-filled saddle and the blanket from his horse and tied the animal to a tree. Medicine Wolf waited beside the tipi, her heart pounding, not sure just what he expected of her this first night. Would he understand her secret fears? White Horse's attack had left its stinging memory, had spoiled her vision of what this moment should be.

Bear Paw had said nothing all the way there. He had simply kept one strong arm about her waist, his lips caressing her hair. He came to her now, standing in front of her, drinking in her beauty with his eyes.

Medicine Wolf felt a sudden overwhelming urge to cry. She struggled against it. What a terrible thing to do on her wedding night! She saw Bear Paw frown at the sight of her quivering lips and misting eyes.

He reached out and touched her face with a big hand. "So," he said, "you think I would just quickly take you for my own pleasure?" He pulled her close, crushing her against him. "I am not White Horse," he told her. "I have waited for this moment for too many years to let it be anything but perfect. No, my wife, I will not take you tonight. Tonight I will only hold you." He moved a hand to the shoulders of her tunic, untying the dress. "But I wish to look upon my beautiful wife."

She shivered, and silent tears of joy mixed with anger at herself for crying slid down her cheeks. He stepped back from her slightly, letting the dress fall. She heard him suck in his breath, but she could not bring herself to meet his eyes. Fire ripped through her when he touched a breast with the back of his hand.

"I am greatly honored," he said, his voice gruff with emotion. "Not only is my wife a sacred woman with great powers, but she is also the most beautiful Cheyenne woman who ever walked." He came closer and picked her up in his arms, carrying her inside the tipi.

A morning mist made the broad horizon beyond the river a gentle haze of green and gold, a soft, almost unreal scene. Medicine Wolf stood in front of her wedding tipi, where Bear Paw still slept. It still seemed incredible to her that he had kept his promise and had only held her last night. It was such a sweet, comforting feeling, and she knew she could always trust his word. But now she worried she might have disappointed him by not yet being fully a wife to him.

She walked farther away to pick up some wood for a fire. She should make Bear Paw something to eat. It seemed men were always hungry, or so it was with her father and brother. They would be camped there for one full week, remaining apart from the rest of the village, talking, getting to know each other. This was their special time. They would think only of happy things, and they would try hard to make a baby. That was most important. She was eager now for a child of her own, and nothing would make her prouder than to give Bear Paw a son. But that meant she must stop being afraid of mating. Last night her husband had shown her she could trust him. Now she would have to trust him to make a woman of her and not be afraid of the pain.

She turned to go back to the tipi when she saw him

standing at the entrance, wearing only his breechcloth. His near-naked splendor almost took her breath away. His right forearm was still bandaged, but he had removed the wrappings from his middle. The long red scar across his belly from White Horse's knife only reminded her of how much he loved her, how he had fought for her. She met his eyes, feeling suddenly weak and hot. She wished she still wore the white tunic, but this morning she had changed into a plainer dress, not wanting anything to happen to the special dress her mother had worked on for so long.

She moved closer to him and set down the wood, and she knew by the look in his eyes that he was a man wanting his woman. She told herself she would make him wait no longer. He walked close to her and took her hand. "We are friends, but still we are not lovers," he told her softly. "Last night I showed you I make no demands, for I honor you. But you are so beautiful, my wife, and I yearn to show you my love in every way."

Medicine Wolf wondered if she might faint. "It is not you that I fear," she answered, her voice sounding small and far away. "Nor do I fear becoming a woman. The only thing I fear is that I will not please you."

He put a hand to her chin, forcing her to look up at him. "I am your husband now. You can look me in the eyes, Medicine Wolf." She studied his handsome face as he spoke, the straight white teeth, the true dark eyes, the way his full lips moved as he spoke. "How could you think you might not please me," he asked her. "Never have I beheld such beauty. And our hearts have been as one since you were but a child. Last night we talked of many things. We know each other's dreams and visions, each other's desires, each other's hearts. All that is left is to know each other's bodies. And I promise you, Medicine Wolf, that in not too many days, perhaps only hours, you will want to share bodies as eagerly and as often as I. Do you think you are the only one who worries that you will not please? I, too, want to please you."

She smiled in surprise, her eyes moving over his magnificent frame. "How could you think . . ."

He put a finger to her lips. "Let me make love to you,

my wife, before I die from the want of you. Last night
was more painful for me than any injury I have ever suffered.''

She swallowed, realizing it would be almost cruel to
tell him no, nor did she want to. There seemed to be fire
in his fingertips when he touched her shoulders to untie
her tunic. She let it fall away from her, and she wondered
if he could hear her heart pounding, hoped that her legs
would not grow so weak that she fell to the ground. She
lowered her eyes again and felt his own eyes moving over
her, drinking in her nakedness.

She was at his mercy now, but it was not like with
White Horse. It was beautiful; gentle. He scooped her up
in his strong arms as though she were a mere feather and
carried her into the tipi, where he laid her on their bed of
robes. She started to curl up, but he asked her to lie still.
His eyes looked watery with a mixture of desire and near
worship. "I have never seen such a beautiful creature,"
he told her, his own voice strained. He turned and dipped
his hands into a wooden bowl holding a mixture of water
and fragrant oils from the stems of certain flowers that his
mother had prepared for him. She had put it in a water
bag for him, telling him it was good to use to relax his
new wife and take away her fears. He had poured it into
the bowl before coming for Medicine Wolf, determined
that before the sun was fully risen, he would have laid his
claim to her.

He turned back to her, touching her shoulders with his
oiled hands. "Close your eyes and think only of good
things," he told her. "Your muscles are tense, my wife,
like mine get before going into a battle." He leaned closer,
his hair loose now, shrouding her face as he touched his
cheek to hers. "This is not a battle, my love. This is the
most wonderful thing we will ever know."

She closed her eyes as he asked, and he began a gentle
massage over her shoulders, down her arms. It was a wonderful feeling. She began to lose her inhibition, feeling
bolder, happy that he was pleased with what he saw. His
hands moved back up her arms, down over her breasts.
She breathed deeper at the touch, fire moving into her

blood. Bear Paw was touching her bare breasts for the first time! His thumbs caressed her nipples, arousing them.

He moved his strong hands farther down, over her belly. She felt him leaning closer, felt a warm moistness at one nipple as he gently tasted it. She gasped at the new sensation the touch created in her. She actually ached for him to touch her other breast. She opened her eyes, and he looked at her, a wild hunger in his own dark eyes. She reached up and grasped his head, bringing it down to her other breast, arching up to him as he tasted of it fully, pulling at it like a hungry calf.

Never had she known such ecstasy, nor had she had the feeling of such power, to know that she could make a man like Bear Paw ache for her this way. She began to realize a woman could have a certain hold over a man in moments like this, and she remembered how her own father, fierce warrior that he was, sometimes seemed like a child around Star Woman.

Bear Paw moved his lips over her belly, licking her, making her groan with the want of him. This first time, she realized, the power was really his, for only he knew what to do. This was all new to her, but she suddenly felt a fierce jealousy for Clay Woman, who she suspected was the one who had taught him these things.

He moved his oiled hands over her thighs, her knees, her calves, her feet, back up her legs. She shivered and moaned when he gently urged her legs apart. "Never have I wanted a woman this much," he said in a near whisper, moving a thumb over that secret place that she had never let any man see before. He touched something that made her gasp. He kept caressing her there, making beautiful circular motions that made her wild with desire for him. He untied his breechcloth and tossed it aside, moving between her legs.

Medicine Wolf opened her eyes, meeting his own eyes boldly as he rubbed his hardness against the magic spot he had aroused with his thumb. He kept up the intimate massage until she felt a wonderful explosion deep inside that made her gasp and arch up to him. A light smile of victory moved over his face, and she knew he had done something magical to her and was pleased that he had done it right. He moved his arms under her knees so that her legs were fully open, resting outside his arms. He grasped her bottom then, massaging it for a moment.

"The pain does not last long," he told her.

She boldly moved her eyes to drink in his manly splendor, and it reminded her of a magnificent stallion. She wondered how he was going to fit inside her, but in the next moment he proved that he could. He pushed himself deep, and she cried out in pain and shock. It felt as though he had set fire to her insides. It was done now, and he was lost in her. She would bear the pain, for she could see that he was greatly pleased. He remained on his knees, grasping her hips and moving rhythmically, his breathing quick, his nostrils flared, every thrust bringing a moan from his lips.

He was soon finished with her, and she was surprised to realize she could feel his life spilling into her. She hoped his seed would take hold and she would soon be pregnant with his son. He shivered, stretching out on top of her then, remaining between her legs. He rubbed his chest against her breasts and licked her neck.

"It feels so good to touch your skin to mine," he groaned. "Most of all, it feels good to be inside of you. You have pleased me greatly, my wife."

She swallowed back the pain, but a tear slipped out of one eye. Bear Paw rose to his elbows and saw it. He wiped it with his fingers. "I have hurt you."

"It is to be expected. My mother told me it would hurt."

"But not for long. Did she tell you that too?"

Medicine Wolf sniffed. "*Ai*. I know that she spoke true, for she is always eager for my father."

Bear Paw smiled. "And soon you will be eager for me." He bent his head and tasted her breast again. He had not pulled himself away from her, and now she could feel him swelling inside of her again. She thought it strange that it could hurt so, yet be so exciting. "We will do this again, my wife, and then I will give you time to heal." He kissed at her breasts. "We will be here many days. By the time we leave, you will know every part of me, and I will know every part of you." He met her eyes. "And you will want me this way. Sometimes it will be *you* who comes after *me*."

He grinned, and Medicine Wolf knew, in spite of the pain, that he was right. She leaned up and kissed his nipples, then lay back as he began again the rhythmic penetration. Outside, the mist began to lift, and in the distant village her People began their daily routines, some of them still weary from a full day and night of celebrating. Far off on a distant hill a wolf howled, something that was never heard this time of morning. Medicine Wolf and Bear Paw both knew it was a good sign. They were one now, and it was good.

Medicine Wolf's screams and laughter filled the air as Bear Paw splashed her. She jumped up to run from him, and he allowed himself the pleasure of watching her nakedness for a moment, studying her firm, round bottom and slender legs. He wondered if he would ever tire of looking at her and could not imagine that he would.

A bath in the cold creek had turned into a dunking and splashing battle, and now she teasingly dared him, looking back once and kicking at the water with her feet. He rose and ran after her, and she screamed again. In seconds he was upon her, gently tackling her and landing with her into the soft bed of the stream.

"Now you are my captive," he told her.

She lay with her hair in the water, and she smiled, looking up at him. "Promise me you will never take another, not a captive, not another wife."

"Why would I want either when I have you?"

Her smile faded slightly. She suddenly remembered her dream of standing by a stream, a wolf on one side and a man on the other. The man had reached for her, but she had chosen the wolf. Black Buffalo had told her one day she would have to choose . . . No, it could not be. She was Bear Paw's wife now. Nothing could change that.

"I would not want to share you," she told him. "Or ever live my life without you."

"And you are enough woman for any man." He

rubbed against her. "Tell me that now you have forgotten the white man called Tom Prescott."

She frowned. "Tom was a friend, a blood brother. He was never anything more. Many times I spoke to him about you."

"He wanted you. I could see it in his eyes."

She smiled softly. "You are jealous of a *white* man!" She splashed him. "How could you think any *ve-ho-e* could ever mean to me what *you* mean to me! He is no warrior. He has never counted coup or taken scalps or caught the eagle with his bare hands!"

Bear Paw finally grinned again, pride shining in his eyes. "*Ai.* I will always remember the look on White Horse's face the day I brought Arrow Maker the eagle!" He grasped her hair tighter in his hands, moving himself between her legs. "I would have killed him before I would ever let him touch you the way I have touched you."

She reached up and traced a finger over the scar on his cheek. "And *I* would have wanted to die if he had. I belong only to you, Bear Paw. There was never a thought for White Horse, and Tom Prescott was a white man with a good heart who was my friend when I had no one else. But you are my *best* friend. More than that, you are my lover."

He bent his head, licking her nipples, which were taut from the cool water. The feel of his tongue aroused her to the point of ecstasy, as it always did. He seemed to always know just the right places to touch and taste, making her want him with an intensity that surprised even her. Just as he had promised, the pain had left her, and now being one with him was the most wonderful, exotic act she had ever known. She had boldly let him use her body to his full pleasure, letting him explore, taking whatever position he asked. He had even let her be the conqueror, the one to master him by being on top and riding him like the great stallion that he was. When he let her take him that way, she felt wild and free and victorious, her head flung back, her body displayed before him in naked splendor.

She gasped when he entered her now. She lay in a shallow part of the stream, soft mud at her back, water running over her breasts. Its chill did little to cool the heat

Bear Paw brought to her blood. He had a special way of rubbing against the secret spot he had toyed with that first time with his thumb, so that when he was mating her, she again felt the exotic urges deep inside that made her cry out with pleasure, and made her insides pull at him in tight spasms that seemed to please him greatly.

This was a wonderful thing, this mating. She wondered now why she had ever been afraid of it, and she was sure no other man was quite as perfect as Bear Paw. His many scars only made him more desirable, for he was a proven warrior with many scalps and stolen horses to his credit. They had waited for each other for ten years, ever since she was six years old and he was only fourteen. So much had changed since that time she spent on the mountain, but her destiny of belonging to Bear Paw had never altered.

Again his life surged into her. How many times had she taken his seed? Surely his life was already beginning to grow in her belly. By this time next year she would give him a child, she was sure.

He pulled away from her, and they both washed again. "We must go back to the village tomorrow," he told her. "It is time to go north and join the Sioux. I do not think we will come back here so often anymore."

She sat down in the stream beside him. "It is hard to know where to go now. Wherever we go, there is trouble."

"The Sioux are strong. In the South the railroad comes ever closer, and the Cheyenne who stay there grow weaker. Black Kettle is a good man, a peace chief, but he is too ready to do whatever the white man tells him. I cannot live that way, nor can your father. We follow Arrow Maker, not Black Kettle. It is good that we go back north."

"I know." She met his eyes. "I do not want to go north or south, or even go back to the village. I wish that you and I could stay right here forever and never have to face what is to come."

"Only good things will come," he tried to assure her. He touched her hair. "We are still strong, Medicine Wolf. And you have the wolf's paws. They will *keep* us strong."

Her eyes teared. "This place will always be special to me. It is here I have known a kind of happiness I fear I will never know again."

He shook his head, "As long as we are together, the happiness you feel now will stay with you. This place will always be with us, in our hearts and memories. Do not look so sad, Medicine Wolf. It pains my heart to see tears in your eyes. Your vision has shown you that we will always be together, and that is all that matters."

She studied his handsome face. "*Ai.* As long as we are always together, life will be good. And soon I will give you a son, Bear Paw. It is all I pray for."

He grinned. "And he will be fine and strong."

"And handsome like his father."

"Full of strength and wisdom like his mother."

"I am so happy, Bear Paw."

"It is the same for me. In all my battles against the Crow and the Pawnee, against White Horse, in all the times I have felt the thrill and excitement of the hunt, I have never enjoyed the taste of victory as much as how I felt the first time I was inside you. When I took you for my own, I felt more of a man than in anything else I had ever done. I am honored to be able to say that Medicine Wolf, the most beautiful and sacred Soldier Girl among the Cheyenne, is my wife."

She pressed her hands against his chest. "And I am proud to call the most honored warrior among the Dog Soldiers my husband."

Bear Paw rose, picking her up in his arms and carrying her out of the stream to their tipi to dress. Medicine Wolf clung to him, savoring the moment, resting her head on his strong shoulder and wishing they could always live like this, in their own quiet little world, unaffected by the troubles that lay just beyond this little stream and this little patch of trees that had been their home for seven days.

White Horse rode through fort grounds and approached the white scout, who he knew understood Cheyenne. He was the hairy-faced man whose white friends had nicknamed him "Blondy," and the Cheyenne called him Yellow Face because his beard was the color of the sun.

Behind White Horse rode Summer Moon, her own horse pulling a travois filled with their few belongings. There were no extra horses, only the two White Horse and Summer Moon rode. The Cheyenne had not allowed him to take the rest of his horses, requiring that he give them to Arrow Maker for offending the man's daughter.

Summer Moon remained stony and silent as White Horse spoke to the scout. A few soldiers glanced at her, noticing her face and arms were bruised. They made remarks about what animals the Indians were, but she did not understand them. She only waited quietly and patiently for her husband to conduct his business.

White Horse had not been kind to her, but she forgave him, for she knew he was still full of anger over what had happened with Medicine Wolf and Bear Paw. She was sure that in time he would grow to love her, and he would not be so cruel. She was beginning to heal from that first night he had taken her. He had been quick and rough, and her introduction to womanhood had not been easy; but by taking her he had made her his wife, and she was proud to finally belong to the handsome, brave young man, even if he was hot-tempered and liked his whiskey. It was not her place to question his ways. It was her place only to serve him, and be grateful to be able to call him her husband.

She listened as White Horse told Yellow Face to inform the leader of the soldiers at Fort Laramie that he wished to work for them as a scout. When Yellow Face asked him in what way, he said that he would willingly help the soldiers find the Cheyenne whenever they wished to hunt them for wrongdoings. Summer Moon made a little gasping sound, and White Horse turned to face her.

"White Horse, you are talking about helping soldiers kill our own People," she said.

He glared at her, and she knew by his look that had they been alone he would have hit her for objecting to something he wanted to do. She lowered her eyes. "I'm sorry."

"The Cheyenne have cast me out," he growled. "I am no longer a Cheyenne, Summer Moon. They are my *enemy*! If I have to ride alongside Pawnee scouts against the Cheyenne, I will do it! I have no home among them any longer, nor among the Sioux or the Arapaho. Here we will be welcome. We will have food and shelter and clothing. I will be given a new rifle and white man's money. Where else are we to go?''

Summer Moon felt some relief at his use of the word "we." Her heart ached to see her father again, and sometimes she even missed Medicine Wolf, realizing now that her friendship had been true. But to go back to her family and friends would mean never being with White Horse again, and she could not bear losing him after finally winning him for herself. She met his eyes.

"I understand, White Horse. It is just that you did not tell me why you were coming here. I was surprised."

He looked her over in near disgust. "Go and prepare our dwelling outside the fort grounds. We will stay right here."

Summer Moon obediently turned her horse and rode off to do his bidding. White Horse turned his attention back to Yellow Face, who frowned and pulled thoughtfully at his beard. "You sure you want to scout for the army," the man asked him.

White Horse grinned wickedly. "I am very sure. The Cheyenne have cast me out for no good reason."

The scout studied the scratches on his face. "Oh, I expect there was a reason," he murmured in English. He saw the scowl on White Horse's face. He knew the young man called White Horse had been a respected Dog Soldier among the Cheyenne. If anyone would be a good scout against them, it would be this one. "I'll talk to the lieutenant in charge," he told White Horse. "If he approves, you'll be issued a new rifle and a uniform."

White Horse grinned even more. "I will do good work."

Several yards away Reverend Prescott watched the sorry-looking young Summer Moon ride past him, wondering what life must be like now for Medicine Wolf. Was she also the abused wife now of some savage warrior? And with all the troubles facing the Cheyenne, were they beginning to turn on each other? Why was that Cheyenne man talking to the scout called Blondy?

It mattered little to him, for he was giving up his work here. He was getting too old for the rough life out on the prairie. He would be leaving soon to join his wife and son, who now resided with Christian friends in Boston. Tom was especially eager for his father to come back east, for he was to be married as soon as the reverend arrived.

The reverend smiled at the thought. He would conduct the ceremony himself. Tom had finally seemed to get over his anger with them. He had finished his schooling and had met a girl of whom Marilyn approved. It would be nice to all be a family again, back home in their own environment. By now Tom had surely put away all those foolish thoughts about wolf spirits and being a blood brother to the Cheyenne.

He took the letter from his pocket again. Marilyn had written it over three months before, urging that he come home as fast as he could, for Tom was "quite anxious" to wed his beloved Elena, and he wanted his father to conduct the wedding. Prescott smiled and headed for the command post to find out when the next supply train was expected. When they returned east, the reverend would go with them.

He paid no more attention to White Horse, who was shaking hands with Blondy. The scout pulled a flask of whiskey from inside his shirt and uncorked it, handing it out to White Horse, who gladly took a swallow, sealing his new pact with the *ve-ho-e*.

White Horse thought maybe the Pawnee knew what they were doing after all, befriending the white soldiers. This would not be such a bad life, but someday . . . someday he would have another turn at Bear Paw, when he was better prepared. Then would come Medicine Wolf! He was determined that someday he would find a way to repay her for turning him away.

Chapter Seventeen

1857

The passion Bear Paw and Medicine Wolf shared was matched only by a new passion among the Cheyenne, a passion to do anything they could to keep the ever-encroaching whites out of their land, especially the Smoky Hill River country, which had remained their only refuge but was now also being invaded by the *ve-ho-e*. Willingness on the part of the Cheyenne to continue to try to remain peaceful was fast fading, especially now that they considered the Laramie Treaty invalid.

On their trip to a newly constructed Bent's Fort to receive their regular annuities, one full summer after Bear Paw and Medicine Wolf were married, the young warriors grew even more angry and restless when they were told that no guns or ammunition had been included this time in the government supplies. Feeling cheated and betrayed, they threatened to scalp Indian Agent Whitfield, and even their former friend, William Bent.

Arrow Maker and his people had reached the point where they felt no white man could be trusted. Because the government had fallen far short in promised annuities, and combined with a scarcity of game, the Cheyenne turned to raiding freight wagons that supplied the various towns and forts springing up everywhere in Indian country. They demanded, and usually received a variety of goods, such as tobacco, sugar, flour, cloth, and the like, feeling they had every right to take what they needed. The *ve-ho-e* had cheated them, so they would cheat the *ve-ho-e*.

Medicine Wolf was afraid for Bear Paw, confused as to how far her People should go in their anger and retaliation. She fully supported the husband she loved, but she was afraid for him, afraid for all of her People. She had not forgotten the big guns at Fort Laramie, or Tom's warning about how many more whites there were in the East. Those of her People who had been invited east after the Laramie Treaty, and who had seen the marvels of the white man's world, had told Medicine Wolf's People and other Cheyenne tribes that they believed the *ve-ho-e* had just tried to fool them, that there really were not so many of them, but that they had moved people from city to city to try to make the Indian visitors believe their numbers were much greater than they actually were. Medicine Wolf considered the theory, wondering if it could be true. But she could not make herself believe that Tom had lied to her.

Confrontations began to worsen. More whites came into Smoky Hill country, penetrating the only prime buffalo country left to the Indians, and the Cheyenne would raid and plunder in an effort to keep them out. Dull Knife, another respected Cheyenne chief, was struggling to keep the peace, making promises to Indian agents and soldier chiefs at Fort Laramie, but he could not speak for all the Cheyenne.

Throughout that restless year Bear Paw and Medicine Wolf made love nearly every night, their youth and their joy over at last being joined bringing on a sweet passion that made them wonder if they could ever get enough of each other. When Bear Paw was off on raids against the

Pawnee or Utes, or on a buffalo hunt, Medicine Wolf ached for him. His return was always a time for heated reunions.

Finally, because of her special powers and the good luck the blessing of the wolf's paws brought them, the Dog Soldiers requested that Medicine Wolf ride with them on some of their raids. It was a great honor for her, and proudly she rode by Bear Paw's side. More and more Medicine Wolf was burying her memories of life among the *ve-ho-e*; more and more she became the wild, proud Cheyenne holy woman, as passionate and determined as the young warriors with whom she rode. They staged several raids into Ute country, in retaliation for the Utes stealing women and horses from the Cheyenne.

Now, on this most recent raid, she had become a true warrior woman. A fleeing Ute warrior had aimed a lance at Medicine Wolf as he passed by her. She had managed to dodge out of the way, then whirled her horse and landed a tomahawk into the Ute man's side, wounding him severely. Bear Paw had ridden to her aid, only to find the Ute man lying on the ground, bleeding badly, the bloody tomahawk that wounded him still in Medicine Wolf's hand.

Bear Paw had quickly scalped the Ute warrior and handed the lock of hair to Medicine Wolf as a trophy. When she took it, she felt a strange new power, a kind of victory she had never felt before. She was not just watching the Cheyenne warriors; she was a part of them in every way.

Now she held up the scalp against the orange night fire, while around her warriors danced wildly, screaming and whooping in victory, and Medicine Wolf knew that in that moment all of Marilyn Prescott's teachings had flown from her like the wind!

"Notaxe he-e," Bear Paw said, calling her Warrior Woman. He had come to stand by her side, looking wild and masculine, his body painted, his eyes glowing with pride. He reached down and took her hand.

With a rushing heart Medicine Wolf rose, and Bear Paw smiled, whisking her up into his arms and carrying her beyond the light of the celebration fire. He whirled around as he held her, laughing, then lowered her to the ground and lay her back in the grass. "You are my warrior woman,'' he repeated. ''I own the sacred woman who has counted coup and who owns the wolf paws.'' He laughed again, nuzzling her neck.

''I am brave in battle only because I am with you,'' she answered. ''I am never afraid when I am with Bear Paw.'' She felt him sliding his hand along her thigh and breathed deeply when he massaged her naked bottom.

''Victory over our enemy has made me a hungry man,'' he told her in a husky voice. ''I have killed three Utes and counted coup on four others. The Pawnee fear us so much now that whenever they even think we are coming their way, they run to the white soldier forts. The whites are afraid now too! Surely they will soon leave and not come back. It is a good feeling. I feel strong and happy tonight.'' He licked her neck, his fingers searching her depths and arousing her.

''Bear Paw,'' she whispered.

Soon her tunic was pushed to her waist and his power was between her legs. He pushed deep, moving with the rhythm of the nearby drumming. The night seemed to melt into dizzying ecstasy as she gave herself to him there in the grass, while not far away other warriors continued to dance and celebrate.

The utter glory of their union was shadowed by only one haunting sadness. In spite of the great love she and Bear Paw shared, and their frequent consummation of that love, Medicine Wolf still had not conceived. It worried her greatly, for Bear Paw was strong and brave and a wonderful lover. She wanted so much to give him sons. Again she took his seed with great hope. Maybe this time, she thought. Maybe this time his seed would take hold.

Problems with the *ve-ho-e* could not help but get worse. The Cheyenne were feeling more sure than ever. They continued their raids on other tribes who tried to hunt on what little land they had left to them, and in so doing they often rode through white settlements. They cared little what the whites thought of it. After all, the *ve-ho-e* were not supposed to be there. If they wanted to risk settling in Indian country, they could face the consequences, including losing horses to any Indian who rode through and decided to take a few.

The Cheyenne attitude invited trouble, but in their minds they were doing nothing wrong. Such trouble was to be expected until the whites and enemy Indian tribes realized they could not steal buffalo and land from the Cheyenne. But they soon found more trouble than they expected when, in another random raid, several confident young Cheyenne warriors, including Bear Paw, surrounded a supply train and demanded tobacco. Medicine Wolf approached the lead wagon with Bear Paw, sitting defiantly on her mount, her dark hair blowing in a light summer breeze. She could see the driver of the wagon looked nervous, and suddenly he reached for a pistol. She reached out to push Bear Paw out of the way, and she felt a hot sting in her left forearm. Her horse whirled, and it was then she saw an arrow in the driver's left shoulder. The wounded man whipped his horses into motion and drove away in a cloud of dust, but the rest of the warriors surrounded the other wagons of the supply train, finding no more resistance to their demands for tobacco and flour.

Medicine Wolf looked down at her arm, seeing a hole ripped through the flesh just under the bone, about an inch in front of her elbow. Bear Paw grabbed her from her horse and pulled her onto his own, keeping a strong arm around her. "Are you all right?" he asked, his eyes frantic.

She looked him over, seeing that he was bleeding near his left armpit. "You are hurt," she gasped.

He held out his arm. "It is only the flesh. See? It went right between my arm and my chest." He held up her arm, quickly taking a red bandana tied around his knee for decoration and tying it around her arm. "Yours is also only a flesh wound." His eyes seemed to tear. "You saved my life, Medicine Wolf. If you had not pushed at me, the bullet would have gone into my chest, perhaps my heart. It went through your arm first, then through me. I was so afraid that—" He did not finish. He only held her close.

"This is a bad omen, Bear Paw. I have never been wounded before. The blessing of the wolf paws always protected me. But today we did not offer the usual prayers.

We were careless. I fear what we have done here will bring bad things to us.''

He caressed her hair. "We have done this many times, and the *ve-ho-e* never come after us or even send their soldiers. It will be no different this time." Several of the warriors returned, whooping and yipping, holding up bags of tobacco and flour and bolts of cloth. "We will go back to the village and divide the supplies we have captured. You should see the Shaman and let him put his herbs and ointments on your wound so it does not become infected.''

He helped her onto her horse, and they all rode away, leaving behind the shaken and bewildered wagon drivers, who drove off then, hurrying to catch up with the lead wagon. Its wounded driver continued to whip his horses into such a frenzied gallop, they were beginning to lather.

The wagon bounced and jolted over ruts and rocks so violently that the driver nearly lost his seating, but he was not about to slow down. Panic filled him at the touch of the horrible arrow still sticking out of his arm, and he was sure he would feel more ripping into his back at any moment. Had the others all been slaughtered? This was the last straw! These fearful raids had to stop, he thought. The Cheyenne had no right to do such things! It was time the army did something about this! They had pussyfooted around the Cheyenne long enough. It was time the savages were taught a good lesson!

Rain had fallen ceaselessly all morning, and the air had grown cold for August. Because of their wounds and the cold, wet weather, Bear Paw and Medicine Wolf remained inside their tipi, lying in each other's arms. Medicine Wolf looked into her husband's eyes, reaching up to touch his handsome face. "Do you still love me, my husband?''

He grinned teasingly. "Why would I not love you? Because of you I lie here still breathing.''

"Not that. I mean, do you still love me like you did

the first time you took me? Would you still love Medicine Wolf even if she had not saved you?''

He frowned. "Why do you ask such a thing?"

She closed her eyes and snuggled against him, moving to keep the pressure off her wounded arm. "Because I still have not conceived. It is a source of great sorrow to me."

He stroked her hair, moving a hand along her naked body. "I am happy just to call you my wife, to lie next to you this way, to feel myself inside of you whenever I have the desire."

She kissed his breasts. "It is not enough for me. You are a brave and accomplished warrior, Bear Paw. Such a man should have sons to carry on. Such a man has strong seed. But that seed does not grow in me. I am so sorry, Bear Paw."

He wrapped his arms around her and rolled onto his back, pulling her on top of him. "All the more reason to keep trying," he told her, his eyes shiny with desire.

She felt his growing hardness and she raised herself up on her knees, grasping him gently and pushing him inside herself. He closed his eyes and sighed deeply, and she thought how easy and right this always seemed. Her breathing quickened as she began moving in an undulating motion as though she were on the back of a horse. He began moving with her, raising his hips to push deep. He grasped her thighs with strong hands, running them up to her groin area, where he pushed his thumbs into the crevices at the tops of her thighs.

He watched her, glorying in her beauty, her slightly parted lips, her full, firm breasts, the way her eyes glazed over with passion whenever he was inside her. He moved one thumb to toy with that part of her that made her gasp and want him more, and he held off his own release until she cried out with her own pleasure and he felt her insides pulsating and pulling at him in her own sweet climax. He held out longer, allowing her the pleasure of taking him with even more eagerness. She grasped his powerful wrists and leaned back, gyrating, riding her grand stallion until the stallion could no longer control his own ecstasy.

Again his life spilled into her. He quickly rolled her over, grasping her hips and staying inside her. "We will keep trying," he told her in a near whisper. He moved in his own exotic thrusts, her master now. In moments the life came back to him, and he took her again. She was still hot and willing from her recent climax, and she responded with equal determination.

Bear Paw shuddered with his release, then leaned down and tasted her mouth. "Only a few days ago you returned from the menstrual lodge. We have many days now to try. Perhaps it will be a long time before you visit the menstrual lodge again."

"Perhaps." How she prayed he would be right this time. They had barely finished their conversation when they heard the shout from outside.

"Soldiers! They come quickly!"

Bear Paw leapt to his feet and quickly tied on a breechcloth. Medicine Wolf pulled on her tunic and grabbed what few items she could cram quickly into a parfleche. Shots were already being fired, and she gasped when one ripped through the top of the tipi.

"Get as many horses as you can gather and run to the hills beyond the river," Bear Paw ordered. *"Hopo! Hopo!"*

There was not time to question the order, not even time to tear down the tipi. Medicine Wolf did as she was told, leaving behind food and clothing and other utensils. She managed to grab a couple of blankets, then darted outside to see soldiers bearing down on the camp. Everyone had been resting, and she knew most would be lucky to escape this surprise attack. She could hardly believe that soldiers would come after the whole village just because one white man had been slightly wounded in the arm, especially when that man had pulled a gun on the Cheyenne. Medicine Wolf could think of no other reason that the soldiers were coming, and she knew her suspicion had been right that her being wounded was a sign of bad things to come.

She ran to where the horses grazed. Many other women were gathering horses and children and fleeing, while some of the warriors tried to hold off the soldiers. Medicine Wolf managed to herd together five of Bear Paw's finest ponies, as well as *Nahkohe* and *Nonoma-e*. She shouted at them, urging them to the river. She could hear gunshots everywhere and expected to feel a bullet rip into her body, but she reached the Platte unharmed and waded across, grateful that the river here was deeper than most of the Platte was this time of year, for she had not had a chance to wash after making love. She walked through waist-deep water, holding up her dress and washing away what was left of the life that had spilled out of her. She wondered if life was always going to be like this now, never knowing when a peaceful morning of lovemaking would turn into a matter of life and death.

She prayed for Bear Paw's safety as she climbed the bank on the other side of the river. She spotted Smiling Girl and ran to her sister, asking about Star Woman.

"She is all right. She is helping Bear Paw's grandfather," Smiling Girl told her. She began to cry. "What is happening, Medicine Wolf?"

Medicine Wolf touched her medicine bag. "The soldiers are getting stronger, the *ve-ho-e* angrier. I will have to do more fasting and praying." She turned to her sister. "Get up on one of the horses. We will ride to the big timbers in the distance. The warriors will meet us there."

"Why can they not just leave us alone," Smiling Girl asked, crying more as she mounted a horse. "If they would just stay out of our land, and if they would keep their promises and bring the things they agreed to in the treaty . . ."

Medicine Wolf looked back to see the soldiers advancing on the village. A sick feeling came into her stomach when she saw several warriors lying on the ground. Bear Paw!

"We *have* no treaty," she almost growled as she watched the soldiers. "All we can do is fight to protect what is ours! Now it is time to stop fighting enemy tribes and turn our attention to the bluecoats!" She turned, running with the horses, helping some of the old ones along the way, using what strength she had to help some of them get up onto the horses. They headed into a wooded area and waited, and minutes later several warriors came running. To Medicine Wolf's relief, Bear Paw was among them.

"Hopo! Hopo," the men were saying. "Run again!"

Bear Paw reached Medicine Wolf's side. "There was no time to gather our weapons. And without our horses we could not fight them, for they are on horseback. Come! We flee! We will pay back the bluecoats another time! For now we go to Dull Knife's village!"

The women did not scream or panic. They simply obeyed orders. Children did the same. In moments those who could not run, or whose legs were too short to run quickly, were on horseback and riding away. A few of the younger, swifter warriors simply ran, realizing that to stay and fight in their present condition was hopeless. They left behind ten dead Cheyenne, including two women and a child. Eight more warriors had been wounded, and several horses and most of their supplies were taken by the soldiers, the tipis burned, the wounded left to die or be helped by anyone who might return to bury the dead.

A Captain G. H. Stewart, who had led the attack, watched the fleeing Cheyenne and decided that the hostiles had been taught a fine lesson. They would think twice now about harassing supply trains and making their mischief. The Cheyenne had lost many valuables this day, and many lives!

Two days after the attack on their village, Arrow Maker's scattered tribe returned to bury their dead. Among them was the young, proud Swift Fox, Medicine Wolf's brother, Arrow Maker's son. It was a time of great loss and great mourning, and Medicine Wolf became even more determined to continue to ride with the warriors, vengeance growing in her own heart. Her brother had been killed! There was no room left now for reasoning or forgiveness, no desire for peace talks. Now the holy woman felt the same thirst for revenge as the fiercest warriors!

She watched her father bravely, watched him slash his arms many times over in his great grief. She took out her own knife, and soon her own blood dripped onto the ground beneath the scaffold that held Swift Fox's dead body. Again, great personal loss had visited her. Any desire she had left to cooperate with the *ve-ho-e* had vanished. It was buried with her beloved brother, who had been unnecessarily cut down in the prime of his life.

   For the rest of the summer and autumn, war cries could be heard everywhere throughout the plains. Settlers could not be sure just where the Cheyenne would strike next in their rage over Stewart's attack on their peaceful village along the Platte. Before the soldier raid, Arrow Maker had even sent a runner to Fort Kearny to explain that the Cheyenne had meant no harm when they stopped the supply train to ask for tobacco; but as in most such confrontations the differences in outlook and understanding between the Indians and whites made it impossible to strike a compromise. In the Cheyenne way of thinking, the white wagon driver should have been grateful he had not been killed on the spot, which the Cheyenne had every right to do to anyone who came into their hunting grounds.
   The soldiers and the "Great White Father" in Washington, of course, did not see this Indian reasoning. They saw only "hostiles," savage, unschooled, animallike natives who thirsted for blood. It was the *Indians* who had broken the treaty, the *Indians* who were roaming where they did not belong. The Indians had no right claiming any land, no right trying to scare settlers and travelers out of that land. And the Indians certainly had no right committing ruthless acts against settlers and travelers in retaliation for any attacks on their villages by soldiers, who were only defending the frightened settlers.
   But revenge had been a way of life for the Indian since the beginning of time. More and more now their attention was drawn from warring with enemy tribes to warring against the *ve-ho-e* and the bluecoat soldiers who protected them. The soldiers were supposed to have been sent west to protect the *Indians*, to keep more whites from coming into their land. That was the original agreement. But now those soldiers had turned on them, and the Cheyenne reacted in the only way they knew how, not with a cowering fear and promises to remain peaceful and stay in one place, but with that vengeance that could not be controlled. Cheyenne women and children had died, so white

women and children must die. Settlements were attacked, and now the Indians did not kill just men. It seemed only fair to fight back the same way the soldiers fought against them, considering the incidences of buffalo hunters and other forms of *ve-ho-e* lowlife who had raped Indian women and shot at Indians of any age or sex just for the fun of it.

It was time to pay back, and pay back the Cheyenne did. White women and children were taken prisoners and held for ransom in return for food for hungry bellies. Taking women and children prisoner and making them work or turning the children into "little white Indians" was as normal to the Cheyenne as breathing. They had been doing the same for centuries with enemy tribes, such as the Pawnee or the Crow or Ute or Shoshoni, just as those tribes had done to them.

For the next four years skirmishes and depredations continued, with only occasional moments of peace for the Cheyenne. In retaliation for their raids against whites after the Stewart incident, the army sent out even more troops, under a Colonel E. V. Sumner, who, aided by Delaware and Pawnee scouts, and also by White Horse, attacked Cheyenne camps with a vengeance. Sumner seized government annuities meant for the Cheyenne, declaring that as long as the Cheyenne were at war, and were very obviously ignoring the treaty, they did not deserve to receive government rations, especially not guns and ammunition that could be used against settlers and soldiers.

The Smoky Hill region, the last peaceful, unsettled area for the Cheyenne, was lost to them in 1858, when the discovery of gold in Colorado created a new rush of whites. To the dismay of the Cheyenne, over a hundred thousand whites moved through the rich prairie grasses along the Smoky Hill, killing game, their horses and cattle consuming the grass. They spoiled the water, cut many trees, scared away the buffalo. To Medicine Wolf it seemed more apparent now that Tom Prescott had been right about how many whites there were in the East, and surely, with this new flow of settlers, the lands in the East must be nearly empty!

Medicine Wolf spent many hours fasting and praying

as well as riding with the warriors on raids. She was becoming known to the soldiers and the more permanent settlers through information that scouts brought back to them. Many whites began to blame Medicine Wolf for much of the trouble, for she had once lived among the whites and she learned to hate them. She knew their ways, and therefore must be directing some of the raids.

The Cheyenne continued to think of her as magical and prophetic, and so, the whites determined, it must be Medicine Wolf who spurred the Cheyenne to continue their raiding. None understood the agony she suffered over the fact that she had not been able to conceive. No white woman thought of her as a loving, gentle wife who wanted only peace, and to be able to give her husband a son. Few whites imagined that any Indian would weep over a lost loved one the way Medicine Wolf had wept and shed blood over the death of her beloved brother.

But one man did know better. Tom Prescott followed the stories, or, rather, the lies that were told in eastern newspapers he received at the small settlement near Fort Laramie, where he and his wife, Elena, had settled to teach. Tom was writing a series of articles of his own, which he hoped an eastern newspaper would accept, articles that told what he knew about the true personality and beliefs of the Cheyenne woman called Medicine Wolf, the woman about whom he had wondered and worried over the years. What did she look like now? Did she ever think of him? Did she have children?

So far, no newspaper had accepted his articles. No one wanted to hear about the human side of the Indian. They wanted to hear only about the blood and violence. He finished another article, then walked out onto the porch of his small cabin, glancing at Elena as she hung up some clothes to dry. She had been a good wife, patient and accepting. She had come west with him not just for his sake, but because she had a desire to help him teach Indian children, to try to find a way to settle the Indian problem without so much bloodshed. At the same time, they both wanted to help teach the children of soldiers who had families around Fort Laramie, and the children of white settlers who for reasons of their own had chosen to settle in this godforsaken land.

He turned his eyes to the vast plains that stretched out to the east.

Somewhere out there Medicine Wolf wandered with her tribe, struggling to find a place where they could have a little peace. Had she gone north, as so many other Cheyenne had done, to join the Sioux? Scouts had informed the settlers that the Cheyenne were dividing more and more now, since the Smoky Hill region had been infested with new travelers, penetrating the heart of the Cheyenne hunting grounds. He was aware that the railroad was also on its way west. He thought about the time Medicine Wolf had dreamed about a train . . . how many years ago now? She had left them in '53. Now here it was 1860. Seven years!

Medicine Wolf would be twenty now. He was thirty-one already, and the one called Bear Paw would be twenty-eight. He knew that they were both still alive, for every time there was talk of another raid, it was rumored it was Medicine Wolf and Bear Paw who led the Dog Soldiers.

The thought brought a sad smile to his face. He had tried to find Wolf's grave once, but couldn't quite remember where it was now. Maybe that was how it would be with Medicine Wolf. Maybe he would not find her either, ever again. She was wild now, wild and free, riding with the Cheyenne, where she belonged. He wondered if she still carried that Bible with her.

Chapter Eighteen

1861

Bear Paw bit off a piece of venison and chewed heartily. He and Medicine Wolf were camped along the White River in the Black Hills of the Dakotas, an area still relatively free of whites. Here, among the Sioux, those Cheyenne who were determined to remain free of the white man's world found at least a little refuge. The vast area in the great plains and prairies of the Platte, Republican, Smoky Hill, and Arkansas River areas that was supposed to have been preserved for the Cheyenne under the Laramie Treaty was becoming overrun with whites and soldiers.

"At least here we still manage to find game," Bear Paw muttered before again biting into the meat he held.

Medicine Wolf tore off a small piece of meat for herself from the deer leg that simmered over the fire in the center of the tipi, grateful for the peace they had found for the present. Fat dripped from the meat into the fire, making little popping sounds. For many months now it seemed they were always running, always having to prepare new skins, store up new supplies. They stayed to the north now, which meant they were not privy to the annuities that were still given out to the Southern Cheyenne. The Sioux often shared supplies with them, but they had their own problems with finding game and feeding their people. Now the government was no longer willing to supply the Indians with guns, so they had taken to stealing them whenever they could, or to trading precious wolf-, bear-, and deerskins to dirty-looking white traders who thought nothing of illegally selling rifles to them. Medicine Wolf wondered what kind of men such traders could be, to sell guns to Indians they knew might use them against their own people. Whatever kind of men they were, it was not for the Indian to wonder or care. They needed the guns desperately so they could kill game and keep bellies filled. Game had become so scarce that to get close enough to use a bow and arrow only made the job more difficult. Rifles were now an important necessity to the Indian, but only white men could supply them. Medicine Wolf thought how strange it was that in many ways they were becoming dependent on the very people who were fast becoming their worst enemy.

Outside, the wind howled, and a winter snow blanketed the ground, drifting up against one side of the tipi. Both Medicine Wolf and Bear Paw sat with buffalo robes wrapped around them, staying close to the fire. From the distant hills came the call of the wolf, one long howl followed by several replies. Medicine Wolf looked toward the tipi entrance, her heart heavy this night, but not because of the problems her people were having with the white man. The sound of the wolf's howl made her think of Wolf, dead for nearly eight winters now.

"What is it that troubles you, Medicine Wolf," Bear Paw asked. "For many days now you have been very quiet." He licked his fingers and laid a bone aside, saved for the poor starving dogs that roamed the camp. "When we make love, you cling to me as though you think I might run away."

Medicine Wolf searched his eyes. Her husband was

nearly twenty-nine summers, a warrior honed hard and strong, a man bearing many scars, a Dog Soldier who knew no fear. She loved him as much as ever, but there was a new distance between them, something she could not name. She had noticed a kind of resentment in his eyes lately when she was specially honored at scalp dances. Was he upset that she was looked upon with as much honor as the most respected warriors? Always he had been so proud, but something had changed, and she was sure it was because he had a deeper resentment over the fact that she had still not given him a son.

She thought of the vision she had had just two nights before. She had talked to Black Buffalo about it, and she did not like his answer. She still had not told Bear Paw about the dream. "Bear Paw, you must . . . take another wife," she said, the words bringing pain to her heart.

Bear Paw frowned. "What do you mean?"

"You know what I mean. If you would wish to take my sister, Smiling Girl, she would be willing. I have already talked to her. She would consider it a great honor. She loves you like a brother, and would not find it hard to love you like a husband."

The fire crackled quietly, and another drop of fat sizzled against a hot coal.

"You know I want no other wife."

She forced herself to be firm. "To say that is to say you want no sons. Can you truly say you do not want children?"

He scowled, pulling the robe tighter around him. "You had no right talking to Smiling Girl without talking to me first. You know that I want children, but I want them with *you*. It will happen."

"It will *not* happen! We have been husband and wife now for almost five winters, and I have never conceived! It is not fair to you, Bear Paw. And even if you would agree to leave it this way, it is not fair to the *Cheyenne*! You are a Dog Soldier. It is your *duty* to let your seed multiply, to bring more young men and women into the clan. Now more than ever we must preserve the children, bear *more* children, or one day there will *be* no more Cheyenne, just like some of the tribes of the East no longer exist! We must not let that happen, Bear Paw, and a man such as you, whose seed surely is strong, has a duty to help our numbers grow!''

He leaned closer to the fire, his dark eyes burning into her own. ''I have no desire for any other woman.''

Medicine Wolf let out a little gasp of frustration. Oh, how it pained her to think of her beloved Bear Paw taking pleasure in another. But she had to think of the People now, and she knew that in his heart she would always be his only beloved. ''You are a man,'' she answered. ''If you lie with another woman who wants you and who offers herself willingly, you will react the way any man would. A man is made to desire such things easily. It is *Maheo*'s way of making sure we continue to bear many children.'' She met his eyes. ''If my sister lies naked next to you, you will not find it difficult to do what you know you *must* do.''

He studied her intently, his eyes showing a deep hurt. ''I cannot say I do not desire children. And I suppose you are right when you say it is my duty. Your sister is a good choice, because a woman is not so easily jealous of her own sister. But what about you? How would *you* feel about me then?''

Her eyes teared. ''I will always love you as I do now. My feelings would not change. And if Smiling Girl bears your children, they would be like my own because they would have my blood in them. Smiling Girl and I could share them. I would help her take care of them, and I would have a baby to hold, a child who comes from the seed of my beloved husband. All I would ask is that you never make love to my sister in my presence. If you decide to do this, I will go and stay with my father and mother until Smiling Girl is with child. It will be better, easier for you, if we do not make love until your seed takes hold in Smiling Girl's womb.''

Bear Paw looked away, hating the idea, even though he knew she was right. Many Cheyenne men took more than one wife, for many reasons. What Medicine Wolf was asking of him was as common to the Cheyenne as breathing. But he had no desire for anyone but Medicine Wolf. Even so, he felt the strange new resentment deep inside growing stronger, a resentment he could not seem to control. He felt strangely angry that it should be Medicine Wolf who should demand such a thing, rather than the idea coming from him. How dare she order him about on such a personal decision. It seemed she dictated many things he did, from when to make war to whether or not she should ride at his side. It was as though she were the leader and he was always the follower, except in one area . . . when they made love. Then *he* was the master. Then she was not the holy woman who had all the answers and all the dreams and made all the prophecies. She was just Medicine Wolf, his beloved wife.

Perhaps that was why he desired her so, why he did not like the idea of taking another wife. To take another wife meant, in his mind, that he was giving up a little more of Medicine Wolf, losing even more of her to that strange spirit world he could not fully share with her. Lately he had thought about trying some of the firewater that so many of the other warriors had taken to drinking. It seemed to make them braver, happier, closer to the spirits. Maybe if he drank the whiskey, he could better share that side of his wife that remained inaccessible to him.

He realized that her sacred position was part of what he loved about her, and he still felt honored that he had been a part of her vision; but he also realized that her special position was also part of something he was beginning to resent. To be married to one such as Medicine Wolf meant a man had to take second place, that he was not fully the master. Now here she was making decisions about his future and his children, practically ordering him to take another wife. He wanted to scream at her, to shake her.

He met her eyes again, and all the little feelings of animosity left him, as usually happened when he saw that look she gave him now. He reminded himself that her special rank as a holy woman was not of her choosing. No Cheyenne, man or woman, "chose" his or her vision. At the tender age of six, a little girl named Sweet Water slept among the wolves and had a vision. He knew that there had been many times when his wife wished someone else had been chosen for the burden she had to bear, but *she* had been chosen, and to deny such a gift was something no Cheyenne would ever consider. He saw the tears in her eyes, and he knew that to have him take another would be harder on her than on him.

"I had a dream," she told him. "I sat and held what I thought was a baby, but when I looked down at it, it was a young wolf. I knew then, even before I spoke with Black Buffalo, that I will never have a child of my own, Bear Paw. Part of me belongs to the Wolf Spirit. Part of me is not even human." She sniffed and swallowed. "You think it is a great burden I put upon you, but you will have the pleasure of lying with another, the pleasure of planting your seed and watching it grow. I am left to loneliness, and to the sorrow only a woman who is barren can understand. Please do not be angry with me, Bear Paw. This is not easy for me."

He sighed, struggling against feelings he considered selfish. In spite of any resentment he might have, in spite of the hurt and anger, one thing he knew was that he loved Medicine Wolf more deeply than he would ever love anything or anyone in his whole life. His jaw flexed in repressed desire, and he looked away. "Go and get your sister, then," he told her. "If she is to be a second wife, we need no ceremony. She needs only to share my bed." He met her eyes, his own full of hurt and love. "Right now I want you more than ever. I will take out my desire on your sister and have it over with! The sooner she is with child, the sooner I can lie with you again."

Medicine Wolf felt the sting of jealousy. She had thought he would wait a few days, but she realized now that he was right. As long as his desire was strong, it would help him mate with Smiling Girl. She had already said herself it was best this way. To not be able to lie with her would keep him frustrated and in need. She rose, packing a few of her things into a parfleche. She wanted to touch him, to hold him, to make love once more. But she sensed that this was his way of having a say in the matter. She knew she had hurt him by practically demanding he take another. She had hurt his pride before, many times, but he never allowed his anger to show, never vented it in words. She knew it could not be easy for a proud, honored warrior like Bear Paw to be married to a woman who was looked to by all others with such prestige and near worship, a woman who at times took a position of authority over him.

She swallowed against a lump in her throat. "When Smiling Girl is with child, I will return to our tipi," she told him, refusing to look at him.

"You will return when I ask you," he answered.

Oh, how deeply he could plunge the knife in return for how deeply she had wounded his pride! She did not answer, for she could not find her voice. She ducked out of the tipi into the cold, stinging wind, pulling part of the robe over her head as she trudged through deep, soft snow toward her parents' lodge.

"It is strange," Arrow Maker told Medicine Wolf, "that the white man has for years tried to stop us from fighting enemy tribes, and now the white men fight a war among themselves in the East. What do you think of that, Medicine Wolf?"

Medicine Wolf sat in council with the Dog Soldiers just outside the sacred Sun Dance lodge. Again the Cheyenne celebrated the summer sun dance among the Sioux, and the ceremony, along with the warmth of summer and the recent find of a huge herd of buffalo, had renewed the drooping spirits of Sioux and Cheyenne alike.

"I think they are fools," she answered, sitting in the middle of the circle. "But let them fight their war. It only makes things easier for us, for they take their soldiers from our land and send them back east. Now there are not enough soldiers to come after us or to stop us from raiding." She kept her eyes averted from Bear Paw, for it hurt her heart too much to look at him. For six months they had not touched or even spoken, except in council meetings.

Several of the warriors nodded. "We must be careful of the talking wires they build through our lands to the south," White Eagle said. "I think we should tear down the wires and chop down the poles."

Medicine Wolf thought a moment. "*Ai*. The talking

wires help them somehow, and the Cheyenne runners from
the South say the railroad comes ever closer.'' She looked
at White Eagle. ''Perhaps we should go south again, and
help our brothers and sisters there try to stop the railroad.
The iron horse is mighty, but without rails it has no
strength. It can go nowhere without the tracks to take it.
The man called Tom Prescott told me the white man uses
these trains to carry supplies. If we can stop some of them,
we can kill those who make it run, and we can take the
supplies. Perhaps some of these trains carry rifles.''

White Eagle nodded. ''It is a good idea. But what of
the treaty Black Kettle and other Southern Cheyenne have
signed?''

She scanned the circle of warriors. ''*We* signed no
treaty. And there are many Southern Cheyenne who also
refused to sign it. The white man can try to push us onto
that tiny piece of land they now say is all that is left to us,
but he will break his part of the promise, as he always
does. His first treaty meant nothing to him, and neither
will this one. And since we did not sign it, we do not have
to abide by its rules. I for one will never agree to settle
like an old woman on the tiny place the white man gives
us and calls a reservation. It was bad enough that they
took away so much land under the first treaty. Now they
take nearly all of that! I am not ready to live like a beggar.
We will hunt and ride and live where we please, and we
will continue to make many problems for the white man.
Perhaps now that so many soldiers are gone, the settlers
will give up and go back if we make much trouble for
them. We are now a people without a home in the land
we once hunted, a land we love. There is nothing left to
us now but to lend ourselves to the Sioux and to the
Southern Cheyenne in any way possible to help both preserve what is left to them.''

There was a general mumble of approval among the
warriors, who had first passed the prayer pipe, many of
them having fasted and used the sweat lodge before coming to council, for such meetings were always important.

''There are many among Black Kettle's band in the
South who do not agree with the signing of the new
treaty,'' Stands Tall said. ''And Little Wolf still fights.

There is much looting and raiding that can be done along the supply trail far to the south that goes from Bent's new trading post into the Mexican deserts and on to the land of the setting sun. With so many soldiers gone, our tipis and our bellies will be full for a while. By the time we are through, perhaps there will be no whites left anywhere in our lands."

They all nodded, and Medicine Wolf's twenty-year-old cousin, Little Bear, now an honored Dog Soldier, raised a knife. "It would be good if our brothers in the South killed that agent man called Albert Boone. Runners say he has no respect for our ways and is very rude and cruel. He cheats any Indian that he can, and he tries to make farmers out of those who have agreed to go to the reservation."

"Reservation!" Bear Paw rose. "Who are they to tell us we must go to a reservation and plant the ground like *women*! *No* Cheyenne should agree to that! Why did Black Kettle sign such a treaty? I think the white people in the South have a plan to try to get rid of *all* their Indians, and we will not let it happen! We will not lose our beloved hunting grounds, where we have lived and roamed since *Maheo* created us! I agree with Medicine Wolf that we should go down there and show the white man that we never agreed to any treaty, that we are not farmers, but *warriors*!"

He raised his fist, and others followed. Medicine Wolf could not help but look at him then, and her heart beat faster. How she longed for him! How she ached at the look of happiness in Smiling Girl's eyes when they worked together washing clothes or tanning hides. Smiling Girl never talked about being with Bear Paw, for she knew it hurt Medicine Wolf too deeply. She knew her place, knew that as soon as she was with child, Medicine Wolf would return to the tipi and be the favored one; but Medicine Wolf could see in her eyes that Smiling Girl also loved Bear Paw. What woman would *not* be able to love him?

"It was wrong of Black Kettle to sign that treaty, and I say that those Cheyenne who follow it and settle onto the reservation like old people should no longer call themselves Cheyenne," Bear Paw was saying. "They bring disgrace to the name!"

The others agreed, except for one man who tried to argue that the Southern Cheyenne had been promised that the reservations would be fully protected, that it would forever belong to the Cheyenne and that no whites would be allowed to set foot on reservation land, except for traders. Bear Paw's face turned into a sneer.

"They promised the same thing in the Laramie Treaty, and now look what they have done! Many whites came into our land and were *not* stopped! And now all the land they promised us in the first treaty has been taken from us! They keep changing the treaties to suit them, and we must show them they cannot do this! Let Black Kettle and his cowards bow to the white man's offer. *We* will *not*!"

A general agreement moved through the circle of men, and Medicine Wolf thought again of the prophecy of Sweet Medicine, that her people would become divided and argue among themselves. How clever the white man was. Surely he knew that the quickest way to defeat the Indian was to turn them against each other and keep them divided. Already many Pawnee, Delaware, Shoshoni, Ute, and Crow scouted for white soldiers; it was even rumored that White Horse scouted for the army. The thought brought her great pain, for White Horse had once been an honored Dog Soldier. She felt somewhat responsible, yet there was nothing she could have done about it. White Horse had chosen his own path of destruction. The sad part was that Summer Moon would go down that same path with him.

The men all agreed with Bear Paw. Arrow Maker suggested that they go on another hunt and stock up as much meat and hides as possible, then head south, where they would cause havoc for settlers who had now lost army protection. They would take the horses they needed, steal rifles and other supplies, and in general show the Great Father in Washington that most Cheyenne were not ready to abide by a treaty they considered illegal and nonrepresentative of the entire Cheyenne nation.

Medicine Wolf prayed over the wolf paws and sang her prayer song, and all felt renewed, full of new hope and new determination. The meeting, which had lasted six hours, finally ended with the blessing of the wolf paws. Medicine Wolf touched each warrior on the shoulder with one of the paws, offering the same prayer, that each man would be blessed with a speedy mount, an aim that was straight and true; that he would be blessed with great courage and strength, that he would count many coup, and that no bullet or arrow or knife would find its way into his body.

She realized as each warrior passed before her that Bear Paw was saving himself for last. It was always hard for her to pray over him, to touch him with the wolf's paw, for to be so near to him made her feel weak and stirred desires long buried. She touched his shoulder, again refusing to met his eyes. "May your horse be swift and sure," she began. He suddenly took her wrist, and she gasped.

"It has been three moons since Smiling Girl has visited the menstrual lodge," he told her.

A wave of joy and relief moved through her blood. She raised her eyes to meet his, and saw that he was smiling, his dark eyes on fire for her. "Come with me, Medicine Wolf," he said, his voice husky with desire. "Your sister is with child, and we are free to be together again."

Her eyes misted, and her throat felt tight. She suddenly felt like a virgin on her wedding night. He squeezed her wrist. "I have already prepared my horse with food and blankets. We will go into the hills for two nights, just you and I. I know a cave where we will have shelter."

She had not known such joy since her marriage. She nodded. "I . . . should finish the blessing," she finally said when she found her voice. A tear slipped down her cheek.

His breathing was already quickened. "Then hurry," he told her.

The remark made her laugh lightly in spite of her tears. She managed to get out the words, hardly able to see because of her blurred vision. She put the wolf's paw back into her medicine bag, and she felt Bear Paw's strong arm around her. He led her to his horse, which stood fettered several yards away.

"Do not worry about Smiling Girl or your parents," he told her. "I have already spoken to them. They will know where we are." She felt strong hands lifting her, felt him mount up behind her. She leaned back against his powerful chest and felt his muscled arms come around her as he took up the reins. He headed his horse toward the deep pine forests of the sacred *Paha-Sapa*, the Black Hills.

Medicine Wolf knew that after all that had happened between them, it was important at this moment to let Bear Paw make all the decisions, all the first moves. This was his moment. She would not spoil it by making even one suggestion or by questioning anything he did or said. She would allow him to simply be the man that he was, and she would enjoy that manliness.

His every move seemed deliberate, as though he meant to make sure she remembered who was the male and who was the female. It hurt to think that her special standing among the tribe had had its effects on him, to know that because she was so spiritually connected to another world that she would never give him children. How much of that had he grown to resent? Yet she knew he loved her.

He led her to the cave, dismounting and taking her down from his horse. He carried blankets inside and spread them out on the cool dirt floor. Sunlight filtered into the entrance, but inside the cave the sun's heat did not affect them, and a refreshing flow of air came from somewhere deeper in the cave.

Bear Paw said nothing. He turned to face her, holding her eyes as he removed his bandolier of cartridges from across his already-bare chest, then removed his knife and pistol, his leggings and moccasins, his breechcloth. He stood before her naked except for his sacred medicine bag, which was tied to the inside of his thigh. "Take it off for me," he told her, a strange, haughty look in his eyes.

Medicine Wolf obeyed, her cheeks feeling hot, her hands shaking slightly as she knelt down and untied his medicine bag. An aching jealousy moved through her at the thought of Smiling Girl enjoying this man of men over the past few months, and hot tears stung her eyes at Bear

Paw's strange expression, as though she were his captive rather than the woman he loved.

She rose, meeting his eyes again. He untied the shoulders of her tunic and let it drop, and his eyes moved down to rake over her nakedness. He breathed deeply, now appearing to tremble slightly. "All these months," he said, grasping her hair and bending her head back slightly, "when I was planted inside your sister, every time I looked at her, I saw your face. Her cries of pleasure were as sweet as yours, but my own pleasure with her cannot match the pleasure I find in you."

He moved his other arm around her bare back, then put a foot behind her ankle and gave it a light kick, just enough to throw her off balance. She went down, and he went down with her. In the next moment he was surging inside of her with deliberate, almost violent thrusts, their eyes holding, a look of strange victory in his eyes. His need for her was so great that his life quickly spilled into her, and he closed his eyes, bending down to bury his face into her neck.

"Bear Paw," she whispered, touching his hair. "Where is my husband? I do not see him in the man who just took me. I saw him for a moment, in the smile he gave me before he brought me here, and then he went away."

He breathed deeply, rising up slightly, and she saw tears in his eyes. "Sometimes, Medicine Wolf, you make me so angry, and I hate myself for what I am thinking. The man who just took you was the angry one. Sometimes he visits me when I least expect it."

She reached up and touched his scarred face. "I do not like this angry man. But I love my husband. He is the bravest, most handsome, most accomplished warrior among the Dog Soldiers, and when I am with him, I am nothing. All the things others think are so special about me leave me, and I am just Medicine Wolf, the woman who needs her man as any woman needs a man, to protect her, provide for her, please her in the night. I have not been a full woman since the night I left our tipi." A familiar look came back into his eyes, the teasing, worshipful look that told her the anger had left him. "Do you still love me as you did before?" she asked him.

He smiled slightly, then bent down to lick her tears, rubbing his chest over her breasts. "Do you need to ask?"

"I need to ask the angry man who just took me almost painfully."

He began moving inside her again. "He is gone. I chased him away." He lowered his head and licked her breast. "Bear Paw has come for you. Bear Paw still loves you. No matter what you do, he can never stop loving you."

He began moving in rhythmic circular motions that brought forth all the heated desires she had had to deny for so long. The thought of him doing this with Smiling Girl stirred a fierce passion deep inside, for she suddenly felt she must prove she could please him more fully than Smiling Girl. Quickly she felt the pulsating climax that made her cry out his name, and he took her deep and hard, yet more gently than the first time. He was hers again, and life was good.

"Ne-mehotatse," she whispered, touching his hair lovingly, arching up to him in sweet surrender. She knew he would take her many times before the night was through, and she did not mind the thought.

Medicine Wolf had no idea how long the moon had been up, or how soon the sun would make its appearance over the horizon. She knew only that the night was deep, and that she and Bear Paw both ached from a round of passionate lovemaking that had left them spent. She was not even sure what had awakened her, for she was bone tired. She looked at Bear Paw, who slept soundly, then realized that somewhere in a dream she had heard the cry of the wolf. Perhaps she had heard it for real, and that was what had awakened her.

She lay motionless for a moment, listening. It was then she heard it, a long wail not far from the cave. She shivered with the feeling that it was not just a common wolf call, but the Wolf Spirit calling to her. She sat up, half expecting to see old Wolf standing at the cave entrance.

She gasped when by the light of the embers of the dying fire not far away she saw yellow eyes, one pair wide-set, as though belonging to a big animal, and another pair set closer together as in a smaller animal.

She told herself not to be afraid. After all, she was a child of the wolf. Surely the Wolf Spirit was bringing her a message. She carefully moved away from Bear Paw, wondering if it was the Wolf Spirit who made him sleep so deeply that he was not aware of the sounds or her movement. Normally Bear Paw slept lightly, ever alert, especially since they had come to a life of running and the fear of surprise attacks.

She picked up another blanket and wrapped it around her naked body, carefully moving toward the eyes. As her own eyes adjusted, she could see by the dim light that a female wolf stood at the entranceway with a pup in her mouth. The wolf's eyes remained fixed on Medicine Wolf until she drew close, then the wolf dropped the pup, which fluffed its fur in a shiver and quietly whined.

"For me," Medicine Wolf asked quietly.

The mother wolf licked the pup, then gave it a shove toward Medicine Wolf. Outside there came another long howl, as though to seal an agreement. The mother wolf turned and trotted off into the night. Medicine Wolf, astounded, reached out and picked up the pup, drawing it close to her breast. Her eyes misted from emotion, for she realized that the Wolf Spirit understood her agony over being childless. This was her gift . . . another wolf pup to hold and love. In a few months she would hold and love Smiling Girl's baby, and it would also be like her own.

Now that she was with Bear Paw again, she knew she could endure other times when they would have to be apart so that he could mate with Smiling Girl, for it meant carrying on Bear Paw's strong seed and bringing more children into the Cheyenne nation. At least for many months to come, it was she who would share Bear Paw's bed, for a Cheyenne man and woman usually refrained from intercourse for many months after a child was born, so that children would not be born too close together, which was a burden and a health danger to the mother.

She stroked the puppy's fur, realizing with even greater

reality and acceptance that she would never know the joys of true motherhood. The Wolf Spirit had reminded her that she belonged first to her duty as a holy woman, belonged to the Wolf Spirit and a world of visions and dreams and service to her People. She knew that it would forever be this way, that even Bear Paw would have to take second place.

She held the pup close and let it lick her neck. Her tears came harder then, in a mixture of joy at having another wolf pup to love, joy at knowing Smiling Girl was at last with child, and with a sadness at knowing she would never know the honor and glory of giving Bear Paw a child from her own womb. Yet suddenly it was enough to know that he loved her, that she would always be first in his heart. What she could not have in her personal life, she would make up for in other ways. She would be a warrior, ride with the Dog Soldiers to give them courage and blessings, for above all else, above being a woman and a wife, she was Cheyenne!

Chapter Nineteen

Medicine Wolf awoke to the stiff, cold morning. The little two-year-old son she shared with Smiling Girl and Bear Paw was already up and toddling toward the tipi entrance. "Standing Bear," she whispered. The boy only looked back and grinned, then scurried outside.

Medicine Wolf quickly rose, wrapping an extra buffalo robe around herself and hurrying to catch the child. The cold, damp air chilled her to the bone, and she caught up with Standing Bear and wrapped her arms around his solid but chubby body, enfolding him in the robe.

"Where do you think you are going, little one," she asked, nuzzling his neck. "You will take sick."

The boy giggled at the tickly feeling at his neck. Standing Bear was big for his age, a bright and obedient child except for the mischief all two-year-olds enjoyed creating. He had stopped breastfeeding much earlier than most Indian babies, walked sooner than most, and was speaking many words. As soon as he was born, Medicine Wolf was certain the decision she had made that Bear Paw should take her sister for a wife had been the right one, for the pride and joy in Bear Paw's eyes made her own heartache worth the pain.

At birth the boy had been called Little Bear, for his first cries were so loud, Bear Paw said it seemed he roared like a bear, and because the bear had been a part of Bear Paw's own vision at his first Sun Dance. Now that the child was walking, he was called Standing Bear. He was a handsome child, with dark, smooth skin, round, dark eyes that always seemed to glitter with mischief, a bright, quick smile, and black hair that was still fine but grown nearly to his shoulders.

Medicine Wolf had loved him like her own from the moment she first held him. She had stayed behind when the Dog Soldiers rode out on the hunt or on raids so that she could be with her "son," for that was how she thought of him. Smiling Girl shared him willingly, aware of the pain Medicine Wolf suffered at not being able to bear children of her own.

Medicine Wolf had learned to more easily accept the thought of Smiling Girl and Bear Paw mating for the sake of bearing children, and once Standing Bear ceased breast-feeding, she had again slept away from the tipi so that Bear Paw could try for another son. Now Smiling Girl was again with child, which was due in early spring. The three of them were happy together, sharing a son, and Medicine Wolf knew that she came first in Bear Paw's heart. Still, there lingered a vague, silent strain between them that she could not quite name. It was not something spoken, not even something she could point out in Bear Paw's actions. He was as good and devoted and attentive as he had ever been. But she sometimes wondered if he had ever quite gotten over her decision that he should take a second wife. Since then there had been a few times when he seemed to resent it when she made any kind of decision that affected him or the family, or even the Dog Soldiers, yet he never actually argued with her. Now that she and Bear Paw could sleep together again, the odd resentment seemed to have vanished, and she decided it was just a passing thing.

She picked up Standing Bear and carried him through

the quiet village to a place removed that had been chosen
for the basic human necessities. The Cheyenne always kept
such a place well away from the village for sanitary reasons, and never near their water supply. She frowned when
the boy rested his head against her shoulder. "Standing
Bear, you are getting so heavy I can hardly hold you,"
she teased. "Such a strong, solid little boy you are. You
will surely be a man in only another winter, you are so
big!"

She touseled his hair, and he laughed as she set him
on his feet. Both of them wore moccasins made from the
shaggy neck area of buffalo skin, the hair turned to the
inside of the moccasins for warmth. This time of year
moccasins were usually left on even in sleep, for tipi fires
burned down through the night so that mornings were
chilly. Standing Bear straddled his legs and pulled up the
knee-length wolfskin shirt he wore, using a chubby little
hand to guide himself so that he did not get his clothes or
moccasins wet. He happily urinated into the lightly snow-
covered ground, smiling at how his urine seemed to turn
to steam when it hit the cold air, then made little yellow
designs in the ground.

Medicine Wolf kept the buffalo skin around her shoulders as she likewise relieved herself. She thought how glad
she was that they had come south to see Red Foot, her
mother's brother, who had chosen to stay among the
Southern Cheyenne. Star Woman and Arrow Maker were
also there, as well as Bear Paw's mother and father.

Because many of the Southern Cheyenne had chosen
to live on the small piece of land that had been promised
them under the Treaty of 1861, things had been fairly
peaceful for them, although they had been blamed for raids
committed by Northern Cheyenne, and by the Arapaho
and Kiowa. Still, for the present, this was the most peace
Medicine Wolf and her family had known for months. Ever
since the Santee Sioux east of the Dakotas had gone on a
wild raiding spree two winters before, soldiers had harassed all the Sioux and Northern Cheyenne relentlessly.

Once Medicine Wolf and Bear Paw and the rest of the
family had reached their relatives in the South, they had
decided to stay awhile to rest and regain their strength, for

it seemed rather pleasant to be able to stay in one place.
Earlier in the year these Southern Cheyenne had also had
devastating troubles with volunteer soldiers in Colorado
Territory, led by a man they called *Zetapetaz-hetan*, or
Squaw Killer, a Colonel Chivington. The Cheyenne had
been blamed for raids committed by other tribes, and had
been harassed and hunted until the peace chief of the
Southern Cheyenne, Black Kettle, finally managed to calm
his angry young warriors and negotiate a peace settlement.

The winter had been relatively quiet for Black Kettle's
band, among whom Medicine Wolf's uncle and his family
lived. They were camped now on Sand Creek, where Black
Kettle's people waited patiently for word from a Major
Scott Anthony about when new rations would be arriving
under a peace agreement Black Kettle had reached with
another white soldier, a Major Wynkoop, called "Tall
Chief" by the Cheyenne.

Medicine Wolf's uncle claimed that Wynkoop was a
good man, a man of his word. But he had suddenly been
called back east, and Major Anthony had taken his place.
There seemed to be some confusion as to where the white
man's government expected Black Kettle's band to settle,
and whether they were free to hunt; and promised supplies
again were late. They waited here patiently, proving their
intent to keep their word and cause no trouble. At times
like this Medicine Wolf sometimes wondered if all the
Cheyenne should surrender and settle on the small reservation left to them in eastern Colorado Territory between
the Arkansas and Smoky Hill rivers. Perhaps if they felt
they could truly trust the white government's promises,
and if promised rations would arrive on time, and if the
food that was sent was not wormy and rotten, perhaps they
could give more consideration to bowing to white demands, for life was getting more difficult, bellies hungrier
every year.

Standing Bear started to run away from her then, in-
terrupting her thoughts. She laughed, chasing after him
and again whisking him up into her arms and wrapping
her robe around him. Just as she did so, she heard the
strange thunder. She barely had time to turn and see what
had caused the sound, when a tipi not far from her own

exploded and collapsed. She realized in that shocking instant that the tipi belonged to her parents.

Everything happened so quickly then that for those first few moments Medicine Wolf could hardly comprehend what she was seeing. Her father had been just emerging from his tipi when it shattered, and she watched his body fly forward as though propelled by an invisible force. Was her mother still inside the tipi? There came the thundering sound again, and another tipi collapsed. Somehow she knew that the big guns that had always frightened her were being used now. But why? Black Kettle and his band had been waiting here peacefully. They had made no trouble. Who was doing this? What had gone wrong?

She began running then, and everything happened in turmoil and terror. She could hear the cries of men hungry for blood, feel the ground shake from the hooves of many thundering horses, horses carrying mounted soldiers bent on destruction. Her heart pounded so hard that her chest hurt as she headed for her own tipi, where she could already see Bear Paw outside, wearing only a shirt and leggings and carrying a rifle. Behind her the horses sounded closer, and she could hear the clanking sound of soldiers' sabers. She held Standing Bear close as shots were fired and bullets whizzed all around them.

Indians were pouring out of other tipis now, children beginning to cry, women screaming. Black Kettle was raising an American flag as well as a white flag, trying to signal the soldiers that they were a peaceful band.

"Each of you, take a horse," Bear Paw told Medicine Wolf frantically as she reached him. "*Hopo! Hopo!* Ride hard, Medicine Wolf! Take Smiling Girl with you!"

"My mother . . . the tipi . . ."

"There is no time! Go! Go!" He quickly hoisted her and Standing Bear onto the back of *Nonoma-e*, glad he had staked a couple of horses near the tipi the night before. It was a habit he had developed over the months of harassment from soldiers in the North after the Sioux uprising, for now they must always be ready to flee.

Smiling Girl, wearing only a tunic and no moccasins, climbed onto another of Bear Paw's mounts. Medicine Wolf felt as though she might vomit any moment. There was no time to save one thing, to grab even a blanket, no time to embrace Bear Paw. He was a Dog Soldier. He would stay behind and fight with the other young men while women and children and old ones tried to flee the hell-bent soldiers.

Who were these men? What had gone wrong? *"Zetapetaz-hetan,"* she heard one woman scream. *Big man,* she thought, *squaw killer Chivington!* Already soldiers were streaming through the village. Tipis were on fire, women were screaming and running. Medicine Wolf and Smiling Girl rode hard, heading north. Medicine Wolf tried not to think about Bear Paw, who should have been blessed first with the wolf's paw. When there was time to pray for the Dog Soldiers and bless them with the paw, they were usually victorious. But now soldiers always seemed to attack by surprise. There was no time to prepare, no time for the Indian men to plan their defense, no time for smoking the prayer pipe and receiving the strength of the spirits of the four directions and the blessing of the wolf's paws.

As though in a dream she saw a soldier run a saber through a small child. She wanted to fight them herself alongside the other warriors, but she had no weapon, and her first duty was to save Standing Bear, for he represented the future. To stop now would mean that she and Standing Bear and Smiling Girl would all die. This was a time when everyone thought only of saving themselves. There would be time later for retaliation, if there were any of her People left to fight. She allowed herself to look back once, and she saw a Cheyenne woman lying naked in the cold snow, pinned there by a saber run through her shoulder. A soldier was raping her.

Medicine Wolf let out a little gasp of horror and kicked *Nonoma-e*'s sides, making the horse ride at a thunderous gallop. Bear Paw's horses were lean and swift. She knew she could outride any mounted soldier. She looked over at Smiling Girl, who face looked almost white from shock. She knew her sister must be freezing cold, and she worried about her pregnant condition; but if she gave her her robe, little Standing Bear would be the one who would be cold. She did not mind for herself, but she could not risk the child getting the lung sickness and dying. There was nothing to do but ride, ride until they could no longer hear the screams, or the big guns.

Medicine Wolf put her robe over Smiling Girl, who lay shivering and coughing between fits of weeping. "Medicine Wolf," the woman moaned to her sister, "you are the holy one, the woman of vision. Why did this happen? Black Kettle's band caused no trouble. Why did the squaw killer attack us?"

Medicine Wolf had no answer. Perhaps the Wolf Spirit meant for her and Bear Paw to stay in the North. She had had a strange, apprehensive feeling about coming south, but her mother had wanted to make the trip, and things had been so peaceful these past few weeks. They had thought they would enjoy a serene winter. Perhaps the Wolf Spirit was upset with her for not obeying her instincts, but she had hesitated, for Bear Paw had wanted to come here, and she had not wanted to interfere with his decision.

She was allowing her love for Bear Paw and her son cloud her deeper spiritual instincts, and this was the result. She had not prayed enough, had not fasted enough, had not been firm enough in stating her feelings and personal decisions.

Somehow she and Smiling Girl had managed to find refuge in a small cutout in the earth along the bank of a tributary of the Republican. The bank afforded shelter from the wind, and Smiling Girl huddled under Medicine Wolf's robe with Standing Bear.

"I do not understand myself what has happened," Medicine Wolf told her shivering sister. "I know only that we must find more robes or blankets before we go on. We will go north, Smiling Girl, as soon as you can travel again. We must find a village of Northern Cheyenne and wait there until we hear what has happened to the others."

Again she felt sick. Not only was she hungry, but it horrified her to think what must have happened to her mother and father, and to Bear Paw. The soldiers had had a tremendous advantage this time. Memories of the child being killed, the Cheyenne woman being speared and raped, kept shocking her brain like bolts of lightning, but there was no time now to weep. She had to devote her energies to deciding how she and Smiling Girl were going to survive. She moved away from the shelter, aware that she could hardly feel her fingers and toes. She had given her moccasins to Smiling Girl for a while to warm her feet, and since putting them back on, it seemed her own feet would not warm up again. She had no robe now, only her winter tunic. Besides the clothes on their backs, they had two horses and one buffalo robe . . . no food . . . nothing else for warmth.

She gazed out at the wide horizon, wondering if they would freeze and die before they found help. She half hoped to see a white settlement, for then she could sneak there when darkness fell and perhaps steal some food and blankets; But there was nothing on the horizon except endless white snow and a gray sky. She moved back into the shelter, getting under the robe with Smiling Girl and putting her arms around her sister to try to warm her.

They lay together for nearly an hour before Medicine Wolf thought she heard a voice, a strange sobbing. Her first thought was that soldiers might have tracked them this far, and she wished she could find something for a weapon, but there was not so much as a stick lying about. She remained huddled in the shelter, waiting, ready to fight with nothing but fingernails if she must. She could feel footsteps on the earth near the shelter, above the bank, feel the stronger vibration of a horse. Again she heard someone sobbing.

She gasped when something charged into the shelter, then realized it was Little Wolf. The animal, not so little anymore, bounded to her side and began licking her face. She cried out his name and pulled him under the blanket for even more warmth, and Standing Bear, too young and innocent to realize the gravity of their situation, smiled and reached out his hand so Little Wolf could lick it. The child lay between Smiling Girl and Medicine Wolf, and Little Wolf straddled him then, licking his face and making him giggle.

Medicine Wolf quickly moved out from under the blanket. This was a good sign! Little Wolf had followed her scent and had led someone to where they were hiding. She crawled out of the shelter, just as a pair of moccasined feet came down the bank. She looked up to see Bear Paw standing there, his hand still holding the reins of a horse, a cut across his nose and lips leaving a scab from frozen blood.

For a moment they just looked at each other, amazed that they had found each other at all. Medicine Wolf saw the horror in her husband's eyes, saw a new hatred that had never been there before. He had apparently managed to grab her wolfskin and another blanket, for the wolfskin was draped over the pony he led, and he wore a blanket around his shoulders. In his left hand he still held a rifle, but blood stained other parts of him, as though he had been cut several times or perhaps fought hand to hand.

There was nothing to be said at first. There was only gratitude they were even alive. Medicine Wolf walked into his arms, and he enfolded her in the blanket, letting go of the reins of the horse. Medicine Wolf allowed herself the luxury of the moment, to enjoy the safe feeling of his arms around her, to quietly celebrate the fact that he was alive. She closed her eyes, breathing deeply of his scent, fighting an urge to finally give in to the horror and terror and allow the tears to come. But she knew she must not do that, not yet.

"Everything is gone," Bear Paw told her. "Never have I seen anything like it." She had never heard such gut hatred and horror in his voice before. There was even a hint of fear, but she knew it was not a fear of fighting and dying, for no Dog Soldier feared such things. It ran much deeper than that—a deep dread felt only by someone who had witnessed something beyond horror. Neither of them could quite believe to what lengths the white soldiers would go to suppress the People. Did they mean to just come and murder them all, even women and children, even those Indians who were trying to live peacefully? What hope did they have against such hatred, or against the soldiers' big guns?

"No Crow or Ute, no Pawnee or Shoshoni . . . has ever done to our People what the squaw killer did today," he said then. She felt him shiver, heard a little gasp from his throat. "The women and children . . ." He gripped her tighter. "I did not know for certain that you had gotten away. When I rode through the ravine where most of the women and children ran for shelter and I saw . . . their bodies . . ."

He let go of her, giving her his blanket, standing back slightly. When she looked at the utter despair on his face, saw the tears on his cheeks, she knew it was as bad as it could be, for Bear Paw had never looked so defeated. "The soldiers followed them into the ravine. They cut the heads off little children and women, cut off arms, legs. I saw women . . . cut open . . . their private parts cut out . . . breasts cut off. When I managed to escape, the soldiers were burning the rest of the lodges, taking our horses, our supplies. They were laughing and celebrating."

He let out another gasp and turned away. It was then Medicine Wolf realized that Sweet Grass, her uncle Red Foot's young wife, sat on the pony Bear Paw had managed to save. The woman's head hung in despair and she wept, looking as though she hardly realized where she was.

Medicine Wolf stepped up to Bear Paw and touched his back. "My . . . mother?"

He only shook his head, facing her then, his eyes dark with pain and sorrow. "She is dead. So is Arrow Maker."

The words seemed to strike her heart like a sword. The sick feeling seized her again and she grasped her stomach, turning away.

"My own mother . . ." Bear Paw did not finish the sentence. How could he tell her what had happened to his own mother! He could not speak the words. It seemed easier to think that maybe it had not really happened if he did not say it. He could still see her, begging him to kill her and put her out of her misery. "I could not find my father, but I saw others. Many good warriors like your father are also dead . . . White Antelope, War Bonnet, Yellow Wolf . . . and your uncle, Red Foot, he is also dead, and his little son. There must be over two hundred of our People lying dead along the creek bottom!"

The sun had not yet gone down, but for Medicine Wolf it seemed that the sky had turned dark, for she could see nothing for the moment. She went to her knees, hardly feeling the snow. Her little cousin had been only six months old. Now she understood Sweet Grass's bitter sorrow. The woman's husband and son were dead. Star Woman and Arrow Maker and Bear Paw's mother . . . all dead.

"All my horses are gone," Bear Paw continued. He walked past her, studying the horizon. "All our belongings, the Pawnee war shield and tomahawk, all my weapons except this rifle, for which I have no bullets; all the food we had stored for the winter, our blankets, our skins . . . everything . . . my horses," he repeated. "All my horses. But I would gladly give all of it over again, many times, if I could have my mother back, and your own mother and father, all of the loved ones who have been lost."

Medicine Wolf struggled to her feet, realizing that in spite of her own horrible grief, this was not the time to break down or give up. On trembling legs she walked close to Bear Paw and touched his arm. "We have Standing Bear. He is alive and well," she told him, struggling to keep her voice strong. "Smiling Girl needs our help, Bear Paw. She is sick. We must find a warmer place for her or she will lose the baby. It is the young who are left we must save. And we must remember." Her voice choked. Oh, how she wanted to scream and scream and scream; how she wanted to get hold of a bluecoat soldier and take a knife to him until he was a bloody pulp! "There must be other survivors. We must help those we find, and we will all need you to lead us to the nearest village of Northern Cheyenne. We cannot stay here long, Bear Paw, or we will die."

He turned to look at her, and his eyes frightened even her. People would pay for what had happened, and she was glad at this moment that she was not Bear Paw's enemy.

"There was no reason," he said, his voice low, his teeth gritted, his jaw flexing in repressed rage. "No *reason*!" He clenched his fists. "Many will die for this! There is *no* peace for us now, Medicine Wolf, no place left for us to go except to the Sioux! For a long time, ever since the soldiers chased down the Santee after the raids two winters ago, the Sioux have asked us to help them fight the white soldiers. Always we said no. We waged our own raids, kept the peace until we were chased and shot at so often that again we had to steal food and horses to stay alive. We have lived much among the Sioux, but we have seldom fought at their side. Now it is time to gather together, to forget about whether we are Sioux or Cheyenne or Arapaho and remember that we are *Indian*! Remember that we *all* have a common cause! Let the peace chiefs go on about how it is hopeless to fight the soldiers and settlers. I will *die* before I let men such as those I saw today turn our own men into women and put us on a piece of land where we are watched like wild animals in a pit and treated like insects, to be stepped on and killed!''

Their eyes held, and she put a hand to her medicine bag, which she was thankful she had been wearing in her sleep this morning. Was it really only this morning? It seemed like many days ago.

"*Ai*, my warrior husband. We will fight them together, for I have lost much this day." Her throat ached fiercely. Star Woman! Arrow Maker! It did not seem possible that her parents could be dead! Smiling Girl cried out her name then, and she turned, wondering how she was going to tell her poor sick sister their parents were gone, along with so many others.

Bear Paw walked past her, going to Smiling Girl and picking up his son. He held Standing Bear close, quietly weeping. Medicine Wolf turned to Sweet Grass, reaching up for her, but the woman only stared vacantly, muttering her son's name. She finally moved her dark eyes to Medicine Wolf, the whites of her eyes red, her whole countenance one of fearful bitterness. "We cannot even . . . bury them," she groaned. "The squaw killer stayed to collect trophies from our People, things they can take home with them and brag about what a brave battle they fought today."

"Come down from the horse, Sweet Grass," Medicine Wolf urged her.

The young woman just looked away. "Go to your husband. Hold him much, Medicine Wolf, for you may not have him long. From now on his hatred for the *ve-ho-e* will come before all things."

Medicine Wolf turned away, not sure how to help Sweet Grass. She looked at Smiling Girl, remembering how she used to smile so often, a young woman who was undemanding, who was quiet and obedient, who had accepted her place as second wife with total joy, and who gave children to Medicine Wolf and Bear Paw with the enthusiasm of a child giving gifts. She did not smile now, and Medicine Wolf wondered how long it would be before any of them smiled again.

She quickly turned then at the sound of a shuddering gasp, followed by a thud. Bear Paw turned at the same time, and to his and Medicine Wolf's horror, they saw Sweet Grass lying in the snow, a knife in her heart, her own hands still clutching it. Quickly the snow beneath her turned red with blood. She cried out her son's name once more before her hands fell away from the knife, her eyes showing the vacant stare of death.

It had been a long time since Northern and Southern Cheyenne had banded together to raid and pillage, nor had they ever been quite so violent as the Sioux and Apache. But now the incident at Sand Creek burned in their hearts and memories like red-hot coals, and their hatred was just as hot. Except for a few Southern Cheyenne who allowed the attack to break them into complete submission, the majority of the Cheyenne had no desire left to try to make peace with the white men's government. Sand Creek must be avenged! Hardly a man or woman or child had survived without losing someone dear to them in the senseless slaughter.

War parties of Dog Soldiers led by chiefs like Tall Bull and Bull Bear raided and plundered as they worked their way north. Another name began to emerge in the headlines of eastern newspapers—a fearsome Cheyenne Dog Soldier called Bear Paw; and it was rumored that a woman rode with him, a woman who had great authority among the Cheyenne. She was called Medicine Wolf.

Other bands of Cheyenne, as was usual for most Indians, shared what they had to help those from Sand Creek rebuild their store of food and other supplies. Towns and settlements were plundered, rifles and ammunition stolen. No settler in the pathway of the enraged warriors was spared, and Bear Paw rebuilt his horseherd at the expense of angry and frightened settlers. Many paid with their lives.

The slaughter at Sand Creek had taken place in the Moon When the Wolves Run Together, what the white man called November, 1864. By the Moon of the Strong Cold, January of 1865, after being joined by Northern Arapaho and by many Sioux, who were led by one known as Pawnee Killer, the warriors were over a thousand strong. They attacked Fort Rankin, killing all but eighteen of the sixty men manning the fort. Nightly war dances were held by the young Cheyenne Dog Soldiers, always preceded by prayers from Medicine Wolf and the blessing of the wolf paws. Smiling Girl had recovered, and she and the few other women who had survived Sand Creek went even farther north to live with Medicine Wolf's band of Cheyenne.

Medicine Wolf and several other women remained behind with the warriors, the women as furious and full of vengeance as the men, for many had lost their husbands or children. Medicine Wolf herself rode with the warriors, directed raids. She even learned to be skilled with a rifle, learned to kill.

Other women who accompanied the warriors did not participate in the actual raids, but they supported their men, prepared tipis, tended the horses, helped repair shields and weapons, and cared for the wounded when they returned from raids. The Dog Soldiers' most successful raid was against the town of Julesburg, Colorado, where they seized thousands of dollars worth of food and other supplies as well as more rifles and ammunition. The camp women helped by bringing extra ponies to use to pack and carry off articles taken from stores and warehouses—flour, sugar, corn, tobacco, ammunition. Even cattle were rounded up and herded away, as well as horses.

With great delight Medicine Wolf remembered one raid in particular. She and Bear Paw and his Dog Soldiers attacked a passenger coach at Julesurg. They discovered a large metal box on board and proceeded to chop it open, discovering it was full of money. To Bear Paw paper money seemed to represent something evil about the *ve-ho-e*, and when Medicine Wolf explained how important this paper money was to the white man, he and the other warriors began hacking the bills into small pieces and throwing them to the wind.

"Wait! Stop!" one of the coach drivers had shouted. "That's the payroll for—" The man suddenly shut up. Medicine Wolf told Bear Paw what he had said, and Bear Paw walked over to him, slamming him against the coach and holding a knife to his throat. He told Medicine Wolf to make the man finish his sentence. Sweat pouring down his face, the man told her, and Medicine Wolf smiled wickedly.

"It is money to pay the soldiers of Colorado, Squaw Killer's men," she sneered. "It is a good thing that we do. Destroy it *all*, Bear Paw!"

Bear Paw barked an order to the other warriors, and they began whooping and yipping, making sure that every green bill was cut into many tiny pieces. They shouted and danced as they watched the brisk wind carry them across the dusty plain. All the while Bear Paw kept his eyes on the shaking driver. "So," he growled to Medicine Wolf, "this man brings the money to pay the men who murdered our People." Quickly his big blade slid across the man's throat. His dark eyes dancing with sweet revenge, he watched the man crumple to the ground. He wiped his knife on the man's shirt, then mounted his horse.

Medicine Wolf stared at the dead body, a part of her telling her that this was wrong, but her sorrow making it impossible to think rationally. The white man had to know he could never again do what he had done at Sand Creek.

After the raids on Julesburg, the warriors headed north, and for the next seventy-five miles along the way they raided and burned stage stations, wagon trains, and small settlements as well as destroyed the "talking wires" that sent messages to soldiers.

It was a time of sweet revenge, a time of stealing back from the *ve-ho-e* what had been stolen from them—food, horses, supplies. It was a cold winter, but the Cheyenne were hot for vengeance. Wounded pride and grieving hearts removed all reason, and together they were strong, so strong that they began to believe they truly could send the white man packing back to the land of the rising sun. In February 1865 Julesburg was attacked for a second time, and Sioux, Cheyenne, and Arapaho alike were again rich in supplies, horses, and rifles.

To their great delight, the Indians seemed to be able to roam free and raid at will. Because of the white man's fighting with each other in the East, there were few soldiers to stop them. Repeated victories and stores of plunder helped ease the pain of the loss of loved ones. The Cheyenne, along with the Sioux and Northern Arapaho, were free, roaming the plains at will, camping in the open, using buffalo chips for fire when there was no wood; or camping along wooded riverbeds, where game was more plentiful. Bellies were full, tobacco was smoked, feet and backs were warm. There were skins for clothing, hides for tipis.

Now even the soldiers did not come after them, but victory was slightly soured for Medicine Wolf by a new enemy, one she did not know how to fight. Ever since the horror at Sand Creek, Bear Paw had turned to drinking whiskey. For years he had avoided going the way of so many others, drinking the firewater every night until their dancing became frenzied, their eyes wild. Some drank it before raids, and it made them bold and careless. Now Bear Paw had fallen into the same practice.

There had always been something about the white man's whiskey that Medicine Wolf did not trust, but because it seemed to make Bear Paw so much happier, and because anything Medicine Wolf said to him in the way of criticism seemed to wound his immense pride, she said nothing. Since he had taken a liking to the firewater, the underlying resentment she had felt those first months after she had told him he must take a second wife had again emerged. It was worse now that she had ridden with the Dog Soldiers on so many raids and often had even been the one to give the orders.

The whiskey seemed to change her husband's personality. Where once he had been proud of his warrior woman, he now sometimes acted as though he thought they were in some kind of competition. In Medicine Wolf's mind there was no competition at all. How could she ever compare to the brave and daring Bear Paw, who had successfully led so many raids of his own, who had sometimes ridden right into the pathway of bullets from soldier and settler guns and had never been wounded?

Many nights Bear Paw had shown her the other side of his manhood. They still shared a wonderful intimacy, a glorious union; but since he had begun drinking the whiskey, he was sometimes more distant, less gentle. Medicine Wolf began to feel more and more alone in spite of the love they shared, for Bear Paw was full of hatred and violence . . . and whiskey. She understood the hatred, felt it herself, but she knew what they were doing had to end soon, that somehow they had to be at peace with themselves again. She sensed that the horror had been worse for Bear Paw, that there was something about Sand Creek that he had not told her, and that it was festering inside him like an old wound. There was a side to him now that she could not reach, as though someone else had taken over her husband's body; she decided she could only be patient. Somehow things would be sweet and good between them again. In the spring following the horror of Sand Creek, Smiling Girl had given birth to another son, called Big Hands. Medicine Wolf had thought at the time that the gift of a second son would help Bear Paw find peace within himself again, but he had only celebrated the birth by drinking so much whiskey that he had not even been able to rise the next day.

Medicine Wolf did not like seeing her husband so controlled by what she considered the evil spirits that lurked inside those brown bottles. But whenever she mentioned it to Bear Paw, he became belligerent and angry, looking at her in a way that he had never looked at her before, sometimes even frightening her. All the young Cheyenne warriors were feeling cocky and confident now, and with good reason. Victory and freedom seemed to be a sure thing. The few soldiers left were farther north, in forts along the road into the Bighorn Mountains that the white man called the Bozeman Trail. The Sioux, and their esteemed leader, Red Cloud, were in the process of raiding and killing in an effort to close those forts and the road leading into the gold fields of Montana. Many white men took that road, all of them after the yellow metal that they seemed to look upon as almost sacred; but they were again coming into Indian country, where they did not belong. Red Cloud was determined to stop them. The Cheyenne, feeling stronger than ever, would help.

A new leader emerged among the Sioux, and his name was becoming as well known as Red Cloud and Bear Paw. He was called Crazy Horse, and under his direction a troop of eighty soldiers from Fort Phil Kearny in Wyoming Territory were killed to the last man after being tricked by Crazy Horse. The story was told often over Sioux and Cheyenne campfires, how Crazy Horse and a few warriors had attacked soldiers who had been out cutting wood, how the soldiers got more men and came after them, thinking there were only a few warriors. Crazy Horse had stayed just out of rifle range, he and his men riding back toward the soldiers and shooting at them just enough to entice them to keep coming.

As soon as the soldiers, under the leadership of a Captain William Fetterman, who had once boasted that with eighty men he could ride through the whole Sioux nation, were far enough from the fort to be out of range of the "big guns," Crazy Horse attacked. Hundreds of Sioux, who had been lying in wait, swarmed over the soldiers, and soon there was not a bluecoat left alive, or left with all his hair on his head. Every man was stripped, all rifles taken.

At last it seemed that the *Indians* were in control! Scalp dances took place often. By the year 1867 the Sioux nation wielded a mighty sword, and Washington was frenzied over what to do about it. The gold fields of Montana had become almost inaccessible from an eastern direction, for that meant riding through Sioux country to get there. Wives who had dared to come to the western forts to be with their husbands were sent south to Denver for safety.

Still, Medicine Wolf could not shake the feeling that victory would be short-lived. Was this lull in white retaliation only temporary? What was the Great White Father in Washington planning? She was disturbed by the howling of wolves at night, for their cry did not seem normal. It seemed more a cry of terrible mourning, and their song always gave her a feeling of desperateness, a feeling that soon no wild thing would be able to roam free. Besides the railroad, a new breed of white man had come into their land, and no matter what the Sioux and Cheyenne did to discourage them, they kept coming, bringing with them their huge rifles, guns that could shoot very far and fire big bullets, big enough to fell a buffalo bull with one shot. These men were rude and dirty and determined, and they were indeed killing buffalo, by the thousands. It seemed everywhere they went now the Indians found the putrid remains of a buffalo, all of it wasted except for the hide and a little meat.

It was a bad sign, but in spite of the problems with buffalo hunters, the Sioux and Cheyenne had much to celebrate. Soldiers were leaving, settlers were fleeing, and the Bozeman Trail was practically closed. Their bellies were full, their blood hot with whiskey. They were winning this war! The whites would forever regret what they had done at Sand Creek!

Chapter Twenty

Elena Prescott looked up from her desk to see Tom coming toward her with a newspaper. "A month old as usual," he told her with a half smile. "But it's the same. Look at how they describe the Sioux who attacked Fetterman and his men. " 'Despicably bold and confident,' " he read from a Denver newspaper. " 'These savages of the West must be restrained before they murder every man and commit atrocities against every woman from the Missouri to the Rockies in their relentless thirst for blood. Our own innocent suffer at the hands of an ignorant people who have no sense of how to manage the land for which they seem so determined to fight; a people whose cunning and whose yearning to murder and pillage cannot be matched. If we are to defeat them, we must think like them. We must do unto them as they do unto us.' "

He tossed the paper into a corner and sat down at one of the wooden desks in the tiny schoolroom. The students, such as they were, had left for the day, Indian children of the few Sioux who stayed around Fort Laramie, children of some of the Indian scouts, including nine-year-old Crow Dog, son of the Cheyenne scout White Horse and his wife, Summer Moon.

"You can't really blame some of them," Elena told her husband. "When men continue to meet revenge for revenge, the vicious circle can never end."

Tom met her tired eyes. "You think it's hopeless, but it isn't, Elena. It will just take time. The key is to help them learn new ways without demanding that they give up everything that is Indian. You can't do it the way my mother tried to do it with Medicine Wolf."

Elena leaned back in her chair, putting a hand to her stomach. Finally, after nine years of marriage and two miscarriages, she was with child again. This one seemed to be hanging on. "I would certainly like to meet this Indian woman who so affected your life, Tom. Sometimes I am glad she has never come around here. I have a feeling if she became a reservation Indian, I would have some competition for my husband's attentions."

Tom reddened slightly and grinned. "Don't be silly." He ran a hand through his hair. "It's just that one on one, Elena, it's easier to understand them, easier to work with them. And Medicine Wolf was so bright, so . . . I don't know . . . almost wise for her age. She had something spiritual about her, and she showed me a beautiful side to these people that the average white man will never understand. They just don't see the real reasons behind what the Indians are doing. They don't understand the fear the Indian feels, the terror that they will lose their freedom. That means more to them than life itself, and they're proving they're ready to die for it."

Elena's eyes dropped to a simple reader she had been using to teach. She thought of how difficult it was to make the Indian children sit still for lessons, how hard it was to even get the fort Indians to send their children to her. "Well, I'm afraid some of the things you saw in Medicine Wolf are lost to the Indians around here. I see a lot of drunkenness, laziness, and restlessness. That scout, White Horse, is no good. He drinks constantly, and he beats that poor wife of his. I don't understand why she takes it so meekly, as though she thinks she deserves to be treated that way. If that's the way most Indian men treat their wives, I see no beauty or spirituality in them.''

"You know some of the others around here don't like White Horse. These other Indian men don't treat their wives that way.''

"Yes, but they don't do anything to stop White Horse either.''

"Indians don't interfere with other Indians' domestic conflicts,'' Tom told her. "But don't go judging them all by the ones around here. For one thing, White Horse was apparently kicked out of the Cheyenne nation in shame, so the story goes. It's obvious the Cheyenne had no more respect for him than we do, so that shows you right there that there is a code of honor among them. And these other fort Indians are just some of the lazy ones who would rather sit around here and get fat on handed-out food and drunk on illegal whiskey than to risk their lives for their people. Ones like Bear Paw and Medicine Wolf, they'd rather starve than live like these fort Indians.''

"They just *might* starve, the way things are going. Those detestable buffalo hunters bring in more hides all the time. You know what that means for the Indians. The soldiers might as well sit back and let the buffalo hunters do their job for them. Without the buffalo, there *is* no Indian.'' She put a hand to her eyes, rubbing them wearily. "I don't know, Tom. It all seems so hopeless sometimes. I just think these fort Indians bring their children to school because they believe they'll get more handouts if they cooperate. They've lost that pride you say the free ones still have. In turn, the free ones would not think of sending their children to school. Either way, they have no conception of how important it is to be educated. I feel like we're fighting a losing battle. And now with the baby coming . . .'' She met his eyes. "I don't want to have this baby out here, Tom. I think I should go home to Boston to have it.''

Tom watched her lovingly. His wife was stronger than would appear by her frail looks. He had met her back east at school, a thin, redheaded, green-eyed beauty whose ideals and dreams matched his own. It took a woman of strong countenance and brave soul to come to this land to teach Indians. Their pay came from a parochial school in Boston, where they had both taught for four years before coming west. There Elena had miscarried twice and had been told she would not conceive again; yet here she was pregnant. It was a source of worry for Tom also, for she had carried the baby for five months now with no problem. Considering the problems she had already had, neither of them cared for the thought of her having the baby at an army fort without a doctor who knew about such things.

"You know how I feel, Elena," he told her aloud. "We've talked about this before. I agree this is a hell of a place to have a baby, but we didn't think it could happen in the first place. And considering how easily you miscarried in the past, you couldn't very well risk that rough trip back east. It's the lesser of the two evils to just stay here."

"But I feel good, and I know this is a strong one, Tom. Maybe I could try the trip now."

"With the way things are with the Sioux and Cheyenne?"

She smiled sadly. "You're a blood brother, remember?"

He rose, a handsome man of thirty-six now, his blue eyes dancing teasingly. "And I suppose if you're attacked you're going to say 'wait a minute! I'm Tom Prescott's wife. Find Medicine Wolf. She'll tell you not to harm me.' " Their eyes held in mutual concern, both realizing the true gravity of their situation. "It's a big country out there, Elena. And it's full of angry Indians. God only knows which ones Medicine Wolf rides with right now, where she is, or if she even cares anymore about this blue-eyed *ve-ho-e*."

She smiled more. "Knowing you, I have a feeling she still cares."

He leaned his big frame over the desk and kissed her cheek. "You've got to stay right here, Elena. There are quite a few women around here who can help, and don't underestimate the value of the Indian women. They've been having babies under a lot worse conditions than this for centuries."

She sighed deeply. "Yes, I suppose you're right. But

after the baby is born, maybe you and I should both go back for a while. I'm not sure I want to raise our child out here, Tom, at least not under the conditions we have now. Maybe once this is all settled, once the Indians are placed on reservations, it will be easier."

"Easier?" He thought about Medicine Wolf again, how impossible it had been to change her ways. Now she was as wild as the others, in spite of all his mother had tried to teach her. Her name had even appeared in Denver newspapers as the infamous holy woman of the Cheyenne, whose ways were as ruthless as the Dog Soldiers. "It will be one thing just getting them to agree to reservation life," he said. "It will be quite another helping them adapt to it." He turned and walked to a window, watching soldiers go through some drilling maneuvers just outside the fort. "There is a long, long road ahead, Elena. I'm not convinced it's right even to try to subdue them. I feel like an intruder out here. My only interest in helping them is that I know in the long run it's their only hope of survival. They think they're winning now, but you watch. Washington hasn't begun to let loose its guns yet. When they do, it's going to be bad for them."

He moved his fingers over the long white scar his mother had never seen. His parents had remained in Boston to teach, giving Tom all the more reason to come back west. He had never quite forgiven either of them for the way they had treated Medicine Wolf. If she had been handled right, perhaps she would have stayed with them after all.

But then, maybe things had all taken place as they should. He had Elena now, although her inability to enjoy sex had often been frustrating and disappointing. He supposed that losing two babies had not made things any easier for her. After the second loss they did not have sex for several months. In a way he almost wished now that he had left it that way, for he was just as afraid for her to have this baby here as she was.

He did so love the idea of having a child of his own, and it meant so much to Elena. She was a good woman, a caring person, strong and brave; but in spite of his love for Elena, his thoughts often moved to another, a woman with dark skin and dark eyes; a woman whose soul sang with the wolves, and who sometimes seemed to visit him in spirit whenever he heard the wolves howling in the night wind.

1867

"So, the Great Father in the East wants a new treaty," Bear Paw sneered. He drank more whiskey, while five-year-old Standing Bear and two-year-old Big Hands played nearby with stones. Smiling Girl sat outside the tipi mending a pair of Bear Paw's moccasins. Medicine Wolf stopped petting Little Wolf long enough to turn a hind quarter of deer meat that cooked on a spit over an open fire.

It was a warm September night, and Medicine Wolf's band of Northern Cheyenne, camped near a huge tribe of Oglala Sioux along the Powder River in the Bighorn Mountains, was enjoying a rare spell of quiet peace. Red Cloud's and Crazy Horse's efforts at closing the area had stopped white encroachment in its tracks, at least for the time being, and now white scouts were being sent out to try to talk the Indians into coming back down to Fort Laramie to sign a new treaty.

"I cannot bring myself to believe these new promises any more than the old promises they made us," Medicine Wolf answered her husband. "I do not think we should agree to this treaty."

She did not see the strange, angry look her husband gave her. She had forgotten how easily he was offended when he drank the whiskey.

"It is not your decision to make," he answered.

"Black Buffalo and your Dog Soldiers will want my opinion," she said without thinking.

Smiling Girl's chest tightened at the dark look in Bear Paw's eyes. He was still a hard, handsome Dog Soldier. The whiskey had not made him weak and lazy like some others, but rather meaner, more determined. She doubted any other warrior in their camp or in the Sioux camps would want to tangle with Bear Paw. She loved him, and she knew Medicine Wolf loved him even more, but ever since Sand Creek he had changed, and Smiling Girl had learned to speak as little as possible when he was drinking.

Medicine Wolf, on the other hand, still sometimes spoke out of turn, as she had done just then. It was not that Smiling Girl feared Bear Paw. He had never struck her or Medicine Wolf; it was his eyes, the anger she sometimes saw there, especially toward Medicine Wolf. Just his look was enough to keep her quiet.

"So, you are saying it is *your* decision whether or not Red Cloud signs a treaty," Bear Paw grumbled, casting angry, dark eyes at Medicine Wolf.

Medicine Wolf realized she had again offended him, something she seemed to do unwittingly and all too often these past months. She studied him, this man she loved more than her own life, and she wondered where the real Bear Paw had gone. He had not been physically killed at Sand Creek, but she had lost him just the same. Now the whiskey was killing what little was left of his soul and spirit.

"I do not make Red Cloud's decisions," she answered, tired of the way he seemed to always put her on the defensive with every word she spoke. She met his eyes boldly, rising. "Nor *yours*. The *whiskey* makes your decisions for you! Tell me, my husband, how long will you go on letting the whiskey be your strength and control your thoughts and actions? How long before you fast and pray and find your strength from the *inside*, where you carry so much power and pride? Only prayers and proper sacrifice will bring you the wisdom and happiness you seek. The whiskey is destroying you!"

She ducked inside the tipi then, and Smiling Girl quietly watched Bear Paw out of the corner of her eye, wondering how he would meet this new challenge. He also went inside the tipi, and Smiling Girl wisely stayed put. Inside, Bear Paw watched Medicine Wolf shove some of his clothes into a parfleche. She took a knife from her belt then and picked up the blanket she shared with Bear Paw. He knew she was readying to rip it in half and throw his half outside, along with his personals, signifying that he was no longer welcome in their lodge. Before she could cut the blanket, he grasped her wrist and whirled her around. He squeezed her wrist until she dropped the knife.

"Are you saying I am weak," he snarled.

Medicine Wolf stood her ground. "Not in body," she answered firmly. "But your mind and heart are weak, Bear Paw! Once your spirit was as strong as your body, and it was that spirit that I love much more than the grand physical man that you are! I no longer know you! Until I see the Bear Paw that I married in your eyes again, I no longer want you in my dwelling!"

Oh, how it hurt to say it, but it did no good to harp at him about his drinking. Perhaps if he could no longer be near his sons, no longer sleep with her, he would give up the firewater.

He suddenly kicked the back of her leg, not in a gentle, teasing way he once had used to get her to the ground, but a painful kick that made her grunt. She hit the ground hard, and he was quickly on top of her. "Again you make the decisions," he snapped. "*I* will decide whether I live here, and *I* will decide when I take pleasure in my wife!"

He rose up to shove her tunic up to her waist, but before he could do anything more, Medicine Wolf brought her leg back and kicked him hard in the chest, sending him sprawling. She started to scramble away, but he grabbed her ankle, twisting it so painfully that she cried out and was forced to move onto her back again. He quickly sat on her legs and grabbed her arms, jerking her up.

"You think you are the only one who has powers," he growled. "*I* have power too, the power of a great warrior, the power the *firewater* gives me! You may be blessed with the Wolf Spirit, woman, and you may be able to bless and prophesy for the Cheyenne, but that does not give you the right to tell me what I should eat and what I should *drink*! Nor do you have the right to tell me where I will live! Must you dictate my every *breath*?"

"The firewater does *not* give you power," she answered boldly, trying to wrench free of him. "It makes you *weak*! If you were the same man I married, I would not think to try to tell you anything that you should do! But you are a changed man, Bear Paw, and I love you too much to let you destroy yourself! I want us to be happy

again! Share your grief and anger with *me*! Do not try to
drown them in the whiskey! It will kill you. It makes you
do foolish things!''

"So," he spat out. "I am not only weak, but I am
also *foolish*! But *you* are the fool, Medicine Wolf, to think
you are above your husband's wrath! You are a sacred
woman to the others, but you are *my* wife. Leave your
preaching at the council meetings! I am tired of sharing
you that way, *tired* of being looked upon as the husband
of the holy woman rather than as Bear Paw, the great warrior!''

"The People *do* look at you as a great warrior, my
husband," she threw back at him. "It is only lately they
have begun losing their respect for you, because of the
whiskey! It has nothing to do—!''

"From now on you will not give me orders," he interrupted as though he had not heard a word she said. "*I*
am the master, the one with the power!'' He raised his
hand as though to hit her, and Medicine Wolf, her own
fury raging at his threats, used her free hand to grasp the
knife that lay near her. In anger and despair she jabbed
the knife into his upraised arm.

Bear Paw cried out, leaping away from her and glaring
at her in shock and disbelief. Medicine Wolf took advantage of the moment and ran outside, hardly noticing Little
Wolf, who had come running from where he had been
scavenging in the nearby hills. The animal turned to follow her, sensing his mistress's distress. Medicine Wolf
kept running as fast as her legs would carry her. A few
others in the village watched, but none followed. This was
a domestic squabble that was not their business, and the
fact that it involved the holy woman and one of their most
prized warriors made it even less their business.

Medicine Wolf finally fell to her knees under a huge
pine tree, panting to get her breath. She lay down in a bed
of soft needles to weep, her disappointment in Bear Paw
overwhelming her. If only Arrow Maker or Star Woman
or Old Grandmother were here to talk to, to give her some
advice. But there was no one, and the loneliness she had
suffered over the years returned to pierce her heart. She

felt Little Wolf licking her, and she rolled onto her back, taking the animal into her arms.

Suddenly she felt like the little six-year-old girl who lived alone among the wolves twenty-one winters ago . . . twenty-one winters since the handsome young warrior of fourteen years called Red Beaver had found her among the wolves. But that was another time, another world, a time of sweet freedom and peace, a time when few white men lived in the land of the Sioux and Cheyenne, a time when their hearts were happy.

She waited, wondering if Bear Paw would come, wishing he would tell her how sorry he was, wishing he would hold her the way he used to; but no one came.

Back at the village Bear Paw stumbled out of the tipi. He glanced at Smiling Girl for a moment, then picked up his whiskey bottle and headed for Clay Woman's dwelling.

Morning broke still and bright. Medicine Wolf awoke to the feel of Little Wolf lying close to her to help keep her warm. The animal raised its head, then licked her face lightly before springing to its feet. Medicine Wolf grasped the thick fur of his chest and rubbed it vigorously.

"You do not change, do you," she said sadly. "The love of an animal is simple and true. You will always be my loyal friend." She sat up and gave him a hug, then got to her feet and shook off pine needles. She smoothed back her hair, breathing deeply of the rich smell of pine sap and wondering what she should do next. She loved Bear Paw, but she could not abide with what he had become. It tore her heart to have to throw him out, but perhaps that was best. Today he would have slept off the whiskey and she could reason with him.

It felt as though a huge stone were lying against her heart. Bear Paw, her mighty warrior, her beloved. She started toward the village when she saw someone coming her way. It was Bear Paw. She hesitated, her heart racing. Last night was the first time he had ever been cruel to her, and she would never have thought she could use a knife on this man she loved so dearly.

She could see that his upper left arm was bandaged.

Little Wolf growled slightly, as though to give warning. "So, you also know how our beloved Bear Paw has changed," Medicine Wolf told him softly. She reached down and touched his head. "It is all right. This morning he will not be full of the whiskey." The wolf, much bigger than his name would imply, stood stiff and glaring, the fur on its back rising slightly.

Bear Paw called her name, and she walked out of the thick grove of pine so that he could see her. Little Wolf followed. Bear Paw spotted her and moved toward her, then hesitated when he saw Little Wolf's yellow eyes boring into him.

"He will not harm you," Medicine Wolf told him, "as long as you do *me* no harm." It seemed strange to have to warn him about the wolf that had been with them now for nearly six years and had been as much a friend and pet to Bear Paw as he had to Medicine Wolf.

Bear Paw came even closer, and for the first time Medicine Wolf became more aware of the lines of aging that were beginning to show on his face. He was a man who had lived a hard and dangerous life, a man who did not know the meaning of fear when it came to combat. He was afraid of only those things he could not control, like the future of his People. Medicine Wolf knew it weighed heavily on him, knew that was why he had turned to whiskey. She realized she had always seen him through the eyes of the sixteen-year-old girl who had married him when he was twenty-four, but he was thirty-five winters now, and he carried many scars, including the thin white scar across his nose and lips that he had gotten at Sand Creek. There were other scars, unseen scars, and it was these inner scars that had not healed. He was looked to as one of those who would save his people from harm, and he had tried to do so at great cost. They had suffered much together; but they had also known much joy, had shared a passion few people were privileged to experience.

She knew by his eyes the pain he suffered over the way he had treated her the night before. He looked at her, his eyes lingering on the bruises at her wrists. He closed his eyes then, breathing deeply before speaking. "Smiling Girl told me what I did." He looked at her again, shaking his head. "I do not even remember. I ask your forgiveness."

She reminded herself she must be firm with him, but it was hard when he was so close. "It is not necessary," she answered. "How could I not forgive my beloved? I did not harm you because I hated you. I did it only to keep you away." She reached up to touch his arm. "How badly did I hurt you?"

He grasped her hand, but not painfully. He gently pushed it away. "It is no worse than other wounds I have suffered, but I suffered those in honorable fighting, not in a cowardly attack on the woman I love."

She took hope in the words, yet the anger was still there in his eyes. She searched those dark eyes deeply, feeling a mixture of anticipation and dread. "What have you come to tell me, Bear Paw?"

He turned away, walking a few feet from her. "In the beginning I thought it would not be so difficult living with a woman who has more powers than I," he said, pain in his voice, "because I loved you so much. But now I see that love is not always enough."

"Love *is* always enough, Bear Paw."

He shook his head. "No. I am a man, Medicine Wolf, an honored Dog Soldier. Perhaps it is too hard for two people of much power and pride to be as one. I feel . . . always challenged by that part of you I cannot reach or possess, that spiritual side that belongs to a different world. A man like myself needs a quiet, submissive wife, one like Smiling Girl. A woman like you . . . perhaps you should never have taken a husband."

Medicine Wolf felt the same sick feeling she had when her parents left her behind at Fort Laramie. "What are you saying?"

He threw back his head and breathed deeply again. "I am saying I have never truly belonged to you, or I should say *you* have never truly belonged to *me*." He turned to face her. "I feel I have loved you from a distance, like that white man Thomas loved you, a woman he could never possess. Sometimes I even fear you." He rolled his eyes. "Me, an honored warrior, afraid of his woman." He sighed and shook his head. "I cannot live with these things."

Her eyes teared. "What do you want of me, Bear Paw?"

He glaced at the wolf, then back at her eyes. "I want you to choose between the Wolf Spirit and the sacred paws . . . or me."

Their eyes held, and in spite of the bright morning, she felt a blackness closing in around her. So, here it was . . . the vision she had dreaded most. The time had come, as Black Buffalo had said it would, to choose.

"Black Buffalo would gladly take the wolf's paws," he was saying. "They bear much power. Any priest would be highly honored to own them. Give them up, Medicine Wolf, and *I* will give up the whiskey."

She struggled to stay in control, one tear slipping down her cheek. "You know I cannot make such a choice. It has never been up to me to do the choosing. The Wolf Spirit chose *me*, Bear Paw. I cannot turn away from my visions, my spiritual gifts. To do so would bring more trouble to the Cheyenne than our people already have. You know as well as I that our visions, our duty to the People, must come above all things."

She saw the agony in his eyes. "I know," he answered in a near groan. He held out his hand and opened it. In it was the wolf's paw she had given him so many years before. "I no longer deserve this or want it. You have chosen."

She recoiled in shock. He was taking a great risk giving back the wolf's paw, and she knew that by doing so he was also dissolving the marriage. She quickly wiped tears, looking at him in surprise. "This could mean your death! Do not do this, Bear Paw! Somehow, we—"

"I do not want it," he said sternly.

She shook her head. "It is not a matter of my powers, Bear Paw. It is only a matter of the whiskey! The firewater has become more powerful than you! Do you not see that? Before you started drinking the whiskey you thought with a clear mind. You were *strong* inside, strong enough to love me as a wife in spite of my powers. We *belong* together, Bear Paw! There is still a vision that has not been fulfilled!''

He walked closer, shoving the wolf's paw roughly into her hand, then stepping back. ''It is time I proved to you and to myself that I do not need your powers or the wolf's paw. And you are *wrong* about the whiskey! When I drink it I am strong and I feel no pain! More than that, when I drink it, *I* am the one with the power! I have found something much stronger than the wolf's paw, and it has made me see that this marriage cannot be, for we are too much the same, Medicine Wolf, always competing for power and honor.''

''No! Only *you* feel that way, Bear Paw! It has never mattered to me! Anything I did or said to you was because I *loved* you and wanted no harm to come to you.'' A desperate, sick feeling engulfed her. She had known herself that perhaps they should part for a while, but not this way. He must not give back the wolf's paw! It was too dangerous for him. Bear Paw turned away and she shouted after him. ''You told me I must make a choice,'' she nearly screamed. ''But it is *you* who has made the choice, Bear Paw! You chose the evil spirits of the firewater over *me*! You have seen what it does to some of the others. Some of our finest warriors are worthless now! The white man gives us the whiskey because he knows that someday it will *destroy* us! It makes our men weak and foolish!''

Immediately she wished she had not uttered the last sentence. Again she had insulted him, yet she knew she was right. He stopped and turned, giving her a dark look. ''We shall see,'' he told her. He turned away again.

''Bear Paw, do not do this! Do you not see that the whiskey destroys my own powers? I cannot help my people this way! They no longer listen to me!''

He turned again, this time smiling strangely. ''So, I *have* found something stronger than the wolf's paws!'' He nodded. ''I will continue to provide for you and protect you, Medicine Wolf. But we are no longer husband and wife. I asked you to give up your powers, but you chose them over me. Now *I* choose the whiskey over *you*. You have my vow that I will never again harm you, and you should know that my sorrow is great over what I did. But

that does not change what must be. You have your place,
your honored duties among the People, and I have mine.
If there is a vision yet to be fulfilled, then somehow it will
be. Let the Wolf Spirit find a way.''

He left her then. She watched him walk, studied the
build of the man with whom she had shared so much joy,
so much passion, the man who belonged in her vision. His
back was still broad and powerful. She watched the familiar hips, the flow of his hair, watched the dancing
fringes of his leggings.

She closed her hand around the wolf's paw, and she
felt the agony she had felt when she awoke from the vision
of standing at the stream, a man on one side, the wolf on
the other. Now she knew who that man was.

With shaking hands she took her medicine bag from
around her neck. She opened it, dropping the fourth wolf's
paw inside. She closed her hand around it and went to her
knees, her tears making little wet marks in the soft earth
over which she wept.

''We will not sign their worthless treaties.'' White
Eagle spoke up at council. ''What say you, Medicine
Wolf?''

Medicine Wolf moved her eyes to Bear Paw. For nearly
a year they had been apart. She lived now with Two Moons
and his wife, Shining Woman, her father's brother and his
wife. She was well cared for physically, but her heart remained sick. She saw the distant yearning in Bear Paw's
own eyes. Pride and whiskey were all that kept him from
her.

Smiling Girl was pregnant again, and Bear Paw had
turned to Clay Woman for his sexual needs. That was what
hurt most of all, for Clay Woman had always wanted to
claim him for herself. She strutted around the village like
a queen, carrying no shame for her behavior, giving Medicine Wolf haughty, victorious glares.

Medicine Wolf turned her attention back to White Eagle. ''I think the new treaties are as much a lie as the old
ones. The runners from the South tell us that the land set
aside by the Medicine Lodge Treaty is only a tiny piece,

and moves our People even farther south into hot, useless land occupied by many eastern tribes. It is land far away from the plains and prairies rich with grass and game that we once called our own. Only the peace chief Black Kettle is willing to sign this treaty. Even after what was done to his People at Sand Creek, he continues to try to keep the peace. It is wrong.'' She closed her eyes. ''I saw him in a dream. He was clutching the flag symbol of the white man's government. In his other hand he held the peace medal the Great Father in Washington gives to those Indian leaders who promise to remain peaceful. But in his heart was a soldier's saber.''

It was night, and a fire crackled nearby, lighting up the faces of the circle of warriors. Medicine Wolf opened her eyes and looked around at all of them. ''Black Kettle will die. All he has done to keep the peace will be for nothing.''

Restless mumbles could be heard, and when Medicine Wolf looked at Bear Paw again, he was taking a drink of whiskey.

''What about the new treaty they want the Sioux and Northern Cheyenne to come into Fort Laramie to sign,'' Stands Tall asked her.

She looked at Bear Paw's father, his face heavily aged now. Sadly, Medicine Wolf realized that all the older warriors looked weary . . . weary of the struggle to cling to their freedom. ''We will agree to that treaty only if and when Red Cloud agrees,'' she answered. ''So far he refuses to sign. The Sioux are one of the last remaining tribes who continue to fight for Grandmother Earth. They are still strong. We will continue to live among them and fight at their side.''

''I say we should go south and give help to our people there,'' Bear Paw put in, as though to challenge her.

Medicine Wolf shot him a look of daring. ''Our people in the South have already given up. There is a great soldier campaign there against them, led by the long-hair Custer. It would be dangerous to go there. Here we have a better chance of preserving what is left of the Cheyenne.''

''The women and children can stay here.'' Bear Paw

looked at her haughtily, taking another swallow of whiskey.

Medicine Wolf felt a strange fear growing deep inside.
"For many years now the Southern Cheyenne have been
like a different people to us. You know what happened the
last time we joined them. Their days are numbered now,
and I feel a great warning that we must stay here. I also
feel we must be very careful of the long-hair Custer. When
I said I saw a soldier's saber in Black Kettle's chest, I did
not tell you all of it. It was the long-haired one who held
the saber."

More mumbles moved among the warriors. Bear Paw
rose. "We have helped the Sioux hold on to the Powder
River country and the Black Hills," he said, strutting
around them like the fearful warrior that he was. "We
have brought the white man's government to its knees.
There are so afraid that now they want us to sign another
treaty! Now we wait to see what Red Cloud will do. I am
getting bored! In the South the soldiers have not yet learned
the lesson we have taught them here in the North. Many
of our brothers in the South continue to fight, and they
need our help. I say we should go down there and remind
them how we feel about Sand Creek! Have all of you *forgotten* what happened there? *I* have not forgotten! *I* remember how it felt to be unable to protect those who *count*
on me for protection! *I* have not forgotten the look on my
mother's face! I say we go *back*!"

"It is very dangerous to go through the country of the
Great Medicine Road," Stands Tall put in. "Now that the
iron horse is there, it is even more dangerous. White men
shoot at us from the windows like we are wild game."

"I will not let the iron horse or the white man's settlements stop me from where I want to go! He does not
belong there!"

"My son speaks foolishly since he started getting his
strength and wisdom from a bottle," Stands Tall retorted.

Bear Paw's eyes widened with indignation. He tossed
the bottle aside and came closer to his father. "And my
father listens too much to the holy woman. I have found
a power greater than hers, and I say we should go south!
We will tear up the iron rails as we have done before! We

will make the iron horse fall from the tracks and we will kill everyone on board and take their guns and anything else of value to us! We will show them they do not belong there! *I* am not afraid to face long-hair Custer or *any* blue-coat!"

Stands Tall rose, facing his son. "We have already done much fighting, yet more trains come, more whites, more settlers, more soldiers. That land is lost to us now, Bear Paw. To go there is to die."

Bear Paw shook his head. "To stay here and do *nothing* is to die!"

"If we are doing nothing, it is only for a while, my son. Do not foolishly think that the white man is done with us. Many battles lie ahead."

"Battles we will win, as we have won them in the past!"

"Perhaps. But for now I am tired of fighting, Bear Paw. This new treaty gives much land to the Sioux and Northern Cheyenne, all of the Black Hills and much of the Powder River country. It is good land. We must stay here, stay strong, protect it, in case the white man finds another reason to take away even more. We will need all our strength and power right here. Allied with Red Cloud and the new leaders, Crazy Horse and Sitting Bull, we are very, very strong!"

Bear Paw tossed his head, looking at the others. "My father is old and tired. But many of us are young, and able to help our people in the South. I am ready and willing to go. Who will go with me?"

"Do not go, Bear Paw." Medicine Wolf spoke up pleadingly. "It will be bad for you. I feel it—"

He whirled on her before she finished. "Be still, woman!"

Medicine Wolf straightened, stepping closer to him. "Fool! You plan your own death!" She walked away, but she could hear Bear Paw asking for volunteers. She felt sick inside, realizing how right Sweet Medicine had been in his prediction that her people would become divided. She left the light of the fire, not even staying for the blessing of the wolf paws, for many of the younger warriors had grown sure and haughty from the whiskey and they felt they no longer needed her powers.

She was sure their attitude was wrong and dangerous, but she had lost them to whiskey and victory. It was not good for her people to lose their way, to turn from rituals and spiritual blessings. She closed her eyes, shivering at the distant sound of Bear Paw's voice. Someone touched her shoulder then, startling her. She quickly turned.

"It is I, Black Buffalo," came a voice.

Medicine Wolf studied the old priest's commanding stature in the moonlight, unable to see him well. "You must let him go, Medicine Wolf," he told her, his melodic voice betraying his advanced years. She wondered how much longer he would be around to give her advice about her dreams and visions. "Remember that he was part of your vision, a vision that has not yet been fulfilled. You are separated now, because he needs time to see his own mistakes, to see that he cannot live without you. He needs time to learn to accept and understand that he will always stand behind you, not beside you. That is a difficult thing for a man like Bear Paw."

"He must stop drinking the firewater."

"Then something must happen to make him see this on his own. He is not ready to listen to what you tell him."

She put a hand to her medicine bag. "I am so lonely, Black Buffalo," she said. "If not for little Standing Bear and Big Hands, I would want to die. The wolf, my sister, the children, none of them can make up for what I lost when Bear Paw walked away from me. He is my life."

"No, child. The Wolf Spirit is your life. And through the Wolf Spirit you will find Bear Paw again."

"But I fear he will die before that happens," she answered. She hesitated, then decided he should know. "You are the only one who knows that many years ago I gave one of the wolf's paws to Bear Paw. You told me I was not to speak of it, but you knew what I would do. Now . . ." She swallowed. "He gave it back to me, Black Buffalo."

In the darkness Medicine Wolf could hear his gasp. "That is very bad medicine," he told her.

Her eyes teared. "It was the whiskey that made him

do it. I could bear this parting if I knew he was still protected by the wolf's paw. But to give back such a sacred fetish . . . and then ride against someone like long-hair Custer . . . it is bad. He will ride away without the blessing of the wolf's paw. Always he has been a great warrior. Always his wounds have not been the kind that could kill. The white man's bullets have never struck him because the Wolf Spirit protected him. Now I fear for him.''

He touched her head gently. ''There is nothing to do but pray for him, Medicine Wolf, and believe in the power of the Wolf Spirit, believe that through that power you can continue to protect him. He must learn his own way. There is nothing more you can do.''

Sadly she left him there. She gathered together a blanket and a container of water, telling Shining Woman she was going into the hills to pray. Little Wolf followed her. She found her way through the darkness, while in the distance she heard the young warriors begin a war dance. She knew that many of them would be drinking the whiskey, and that Bear Paw would easily rally them to his side, for they were young and eager to count coup.

On a hill above the village she spread out her blanket. She could hear the rhythmic drumming, hear the war cries of frustrated young men who knew no other way to live than to hunt and make war, to count coup and bring trophies home to their women. The white men wanted them to settle down and learn to farm. Even if the government awarded them all of the plains and prairies, to be told they must give up their way of life and accept handouts was something her People, especially the young men, simply could not do.

She knelt onto the blanket and raised her arms, lifting her eyes to the heavens and singing.

Oh, Grandmother Earth, hear me!
Oh, Grandfather Wolf, hear me!
Oh, great Maheo, hear me!
I sing my thanks to you!
Forever the wolf shall be sacred to me.
Forever the earth shall be sacred to me.
Forever I will please Maheo.

She sang her prayer song over and over, adding words to ask the Wolf Spirit to continue to protect Bear Paw, for she had been loyal to her duties, loyal to the Cheyenne. She had chosen the wolf paws over her beloved; but her beloved had chosen another way, and she greatly feared for him. She would stay here in the hills and fast and pray for many days.

All night she prayed, and beyond, even while Bear Paw and ten young braves rode out of the village and headed south. Some took their women with them. Bear Paw took Clay Woman.

Chapter Twenty-one

Medicine Wolf!

Medicine Wolf gasped, sitting up from a deep sleep. Who had called to her? She grasped her right side. In her still-sleepy state, she was sure she had somehow been injured; but as she came more awake she realized she was fine. She blinked in astonishment, for the pain had been very real.

She looked around the tipi, and by the light of a dimming fire she could see Smiling Girl and the boys slept peacefully. Since Bear Paw was gone, she had returned to stay with her family, but she had remained uneasy. Now that uneasiness was intense.

She touched her side again, and Little Wolf suddenly jumped to his feet. He went to the tipi entrance, sticking his nose through the edge of the buffalo-hide flap and whining. In the distant hills several wolves began howling. In spite of the quiet night, Medicine Wolf felt something was very wrong. She rose and folded open the buffalo skin to let Little Wolf outside, then stepped out herself, gazing around the village, listening intently.

She saw and heard nothing unusual, except for the continued howling of the wolves, a strangely mournful wail, as though they were trying to tell her something. "Bear Paw," she whispered. Was he hurt? Had it been his pain she felt? A sick feeling of dread overwhelmed her. If he was injured, *she* should be with him, not Clay Woman. She tried to imagine what could have happened. Bear Paw had been gone for only a week. There had not been time to reach the Southern Cheyenne and long-hair Custer.

She tried to reason that he was probably fine, but she could not deny the pain she had felt in her side, so sharp it had brought her out of a deep sleep. And what about the voice? She was sure someone had called to her. If she were an ordinary person who had ordinary dreams, she could perhaps dismiss this feeling. But she was Medicine Wolf, the holy woman, the keeper of the wolf paws. Most everything she dreamed had meaning, and to wake up with such a distinct pain, to hear someone calling her, could mean only that someone she loved was hurt.

The night was warm and mild, the smell of a coming spring rain in the air. She walked into the darkness, leaving the village to go into the nearby hills to pray, convinced Bear Paw was in trouble. Even under their present separation, she could not imagine life without his presence. He had been all she had lived for since she was six years old. Tears stung her eyes. He could be lying somewhere, needing her. If only she knew exactly where he was she could go to him; but she could only wait and wonder . . . and pray.

An hour passed, but the morning remained dark, for black clouds had gathered in the sky, shrouding the rising sun. To Medicine Wolf they were an ominous sign—no sunrise, no life, no Bear Paw. Thunder rumbled to the west, and the wind grew stronger. A storm was coming, not just to the land, but to her heart. Rain began to sprinkle against her face, and she raised her eyes to the heavens, praying then to the powerful Thunderbird, Lord of Storm and Wind. Perhaps Thunderbird would help her.

She would appeal to all the most powerful spirits, and to her own protective Wolf Spirit, and to *Maheo*.

Lightning lit up the forest, leaping from the clouds as though angry. She remembered when she used to be afraid of storms, but this time she wanted the storm to come, wanted to feel its power! To her the earth-shaking thunder and the shattering lightning proved that the powers of Grandmother Earth and the great heavens were with her. She was knelt in a grove of tall pines, and as the rain began to fall, the sweet smell of a damp forest was soothing to her.

She raised her arms, throwing back her head, letting the warm rain run over her face, feeling surrounded by powerful Beings. Yes, she would stay here. She would fast and pray until Bear Paw came back to her. She would pray to *Ahktunowihio*, God of the Earth, to *Heammawihio*, God of the Sky. She would pray to the four directions and sing her prayer song. Perhaps the first prayers she had offered when Bear Paw left had not been enough. She would pray again; she would suffer starvation; she would do whatever she must do to bring Bear Paw home to her alive.

The rain poured harder then, soaking her hair and her tunic, mixing with her tears. She did not need anyone to interpret her dream this time. She knew its meaning. How she wished she did not have this strange insight, these premonitions. Of all her spiritual connections, she was closest to Bear Paw. His pain became her pain.

She was totally unaware that other wolves had gathered around her, some lying down, others sitting, a few pacing nervously. This strange human had called to them, had called upon the great Wolf Spirit that guided them and filled their souls. They watched Medicine Wolf weep and pray, and none thought to harm her, for she was one of them.

The cry carried through the village as scouts rode in. Bear Paw was coming! Their fiercest Dog Soldier was badly wounded. Bear Paw's father, Stands Tall, quickly mounted a horse to ride out to his son, who the scout had said was still at least two miles from the village. Since

Arrow Maker's death at Sand Creek, Stands Tall had been looked to as the leader of Arrow Maker's band of Cheyenne.

A runner headed toward the hills, and Smiling Girl, big with her third child, stopped pounding the spring berries she had been preparing to make pemmican. Tears formed on her chubby cheeks, for the scouts had said her husband was badly hurt. She wept not only for Bear Paw, but also for Medicine Wolf, for her sister had been fasting for many days now, praying for Bear Paw's return. Now they all knew that Medicine Wolf's predictions that something had happened to Bear Paw was true.

Six-year-old Standing Bear and three-year-old Big Hands stood near their mother, both of them strangely quiet, sensing something was gravely wrong. All through the huge village and its circles of tipis, women and children and the older men began to gather to wait, wondering what could have happened, for Bear Paw and the others had not had time to reach the South.

Smiling Girl turned then to see Medicine Wolf walking through the open grassland between the village and the distant hills. Black Buffalo seemed to be helping her. Smiling Girl remembered the morning she had awakened to discover her sister missing. Scouts had found Medicine Wolf praying in the nearby hills. Black Buffalo had been summoned, and no one in the village had seen Medicine Wolf or the priest since then.

Smiling Girl hurriedly gathered together some dried meat and some Indian bread and turnips. She nearly gasped at Medicine Wolf's gaunt, hollow-eyed look when she finally reached the tipi, and Standing Bear and Big Hands both stared at their other "mother," wondering why she looked so thin.

"You must eat," Smiling Girl told her. She handed her a tin plate with the food she had prepared. "Your prayers have been answered. Bear Paw comes, and he will need you to be strong. I will go inside and prepare a place for him."

"No," Medicine Wolf objected in a weak and raspy voice. "You and some of the other women, prepare another dwelling where Bear Paw and I can be alone. It is better for you and the children. If Bear Paw is badly wounded—'' How she hated the sound of the words! ''He will need quiet. And also, you will deliver your new child any day now. It is better you have this dwelling to yourself. Shining Woman and Two Moons will look after you.''

Smiling Girl nodded, trying not to cry. She hurried to Shining Woman, and quickly the two of them were joined by other women, using extra poles and skins borrowed from here and there to build a separate dwelling for the wounded Bear Paw. With a skill and speed no woman of any other race could have accomplished, the women had laced together skins and erected another tipi within the hour.

Others came to help, volunteering food, blankets, herbs, and medicines. Finally the straggling remains of what, nearly two weeks ago, had been a proud group of Dog Soldiers, appeared on the horizon. Of the ten warriors and five women who had left, only four men were returning. They realized then that there was one more, someone being dragged behind one of the horses on a travois.

Medicine Wolf set aside her plate of food, most of the meat and bread still untouched. She rose, her legs weak. She knew without looking who was on the travois. Never in all the years she had known Bear Paw, in all the battles he had fought, of all the times he had been wounded . . . never had he returned flat on his back. Always he had ridden his mount, straight and proud, ignoring his pain. Surely, then, this was a pain that could not be ignored. Surely this was a very grave wound. If only he had not given back the wolf paw! If only he and the others had waited for the blessing of the wolf paws before riding south! Although she had been right in her fears, she did not feel victorious.

She began walking then, Little Wolf trotting behind her. Black Buffalo stayed beside her, holding one arm in case her weak legs betrayed her. The sad procession of warriors came closer, and Medicine Wolf walked faster, anxious now, too anxious to wait for them to reach the village.

Finally she reached the travois, where Bear Paw lay

shivering and moaning her name in a voice that betrayed his agony. She saw a cut down his right cheek and one on his neck, but the rest of him was covered with a blanket. She looked up at Little Bear, her cousin and one of those who had gone with Bear Paw. Little Bear Rode the horse that led Bear Paw's travois. He appeared to be unscathed. "What happened?" she asked.

"Buffalo hunters," he answered, his face drawn, his eyes showing remorse and grief. He dismounted and came to stand beside her. "We were a few days south of here. I and those with me spotted some deer and we rode after them. While we were gone, Bear Paw and the others made camp. I know only what Clay Woman told me before she begged me to kill her."

"Clay Woman is dead?"

Little Bear nodded, and in spite of what Medicine Wolf thought of the woman, she could now feel only pity and sorrow for her. "She said that buffalo hunters came, many men, leading many mules piled high with buffalo hides," Little Bear continued. "They had their big, long guns, and because they did not shoot at them from afar, Bear Paw and the others thought they had come to trade. They knew that if they tried to attack them they could kill them from a long distance with their buffalo guns, so they waited until they were closer. If there had been more of us and if we had not ridden off after the deer . . ." He breathed deeply before continuing. "Those buffalo hunters set their eyes on the women. They tried to trade some buffalo hides for them, but Bear Paw would not trade. He told them Cheyenne women were not for sale to white men at any price. Without warning or any more argument, the hunters began shooting. Those big guns can kill a buffalo from a great distance, so you know what they would do to a man."

Medicine Wolf looked down at Bear Paw. "They shot him in the right side," she said.

Little Bear looked surprised. "How did you know?"

She met his eyes. "I felt it."

Little Bear nodded. "The bullet went through him," he explained. "It killed my brother, Young Pine, who stood behind him. Clay Woman said that in the blink of an eye

every man was down. Some of the buffalo hunters laughed
and yelled, jumping from their horses and stabbing at Bear
Paw while he lay wounded. They took turns raping the
women, then killed them slowly.''

Medicine Wolf closed her eyes, imagining the horror
of it. Not even Clay Woman deserved such a death.

''When we found them, all were dead but Clay Woman
and Bear Paw,'' Little Bear continued. ''Perhaps they
thought they were dead too. Clay Woman lived long
enough to tell us what happened, then begged me to kill
her, for she was greatly ashamed and her breasts had been
cut off.''

Medicine Wolf uttered a choking gasp. ''So, this is the
white man's way of saying they want peace.''

''I do not know how Bear Paw has lived,'' Little Bear
told her. ''I know it can be only because the holy woman
has been praying for him. He calls for you constantly.
Perhaps since he has lived this long, you can save him,
Medicine Wolf, or perhaps he clung to life just long
enough that he could die here with his People, with his
woman.''

Medicine Wolf knelt beside the travois, carefully lifting the blanket. Her eyes widened at the horror of what
she saw, an ugly black festering hole at Bear Paw's right
side, and an array of knife wounds about his entire body,
some scabbed over, some so grave that they still leaked
blood and puss.

''Medicine . . . Wolf,'' Bear Paw groaned. His whole
body shook, and for the first time in his life he could not
pretend he felt no pain. She was shocked to see a tear slip
out of one eye and run down the side of his face into his
ear. She leaned closer, brushing it away.

''I am here, Bear Paw. You are with the People again.
We will make you well.''

''Medicine Wolf,'' he groaned again, as though he had
not heard her.

Quickly she opened her medicine bag and took out a
wolf's paw. She opened his hand and placed the paw into
his palm, then closed his fingers around it. ''Keep hold of
it, Bear Paw. It is yours again. It will make you strong
again.'' She leaned close, speaking softly into his ear. ''I

am here, Bear Paw,'' she repeated. ''You are with Medicine Wolf, and the wolf's paw is again yours. Let its strength move through you. Draw on the spirit of the wolf. Hear his song in your heart. Feel my love.''

She covered him again, noticing then that his eyes were open and he was looking at her. ''Forgive me,'' he shuddered. ''You were right, and I was . . . foolish . . . weak . . .''

She put her fingers to his lips. ''You will be strong again.''

''Help me,'' he mumbled. ''The pain . . .''

''Keep hold of the wolf's paw. Feel it in your hand, my husband. The Wolf Spirit is with you. And *I* am with you.'' She rose, looking at Little Bear. ''I will take care of him now.''

Little Bear nodded. ''I will go into the hills to pray and make a blood sacrifice. We were wrong not to listen to you, Medicine Wolf. When we rode after the deer, we were full of firewater, forgetting we should stay together, paying no attention to who else might be near.''

''You must give up the whiskey, Little Bear. It is bad medicine.'' She left him, taking hold of the horse's bridle and leading it to the village. Little Bear walked off to be alone. Everyone watched in near silence, even the little children. Their holy woman walked past them, leading her beloved, whose only chance of survival was the sheer strength of the love he shared with his Medicine Wolf.

Medicine Wolf had never seen such suffering, and to have it be Bear Paw meant that she suffered right along with him. For two weeks the village could hear her chanting and singing. She sat at Bear Paw's head, offering up prayers while Black Buffalo kept a holy fire burning, covering the hot coals with sweet grass and sage to fill the tipi with the ''magic'' smoke. The old Shaman, Stalking Bear, worked over Bear Paw with special herbs and chants; and because the wolf was Medicine Wolf's spirit connection, and because it was known to all Indians that the saliva of animals' tongues contained a healing ingredient, Little Wolf was allowed to lick Bear Paw's open wounds, thus fulfilling Bear Paw's vision of wolves licking the wounds of a bear.

Little Wolf stayed right by Medicine Wolf's side, as though he understood he was needed. Through it all Bear Paw clung to the wolf's paw, suffering the hideous pain, vomiting when he tried to eat, begging for water, only partially aware of where he was. He dreamed of wolves gathering around a bear to protect it from giant white men who threatened it. He dreamed of another time, when the Cheyenne rode free over the grasslands and mountains for as far as the eye could see, from the Queen's country in the North to the place called Texas; from the Rocky Mountains to the great river of the East. He dreamed that he was a young boy again, running across the prairie, holding a pretty little girl's hand. And he dreamed he was standing on a mountaintop, a beautiful woman in front of him, the sun behind his back, wolves gathered around both of them.

Through his agony he clung to the sound of Medicine Wolf's voice, the one thing that made him want to live. He did not argue when she said he could not have whiskey to kill the pain. "The whiskey is the reason you lie here," she told him. "You must learn to depend on your own great strength, Bear Paw. You must draw on the inner spirit, that part of you that helped you survive two Sun Dances; that part of you that made you the great warrior that you are. You did it on your own, Bear Paw, not with the help of firewater. The spirits of the bottle are evil. They destroy you."

He knew now that she was right, but it was not easy to suffer this pain without wanting the whiskey to dull his senses. More than that, besides the pain he was suffering, he experienced a terrible craving that made him shake. Sometimes he cried out, waving his arms, trying to chase away bats that he was sure were attacking him, or trying to brush off spiders that swarmed over him. Always he heard Medicine Wolf telling him these things were not there. They were only in his mind.

"It is the spirits of the firewater trying to gain control of you," she told him. "Fight them, Bear Paw! Fight them! They cannot have you! You are a strong and brave warrior! You are *stronger* than the bottle spirits! Let the

Wolf Spirit attack the evil spirits that fight for your soul. The Wolf Spirit will kill them so that they can never return!''

By the third week, after many applications of moss and herbs, the wound from the gunshot began to heal. The black look was gone, but it was obvious there would be an indention left in Bear Paw's side where muscle had been shot away. It pained Medicine Wolf to realize how many scars he would bear now from the many cuts and stabs, but at least now they were all healing. After three weeks Bear Paw was able to eat a little without throwing up the food. He was able to sit up, and Stalking Bear and Black Buffalo left the dwelling. They were no longer needed. All Bear Paw needed now was Medicine Wolf.

Bear Paw awoke to see Medicine Wolf entering the tipi with a pan of water. He was still a little confused, but from the light that came into the tipi when she came inside, he guessed it was very early in the morning.

Medicine Wolf looked at him and smiled, and to Bear Paw she was the most beautiful sight he had ever seen. She was freshly bathed, her hair still damp. She wore a simple tunic, and he marveled at her exotic beauty. Her shape was still supple, her face looking much younger than her twenty-eight years. She seemed hardly changed from the young woman he had married.

"You are thin," he told her, his voice still weak.

She set the pan down beside him. "Before you returned, I fasted for many days," she told him. "I dreamed and felt a pain in my side. I knew you had been hurt. I went to the hills to pray for you. Since you returned I have hardly been able to eat because of my concern for you."

He studied her, realizing then that all the anger and resentment he had felt for her the past few months was gone. "You saved my life, Medicine Wolf."

She turned to wet a rag. "The Wolf Spirit saved you. But it was not just that. You drew on your own strength. You let yourself heal from within, and you did not need the firewater to help you." She wrang water from the rag. "You are a strong man, Bear Paw. In many ways you are much stronger than I. Why could you not see that? Why did you think you needed the whiskey?''

He searched her eyes as she started to wash him. He grasped her wrist then. ''Something happened to me,'' he told her, his voice strained.

She met his eyes and saw they were teared. She set the rag aside and took his hand. ''Tell me, my husband.''

He swallowed. ''At Sand Creek . . . what I saw there was not just the dead bodies of the women and children. My mother, she was . . . still alive. They had . . . cut her open. Her eyes . . . she begged me to kill her.''

His mouth quivered, and Medicine Wolf felt as though something were squeezing painfully at her heart. Her throat ached. ''My beloved, I am so sorry. Why did you not tell me this? I would have understood your pain and anger so much better. This is a terrible thing to keep to yourself.''

He squeezed his eyes shut. ''It was not just that I . . . killed my own mother to end her pain. It was . . . something more.'' He shuddered and took a deep breath. ''When I put my knife into her heart . . . it was as though . . .'' He began to shake, and she took hold of both his hands.

''Tell me, Bear Paw. You must talk about it. Do not let these things fester in your soul. It makes you weaker, makes you turn to things like the whiskey.''

A tear slipped down his cheek. ''It was like I was putting to death . . . the entire Cheyenne nation. At Sand Creek I saw. I saw, but I did not want to face it . . . so I turned to the whiskey, because it made me happy. It . . . helped me forget what I saw.''

She squeezed his hands. ''What did you see?''

He sniffed, another tear making its way down his face, over a scar. Many times Medicine Wolf had seen his eyes tear, but she had never seen him cry this way. ''I saw that it was over . . . that there was no hope. I saw that it was only a matter of time before the same thing happened to all the Cheyenne and the Sioux . . . all Indians. Never before have I known such a helpless feeling. It frightened me . . . to feel so helpless.''

Her own throat felt tight. ''Perhaps we cannot help what will come, Bear Paw,'' she told him. ''But if we are to die, let us die like the proud Cheyenne that we are. Let us not die as women who sell ourselves so that our men can have the whiskey that turns them into weak beggars. If we are to die, let us leave in the memories of others a picture of a people who were fierce and proud. Red Cloud may sign this new treaty. If the white man keeps his promises this time, we will still have much land left to us, including the sacred Black Hills. We will live here in peace. But if the white man breaks his promise to keep other whites from coming into this land, then we will fight, even if we know it is hopeless and will lead to our deaths.'' She held her chin proudly. ''We will fight this together, Bear Paw. Above all things, we will not let the white man and his firewater destroy our love for each other, and the strength that love gives us. It is that love that saved you, Bear Paw. And all is not hopeless, not as long as children like Standing Bear and Big Hands still live.''

She touched his tears with the back of her hand and smiled. ''You are going to live, and that is a good sign. Now I can tell you of an even better sign. I have just learned that Smiling Girl has gone into labor. Soon she will deliver a third child of your seed. It is good. Even if you should die, Bear Paw, you will live again, in your sons. As long as there are children, all is not hopeless.'' She leaned closer, sitting down near him and putting her arms around him so that his head rested on her shoulder. ''To weep is not a sign of weakness, my beloved. It is the greatest expression of the love you have for your People. Sometimes it is good to weep. Sometimes when we are through weeping, we are stronger.''

She felt him tremble, felt his tears on her shoulder.

Bear Paw knelt beside the stream, cupping his hands and dipping them into the water. He filled them and splashed his face with the cool water. Medicine Wolf spread out a blanket and set down the parfleche full of jerked meat and summer berries.

''It feels good,'' Bear Paw told her, ''good to walk and feel strong, good to feel the sweet water on my face.'' He turned to face her, and she knew by the look in his eye that she had her Bear Paw back. He had been a changed man since he had healed. He was the proud warrior she had married, and he was strong, strong from the inside, strong in spirit. "I have two fine sons, and now a daughter," he said, referring to six-week-old Little Flower, the daughter to whom Smiling Girl had given birth.

"And there will be more sons, more children to carry on the blood of Bear Paw long after he is gone," Medicine Wolf told him. She came closer, unlacing the shoulder of her tunic. "Why don't we bathe in the stream, Bear Paw? It is a hot day. The cool water will feel good."

She gave him a sultry, teasing look then, letting her tunic drop so that she stood naked before him. She watched his smile fade, watched desire move into his dark eyes. He was thinner, but lean and hard. So many scars he carried now, but he was alive! Alive! And he was growing stronger. More than that, he was Bear Paw, her husband again, the man who loved her more than his own life, as she loved him. He was her husband again in every way but one. She saw his lips quiver slightly, saw the strange apprehension in his eyes. She moved closer, touching his chest, opening his vest to pull it off his shoulders and down his arms.

"You think you are not ready," she said softly. "Or perhaps you think your injuries affected your ability to make love to me." She tossed the vest aside and knelt to her knees, unlacing his leggings. "You forget, my husband, that I have been bathing you. I have seen the life try to come to you when my hands touched you." She pulled the open-sided leggings away and began untying his breechcloth. "We are together again in spirit, Bear Paw, but we have yet to be one again in body."

She tossed the breechcloth aside and caressed him, closing her eyes and resting her cheek against that part of him that represented all that was man about him, all that was intimately Bear Paw's. He had lain with others, but she knew it had not been with the same passion he felt for her.

He grasped her hair, and his hands were cool from the water. She moved her hands over his thighs and hips, letting her lips touch him teasingly until he groaned her name. He grasped her arm then, forcing her to rise. She cast down her eyes and he pulled her close, caressing her hair with his lips. "It has been so long," he said softly. "I hope I can still please my wife."

She turned her face to taste his neck. "How could you not please me? You are Bear Paw, and I have my husband back, the proud warrior that he was when first he took me. That is all I need."

He reached down and grasped her bottom, hoisting her so that she wrapped her legs around him. He thought how light and supple she was, not tall and big-boned like Clay Woman had been; short and heavy like Smiling Girl; but just right, with curves that made a man ache, a slender waist, her dark skin so soft.

He carried her to the blanket, where he went to his knees. Little Wolf, who had been lying nearby, got up and trotted to the stream to sniff around for something to chase. Bear Paw moved over his woman, glorying at the realization he was indeed still a man in every way. How could he not respond to this creature who so easily aroused his passion?

He groaned with ecstasy as he entered the sweet depths of this wife he so cherished, this wife who had loved him even in the bad times. He wondered at how this time seemed almost more exciting than that first time. This time they had suffered much together. This time they had nearly lost each other, and he had nearly lost his life. He had hated being apart from her, hated himself for allowing it to happen; but he had been unable to stop drinking the whiskey until she gave him the strength to do it. Medicine Wolf had shown him the way, and he no longer resented her wisdom and power, for he realized now that it had nothing to do with the love they shared. This part of her belonged only to him.

Medicine Wolf groaned with the ecstasy of finally being one with her Bear Paw again. She had not stopped loving him or wanting him for one moment. She ran her hand over his many scars, remembering how horrible it felt to think that he might die. She knew that one day he *would* die, but this was not the time. The Wolf Spirit had given him back to her, and it was good.

They made love with all the passion they had known in their younger years, and Bear Paw knew that he was fully healed, fully a man again. He realized that he got part of his strength from this, from being one with his woman. They moved in wild rhythm, giving, taking, enjoying. When they finished he carried her to the stream and they bathed, splashing and laughing in the cool water like two newlyweds. They ate a little, but suddenly the food was unimportant.

"I would rather taste the fruits of your breasts," he told her, leaning down and taking her full nipple into his mouth.

Medicine Wolf laughed lightly, grasping his head. "And I would rather feed you than eat," she answered.

He moved to her other breast, licking it, moving his tongue down over her belly and tasting the sweet crevices where her thighs tried to hide that part of her he had recently invaded. She opened herself to him, shuddering at his touch. He moved back to her breasts, his long black hair brushing her skin as again he entered her, rubbing against her so that he brought forth a lovely, almost agonizing hunger for him. Finally she felt the pulsating climax she had gone so long without.

He rose up on his knees and she sat, moving to straddle her legs across the tops of his thighs so that they sat facing each other while he was yet inside of her. She moved rhythmically while they touched lips, tasted mouths. She threw back her head and he licked her throat, lowering his head then to lick the whites of her breasts as again his life spilled into her.

She had long ago accepted that that life would never take hold in her own womb. It was enough that he still wanted her this way, that he was here with her, his own man again, her husband again. Smiling Girl would give him children, but she would give him something no one else could give him. She would give him his very life. She would give him gentle understanding. She knew him intimately, understood his soul, had held him when he wept.

She was the one for whom he had cried out when in pain. She had helped him stop drinking the whiskey.

He was Bear Paw, the man of her vision, and she was Medicine Wolf, the woman with whom fate insisted he share his life. Nothing could change this. He carried her again to the stream.

Chapter Twenty-two

November 1868

The large contingent of Oglala Sioux and Northern Cheyenne made their proud entrance into Fort Laramie. Red Cloud, convinced that he had much more power and more men than the white government did, had agreed to sign the new Laramie Treaty, even though the rising Hunkpapa Sioux leader, Sitting Bull, still refused to sign.

Medicine Wolf was not fully convinced that their numbers were strong enough to continue to defeat the Great White Father's forces, although together the Sioux and Northern Cheyenne were a mighty force indeed. Recently army authorities had ordered the abandonment of forts Reno, C F. Smith, and Phil Kearny, all forts established along the Bozeman Trail into Montana Territory. This was considered a great victory by the Sioux and Cheyenne, who immediately burned down all three forts, and even Medicine Wolf and Bear Paw were taking hope that this was the beginning of a new era for the Sioux and Cheyenne.

It felt good to have something to cling to, some sign that their struggles and all the cruel deaths had helped them preserve the freedom they so dearly wanted. It was not so for the Southern Cheyenne, who runners had told them were hunted like dogs now. Long-hair Custer, who they had also begun calling "Hard Backsides" because it was rumored he could stay in the saddle for days on end when he was chasing Indians, had attacked an innocent village of Southern Cheyenne along the Washita in the new Indian Territory to the south. Black Kettle, the peace chief who had struggled so hard to stay on good terms with the white man's government, was finally killed.

Hearing of the bloody massacre left Medicine Wolf and Bear Paw apprehensive of signing the new Laramie Treaty, but after the army abandoned the forts along the Bozeman Trail, it seemed they had finally won a war against the white man's government. It was a sign of great hope, and it was with relief and happy hearts that they rode into the fort with Red Cloud and many of his people.

Bear Paw sat straight and proud. They were victors! They were not crawling on hands and knees, begging for handouts. Red Cloud was convinced that at least here in the North they could set their own rules. This new treaty might set new boundaries, but the Sioux would continue to ride wherever they pleased. Those few who wanted to learn to farm could do so, but it was ridiculous to think that one could survive in this land on the mere eighty acres the government wanted to give each family. How could a person graze his many horses plus raise all the food he needed on eighty acres, when much of it was barren, arid land?

Most had no intention of going to settle on the new reservations that had been established for them in northwest Nebraska Territory and the southern Dakotas. Each man would take his time and decide what was best for him. The Sioux were still left with a vast amount of land, and now that they had chased off the soldiers and burned their forts, their power seemed unlimited! The white man's government was afraid of them now. By the treaty they had promised that no whites would be allowed onto the land awarded them, including the sacred Black Hills. Other tribes may be folding under bluecoat power, but not the Sioux or the Northern Cheyenne!

Medicine Wolf rode beside Bear Paw, who had learned to accept her equal importance, for privately she was just Medicine Wolf. A woman, *his* woman. He had learned that without her he was not the same man. Their love was his strength; her power, his shield. She had brought him back from the dead, had loved him in spite of how he had abandoned her, had helped him gain control over his dependency on the firewater, which he no longer touched. He felt good, better than since before he had begun liking the whiskey. He was strong again, not just on the outside, but on the inside. He was ready for any soldier or white man who might break this new treaty, including long-hair Custer, if he should come north.

From a distance Tom Prescott and his wife watched, along with the few wives of soldiers who were present, some traders, and the few whites who had dared to settle around the fort. Tom had heard from scouts that this time the Cheyenne band belonging to Medicine Wolf's clan were coming in with the Sioux.

Tom studied the grand-looking procession of Indians as they came through, searching, hoping to see Medicine Wolf again. It had been fifteen years since she first rode out of his life. With all that had happened, all the battles, all the stories about the warrior woman who was considered sacred, the woman who rode alongside the Dog Soldiers on many raids, he was eager to see her again, trying to imagine what she must be like by now.

He glanced down at Elena, who held ten-month-old Rebecca in her arms. To Tom's relief their daughter had been born with no complications, and having the baby with her helped ease the loneliness a woman suffered in this savage land so far removed from the pleasantries of the cities back east. Elena devoted her time to her child, and still she talked of taking her home to Boston to raise her; but Tom could not quite bring himself to leave. Red Cloud was signing a treaty today, a treaty that could mean more Sioux would come into the reservations. More than

ever the Indians needed men like himself to teach them a
new way. But he knew it was hard for Elena, and now that
a transcontinental railroad was well on its way to comple-
tion, perhaps he could send his wife home for the winters
and she and little Rebecca could come and spend the summers with him.

"Do you see her?" Elena asked, surprised at the odd
jealousy she was feeling. Tom had always had a fascination for the Cheyenne woman called Medicine Wolf, and
she sometimes suspected he had even thought he loved her
once.

"My God," she heard Tom say in a near whisper.

She followed the direction of his eyes. Most of the
Sioux who had ridden in with Red Cloud had gone by.
Behind them came the Northern Cheyenne, and leading
them was a handsome but scarred savage-looking man who
Elena knew would frighten her to death if she were to
confront him alone. Beside him rode the most exotically
beautiful Indian woman she had ever seen. The woman
rode a big Appaloosa gelding painted with paw marks. A
large white wolf trotted beside her horse. The woman was
dressed in a white tunic, with very long fringes at the
bottom that draped and danced over the dark skin of her
exposed knees and on down over her knee-high winter
moccasins. She wore a white wolfskin draped over her
shoulders, the head of the wolf hanging over her right
shoulder. A gentle wind blew her waist-length black hair
away from her face, an exquisite face that displayed a small
upturned nose, full lips, high cheekbones, and wide-set,
dark, exotic eyes.

Although it was November, a warm wind had swept
across the plains from the western mountains, bringing the
temperature to the sixties; still, that same wind did not
fool anyone who had lived for long in this country. Tom
and Elena both knew that at any time that wind could turn
to devastating cold and carry enough snow to bury them
within a day. But for now the sky remained blue, and one
needed only a woolen cape for warmth.

Apparently for the Indian woman she watched now,
the wolfskin was enough. She knew without asking that it
was surely the same wolfskin Tom had helped Medicine

Wolf cut away from her murdered pet wolf all those years ago. Tom stepped forward, and the jealousy Elena had felt earlier returned, surprising her, for she had never felt this way about her husband before. Tom called out Medicine Wolf's name hesitantly. She did not turn at first. He called it louder, and the woman finally looked his way. She stared at him a moment, and then her face lit up with a ravishing smile. She said something to the savage-looking man who rode beside her, then left the procession and trotted her horse over to Tom. The warrior followed, but held back as the woman dismounted.

"Tom," she said, an amazing note of love and joy in her voice. She embraced him, and onlookers whispered and stared in amazement. They all knew Tom Prescott had known the holy woman of the Cheyenne, knew this must be the infamous warrior woman who was held in such high regard by her people, but who was hated and actually feared by many whites.

"That's her," she heard one woman telling another.

"I'm told she's as savage as the rest of them," another said.

"She was at Julesburg!"

"She has killed white men!"

"She's said to have magical powers."

"Look at that wolf, standing guard. He looks ready to light into anyone who might want to do her harm."

"They say she once lived among wolves . . . that she's part wolf herself."

"She don't look like no wolf to me," one trader said with a hungry hint to his voice. "I ain't seen somethin' that looked that good in my whole life."

Tom was bringing her toward Elena now, and Elena was not surprised to see that both of them seemed to have tears in their eyes. She could hardly believe she was looking at the woman about whom her husband had carried on for years, the woman who was the reason he had come back west to teach Indians. She was certainly not the thirteen-year-old girl he had described, and she could tell by Tom's red face that he had been himself surprised at her beauty. She was sure Tom had pictured this woman the way Elena herself had pictured her, hard and worn from years of life on the plains, years of making war and living with the harsh elements. She had supposed Medicine Wolf would look much older than her twenty-eight years, growing fat and developing harsh age lines on her face like so many other Indian women.

But before her stood something that looked more like a fantasy from a book that might be published back east about the "noble Indian." Her complexion bore not a mark, her skin looking like brown velvet. It was obvious that under the tunic stood a slender, supple body with curves in all the right places. Elena wondered then if Medicine Wolf was indeed blessed with magical powers, perhaps not fully human at all, for she was surely watched over by some outside force that kept her so flawless, had kept her alive and unscathed in spite of the hard life she must lead.

Tom introduced her, and it took a moment for Elena to find her voice. "How do you do," she said. "I am so proud to finally be able to meet you. Tom has talked about you so much over the years."

Medicine Wolf studied her a moment, thinking how thin and pale this woman was. Her hair was as red as sandstone, her eyes as green as prairie grass. "And I am honored to meet the wife of Tom Prescott," she answered. She touched the little girl's chubby hand, her own looking so very dark next to it. "And this is your child. I am happy for you."

Rebecca smiled, seeming to be completely unafraid of this strange, dark woman. She actually reached out for her, and Medicine Wolf took her into her arms, uttering something in the Cheyenne tongue and smiling as she brushed cheeks with the child. Elena looked helplessly at Tom, not sure it was quite right to let an Indian woman hold Rebecca, especially one as supposedly wild as this one. Tom gave her a look that warned her not to object, and moments later Medicine Wolf handed the girl back to her mother. She looked at Tom.

"Such a beautiful wife and daughter you have," she told him. She moved her eyes to Elena. "You are a woman blessed to be able to have children. I was never able to have my own, but I have three children through my sister.''

"*Through* your sister," Elena asked while others gaped at them.

"*Ai*. My husband Bear Paw took my sister for a second wife so that he could have sons. Now he has two sons. Standing Bear is six summers, and Big Hands is three. Only this past summer my sister gave birth to a little daughter, called Little Flower.''

Elena blushed, struggling not to show her shock. Apparently this woman thought nothing of her husband taking a second wife, her own sister! She knew it was a common practice, but to be confronted with it as though it were as natural as breathing was quite something else.

Tom touched Medicine Wolf's arm. "I'm sorry you never had children of your own, Medicine Wolf. I know how much that would have meant to you.''

She studied him lovingly. "Yes. But I belong to the Wolf Spirit. It was difficult for me to understand and accept, difficult for me to allow a second wife into our lodge; but a warrior like Bear Paw should have sons. It is important to carry on through our children, so that the Cheyenne never die. In Bear Paw's heart I am still his first and most loved. And he is still *my* only love.''

Elena glanced up at the warrior who had been with Medicine Wolf. He had ridden slightly closer, and was watching the reunion carefully, his eyes studying Tom intently. Was such a wild-looking man truly capable of love? It was difficult to imagine. He sat straight and proud on his mount, his handsome but scarred face showing no emotion until his eyes fell on his "first" wife. He said something in the Cheyenne tongue, and Medicine Wolf looked up at him, answering him in turn in their own language. She turned to Tom. "This is Bear Paw. Do you remember him?''

Tom swallowed, studying the savage-looking painted warrior who looked down at him from a the huge white stallion he rode. "How could I forget," he answered. He managed a smile and a nod, and Bear Paw nodded in return, but he did not smile. He said something to Medicine Wolf, and both Tom and Elena were surprised at the gentle way in which he spoke to her. She answered, holding Tom's eyes, and Bear Paw said something more to her.

"I must go and join the others," she told Tom, "but Bear Paw says to tell you we will make camp outside fort grounds tonight. You are welcome to come and feast with us so that we can talk."

Tom smiled and nodded. "I would like that." He reached out and touched the wolfskin. "I tried to find his grave, but the ground is all changed, Medicine Wolf. It's hard to tell now where we buried Wolf."

Medicine Wolf reached down to touch Little Wolf's head. "It no longer matters. The Wolf Spirit sent me another pup, but now he is grown even bigger than Wolf. He is my guardian and companion."

Others stood back from the wolf, some sure Tom would be attacked when he reached down to pet the animal, but Little Wolf showed him no animosity. "I am glad that this one came to take Wolf's place," Tom said.

"He came to me after Bear Paw's first son was born. It was a sign that the wolves are my children. I will never have any other." She met his eyes again.

"Are you happy, Medicine Wolf?"

She saw the lingering love in Tom's gaze. "I am with my People, and with Bear Paw. I could be happy no other way," she told him. "No matter what happens to my People, I am where I belong. I would rather die with them than live to be an old woman in a world that is foreign to me."

He smiled softly. "Yes, I suppose you would. Tell your husband I thank him. I will come and find you tonight."

Medicine Wolf turned, climbing up onto her mount in one swift bound. She smiled for Tom once more, then looked at Elena. "Elena is a lovely name for a lovely woman. Take good care of him. He is very special." She looked back at Tom. "I did not think I would ever see you again. I am glad you are well, Tom Prescott."

She rode off with Bear Paw. From across the parade grounds White Horse watched the procession, feeling a hot anger and jealousy that these people with whom he belonged had turned him out. He had seen many Sioux and Cheyenne, had scouted against them many times; but this was the first time in twelve years he had seen his own clan.

He spotted Medicine Wolf, his heart racing with a mixture of hatred and desire. It was easy to recognize her, for she had hardly changed, except that she had grown even more beautiful. Summer Moon had grown only fatter and was always quiet and frowning. She did not even seem to enjoy his sexual attentions anymore, nor did he have much use left for her. But if Medicine Wolf could have been his wife as he had once planned . . .

Medicine Wolf glanced his way, then said something to the man riding with her. The man turned. White Horse could tell, in spite of the years and the scars, that it was Bear Paw. Their eyes met in heated challenge, their fight twelve years before suddenly seeming as though it had happened only yesterday. For years White Horse had tried to lead soldiers to Medicine Wolf's band to have some of them, especially Bear Paw, arrested. He was sure they had led those who attacked Julesburg after the Sand Creek massacre, and if he could have captured Bear Paw and brought him to that town, he would have been hanged!

But always Bear Paw and Medicine Wolf had eluded him. Now here they were, riding freely into the fort to sign a new treaty. If it were not for this new peace effort, Bear Paw could be arrested, and that would leave Medicine Wolf unprotected. How he wished it could be so! Still, he knew the white man well now, knew they would not hold to this treaty anymore than they had held to any other. They had tricked Red Cloud, had managed to make him think they were finally giving in to him. Once the Sioux and Cheyenne discovered the white man's deceit, there would be more trouble, and White Horse would have to again scout for soldiers hunting his own people. Now that things were so bad for the Southern Cheyenne, he knew Bear Paw and Medicine Wolf would stay in the North. They would not move around so much. They would be much easier to find and kill!

The hatred in his heart had never gone away. He turned away from Bear Paw's glare and left the fort grounds to go to his dwelling, which was centered among the many "stay-around-the-fort" Indians who liked the white man's

handouts and liked his whiskey. This place had become
his home, and he had managed to supplement his meager
scouting income by trading Summer Moon to white traders
and soldiers in return for money or whiskey. White men
always seemed hungry for a woman, any woman, and they
readily gave up their money for a night in bed with Summer Moon, in spite of her plain face and hefty size.

Summer Moon did not like to have to go to the white
men, who she said were dirty and smelled bad; but White
Horse had soon taught her it was easier to lie with them
than to suffer his beatings. He was himself sick of her,
and now that he had seen Medicine Wolf, the sight of
Summer Moon only made him sicker.

Before he reached the sagging cabin he shared with
her, he drew a bottle of whisky from a pack on his horse
and swallowed some, watching his several children playing outside the cabin. The only one he cared about was
his eleven-year-old son, Crow Dog. He considered his
daughter a useless girl child, except that in a few more
years he would be able to sell her to men for good money,
for she would be young and slender. His other son, Red
Beaver, was only five summers, too young and too much
of a troublemaker for him to spend any time with for the
present.

His dark eyes narrowed when he spotted Summer
Moon's half-blood children, two worthless little bastards
she had borne from the nights she had been forced to sleep
with a soldier or a buffalo hunter or a whiskey trader. It
was impossible to know which men might be the fathers
of the children, and it didn't matter, since they would never
want them anyway. White Horse was struck with having
to feed them, but he made sure his own got fed first. They
both ran as he came closer, afraid of the man who often
beat them or tossed them out in the cold with no food
whenever they did the slightest thing to upset him. The
girl, though, White Horse thought, she, too, could at least
bring him some extra income when she was old enough to
sell to men. That was all she would ever be good for.

Before he even reached the cabin he turned away again.
He did not want to look at Summer Moon or her pitiful
half-breeds just yet. He would go back and maybe get

another look at Medicine Wolf. That one gave a man an ache, a very pleasant ache he had not felt in years. She was here! Maybe somehow . . . Oh, how he hoped that one day soon she would find herself on one of the reservations. If Bear Paw were to be killed . . . if Medicine Wolf was placed on a reservation . . . ah, the possibilities were endless! One day all the Cheyenne would be on reservations, and the ones like himself, who helped the soldiers and were good scouts, would be free to do as they liked. He would be free to go where he pleased . . . free to find Medicine Wolf and have his way with her. This treaty would last no longer than the others. The Sioux and Cheyenne would fight again, and men like Bear Paw would die!

He swallowed some more whiskey and decided to go and find some off-duty soldiers who might want to do a little gambling. This visit was going to be very interesting. There was too much excitement here to go back to the cabin, to children he couldn't stand and a wife who glared at him most of the time and seldom spoke. He watched the continuing procession of Indians in the distance.

"So," Bear Paw was saying to Medicine Wolf as he looked back to see where White Horse had gone, "it is true. He wears a bluecoat uniform and scouts for them," he sneered. "He is a worse enemy than the soldiers, for he is a traitor to his own kind!"

Medicine Wolf remembered a time when White Horse had been an honored Dog Soldier. How sad that he should turn against his own people. She wondered what had happened to her good friend Summer Moon.

Tom walked through the Cheyenne camp, his spine slightly tingling with the surrounding sense of animosity and distrust. Was he a fool to come here alone? The camp was rather quiet, and there was not the same air of celebrating that had taken place back during the treaty signing of '51, when so many different tribes had gathered . . . and where he had first set eyes on the mysterious young girl called Medicine Wolf.

So much had happened since then, so much tragedy

for the Cheyenne. But Medicine Wolf had been left untouched. He had been shocked and amazed when he first saw her, not expecting to see her still so beautiful, so exotic. He knew now more than ever, by her beauty, and by the magical aura that seemed to surround her, that she never could have belonged to him. She not only belonged to that "other world" of the Indian, but was even farther removed, a part of a world of mysticism and supernatural powers. She was as much a part of nature as the trees and the mountains, the wind and the wolves. There was something about her that made her seem almost unreal; even in looks she was like a dream.

He moved through the camp, asking for her in the Cheyenne tongue, for he had learned more of their language, although there was much of it he still did not understand. Elena had chosen not to come. She did not mind teaching Indians in her own classroom, but to go out into the camp of Indians who had so recently been so hostile was another story. She had asked Tom not to go, but he was not about to let Medicine Wolf leave without seeing her once more. Besides, she had invited him there. She would not let any harm come to him.

Women and children stared at him curiously; men watched him warily. Dogs ran about, and smoke from tipi fires curled lazily into the cold evening air. The smell of sage and smoked meat and horse dung was pungent. He finally spotted Medicine Wolf talking to a heavyset young woman whose face resembled her own. Medicine Wolf wore only her tunic, as though the cold of the evening did not bother her. She turned then and saw him. She smiled, introducing him to her sister, Smiling Girl.

So, Tom thought, this was the "second wife" who had given Bear Paw children. Again he envied Indian men the luxurious freedom they enjoyed—to have more than one wife, to be waited on hand and foot, to have many children, to ride free on the hunt and be unencumbered by schedules and rules.

"It is getting colder," Medicine Wolf told him. "Come inside. There is a fire." She led him into a warm, roomy tipi, which was much cozier and cleaner than he had anticipated. Inside sat two small boys quietly playing with a long string of beads. Near them was a cradleboard.

"These are my sons, Standing Bear and Bid Hands," Medicine Wolf told him. "And my daughter, Little Flower."

Tom admired them, saying nothing about how strange he thought it was that she called them her own children. He realized she must have read his thoughts then when she smiled and told him they were hers because her own blood ran in their veins, and because "anything that comes from Bear Paw's seed is as much mine as his."

Smiling Girl had followed them inside, and she took her papoose from its cradle and opened one shoulder of her tunic, exposing a breast to feed the baby. Tom had gotten used to such sights and simply glanced away, studying Medicine Wolf again.

"You have no idea how many times I have prayed I would get to see you again," he told her. He looked around. "Where is Bear Paw?"

"He meets with other Dog Soldiers and with the Sioux to talk about the new treaty. He will come soon." She leaned over to stir something that looked like stew. "We will all eat." She looked over at him. "Your wife did not come?"

"No. She, uh, the baby was a little fussy and she—"

"She was afraid to come. I understand." She turned her eyes back to the stew.

"Don't feel insulted, Medicine Wolf. Elena is a good woman. She teaches Indian children with much kindness and is very dedicated. It wasn't easy for her to come here."

"I am not insulted. It is all strange to her, just as it was all strange to me when first I stayed at the fort with your family. We are always afraid of a people we do not fully understand. I would have liked to talk to her more, get to know better the woman who married my Tom."

He thought it strange the way she said "my" Tom. Had she thought of him as often as he had thought of her? He glanced around the tipi, studying the many paintings on the inner lining. Parfleches and deerskin clothing hung from rawhide ties attached to the tipi poles. Backrests made of woven strips of wood and grass provided pleasant seating. Two or three buffalo robes were stacked in one corner. He thought how simply these people lived and traveled, turning their tipis and poles into travois that were tied to horses and used to carry all their belongings.

His eyes moved back to Medicine Wolf, who continued to stir whatever it was she was cooking. He watched her lovingly, studied the way her hair glowed in the firelight, the way her body moved, the way her tunic clung lightly to her round hips. He noticed her precious medicine bag still hanging around her neck. "You look wonderful, Medicine Wolf," he told her. He removed a woolen jacket. "I was so afraid, after all the things I've heard, that you'd be somehow scarred or, I don't know. You just don't look like I thought you would."

She smiled, sitting back and meeting his eyes. She studied his thinning hair. "And you still have the same blue eyes and soft smile. I also prayed that somehow I would see my blood brother again." She moved closer to him, and he wondered if she realized what her exotic presence did to him. "Are your mother and father well?"

He felt lost in her dark eyes. "Yes. They're back in Boston. After they first went home, they never came back, but I did. I'm teaching now, Medicine Wolf, like my mother taught. But I don't use her same methods. We're doing what we can, my wife and I both. Perhaps one day we'll be teaching your children."

She gave him a rather haughty look, and he could see the wild in her then, the Indian side that had grown more fierce over years of fighting whites and living and sleeping with one of the most notorious warriors among the Northern Cheyenne. "Perhaps," she answered. "But it is not likely. We have burned the soldiers' forts in the Powder River country. We have signed a new treaty that gives us much land. Long ago Bear Paw and I decided we would always live as free as always, or die. I do not think Bear Paw would ever let any of his children go to a white man's school . . . not after Sand Creek."

"Sand Creek! Were you there?"

Her eyes saddened as she looked at the dancing flames of the fire. "Ai. I was there. Both of my parents were killed there. My brother, Swift Fox, was killed by soldiers

seven winters before that." She looked at Tom, her eyes
holding a mixture of bitter hatred and terrible sorrow.
"Bear Paw also lost his mother at Sand Creek. She had
been raped many times, and was so badly wounded by the
soldiers that she begged him to kill her. He granted her
her wish."

The air hung silent for a moment. The two little boys
toyed with the beads and laughed quietly, and the baby
girl sucked away contentedly at Smiling Girl's breast. "I'm
sorry, Medicine Wolf."

Medicine Wolf stared at the fire a moment. "It left
him a very bitter man," she said quietly. "He turned to
the whiskey, and it tore us apart. Then, because of his
drunken foolishness, he was badly wounded. Buffalo hunters almost killed him, and he carries many scars from their
attack. He nearly died, but the medicine of the wolf's paws
saved him. Since then we have been very close, and he no
longer drinks the whiskey."

"That's good. You must see how bad it is for your
people, Medicine Wolf. My wife and I talk to the children
about it often." He sighed. "I can't believe how much
time has passed since that day you left us. I know you
have suffered much, Medicine Wolf, but maybe under this
new treaty the suffering can end."

She looked at him again, her eyes sad. "Do you really
believe this?"

His throat began to feel tight. "I have to believe it,
just as *you* have to believe it. We have to try, Medicine
Wolf. The bloodshed has to cease."

"It will if the white man keeps his word this time and
lets no more whites come into our sacred lands. We made
much trouble for the soldiers and miners in Powder River
country. Now their forts are closed, and we have won. I
think the whites would be very foolish to break this treaty,
for we will not settle for anything less than what we have
now. We will die first."

He nodded. "I know." He smiled then. "Still the same
stubborn, determined Medicine Wolf, aren't you?"

She finally smiled herself. "I have not changed." She
touched his hand, and he felt a warmth move through him.
"Nor have you, Tom. You are still the same caring, de-

voted man I once knew. You came back, just like you promised you would. Your heart is still good.''

He could not help imagining what it must be like to lie with a woman of such beauty and inner spirit. Surely someone like Medicine Wolf was as passionate in her lovemaking as she was in all her beliefs and her determination to fight for all that was Cheyenne. He felt drawn to her, felt a terrible urge to kiss her, but then someone else entered the tipi.

Tom looked up into Bear Paw's dark, possessive eyes. The warrior's presence seemed to fill the dwelling, making it seem suddenly much smaller. He removed a deerskin jacket, under which he wore only a vest. He said nothing until Medicine Wolf spoke to him. Tom recognized the word for *eat*, and Bear Paw nodded.

Tom could not help staring for a moment at the many scars on Bear Paw's arms and on the parts of his chest that were exposed. So, this was what the buffalo hunters had done to him. It was no wonder men like Bear Paw hated the whites so badly; no wonder they wanted their children to have nothing to do with white man's schools.

Bear Paw moved to where his two sons played, and he sat down beside them while Medicine Wolf dished out some stew. Tom immediately saw a transformation in Bear Paw. The wild-looking warrior turned into a soft, attentive father, speaking softly to his sons, playing for a moment with their string of beads, teaching them to count the Cheyenne way. The older boy said something, and Bear Paw laughed.

So, this was the fearsome Bear Paw, Cheyenne Dog Soldier who was married to the tribe's holy woman. Here he was, being a loving father. It struck Tom almost painfully just how much these people must want peace and a normal life like any other family would want. Would this latest treaty bring them that peace? How he prayed it would.

Medicine Wolf handed Tom a plate of stew. He did not question its contents, realizing it could be anything from buffalo meat to dog meat. Whatever it was, it tasted good. Bear Paw leaned over to touch Smiling Girl's cheek with his own, then touched the cheek of the baby that fed at her mother's breast, and Tom noticed Medicine Wolf did not seem the least bit jealous of his attention to her sister and their new baby.

"You didn't mind when Bear Paw took a second wife?" he asked her.

Medicine Wolf smiled. "It is as I told you. It is important to have many children to carry on the blood, especially the blood of a warrior like Bear Paw." She dished up more food for the rest of her "family." "I am the one who urged him to take my sister. He wanted no wife but me, but after five winters and much lovemaking, I knew that I was barren."

Tom reddened a little at the remark, spoken as naturally as she might tell him of the day's latest events. He realized that he would never have been any match for Bear Paw, who probably made love with the same violent passion as he made war. The man was apparently reasonably gentle with Medicine Wolf, for she certainly looked none the worse for wear, and she glowed with happiness.

Bear Paw sat down near her then, and she handed him a dish of the stew. When she did so they touched cheeks, and they shared a look that told Tom she was reassuring Bear Paw that he had nothing to worry about. Did the man actually think that he, Tom Prescott, was some kind of challenge to him? Heaven forbid that the man should think of him as an enemy, some white man come to seduce his wife! If Bear Paw should ever think to pick a fight with him, Tom figured he would last perhaps ten seconds, if he was lucky, and then only if he could get Bear Paw to tie at least one hand behind his back!

The two little boys joined them in the meal, after which they returned to their string of beads. Bear Paw lit a beautifully painted stone pipe and offered it to Tom, surprising him with the gesture. Tom recognized the honor such an offering carried, and he took the pipe reverently, lightly smoking the sweet mixture of tobacco and sage with which the pipe had been stuffed.

Bear Paw proceeded to speak to him in the Cheyenne tongue, Medicine Wolf interpreting for him. He remained slightly aloof, keeping an air about him that Tom had noticed many Sioux and Cheyenne warriors had, a fierce pride that came before all things. The man barely cracked a smile, except when speaking to his sons. He asked Tom many questions about the treaty and if he thought the whites would stick to it. He then proceeded to tell him that if they did not, they would die, plain and simple. Tom did not doubt it, but he did doubt how long the Indians could enforce such a policy without hordes of soldiers teaching them one last bitter lesson.

Tom considered telling them what he thought was the real truth, that he doubted the soldiers could really control any further white settlement; that this treaty was just another attempt at buying more time until the government could get organized now that the War Between the States was over; that he still felt the days of even this limited freedom for the Cheyenne were numbered.

Still, these People had so little to cling to. They wanted so much for their children and grandchildren, but Tom saw no future for them. He did not want to come here tonight and destroy that hope. He enjoyed seeing Medicine Wolf happy, enjoyed seeing her and Bear Paw in a family setting that evoked peace and love. Life could be good for them, if indeed this treaty would hold.

He finished the stew and thanked Medicine Wolf, telling her he had better get back to Elena. He rose, and Bear Paw also rose, overshadowing him. Tom was surprised to realize Bear Paw was no taller than he, but he had such an aura of fierceness about him that he gave the impression of being much bigger. His muscular arms did show a hardness about them that Tom knew his own arms did not have. He put out his hand and Tom returned the gesture. They grasped wrists, and Tom knew by Bear Paw's grip that he was sending a message. Tom needed no interpretation. He thought about what Medicine Wolf had told him about how Bear Paw had had to kill his own mother, how it had nearly destroyed him.

Yes, he thought. *You are fierce and cruel when you need to be, Bear Paw. But you are a man with as much heart as the best of our own. If only those in Washington who try to direct your lives could understand how human you are.*

He released his grip and looked at Medicine Wolf.

"Thank you for the invitation. Perhaps I will see you tomorrow at the signing," he told her.

She nodded. "I will be there among the Dog Soldier Society. When the signing is done, we will leave. My husband does not like to stay too long where there are many soldiers. He does not trust them."

Tom glanced at Bear Paw. "I can understand that." He turned his eyes back to Medicine Wolf. "I missed you so much over the years, Medicine Wolf. I suppose it could be another fifteen years before I see you again, maybe never."

"It is as I told you the first time. Always we will be together here." She touched her heart.

He wanted to hold her again, hold her for a very long time, but Bear Paw was watching. His eyes teared slightly. "Good-bye, Medicine Wolf."

She smiled softly. "Good-bye, my brother. We will meet again in another world, where there is no war, no sickness, no hatred."

He smiled. "Yes. That will be nice, won't it?" *I love you*, he wanted to tell her. *I have always loved you.*

She came closer then and touched her cheek to his own. "It is good to know there are still some white men who are good."

She backed away. Tom could not find his voice. He looked at Bear Paw and nodded, then turned and left. He breathed deeply of the cool night air, hurrying through the village, which seemed more menacing at night. He mounted the horse he had left tied at the fort after taking Elena home earlier in the day. He rode at a slow gait toward home, being careful because it was now dark. His heart and mind whirled with images of Medicine Wolf sharing her passion with the handsome Bear Paw.

By the time he reached home, Elena was already in her nightgown, ready for bed. Rebecca was asleep. He put up his horse and came inside to find Elena full of questions. She seemed nervous and animated, not quite herself. When they finally went to bed, she snuggled close to him, kissing his neck, and moments later he found himself unbuttoning his longjohns to accommodate her.

What was this strange thing that had happened to

Elena? Had his going to see Medicine Wolf actually made her jealous? Whatever it was, he did not mind, for being so close to the Indian woman of his dreams had aroused his baser needs. He entered his wife eagerly, felt her stiffen some then, as she always did. She spoke his name, but in Tom's mind it was Medicine Wolf speaking to him, calling him *na-ehame*, the Cheyenne word for husband. Tonight he was Medicine Wolf's lover.

Chapter Twenty-three

"So, your white man did not forget you," Bear Paw said quietly.

They lay snuggled under a buffalo robe inside the tipi, Smiling Girl and the children sleeping on the other side of the fire.

"*My* white man?" Medicine Wolf asked teasingly.

"That is how I think of him. He is special to you. The rest of us respect that he has a good heart, but for you it is more than that. If I saw him in battle, I would want to kill him for the way he looks at you, but I would not, because he is your blood brother. If things were different, he would have wanted to be more than that. It is still there, in his eyes."

Medicine Wolf smiled, turning to press against him. "He has a wife and a child now. I have seen his woman. She is very pretty, for a white woman. I have never seen such red hair on anyone before."

Bear Paw wrapped his arms around her, rolling her

onto her back. "There is not a woman in all this land who looks like you. Do you think I do not know this? I saw how the soldiers watched you today. I saw how Tom Prescott looked at you. It makes me want to keep you closer to me."

She studied his dark eyes by the dim firelight, the teasing smile still on her face. "We cannot get much closer, my jealous husband," she told him.

Bear Paw smiled, reaching down to push up her tunic. Because of the colder weather, they chose not to sleep nude. "I think we can get a little closer," he answered, both of them speaking in a near whisper.

Medicine Wolf laughed lightly, opening her legs so that he lay between them. "I like to be as close to you as I can get."

He moved to untie his breechcloth, leaving on the calico shirt he had worn to bed. He had stolen several of the white man's cotton shirts in a raid, deciding that to wear them meant fewer animal skins were needed for clothing. In this time of scarcity of game, it was important to save wherever they could. He did not, however, like white men's pants, which he considered confining and unsanitary, as did most Indian men. A simple breechcloth and open leggings were much more comfortable, with knee-high moccasins and extra-long shirts and wolfskin or bearskin jackets in winter.

Medicine Wolf breathed deeply when he gently pushed himself inside her. "Is this close enough," he asked, his eyes glittering with pleasure.

"*Ai,*" she gasped, arching up to him.

They moved in quiet rhythm, not wanting to wake the others. Bear Paw leaned down, licking her mouth, her eyes, back to her mouth, moving his tongue into her mouth in an imitation of intercourse, while he surged inside that secret place that had always belonged to just one man. Medicine Wolf lay nearly limp in sweet surrender, recognizing his need to master her this way. Only one man was allowed to invade the sacred woman of the Cheyenne.

He raised himself up then, looking down at her like the conquerer he was, for in his arms she was helpless. He grasped her hips and pulled her to him, surging inside her until she felt his grip tighten on her bottom, felt his life spill into her again. He stayed rigid for a moment, then relaxed, pulling away from her and lying down beside her. "Now you will not go to sleep thinking about Tom Prescott," he told her.

She smiled, deciding to indulge him, feeling special because of how easily this great warrior became jealous of a white man who could never compare. "I never go to sleep thinking of anyone but you," she answered, snuggling into his shoulder. She closed her eyes, deciding not to tell him what a sad feeling she had over seeing Tom again. It had reminded her how swiftly time passes, reminded her again how very different Tom's world was from her own; it made her wonder about the treaty, wonder if it was really possible this would be the end of the troubles between her people and Tom's people. As long as their cultures remained so far apart, maybe to think they could always live at peace was just a foolish dream.

Medicine Wolf walked toward the fort with a determined gait. There was much activity today as representatives of the white man's government prepared for Red Cloud's signing and Indian women prepared the regalia for their warriors to wear to the ceremony. Smiling Girl prepared paints for Bear Paw, who had ridden off earlier that morning with several other Cheyenne men after a herd of antelope they had spotted. He would be back soon, and later in the afternoon the Indian leaders would put on their finest buckskins and paint their faces with their prayer colors. They would smoke the pipe with the white leaders, and again they would try to make peace with the *ve-ho-e*.

But that would all come later. This morning Medicine Wolf was determined to find her old friend Summer Moon and see how she was doing. She ordered Little Wolf to stay behind, for always she feared for her beloved wolf when he was near soldiers. She had bad memories about this place and would be glad when they could leave it. She felt the soldiers' eyes on her, and she pulled her bearskin cape closer around herself. It was colder today, and the skin of the white wolf who had been killed here was not enough warmth now. She wore knee-high winter moccasins, and hardly anything of her showed besides her face, yet she felt naked as she walked through the fort grounds.

She headed toward the officers' quarters to inquire where she might find White Horse's wife, little realizing that White Horse himself had spotted her when soldiers with whom he was talking pointed her out. White Horse smiled. "She was to be my woman once," he bragged to the soldiers. He knew the white man's tongue now, liked the white man's whiskey, liked the money these white men paid him to sleep with his wife.

"Then how come she belongs to that renegade Bear Paw?" one of the soldiers asked him.

White Horse shot him a warning look. "Because she had a vision that they must be together," he answered. "But *I* am the one she wanted," he added, trying to save his pride in front of the men. "You see? Even now she looks for me. I will go to her and take her to my dwelling. I will take her to my bed easily, for she has surely missed me and longs for me."

The soldiers watched White Horse with wry grins and doubtful minds as he mounted his Pinto gelding and rode toward Medicine Wolf. "You think he's telling the truth?" one of the soldiers asked the others, watching the beautiful holy woman of the Cheyenne about whom nearly every man in the fort had been talking.

"He's daydreaming. Everybody knows there's only one buck for that squaw. I sure as hell would like to run across her in an attack and get my hands on her though."

"Yeah? Well, you'd better make damn sure that son of a bitch Bear Paw was good and dead first, or you'd find your balls missin'," another answered.

They all laughed as White Horse rode closer to Medicine Wolf, charging his horse directly in her path. Medicine Wolf, startled, stopped and looked up at him, her eyes quickly showing the hatred that had never died. White Horse dismounted, standing in front of her challengingly. "So," he said, his gaze wandering pleasurably over her, his breath showing in the cold air as he spoke. "You come to find White Horse."

He grinned, and in spite of the early morning hour,

Medicine Wolf could smell whiskey on his breath. She remembered the smell from when Bear Paw used to drink it, hated what it did to men. She held her chin high, facing him boldly. "I come to find Summer Moon and visit with my old friend. As for you, White Horse, I would rather never set eyes on you again."

White Horse's smile faded slightly. "Summer Moon does not want to see you."

"How do you know?"

"She told me. If she wanted to see you, she would have asked to come to your camp. She has said nothing about you."

"Take me to her. I might never get the chance to see her again, and I wish to mend old hurts."

White Horse studied her a moment, then brightened a little. He realized this was his chance! Bear Paw was no-where about. She did not even have her guardian wolf with her. If she wanted to see Summer Moon, he would take her to his dwelling. Once inside, perhaps he could finally realize the ultimate victory over Bear Paw! This woman owed him a great deal for the way she had tricked him years earlier into giving all those gifts to Arrow Maker to try to win her fickle hand.

For years he had thought of nothing else but finding her in a raid, killing Bear Paw and taking her as his captive. How many times had he daydreamed about planting himself inside this haughty woman who thought she was so sacred? Now, here she was, wanting to go to his dwelling . . . alone. Bear Paw would not dare try to do anything about it or make trouble, not at a treaty signing, not at a soldier fort!

"All right," he told Medicine Wolf. "I will take you. But do not try to talk my wife into going back with you, or I will make much trouble for you and Bear Paw with the bluecoats. I can do it. I have been with them many years. They listen to me. I am a good scout. I share smokes and whiskey with them. If I say they should shoot your wolf or kill Bear Paw, or if I say you should again be forced to stay here, they will do it."

Medicine Wolf watched his eyes. She suspected he was only playing on her own fears and bad memories. He knew she hated and feared this place. "I do not think you have so much power with the bluecoats," she answered. "I think you lie and brag, as you always did. And I think the firewater that controls you makes you say foolish things. But I will not try to make Summer Moon come with us. I want only to talk with her again. Do you have children?"

White Horse puffed up proudly. "We have a son, eleven summers, called Crow Dog. Another son, Red Beaver, is five summers. A daughter, Little Beaver is nine summers." A sneer moved across his lips. "And there are other children . . . half-breed children."

Medicine Wolf's eyes widened. "Half-breed! How is it that Summer Moon has children with white blood!"

White Horse's eyes narrowed, and Medicine Wolf noticed he smelled bad, like a man who seldom bathed. He no longer carried a pride in his appearance. His leggings were badly worn, the knees shiny; and the soldier jacket he wore was soiled. He wore a flat soldier cap over hair that was greasy from its own oils.

"Summer Moon is a loose woman," he told her, leaning closer. "Sometimes I have to beat her for finding her sneaking around the fort offering herself to the soldiers."

Medicine Wolf scowled, her lip curling in disgust. "I do not believe you! I think you have *forced* her to go with the white men, in return for whiskey and tobacco! You are the same coward and traitor that you were when the People disowned you!"

She could not quite read the look on his face. She suspected he would like to hit her, but he held back. She knew he was trying to frighten her, but she did not fear him. He would not dare bring her any harm when so many of her People were right there. "I want to see Summer Moon," she demanded. "Take me to her now!"

White Horse looked over at the soldiers, who watched curiously. He had told them he could talk Medicine Wolf into going to his dwelling. Even if he never touched her, the soldiers would think the worst. They would envy him. He would be a big man in their eyes. He grinned, looking back at Medicine Wolf. "Follow me," he told her. He took hold of his horse's bridle and headed away from the fort, looking over at the soldiers again and grinning.

Medicine Wolf stayed behind him as they walked nearly a quarter of a mile to a crudely built cabin that looked ready to fall in. Smoke curled from a tin chimney that protruded from a sod roof. A young boy lolled on the sagging front steps, giving Medicine Wolf a rather vacant stare as she came closer. White Horse tied his horse and introduced the boy as his oldest son, Crow Dog. "Crow Dog is learning to be a good scout," he told Medicine Wolf.

Medicine Wolf looked sadly at the young man, thinking how children like this, Indian children brought up away from the influence of their proud elders, were such a waste, for they would never know the Cheyenne pride, the Cheyenne ways. She realized it would be this way for children of those Cheyenne who chose to live on the reservations being made for them. Crow Dog showed no pride, nor did he show her any respect as she came closer and mounted the steps. He simply returned to the piece of wood he was whittling.

Didn't he know who she was? Didn't he realize she was the sacred woman of the Cheyenne? Had he no respect for the People from which he had come? But then, why would White Horse teach him any respect for a People he now hated? She could see how living among whites had influenced White Horse. He had become slovenly, probably a drunkard. She was certain he had taken to selling his wife to white men, and her heart ached for Summer Moon.

Two more children came from behind the cabin. One looked perhaps six or seven, a boy who carried a little girl of only about two. The boy had blue eyes, and although the little girl had dark eyes and skin, her hair was light. Medicine Wolf's heart ached at the sight, children of two worlds who could never belong to either. She knew of other half-breed children, children seldom accepted by the Cheyenne and looked down upon by whites with even worse scorn than were full-blood Indians.

"They are not mine," White Horse said casually. "I have nothing to do with them. My children get fed first. If there is anything left over, the half-blood dogs can have it."

He opened the door, and Medicine Wolf felt haunted by the forlorn look she saw in the eyes of the little half-breeds. She followed White Horse inside, where Summer Moon was cooking on an iron stove. A young girl who Medicine Wolf surmised was Little Beaver helped her, and a younger boy sat on the wood floor, carving designs into the wood with a knife much too big for such a child to be playing with.

Summer Moon looked toward the door when they came inside, and her eyes widened with surprise and joy. But just as quickly her eyes filled with shame, and she looked away. Medicine Wolf moved past White Horse. "Summer Moon, my good friend," she said. "It has been so long."

Summer Moon looked the other way. "Go away. I am no longer worthy to be called your friend," she answered quietly. She slowly turned back around, glancing at White Horse, afraid she might say the wrong thing and get another beating. How much whiskey had he already had this morning?

Medicine Wolf noticed a bruise near her left eye. Summer Moon was just as unkempt as her husband and children, and she had grown fat. Medicine Wolf instantly sensed there was no joy left in her, no pride. Medicine Wolf shook her head, her eyes tearing. She reached out and touched Summer Moon's arm, but Summer Moon pulled away.

"Summer Moon, I will always think of you as my friend, no matter how you feel. Never did I betray you, or do anything to try to hurt you. None of it was my fault."

Summer Moon met her eyes, and Medicine Wolf was sure she saw a look of agreement, a look that told her she understood now, but that it was too late.

Summer Moon studied Medicine Wolf quietly, wiping a tear with fat fingers. "You have not changed. You are as beautiful as the day—" She hesitated. The day they parted, Medicine Wolf had been attacked by White Horse. She turned away again. "Go away, Medicine Wolf. Do not call me friend, and do not stay here a moment longer."

Medicine Wolf sighed. "I came to tell you that all these years I have thought of you often. Your friendship and forgiveness mean much to me, Summer Moon." The woman sniffed and began stirring something on the stove while the two children in the house stared at Medicine Wolf. "Tell me, Summer Moon," Medicine Wolf said softly. "Tell me why you let yourself go this way. And tell me it is not true what White Horse told me . . . that you go begging to the white men."

Summer Moon quickly turned, shooting a look of deep hurt at White Horse. "You told her this?"

A menacing look came into White Horse's eyes. She knew what it meant. "I told her the truth," he warned.

Summer Moon swallowed, glancing at Medicine Wolf, turning away again.

"He lies, doesn't he?" Medicine Wolf asked her.

"Be still woman," White Horse growled, stepping closer. "You wanted to see your good friend! Now you have!" He grasped Medicine Wolf's arm. "Now it is time to do what you *really* came here for!"

Medicine Wolf yanked her arm away. "What are you talking about!"

White Horse grinned. "Did you think I cared about you seeing Summer Moon again?" This time he grasped both her arms. "Did you think I had forgotten how we last parted, forgotten how you scorned me and shamed me in front of the Cheyenne! You *owe* me, Medicine Wolf." He sneered, bending closer. "You came here alone, without even your wolf! Your man is not here to protect you now, and when I am done with you, you will no longer be *worth* protecting!"

Medicine Wolf kicked at his groin but did not quite hit her target. She struggled violently, but White Horse whirled her about, wrapping one strong arm around her from behind and dragging her toward a curtained-off room. Summer Moon tried to object, grabbing him, begging him to let Medicine Wolf go, but White Horse landed a fist against the woman's face that sent her sprawling backward. She fell against a table, shoving it across the floor as her hefty body plunged to the floor.

The young boy who had been carving in the floor screamed a scream that told Medicine Wolf the child had seen this many times before. He ran for the door and hurried outside without even taking a jacket. Summer Moon lay groaning on the floor, her nose and mouth bleeding and her young daughter, in tears, went to her side.

Medicine Wolf continued to fight wildly, until White Horse swung her around and landed two hard blows that sent her reeling. She remembered hitting a wall, felt a pain in her side as White Horse grabbed her and hit her again, sending her sprawling over a chair. Her jerked her up by the hair then, and slung her onto the bed as though she were a mere sack of flour.

Medicine Wolf felt her arms being torn painfully backward as he yanked off her bearskin coat. He did not bother with her moccasins, but merely shoved her tunic up over her breasts. By then Medicine Wolf was overcoming her confusion and near unconsciousness. She kicked out viciously, making White Horse grunt when she caught him in the stomach, but she failed to deter him. He grabbed her ankles and pushed her legs wide apart. "I have waited a long time for this," he snarled, planting a knee on each of her thighs so that she could not move her legs. He punched her hard in her already-bruised ribs, again across the side of the face, quickly rendering her helpless.

Medicine Wolf felt her wrists being tied then to the bedposts. "After I have had my fill of you, Bear Paw will no longer want you," he told her, his voice raspy with heated desire. "I will tell him you came here willingly, wishing you had chosen me all those years ago! And once you are mine, the white soldiers will pay a lot of money and whiskey to lay with you! I will live like the richest white man, collecting money for my sacred whore!"

Medicine Wolf opened her eyes, seeing only his blurred figure then. Through a haze she felt him grab an ankle to tie it to the foot of the bed. She tried to scream, but nothing would come. Then she saw another figure behind him, someone heavy, someone with arms upraised. She heard a clang, two, three. White Horse cried out and fell across Medicine Wolf's nearly stripped, partly tied body.

Medicine Wolf tried to clear her mind as the heavy figure pulled White Horse off her and let him slump to the floor. Medicine Wolf's eyes cleared enough that she could see it was Summer Moon. The woman told her daughter to get a knife. She leaned over Medicine Wolf, pulling her tunic back down over her nakedness. Medicine Wolf could hear her crying.

"I am sorry," the woman sobbed. "Forgive me, Medicine Wolf, for the things I said . . . so many years ago. I was wrong."

The young girl came into the room, handing her mother a knife. Summer Moon quickly cut the rawhide strips that held Medicine Wolf to the bed. She helped her sit up, then took her arm. "Come quickly! You must leave before he wakes up."

Medicine Wolf noticed a black iron fry-pan lying near White Horse's unconscious body. Both women stumbled over the man, and the little girl grabbed Medicine Wolf's coat.

"I am so sorry, I am so sorry," Summer Moon kept saying. "I am ashamed that you find me this way, but there is no money, no food. Always he beats me. He makes me sleep with the white men so that he can buy whiskey. I am this way because I have no pride left in me," she sniffled. "Go now. He will be very angry. Go and take my daughter with you, please! Soon he will begin letting white men sleep with her also. I do not want that for my Little Beaver."

Medicine Wolf scrambled with her thoughts. White Horse would sell his own daughter to white men? What kind of horror had Summer Moon been living with? Her head screamed with pain, as did her side from injured ribs. She felt Summer Moon helping her get her coat on. The room seemed to swirl around her. She knew she must get away quickly, but she could not bear the thought of leaving Summer Moon behind. She grasped Summer Moon's arms for support.

"You must . . . come with me," she gasped, struggling to see more clearly. She realized then that she tasted blood in her mouth.

"No! White Horse would make much trouble! It is too late for me now, Medicine Wolf," Summer Moon sobbed. "Why do you think I did not come to see my People or to see you? Many years ago I stopped hating you and started hating my husband. But I had no place to go, no way to live without doing as he asked. He is full of the evil spirits now, Medicine Wolf. To try to leave him would mean death for those who tried to help me, and I am ashamed. I am not worthy to come back to my People.''

''You *are* worthy! You chose White Horse because you loved him. You did not know it would be this way,'' Medicine Wolf told her, clinging to her. ''Now you must come with me, Summer Moon. I did not know I would find you this way. Now that I have, I cannot leave you here. Come, please! Bring the children, *all* of them, even the half-bloods.''

''No! No!''

With all the strength she could muster, Medicine Wolf dug her fingers into the woman's arms. ''I will not leave . . . without you,'' she nearly growled. ''If you do not go, I will stay here, and White Horse will have his way with me! Is that what you want!''

Summer Moon began crying harder. ''You are the sacred woman. This is a terrible thing White Horse has done. It will mean much, much trouble!''

''Let Bear Paw and the elders worry about that. They would all want me to bring you with me, Summer Moon! Now, hurry! Get a coat and a few clothes!''

Summer Moon jerked in a deep sob, suddenly hugging her tightly. ''My good friend,'' she blubbered. ''You should hate me.''

Medicine Wolf felt a painful lump in her throat. She stroked Summer Moon's hair. ''I never hated you . . . and you never hated me, Summer Moon. You only loved White Horse so much that you could not see beyond that.''

White Horse groaned, and both women stiffened. Medicine Wolf gave Summer Moon a light shove. ''Hurry,'' she whispered.

The woman began to scramble then. Medicine Wolf spotted a handgun hanging on a hook near the door. She quickly took it down, hoping she was not shaking too much or too dizzy to hit her target if she had to. She watched White Horse, remembering what a proud, handsome young warrior he had once been. He groaned again, trying to get to his knees but unable to do so. Medicine Wolf saw something terrible in him, a dark foreboding for the future of

ner People. New tears stung her eyes. She realized that
somehow, even if they had to fight to the death, the Cheyenne had to keep their People from too much white influence, keep them from reservation life.

Summer Moon hurried toward her then, half dragging
the young girl by the arm. "There is no time to gather all
our clothing and some food."

"We will share. There are many among us who will
help you," Medicine Wolf told her.

Their eyes held, Summer Moon's puffy from crying.
"I should have realized the friend that you were," she
told Medicine Wolf.

Medicine Wolf licked a bleeding lip. "Perhaps we
should all have tried harder to stop you," she answered.

"My father, my brother, they can take care of me."

Medicine Wolf shook her head, taking her hand. "They
were killed at Sand Creek."

The horror of it, the realization that what she had done
had cost her so much, moved through Summer Moon's
eyes. She started to turn away.

"Come," Medicine Wolf told her. "There will be time
for mourning later. Then you will rejoice that you are home
with your People, and they will rejoice at having you back.
Come now. Hurry!"

The three of them hurried out, and Summer Moon
called to little Red Beaver, who sat huddled under the
porch. The boy came to her, still holding the knife. Summer Moon quickly wrapped a woolen jacket around him,
a small jacket like little white boys wore. She lifted him
to White Horse's pinto and untied the animal.

Medicine Wolf kept hold of the revolver and watched
the doorway as Summer Moon gathered up the two half-
bloods, lifting them also, one by one, to the horse's back
so that the three smallest children were on the horse. She
looked at Crow Dog. "I am leaving your father. I go back
to my People," she told the young man.

Medicine Wolf noted a distinct sense of new pride in
Summer Moon's use of the term "my People."

"They are also your People," Summer Moon told him.
"Come with us, Crow Dog."

The boy remained sitting on the steps, and Medicine

Wolf realized he had not budged through all the commotion inside. He gave his mother a dark look. "He is my father," he answered. "I stay. I like the white man's ways." He moved his eyes to Medicine Wolf. "I would rather hunt the Cheyenne than live with them," he added sarcastically.

So, Medicine Wolf thought, *your father has done a good job of making you hate your own people.* She thought again of Sweet Medicine's prophecy that her People would turn on each other, and the cause of all the strife would be the troubles brought to them by white men.

Both women turned away. There was nothing more to be said to Crow Dog, no time to argue the issue. They had to get themselves and the other children to safety. Medicine Wolf began to shake from the shock of her beating. She pulled the hood of her fur coat over her head, not wanting any of the soldiers to see her bruises and her bleeding lip. She quickly checked to be sure she still had her medicine bag. It was around her neck. Young Little Beaver put her arm around Medicine Wolf's waist for support and helped her walk.

They left the sagging cabin, White Horse still lying inside with a nearly cracked skull. Crow Dog watched until they were well near the fort, then decided he had better go inside and see what had happened to his father. He usually stayed out of his parents' fights, having learned early on that when he interfered he usually also got hit. He had no feelings left for his mother and couldn't care less that she was leaving. After all, his father had explained many times over that his mother was a bad woman who enjoyed sleeping with the soldiers. Crow Dog was convinced it was true, convinced his mother deserved the beatings she got. He had grown so accustomed to them that he no longer paid any attention.

"Father?" He walked into the bedroom, where White Horse was finally getting to his knees. The man held his head and groaned, and when he took his hand away, Crow Dog saw blood on his father's palm. "What do you want me to do, Father?"

"Where are they?" White Horse growled.

"They are gone, all but me. I stayed with you, Father."

White Horse glared past him toward the door. "They will die for this," he yelled. "Bear Paw, Medicine Wolf . . . your mother. They will *all* die!" He tried to get to his feet, but dizziness made him sink to his knees again.

Bear Paw charged inside the tipi, looking even more foreboding in the buffalo-hide coat he wore for warmth. He glared at Medicine Wolf, who quickly looked up at him from where she sat letting Smiling Girl apply an ointment to her cut lip. Rage swept through Bear Paw's eyes as he studied the several bruises on Medicine Wolf's face.

"So, it is true what they told me when I got back," he said, his voice low and menacing.

Medicine Wolf lowered her eyes. "I am sorry, Bear Paw. I only wanted to see Summer Moon. I did not think White Horse would make so much trouble, not with nearly our whole village here, and not so near the fort and the soldiers."

"Those soldiers would not have cared if he had *killed* you!" He threw off the robe and came closer, kneeling down beside her. Outside, the wind howled menacingly. As many had suspected would happen, the unusually mild weather they had been experiencing was suddenly turning into the season's first snowstorm. Heavy flakes were beginning to spit around in the air. Bear Paw touched Medicine Wolf's chin, making her meet his eyes. He pushed back her hair, studying the dark swelling at both sides of her face. "Are you hurt anywhere else," he asked, his heart aching at the look of sorrow in her eyes.

"My ribs," she answered. "I fell against a chair when he—"

Bear Paw grasped her hair. Medicine Wolf could feel his tension and rage. "Did he rape you?"

She closed her eyes and shook her head. "No. I swear it. He tried. I fought him, but he was so strong, and he hit me until I could not see or think or move. Before he could do what he intended Summer Moon came into the room and hit him many times in the head with an iron pan. While he lay unconscious, we ran away." She met his eyes again. "I know I should not have gone there, but now I am glad, Bear Paw," she told him, determination in her eyes. "White Horse has become a cruel, worthless man! He was forcing Summer Moon to lie with soldiers in return for whiskey and tobacco! She has two half-blood children. He beat her many times. They were living in a terrible place, dirty, hungry. Summer Moon did not know how to get away from him! I said she could come back to us, that we would take care of her. She is staying with Two Moons and Shining Woman." Her eyes teared. "I know this will bring much trouble, but I could not leave her there."

He sighed, wiping away her tears with his thumb. "You should have waited for me to come with you. It is done now, and White Horse will pay!"

She grasped his wrist. "I do not want trouble for you, Bear Paw, not here! I am afraid. White Horse has many good friends among the soldiers. He might convince one of them to shoot you."

He grinned a little, shaking his head. "Here? At a treaty signing? There are more Sioux and Cheyenne here than soldiers, Medicine Wolf. They know they do not dare harm one of us, and none of them can raise a weapon to us without permission from the commander. He would never allow such a thing to happen under these conditions." He rose, relieved to know White Horse had not invaded what belonged to him alone. "Have Summer Moon and Two Moons' families pack and be ready to leave as soon as the signing is over. It is right after the ceremony is finished that I will repay White Horse for what he has done!" He knelt to warm his hands over the fire. "When I am finished, we will leave right away. We will camp at Horse Creek and wait for the others. The soldiers will not stop us. They will be glad to have us off their hands so they do not have to worry about it. They will recognize it is a personal thing between two Cheyenne men." He looked at Smiling Girl. "When I dress for the ceremony, I will not wear my prayer colors." His dark eyes sparkled with a desire for revenge. "I will wear my war paint."

Smiling Girl nodded. "I will prepare it for you, my

husband." Finished with Medicine Wolf, she moved away to finish preparing things for Bear Paw, who turned to his wife.

"It is not a wise thing that you did," he told her, "but your heart is good. I know you intended only good to come of it."

"I am afraid for you. I do not like this place. Every time I come here, something bad happens. I am afraid of the soldiers. White Horse said he could make them force me to stay here again."

Bear Paw smiled wryly. "Do you really think I would let that happen, or that I would not come in the night and take you away from here?"

She managed a limp smile, her lip hurting. "Once we leave here, I never want to come back, Bear Paw, not for any reason."

"Not even to see your white man?"

She sniffed. "I already know I will never see him again. It was enough to be able to speak to him, to know that he has a family and is well." She put a hand to her sore ribs. "If something happens to you because of this, I will never forgive myself."

"The only one who is going to suffer from this is White Horse!" He picked up another piece of wood and placed it on the fire. Smiling Girl came over to sit down beside him, dipping her fingers into a red paint made from clay and red berry juice that was saved for such purposes. She touched her fingers to Bear Paw's left cheek, carefully drawing three stripes across the cheek, his nose, over to his other cheek, across the scar he had received from the Crow warrior so many years before, and the scar from Sand Creek that traced from his nose across his lips, over scars put there more recently by the buffalo hunters. While she worked on his war colors, he kept his eyes on Medicine Wolf. He wanted to remember how she looked, wanted to keep this hatred fiery-hot. It was all that much more fuel for the battle ahead.

Chapter Twenty-four

Everyone bundled up in winter moccasins and animal-skin cloaks, arming themselves against the cold wind that hinted at the onslaught of winter. Many came to Two Moons' tipi, where Summer Moon and her children hid from White Horse. They brought clothing and other necessities for the children, and because this was Medicine Wolf's friend and it was Medicine Wolf's desire that Summer Moon and her children be accepted back into the clan, no one objected. Even the half-bloods were accepted and clothed. It would be decided later just who would end up being responsible for Summer Moon's provision, but it was understood that Bear Paw would always help in the way of food and protection.

Summer Moon helped Shining Woman pack everything onto two horses and a travois. She helped take down the tipi, remembering the day so many years earlier when she and Medicine Wolf worked together with Old Grandmother, learning how to do this. Those had been good times, happy times, before her love for White Horse had caused her to turn against her friend. It felt good now to be back where she belonged. She felt safe here, free of the horrible fear with which she had lived for so many years, free of the beatings, free of the stinking bodies and groping hands of the white soldiers who had used her like the shameless painted white whores who sometimes came around the fort. She only hoped Bear Paw was able to make sure White Horse never came for her. If he got hold of her now . . .

She could not even think of it. She must just be happy now to be leaving this place. Bear Paw had ordered that they should get a head start before the treaty signing. He and Medicine Wolf would stay for the signing, as would Black Buffalo and most of the other men. But because of a fear of some kind of trouble with the soldiers now, all women and children, as well as enough men to guide and protect them, would head for Horse Creek.

Summer Moon felt bad that this was all on account of her, yet she was happy to know that her People were still so willing to do this, that they had welcomed her with open arms. Their loving acceptance, combined with her sorrow over knowing the rest of her family had been killed at Sand Creek, made it difficult to see what she was doing for the tears that kept clouding her eyes.

This had been a strange day, sad in many ways, happy in others. She thought about the grand warrior White Horse once had been, how the white man's whiskey and his own pride and selfishness had destroyed him. She thought about what Shining Woman had told her about Bear Paw, about how the firewater had also earlier destroyed him too; but he had conquered the evil spirits of the bottle. It was Medicine Wolf's love that had helped him. She had not been able to do that for White Horse, but she realized now that he had never loved her the way Bear Paw loved Medicine Wolf. It made her heart very sad, but she knew now she must accept the truth and save herself and her children.

With a cold wind whipping at them, Summer Moon and the others finally were prepared to leave. Snow stung their faces, but most were wrapped in warm animal skins. Medicine Wolf approached Summer Moon, and they embraced. Summer Moon looked past her friend at Bear Paw, who stood watching. She gave him an apologetic look and he nodded. She could see by his eyes that he would show no mercy for White Horse today, but it no longer mattered to Summer Moon. White Horse had made his own troubles for himself.

She turned and took hold of the bridle of the horse she had taken from White Horse. On it sat Little Beaver, Red Beaver and her seven-year-old half-blood son, who White Horse had refused to name. He had simply called him "that boy," and called her two-year-old half-blood daughter "that girl." The two-year-old was bundled onto the travois. Beside her stood Smiling Girl, leading a horse that carried Standing Bear and pulling a travois on which Big Hands and Little Flower rode.

Summer Moon looked back at Medicine Wolf once more, and it felt good to be friends again. She left then, heading south. Most of the Cheyenne and several Sioux families went with them. Medicine Wolf turned to Bear Paw, keeping the hood of her bearskin coat pulled over her head. She walked closer, looking up at his painted face. He did indeed look fierce and menacing. She had already given him the blessing of the wolf paws inside the tipi before it was taken down.

"You will be protected today," she told him. "I have no fear of White Horse. I know my husband can easily defeat him."

A look of deep pride came into his eyes. "Let us go," he told her. They each mounted a horse, she on Thunder, Bear Paw mounting a fine black stallion he had captured wild a few months before and had managed to tame. Since Sand Creek, because of so much running and warring, it had been difficult to rebuild his wealth of horses, but through raids and through many hunts for wild mustangs, Bear Paw again owned several fine steeds, some used for hunting, others for raiding, others simply for carrying supplies. Younger men, boys dreaming of one day becoming as grand a Dog Soldier as Bear Paw, gladly helped him tend the horses. One young man had taken most of the horses along with the women and children; another, Big Bear, who was fourteen summers, watched after four more

horses that Bear Paw had kept at what was left of the
Cheyenne village. As soon as he finished with White
Horse, he had told Big Bear and Medicine Wolf, they
would quickly leave.

They approached the tent where the signing was to
take place, dismounted and tied their horses to a hitching
post. They ducked inside the tent, where an array of soldiers, government representatives, and Sioux leaders, Red
Cloud being the most prominent, sat in a circle smoking
a prayer pipe.

Bear Paw and the other Cheyenne recognized that this
treaty was between the white man's government and the
Sioux, but whatever was the fate of the Oglala was also
the fate of many Northern Cheyenne. They had accompanied Red Cloud to this signing to warn the government
of their number and their close alliance with the Sioux,
hoping to make enough of an impression on the soldiers
and government men to insure they would adhere to the
treaty stipulations. Medicine Wolf noticed Tom standing
off to one side, watching the proceedings and taking notes.
Tom looked over at her, unable to see her face clearly
because she kept her hood up. He wanted to go and talk
to her again, but the solemness of the occasion forbade
socializing for the moment. This was a very important
occasion, one that might go down in future history books.
He felt privileged to be present, privileged to be involved.
He turned his gaze to the infamous Red Cloud, who sat
nearby. Here was the man who had wreaked so much havoc
along the Bozeman Trail that he had caused forts to be
abandoned, had caused the government to seek a new
treaty. But if this new treaty was broken, as others had
been, what then? Apparently some Indian leaders already
did not trust the white man's promises, for Sitting Bull,
the new leader of the Hunkpapas, had refused to sign this
new treaty.

Much as he would like this to be the end of all raiding
and warring, Tom feared it was not. Still, a man had to
take hope in these things. At least both sides were trying.
Everyone quieted then, and a prayer pipe was passed
among all men present. Then Red Cloud rose to speak.
He looked around the circle of Indian leaders and govern-

ment dignitaries, and Tom could not help smiling at the arrogance the Sioux leader showed. For the moment the Indians had won the battle. This treaty had been called by the government in response to Red Cloud's unending war to keep whites out of the Powder River country. He took his time now, measuring his words.

"Two winters ago the Great Father in Washington wished only to make a path through our hunting grounds," he began, pausing after each phrase to wait for the interpreter. Tom quickly wrote down as much as he could. "The white man wanted to be able to go north of the Powder River to his gold fields. A promise was made to us, that the white man would only pass through our land and not settle there, a promise that soldiers would protect my People and the game that we need to survive. As with so many other of the white man's promises, they were broken. We have shown the Great Father in Washington what happens when he breaks his promises."

Several other Indians nodded, all of them looking haughty and proud. Tom scribbled rapidly, impressed with Red Cloud, who through all the talks had shown eloquence and a simple logic that had often left the government representatives speechless.

"The Sioux wanted only peace. We showed our goodwill and our trust. But the white man's government began building its forts in our midst, and the white man began settling among us, killing our game, killing our People, plowing up our sacred land. This was not what was promised, and so we waged war. We brought your soldiers to their knees, and now the Great Father wishes to make yet another treaty. We will see if this time the white man can be truthful and honest and can keep his word. My people and I will accept the great amount of land that has been promised us, and again we will trust the white men to stay off that land. If he does not, he will again feel our wrath. The bluecoat soldiers have fled from their forts, and we have burned those forts and will keep the bluecoats from our land forever!"

A round of war whoops burst forth, fists and weapons raised, and Tom felt a chill. He continued writing as Red Cloud spoke for nearly an hour, holding both Indian and white spellbound. The great Indian leader finally sat down, and Tom glanced at Medicine Wolf, who had removed her hood. He frowned, lowering his pad, studying her with alarm. Although it was not very bright inside the tent because it had been closed against rising winds and was lit only with lanterns, he was sure he detected bruises on Medicine Wolf's face.

His first fear was that it was his fault. Had Bear Paw beat her after he left, accusing her of having eyes for a white man? He could not believe Bear Paw would ever lay a hand on his beloved wife. He moved his eyes to Bear Paw, who had quietly removed his buffalo robe. He noticed with alarm that Bear Paw's face was not painted in prayer colors, but looked more like a man painted for battle. He had seen plenty of Indians, knew much more about their customs now, and he knew war paint when he saw it. He frowned, noticing Bear Paw kept dark, hate-filled eyes turned on one particular man. He followed the look to see the scout, White Horse, glaring back at Bear Paw. White Horse, however, appeared to be frightened. He stood in the middle of six soldiers, as though he were using them for protection.

The government representatives were rolling out a piece of paper, reading the treaty to Red Cloud through an interpreter. Tom kept watching Bear Paw. If there was going to be trouble, he prayed for Medicine Wolf's sake that it would not involve Bear Paw and soldiers. He suspected that White Horse had something to do with Medicine Wolf's bruises. He had never liked White Horse. Everyone in the fort knew he beat his wife and sold her sexual favors to any soldier or trader who would trade whiskey or tobacco for them. He also knew that there had been some kind of conflict years before between White Horse and his People that had caused him to be banished from the tribe. Had it involved Medicine Wolf?

The ceremony was finally finished. Red Cloud shook hands with the government representatives the white man's way. He was given a copy of the treaty, tied with scarlet ribbon, and Tom wondered if that ribbon would one day represent Indian blood. Did Red Cloud really understand the treaty provisions, understand that the Sioux were expected to stay within new reservation boundaries and stay out of Powder River country? And as long as Sitting Bull still roamed free, refusing to recognize any treaty, and as long as the treaty did not actually involve the Northern Cheyenne, just how peaceful could the government expect things to be?

Finally everyone began filing out, soldiers, Sioux leaders, government men, all walking into a stiff wind and heading for tipis and barracks. More soldiers left, and White Horse started to leave with them, but Bear Paw barked something to him in a deep, growling voice. Tom sensed he had called White Horse a foul name. White Horse paused, meeting Bear Paw's eyes and saying something back to him but looking afraid.

Some of the soldiers around White Horse laughed, but their smiles quickly faded when Bear Paw pulled a huge knife. Tom glanced at Medicine Wolf, who stood proud and silent. The soldiers stepped back, and Bear Paw waved his knife under White Horse's nose. He hissed something in the Cheyenne tongue, then moved outside.

White Horse looked at Medicine Wolf, who held her chin defiantly. "You think you are a big man," she told him in English. "But only a coward attacks a woman. You were a coward when the Cheyenne disowned you all those years ago, White Horse, and you are *still* a coward," she said with a sneer. "If you want to prove to your soldier friends you are a real man, then go out there and face Bear Paw." She spit at him. *"Voxpas,"* she hissed. "A *snake* stands taller than you!"

Bear Paw continued his taunting from outside. Tom could see him standing ready, his shoulders hunched, the big knife in his hand. He seemed to be oblivious to the cold wind, which was carrying more snow in it every minute. White Horse looked helplessly at the soldiers who had been standing with him, and they backed farther away.

"This is your fight, White Horse," one of them told him. "This ain't the time or place to get bluecoats involved in any kind of fight with those cocky Indians out there."

Medicine Wolf strutted closer, and at the moment Tom thought how wild and almost frightening she looked, as full of hatred and probably as capable of killing as any male warrior. "You always wanted another chance to fight Bear Paw. Now you have it. Defeat him, and I will come to you. That is the only way you can have me," she spat out.

The remark made his eyes light up, but Tom nearly gasped. He knew Medicine Wolf would rather die than leave Bear Paw and her People and live with someone as low and worthless as White Horse. *So,* he thought, *you have that much confidence in Bear Paw's abilities.*

White Horse looked her over. "Then before the day is over you will be sleeping in my bed," he glowered. He threw off his wool jacket and stormed outside, his soldier friends quickly following. Medicine Wolf looked apologetically at Tom. "I will never come back to this place, Tom. I will never see you again." She blinked back tears. "Good-bye, my good friend."

Before he could say a word, she was outside. Tom followed, to see Bear Paw and White Horse circling each other. He wished he knew just what had happened, how and when White Horse had apparently attacked Medicine Wolf. For that reason alone Tom was hoping Bear Paw would indeed be the victor, for the thought aroused Tom's own anger.

Soldiers began to gather around White Horse and Bear Paw. Tom spotted the fort commander and quickly headed his way. "This is a domestic thing," he told the man. "You'd better make sure your men stay out of it, or that treaty won't be worth the paper it's written on."

The commander nodded. "Agreed. As long as no Indian makes a move toward any of my men, there won't be any trouble."

The Cheyenne who had stayed behind for the treaty signing began to gather, mixing with Sioux men and women as well as more soldiers. Already Medicine Wolf was untying two horses. She mounted one of them, keeping hold of the reins of the other horse while she watched her husband continue to circle White Horse challengingly.

Indians began shouting derisive remarks toward White Horse in their own tongue, and Tom suspected they looked upon him as a traitor to his own kind. White Horse eyed

Bear Paw carefully, his hatred and jealousy obvious. He
and Bear Paw had both thrown aside their pistols and
would duel only with their hideously big knives. White
Horse's head still ached, and he knew the injury he had
suffered would be a disadvantage, but the thought of Medicine Wolf's promise was all he needed to spur him on.

He lunged first, and shouts went up from the soldiers,
who could not help getting involved. Bear Paw sucked in
his middle and jumped out of the way, but the tip of White
Horse's blade managed to tear at Bear Paw's buckskin shirt.
Bear Paw only smiled. White Horse lunged again several
times, but Bear Paw did not stab back at the man.

In his cunning, Bear Paw had decided to let White
Horse tire himself out. *Come to me,* he thought. *I will let
you think that you are winning.* His hatred was as intense
as anything he had felt for any white man, even more, for
the one thing that was worse than a natural enemy was a
man who was a traitor to his own kind. He danced and
whirled, teasing, goading. He let White Horse cut him
across the stomach, then across one arm.

Tom's eyes widened in astonishment. Would Bear Paw
actually lose this fight? Still, the man actually seemed unconcerned about the cuts or the blood that was beginning
to stain his shirt and leggings, and Tom wondered if a
more awesome spectacle of man existed.

The crowd grew even more excited, and Tom noticed
Medicine Wolf back off slightly. She appeared to be prepared to ride fast once this was over. The wind began to
blow harder, but the circle of men helped shield Bear Paw
and White Horse as the fighting grew more vicious. White
Horse took another lunge, growing more confident now;
but Bear Paw grasped his wrist at the last moment. White
Horse grabbed Bear Paw's knife hand, but not quickly
enough. Bear Paw rammed his knife into White Horse's
left forearm and quickly jerked it out again.

Indians cheered and soldiers urged White Horse to fight
back. Bear Paw gave him a shove, letting go of his knife
hand and waving his big blade. "Come to me, coward,"
he growled in language Tom could not completely understand. "Traitor! Rapist! You are a *woman*! My own *wife*
is a better warrior than you!"

Whatever he had said, the words brought frenzied war whoops from the Indians, who themselves added to the apparent insults. White Horse looked at his arm as though astonished he had been hurt. He came wildly at Bear Paw then, and again Bear Paw grasped his wrist. This time both men tumbled to the ground, wrestling in dirt wet from snow. They rolled and grunted and held off each other's knife hand until Bear Paw finally managed to get a leg around White Horse's middle and literally flip him onto his back. As he rose, White Horse stabbed him in the right calf, making Bear Paw collapse to the ground.

Medicine Wolf gasped, and the soldiers' cheers grew wild. White Horse quickly stomped on Bear Paw's right arm, making him release his knife, which White Horse kicked out of the way. The crowd quieted then as White Horse stepped back, waving his knife. "Now I have you," he snarled. "You will lose, Bear Paw, and Medicine Wolf will be mine, as she should have been from the beginning! You think you are such a grand warrior! Look at you now!" He shouted the words in English, as though to further defy his Cheyenne blood. He strutted around Bear Paw as Bear Paw managed to get to his feet in spite of the wound to his leg.

Bear Paw faced White Horse, his eyes more menacing than any look Tom had ever seen. He actually grinned again, beckoning White Horse to come for him. White Horse seemed to hesitate, and Tom could see the confusion and fear in his eyes. It was only then that he began to realize Bear Paw had deliberately held back, leading White Horse into a last charge. His long black hair danced as he crouched and moved sideways, and blood poured from his wounds. Tom could not imagine what he would do now that he had no weapon.

"You are a traitor to the Cheyenne," Bear Paw spat out. "This day I will take your scalp!"

Tom struggled to understand what had been said. White Horse charged again, growling like a bear. At the last moment Bear Paw brought his right foot up hard into White Horse's crotch, ending his growl in a thud and a grunt. White Horse went down, and Bear Paw landed a foot hard against the back of his neck, shoving his face into the snow and mud.

Bear Paw had moved so quickly, Tom hardly realized what had happened. The terrible wound to his calf seemed not to affect him at all. As soon as White Horse's face landed in the earth, Bear Paw came down, slamming his knees into the man's back. White Horse's face was so smashed into the snow and mud that Tom wondered if he could even breathe. The crowd had quieted, and there came a muffled grunt from White Horse at Bear Paw's blow.

Quickly Bear Paw grasped White Horse's knife arm and wrenched it up behind him, bending it painfully, enjoying White Horse's screams as the man managed to turn his face sideways enough to get some air. His face was covered with mud. Bear Paw bent his arm until he finally let go of the knife.

In a flash Bear Paw grasped the knife and took hold of a fistful of White Horse's hair, cutting a circle in his scalp while White Horse lay facedown and helpless. He ripped at the scalp, and White Horse screamed as Bear Paw yanked off a good chunk of hair and held it up victoriously. He rammed the knife through the back of White Horse's right ear then, pinning the man to the ground with his own knife by shoving the blade through the skin of the right side of his face and on into the snow and dirt. The handle of the knife protruded from the back of White Horse's right ear, and further screams of horror from White Horse made Tom's stomach churn.

"I should kill you," Bear Paw shouted. "But I would rather let you live with this shame!"

The Indians whooped and yelped victoriously as Bear Paw rose, holding up the scalp. He seemed hardly aware of his own wounds as he carried the scalp over to Medicine Wolf. Their eyes held, and Tom stared in near shock as she took the scalp from her husband without a cringe, holding it high in the air the way a victorious warrior might.

She tied the scalp onto her horse's bridle then. Another Indian ran up and handed Bear Paw his knife, while White Horse lay groaning and unable to move, blood running profusely from the wound in his scalp and face, staining the snow. The fort commander ordered all soldiers to stand back and let the Indians leave peacefully, insisting no one help White Horse until the Indians were well away from the area. Tom held his stomach at the sight of the writhing White Horse, finding it amazing that just the night before the man who had done this had played lovingly with his children.

Medicine Wolf handed Bear Paw his buffalo robe, worried at how pale he was beginning to look. "Let us hurry and leave," she told him softly, "so that I can tend to your wound. You are bleeding badly, Bear Paw."

He put on the robe and mounted his horse, but just as he turned, a young man grasped the bridle of Bear Paw's mount. Medicine Wolf recognized him as Crow Dog, White Horse's oldest son. She told Bear Paw who he was, and Bear Paw seemed to soften.

Tom moved through the crowd of Indians to watch as Crow Dog, who understood little Cheyenne because his own father had forbidden he speak the language, told Medicine Wolf to interpret for him. "I wish to go with you," Tom heard him say.

Medicine Wolf explained to Bear Paw, and Bear Paw extended his arm. Tom was astonished at the sudden fatherly attitude the man was taking toward the son of the man he so fiercely hated. Crow Dog grasped his arm and used it for support to mount up behind Bear Paw. Bear Paw turned and rode off. Medicine Wolf looked at Tom once more, saying nothing, saying good-bye with only her eyes. He knew this time he truly would never see her again. She turned her horse and followed her husband, as she had always done. Together they disappeared into thicker snow that quickly made them appear ghostly.

The wind blew even harder, bringing the year's first blizzard. Tom stood alone while everyone else departed, the rest of the Cheyenne hurrying to break camp and follow Bear Paw, the Sioux going to their own lodges to wait out the storm. Soldiers hurried for their barracks, and the fort commander ordered two of them to remove the knife from the side of White Horse's face and help him to the doctor's quarters.

Tom watched Bear Paw and Medicine Wolf disappear into the wall of snow, the wind pricking his ears, snow settling then melting on his face. His heart felt heavy, and he actually felt like crying, but nothing would come. Finally he turned to go home to Elena. He raised the collar of his woolen coat, then felt a shiver move up his spine that did not come from the cold. On the wind he heard a wolf's howl, a long, mournful wail that made him wonder what lay in Medicine Wolf's future. Was that old Wolf out there, howling a good-bye to the woman who had loved him so faithfully?

"Good-bye again," he muttered. He knew this time it truly was for good.

Part 4

Chapter Twenty-five

1874

Bear Paw and Medicine Wolf watched from the hills as the regiment of soldiers weaved its way in single file through the trees and foothills below. Bear Paw raised the telescope he had found left behind at Fort Reno when he and his Cheyenne warriors had helped Red Cloud and his Oglala Sioux burn the fort. He looked through the magic glass quietly for a moment, then lowered it, a somber look on his face. "It is he." He turned worried eyes to Medicine Wolf. "Hard Backsides."

"It is true then that the scouts saw him at Laramie," she told him. "Why do you think he is here in the Black Hills?"

Bear Paw raised the glass again, watching the procession with a mixture of hatred and dread. Until now the Sioux and Northern Cheyenne had managed to rule the vast domain awarded them in the Treaty of '68. When surveyors for a proposed new railroad that was planned to be built through the heart of Sioux country had come here, the Sioux and Cheyenne had attacked them and the soldiers who protected them so often that the railroad builders had given up. Bear Paw himself had led many of the attacks, shooting at surveyors, destroying their equipment, looting their supplies.

A victory over the mighty railroad builders, following their victory at winning the Powder River country, had left Bear Paw and others feeling more confident than ever. But now here was long-hair Custer, who had a reputation of being daring and persistent. Bear Paw knew by the many descriptions he had heard of this man, and by the shoulder-length golden hair he could see showing beneath the hat of the commander below, that it was indeed Hard Backsides. It gave him an uneasy feeling to see the man in the sacred Black Hills.

"I see picks and shovels, tools that miners use," he answered Medicine Wolf. "There are other men with him, men who are not soldiers." He lowered the telescope, his jaw flexing in anger. "I cannot believe it, but it looks as though they are here to look for gold." He turned to look at Medicine Wolf again. "Why would he do this? He knows this is sacred land, land promised us under the treaty."

Medicine Wolf shared his dread. "Again the treaty means nothing to them. Whenever the ve-ho-e want to build their railroads or dig for gold, suddenly they forget about the treaty." She dismounted, standing on the ledge from where the two of them watched. They had come here because this was a favorite spot of theirs, where they could be alone and listen to the splashing waters of a nearby waterfall, watch eagles circle overhead. Here in this pristine shelter of thick pine and soft grasses they could pretend they were very young, and the land was virgin and free, their private domain. "We could fight the railroad surveyors and the few soldiers who protected them," she added, watching the procession of soldiers disappear around a bend. She turned to look at Bear Paw. "But if they find gold . . ."

Both knew what that could mean. Gold would bring the ve-ho-e by the thousands. There was no stopping them when it came to their strange craving for the mineral that meant nothing to the Indian. If gold was discovered here in the Black Hills, this last huge sacred preserve of the Sioux and Northern Cheyenne, there would be nothing left to the Indian, nothing sacred, nothing untouched by white men's foul hands. "So," she said softly, "the treaty meant nothing, just as we suspected. We were promised the army would keep out all whites, yet the army itself sends one of our worst enemies here with picks and shovels and prospectors. This is how they protect us."

Bear Paw also dismounted, tying both horses. "It is long-hair Custer who drove our sisters and brothers to the south onto the small reservation far off in that worthless land where they die like flies! It is Custer's fault the peace chief, Black Kettle, is dead—a man who wore the President's medal around his neck and carried the white man's flag! Now the long-hair is here, where he does not belong! We must tell Crazy Horse and Sitting Bull. We must send out scouts to find out why he is here."

"Our own land is to the north and the west," Medicine Wolf reminded him. "Perhaps we should leave this to the Sioux."

Bear Paw studied the hills below, trying to spot the soldiers again. "You know better. Whatever happens to them comes to us. If white men invade the Black Hills, they will also invade our lands, the last place we have left to live as we wish. We cannot let it happen. Whoever Crazy Horse and Sitting Bull fight, we also fight."

Medicine Wolf felt a strange foreboding. She touched the medicine bag at her neck. Was her medicine strong enough to fight the long-hair; strong enough to keep white men out of this land if gold was found on it? And unless they were strong together against a new invasion, they could not win. Many of the Oglala had followed Red Cloud onto the new reservation and were trying to live a new way. Red Cloud had visited the Great Father's land in the East several times now, and it seemed to have changed him. Something had happened there to take the fire out of him. Some said he was just getting old; others said that once he had seen the great numbers of white men in the East, and had seen their many magnificent buildings and machines, Red Cloud had just given up, realizing that the white men were much more powerful than any combined forces of Indians.

Bear Paw and others did not want to believe such a thing. They had proven such rumors wrong when they forced soldiers out of the Powder River country, and again when they put a stop to railroad building through the Black Hills. They were convinced Red Cloud had somehow been tricked. Whatever happened, Red Cloud, who had won such magnificent victories in the past and had been such a respected leader, was now a quiet, peace-talking man; he had been replaced by Sitting Bull of the Hunkpapas, and Crazy Horse of the Oglala, who now led those more warlike Sioux who were still unwilling to settle on reservation land and chose to remain free on the vast unceded areas that still belonged to Sioux and Cheyenne but were not a part of the designated reservation confines.

Indians who lived on specified reservation lands were given plots of land and were being taught how to farm. They received weekly rations and were to be well cared for; but Medicine Wolf and others who refused to go to the reservations had heard many rumors of corruption among those who were sent out by the white man's government to run the reservation programs. Annuities never arrived on time, meat was wormy, farm tools were inadequate. Those reservation Indians who had fled told of Indian agents who sold the new government goods to area white citizens, or had them sold at towns through which they passed on the way to the reservation. They would then purchase used equipment and clothing, as well as unsalable beef, and present the worthless merchandise and food to the Indians, pocketing the tidy profits they had made. It was a source of constant irritation among the Indians, making it very hard to remain peaceful in the face of such blatant treachery. The Indians were virtually helpless to change the situation, as they were under the thumb of the agents themselves and had no one to whom they could complain; nor did they believe their complaints would be taken seriously.

Medicine Wolf walked to where Bear Paw stood, still watching to catch another glimpse of the soldiers. "I see them again now," he told her. "They are going on to the north, away from us." She touched his back, bare today, for it was very warm, and he wore only a breechcloth and open leggings; a bandolier of ammunition hung over his shoulder with a pistol at his side. His hair hung long and loose, a simple bandanna tied around his forehead. He wore no paint, no jewelry.

He turned at her touch. Medicine Wolf thought how, in spite of the many scars he bore, he was still a handsome man. It seemed that the little age lines about his eyes and the hint of white at his temples made him even more handsome. She smiled for him, reaching up and touching his face.

"We came here to be alone," she told him, "and to pretend that men like Hard Backsides do not exist. We came here to make love." She traced her fingers over his full lips, thinking how fierce and frightening he must look to those who did not know him as she did. "I do not want to talk about the reasons long-hair Custer might be here; and Crazy Horse's own scouts will tell him soon enough. Moments like this are precious and few, Bear Paw. Let us not waste them."

He remained rigid for a moment, full of worry, eager to banish intruders from what little land he had left to him. She saw a twinkle come into his dark eyes then, noticed a smile tickling the corner of his mouth. He took hold of her wrist, licking the palm of her hand. He drew back then to gaze at her beauty. "There are times when I feel as though I am seeing the young girl who married me standing before me. It is as though you do not age. You only get more beautiful," he told her. "Always you know how to make me feel happy inside."

"Your happiness is all I have *ever* wanted, my beloved."

They both sensed an urgency to the moment, a premonition that there were few moments like this left to them. Bear Paw removed his bandolier and pistol and left her to hang them over a low branch of a nearby tree. When he turned back, Medicine Wolf had untied and dropped her tunic. She was naked except for the small medicine bag she kept around her neck to keep the precious wolf's paws close to her.

He remained a few feet from her, drinking in her dark beauty, struck by how lovely her form remained. She had kept her shape partly because she had never had children. In one sense he was glad, for her breasts were still firm, her waist small, her belly flat. Still, for her own happiness and fulfillment, he would not have cared if she had lost some of that shape if it meant she had been able to have a child. He knew it was something that would always bring her an inner sorrow she could share with no one.

She was as much a mother to twelve-year-old Standing Bear and nine-year-old Big Hands and six-year-old Little Flower as Smiling Girl. Soon there would be another baby. They had been apart again for several months while Smiling Girl again worked at getting pregnant, not that she could call it work, for Smiling Girl always took her shared husband like an eager child. Now that Smiling Girl was pregnant again, it was time to be alone for a while with his beloved, time to catch up on the things that pleased them most.

He kicked off his moccasins and unlaced his leggings. In moments he stood before Medicine Wolf in naked splendor, then swept her up into his arms.

Medicine Wolf screamed as he began running with her toward the waterfall. Little Wolf, who had curled up in soft grass as soon as Medicine Wolf and Bear Paw first dismounted, opened one lazy eye to watch Bear Paw jump into the cold creek with his woman. The wolf simply yawned and stretched, rolling onto his back and wiggling to scratch himself.

Bear Paw pulled Medicine Wolf under the waterfall, where she screamed and laughed as the cold water soaked her hair. It was a wonderful relief from the heat. She splashed at him, then kissed his chest. She felt his limp manpart and teased him that the cold water had quickly cooled his passion. Bear Paw grasped her about the waist and lifted her so that her breasts were near his mouth.

"It will not take long for my passion to overcome the cold," he told her. He tasted her taut nipples, and she wrapped her legs around his waist. He carried her to a sandy spot at the edge of the creek, where there was a large flat-topped boulder that came to his hips. He set her on it, remaining between her legs. "See what I told you?" he asked.

Medicine Wolf looked down to see he was ready for her. She met his eyes boldly as she grasped hold of him and guided him inside her. She leaned back on her elbows, putting her head back and letting her wet hair hang behind her, stretched out in naked glory before him. Bear Paw took her hard and fast, as he always did the first time after being apart for so long, but she did not mind, for she knew he would take her many more times today, tonight, tomorrow. He could never quite get his fill of her after being apart, and she could never quite get enough of him.

He pulled away from her and carried her back into the creek, where they washed. They laughed and splashed each other, feeling like the young couple who had first become husband and wife eighteen summers earlier. She loved these moments, for at such times she was not Medicine Wolf the holy woman, or Medicine Wolf the Soldier Girl. She was simply the wife of a great and respected warrior who had defied death many times.

She hugged him, kissed his nipples, his scars, moved to her knees while he still stood. She caressed that part of him that she had been so long without, wanting to taste him. He grasped her hair and groaned at the daring yet submissive gesture, feeling a strange power at the realization that this was the sacred woman, yet also his wife, a woman who hungered for him, a mere mortal. She moved back up to meet his mouth, and he slaked his own tongue into her mouth, tasting his own life, then lay her back against a grassy bank and entered her again. This time he would make it last longer. He would put the ominous presence of long-hair Custer out of his mind. This was their time, a rare moment of being alone together, a time of peace. Soon they would go farther north for the Sun Dance celebration. In two more summers his own firstborn son would take part in the ritual and he would be a man.

• • •

"I don't believe this!" Tom continued to pace. "Has the man gone mad? Who the hell does he think he is, telling the whole world there is a 'strong likelihood' of gold in the Black Hills! *Damn* him! This is the worst thing that could have happened!"

"Don't swear in front of Rebecca," Elena told her husband quietly. Eight-year-old Rebecca Prescott looked up at her father from the table, where she sat studying the lessons her mother had given her earlier in the day.

"What will happen, Father?"

Tom let out a sigh of irritation. "War, most likely, worse than anything we've seen so far. And I don't blame the Sioux and Cheyenne one da—one bit! They *trusted* us, Rebecca. They trusted our promise to keep whites out of their sacred lands, and now this braggart of a general who's out to glorify his own name comes here and claims there's gold on Indian land."

Elena studied the article in the Denver newspaper they had just received. It was dated December 1874, although it was now January 1875. Elena and Tom had both met General George Armstrong Custer, the man the Indians called Long-Hair and Hard Backsides. Elena had never decided whether or not she liked the man, for he was pleasant and charming on the one hand, but terribly brash and reckless on the other. She knew he was responsible for the slaughter of innocent Southern Cheyenne at the Washita near Indian Territory, and it was obvious he had no respect for Indians' rights. The newspaper article touted bold headlines—GOLD IN THE BLACK HILLS!—and went on to say that General Custer, supposedly at the request of his own government, had led protective forces into the Black Hills to build a fort that would be used as home base for soldiers who would guard surveyors for the Northern Pacific Railroad, which was again attempting to build its way through Indian lands. Geologists, with help from Custer's own men, had found traces of gold, and Custer had wasted no time in announcing the find.

"This is probably in all the newspapers back east," Elena said suddenly.

"Of course it is!"

"It says here the government is going to offer to buy the Black Hills through Red Cloud."

Tom rolled his eyes, facing her. "Do you really think Red Cloud would go so far as to sell his People's sacred lands? He might be a lot more peaceful now, but he's a smart, wily man. He knows damn well that land is theirs by right of the treaty, and the Indians know enough now to realize that by law of that treaty, the government can't touch it—and white men don't belong on it! They're learning their rights now, Elena, and they'll by-God fight for them! Red Cloud will try to do it the peaceful way, but not Sitting Bull and Crazy Horse . . . and not Bear Paw. They'll fight the way their People have always fought."

He shivered and turned away, his voice betraying his sorrow. "Blood is going to be spilled over this, and a lot of it. The worst part is, I think the government *wants* this. They know miners will flood in here like a waterfall. By midsummer the Black Hills will be swarming with miners, and the Sioux will be furious! That will be just fine with the government. Let the Indians kill a few miners and they can say the *Indians* are the ones who broke the treaty! It's the same old ploy every time. If Red Cloud won't sell the land, the government will simply take it. Heaven forbid that honesty and promises should get in the way of getting to that gold!"

He walked to look out a window at Crow and Pawnee scouts riding toward the fort. He wondered how things would have turned out if all Indians, even enemies, had stuck together. Now the Sioux and Cheyenne were left alone to defend what was left of their lands. The sun shone brightly against hardened white snow, and it hurt his eyes; he turned back around to face his wife and daughter. "And we wonder why the Indians don't trust us."

"May I read it, Mother?"

Elena handed her daughter the newspaper article, keeping her eyes on Tom. She suspected his real worry. If this turned into all-out war, Medicine Wolf and Bear Paw would surely be heavily involved. She sighed, rising from the table. "Tom, I think come spring we had better go back east, at least as far as Omaha, where we'd be far away from all of this. If you can't bring yourself to leave, at least Rebecca and I should go."

Tom glanced at her stomach. She did not show yet, but by some miracle Elena was again with child, something neither of them thought could happen again after Rebecca was born. He nodded. "You could at least get to Omaha before you're too far along, now that we have a cross-country railroad. It's only a few days ride south to Cheyenne. You could even stay there, but they probably have better doctors and schools in Omaha." *Those cities were barely more than tiny log settlements when I first came here,* he thought.

He ran a hand through his hair. "I hate to leave yet, Elena. I don't have one doubt in my mind that the government will end up sending more soldiers out here. They'll try to force Sitting Bull and the others who refuse to give up their freedom to come onto the reservation areas and stay out of the Black Hills and surrounding mountains. They won't do it, but at least some will come, and I feel I should be here. I'm going to keep trying to get appointed as agent at Fort Robinson. Somebody has to do something to stop the corruption. The reservation Indians are going to need someone serving them who understands and cares."

Elena rose, walking over to take his hands. "I know how hard you're trying, and how much it means to you," she told him. "But I do think Rebecca should be around other children her own age. And I agree that things could become very dangerous by this summer. I don't want to have a baby in the midst of all that."

He squeezed her hands. "I can't leave here right now, Elena."

"I know that."

"I'm sorry. After a time, things will somehow get settled. If I can get set up at Fort Robinson, maybe eventually you can come back to Cheyenne. That wouldn't be so far for me to come and be with you. Eventually, when the baby is good and strong, you could come to me in the summers, help teach the Indian children. Maybe the area will get settled enough eventually that you can stay."

"We can't think about maybes right now, Tom. We have to take one step at a time. For now I'll go to Omaha and we'll pray I have a nice healthy baby, maybe a son this time. After that we'll decide what to do next.''

He leaned down and kissed her cheek. ''Omaha it is, then. At the first sign of spring I'll have soldiers escort you to Cheyenne, where you can catch the Union Pacific.''

They could make no other decision. The most sacred land of the Sioux was about to be invaded by men seeking gold. The Sioux were not going to take the invasion lying down.

''Custer needs to be taught a good lesson in how to handle Indians,'' Tom grumped.

''I agree,'' Elena replied. ''I just hope he doesn't learn it the hard way.''

The miners came, swarming through the Black Hills and beyond so that Bear Paw claimed they were like ants swarming over something sweet. He and Crazy Horse and others who were willing to die for the last bit of land promised them by a treaty reacted as would be expected, and all those who came to prospect for gold knew they did so at the risk of their lives, or worse . . . captivity and torture. It was only fitting that these men who so flagrantly violated treaty promises should suffer for it. They must be taught a lesson, and Sioux and Northern Cheyenne gladly did the teaching.

Blood ran, and tempers flared. The government offered to buy much of the land promised to the Sioux. Red Cloud, with a twinkle in his eye and a sly smile on his lips, said he would sell it . . . for six hundred million dollars. He claimed that Sitting Bull and Crazy Horse would think even that amount was not enough.

The commissioners who had requested the purchase were left speechless and angry, realizing Red Cloud thought them fools. They countered his offer with six million. Red Cloud would not accept. He was told that not selling the land could mean much trouble for his People. ''My People are not unfamiliar with the trouble you whites bring to them,'' Red Cloud told them. ''I am no longer their spokesman. Go and talk to Sitting Bull and Crazy Horse. Make *them* your offer.''

Faces red with anger, the commissioners left, fully aware that Sitting Bull and Crazy Horse would kill them before they could open their mouths. There would be no sale. President Grant ordered that all Indians must report to reservation areas or be "deemed hostile and treated accordingly by the military force."

Tom put his wife and daughter into a stagecoach that was leaving Fort Laramie for Cheyenne. Two frightened traders who no longer wanted to do business in the area also boarded the coach.

Times were bad. No Indian was trusted now, not even those who hung around the fort, unless they were scouts like White Horse. White Horse himself gladly led troops into the hills to help protect miners, but he always wore a hat now to hide the ugly bald spot on his head where Bear Paw had cut away his scalp. The right side of his face bore an ugly scar that could not be hidden.

In tears, her belly swollen with child, Elena said good-bye to her husband. Tom hugged Rebecca, hating to see either of them go, but relieved to know they would be out of danger. Six soldiers would escort them. Elena was leaving much later than originally planned and would stay in Cheyenne until the baby was born rather than try to get to Omaha. She had only about six weeks left. A Christian family who taught school in Cheyenne had agreed to take Elena and Rebecca into their home until Elena and the baby were strong enough to go on to Omaha by train.

Tom watched the coach clatter off, waving one last time. His heart felt strangely heavy. He hated good-byes, and he thought of another good-bye . . . the day Medicine Wolf had first left this place, and when she left again seven years ago for good. She had said she would never come back, and she never had.

He looked off toward the mountains. She was out there somewhere. She would be hunted now, like the buffalo, which were nearly extinct already; hunted, like the wolves; hunted, like so many other wild things in this land.

·   ·   ·

Four days passed with no wire from Cheyenne informing Tom and others at the fort that the coach carrying Elena and Rebecca had arrived safely. Sick with worry, Tom joined a regiment of soldiers deployed to find out what had happened to the coach. Two days into the search the coach was found overturned in a desolate stretch of country a few miles from Cheyenne. Around it lay the bodies of dead soldiers, some stripped and mutilated, their horses gone, as were the team of stagecoach horses. Baggage lay strewn about, some of it looted. The commander of the regiment studied one of many arrows found at the site. "Cheyenne," he said with disgust.

Tom so dreaded what could have happened to Elena that he felt sick. A soldier climbed up onto the side of the coach and pulled open the door. It was then that Tom heard a young girl's scream.

"Mr. Prescott! Here!" the soldier yelled. The man pulled on the arm of a young girl with red hair, but a terrified Rebecca screamed and fought him, seeing him in her hysteria as an Indian. Tom ran to help pull her from the coach, and he quickly embraced her, weeping. "It's all right, Becky, it's all right." He held her tightly. "It's me, your father. Oh, thank God! Thank God!"

The soldier climbed down into the coach again as others gathered around. "The traders are in here," he yelled. "They've both been shot!" There was a moment of silence, as everyone waited anxiously to know if Tom Prescott's wife was inside. Rebecca clung to her father, still too hysterical to explain all that had happened.

Tom's chest tightened then at the look on the soldier's face when the man finally emerged from the coach. He removed his hat as he walked close to Tom. "Your wife is in here too, Mr. Prescott," he said. "Doesn't look to me like the Indians did her any harm at all, but from what I can tell—" He swallowed, watching Tom's eyes quickly tear with horror and sorrow. "I'm afraid she's dead, Mr. Prescott. Looks like she lost the baby and then bled to death."

Tom squeezed his eyes shut, breaking into deep, wrenching sobs. He had thought it was so right to send her away, and no one thought there was any danger in going south rather than north, especially in summer.

"A man," Rebecca sobbed. "A wild-looking Indian man! He shot the traders," she finally was able to explain. "He reached inside for Mother and she . . . shouted your name. He pulled away . . . and his eyes looked almost afraid and sorry. He left us . . . without harming us. He even . . . left water for us."

Tom breathed deeply to stay in control. He would not let go of her. He grasped her hair in his hand, gently swaying with her. "Did the man have a lot of scars on him?"he asked.

"Y—yes," she sobbed. "I was so afraid, Father! But he just . . . left us! I waited while I heard men crying out . . . and Indians crawled all over the coach, taking things from our baggage. I heard horses riding off. Finally I looked out . . . and all the soldiers were dead and the Indians were gone." She clung to him tightly, sobbing. Tom kissed her hair, thinking how lucky he was that he at least still had his precious daughter. "I couldn't pull the dead men out of the coach," the girl sobbed, near hysteria. "And Mother . . . the attack made her go into labor. I didn't know what to do to help her!"

"There, there, Becky." His own tears trickled down his cheeks and into her hair. "You stayed with her, and that was a brave thing."

"It was . . . so terrible. The baby came out dead . . . and Mama kept bleeding. I couldn't stop it. Oh, Father, I had to just sit there and watch her die! Why, Father! Why did they do it? I don't understand!"

Tom had never felt so torn with emotion. He already understood why, had been trying to tell the fort commander what would happen, had been writing letters to congressmen, sending articles back east pleading with people to understand how the Sioux and Cheyenne felt about miners invading land that was sacred to them.

Now it had all come home to him. Now the tables were turned. It was so much harder to understand when it was your own loved ones who suffered. Elena was gone. She had died a slow, horrible death, and all because of an Indian attack. They had killed her just as surely as if they had taken a knife to her.

Yet they had not. An Indian man had held back when

she yelled out Tom's name. Becky had said he had many scars. There was no doubt in his mind that it was Bear Paw. Only he would have realized why Elena called out his name. Only he would have spared the wife of Tom Prescott, because he would have remembered that Tom was a blood brother. But that was not the only reason. He had done what he knew Medicine Wolf would have wanted him to do.

But what would he have done if Elena had been just any other white woman? Others would suffer much worse fates if the Indians were not stopped. This was just one example of why this all had to end, why, right or wrong, the Indians must come in to the reservations and give up the fight. It was true their own women had suffered rape and mutilation, but how much longer should this retaliation be allowed . . . until a hundred people were dead? Two hundred? A thousand innocent people, like Elena?

For the first time in all the years he had been trying to help the Indians, he felt hatred for them. He did not want this feeling to exist, but his wife lay dead in that over-turned coach. When he thought of what might have been done to them if Elena had not called out his name, if the man who found them had not been Bear Paw, the horror of the possibilities overwhelmed him.

He looked at the commander. The fighting was getting worse, just as he had predicted. This was all the fault of Custer and the President; but there was no changing the facts. The Indians were as angry as they had ever been, and with Elena dead, he already knew he could not sit around at the fort waiting to find out what would happen next. Maybe there was something more he could do, something in the field.

The next several hours were like a nightmare. He helped bury Elena and the baby, a boy, the son he would never hold now, never watch grow. Elena had given up much to come here. How he wished he could have her back, talk to her once more, hold her once more.

He suddenly could not control a need to vomit. When he got control of himself again, he knew he had to some-how be active, somehow do something about all of this, or go crazy. At the moment he could do nothing but vent his hatred by turning it to the very Indians to whom he had dedicated his life.

He watched his daughter weep over her mother's grave, and he turned to the commander. "Do they ever let civilians ride with the soldiers? I'd be one more man, one more gun," he told the man.

The commander, who did not seem old enough or experienced enough to be in charge of anything, met Tom's hollow eyes. He was surprised at how a person could literally age in a matter of hours. "We've had civilians ride with us before, usually men like yourself, men with a need for revenge. I have to say, though, Mr. Prescott, that I never thought you were capable of such feelings. From what I'm told, you've given half your life to the Sioux and Northern Cheyenne."

Tom moved his eyes to the grave again. "All for nothing. This is our fault, you know, not theirs. But there is no hope for them, Lieutenant, and the sooner they're forced onto the reservations and made to stay there, the better. We might as well have it over with."

The lieutenant sighed. "Word is President Grant is sending Custer back to this area to go hunting . . . for Indians. You'd probably be welcome to join us."

Tom nodded. "I'll ride with you." He looked to the north, toward the range of Bighorn Mountains that lay purple on the horizon. He heard a wolf's howl. Another answered. Did Medicine Wolf know about this? Were the wolves only reflecting the cry in her soul? How ironic that the woman he had loved all these years was indirectly responsible for killing his wife, his baby. He would probably never know how this had happened, or if Medicine Wolf had been with Bear Paw. What had they been doing this far south? He felt void of all feeling, all except this sudden burning hatred and frustration.

He walked over to Rebecca, gently forcing her to come away from the grave that held her mother and baby brother, and for the first time, unreasoning passion put him on the side of his own people.

Chapter Twenty-six

"It is a bad sign, a bad sign," Medicine Wolf lamented to Black Buffalo.

The old priest added sage to the flames of the sacred fire he had made inside his tipi, waving his hands over the "magic smoke" and letting it waft over himself and Medicine Wolf. Medicine Wolf thought how terribly wrinkled were his old hands now.

"I did not know." Bear Paw spoke up. He sat near Medicine Wolf, watching the fire, his heart heavy. How many times had he said that he did not realize Tom Prescott's wife was in the coach he had attacked? He did not know there would be a woman and child among the soldiers and male travelers. Even if there had been, they would have had to die, for that was the way. They were the enemy. But Tom Prescott was a blood brother. To kill his own would have been to kill a Cheyenne brother's wife.

Bear Paw and Medicine Wolf and their entire village had come farther south than usual, following the fresh tracks of a herd of buffalo. They needed the meat. The herd was finally spotted by the hunters, and Bear Paw had sent a messenger back to the village to tell the women to prepare for a kill. For once they might have enough meat to survive another winter without having to go to the reservation for handouts.

"We came over the rise and saw the coach and the soldiers," he told Black Buffalo. "We had to go past them to track down the herd, so we waited for them to pass. They were going south, away from Sioux and Cheyenne country, so we let them go. But one of the soldiers shot at us, then another." His hands folded into fists. "When I thought about how it was people like this who make life so hard for us . . . for my family . . . They had no reason to shoot at us. We were letting them pass."

Medicine Wolf listened to the story again, her heart aching for Bear Paw, who knew he had inadvertently created bad medicine for his People. She felt torn, for her heart also ached for poor Tom. A sick feeling engulfed her at the realization that her own People had attacked his wife. And Bear Paw had said she had been great with child!

Had she died, left alone out there that way? Had she lost the baby? Did Tom blame the Cheyenne? Did he think she had betrayed him? Oh, how she hated the thought of bringing him such unhappiness!

"Suddenly I saw in them all that I hated," Bear Paw went on. "They had no right even being there, none of them! The soldiers are supposed to be protecting *us*, keeping the miners out of our land. But instead they shoot at us and protect their own. We attacked them, and we killed them all! We took their horses and guns, their boots and shirts and other clothing. It was a good feeling. As they fled during the attack, the coach overturned. I went to it and I opened the door and killed the two men inside. In my anger I thought to take the woman and child as prisoners to hold for ransom. I thought maybe we could use them to make the soldiers keep their promise to keep the miners out of the Black Hills. But then the woman began screaming Tom Prescott's name. I think she remembered me, or perhaps only hoped I was some Indian who knew about her husband being a blood brother to us. I saw she was carrying a child in her belly. The young girl had red hair like her mother. I did not remember the woman so well, for I had seen her only that one time many years ago; but when she said his name, I realized who she had to be, who the young girl had to be. We let them live and we came back here, for we knew it was dangerous then for us to go after the buffalo. There might have been more soldiers coming." He let out a sigh of disgust. "Now we have lost the buffalo herd. We must find more meat soon to begin storing up for the winter."

Medicine Wolf's eyes misted. "Are you sure Tom wasn't among the men who were killed," she asked Bear Paw again.

He shook his head. "He was not with them. I searched every man's face, looked at their hair."

The fact that Tom himself had not been killed was Medicine Wolf's only relief. "He must have been sending her away because of all the trouble."

"Or perhaps because he knows of more trouble coming," Bear Paw answered. "Scouts say that Hard Back-sides is again coming to the Black Hills under orders from the Great Father in Washington. He will try to make all of us go to the reservations, but we will *not* go!"

Medicine Wolf looked at Black Buffalo, who had been breathing deeply of the sweet-smelling smoke of the holy fire. "What say you, Black Buffalo?"

The man turned drooping, aged eyes to meet her own. "Bear Paw did not kill the woman or the child; nor did he take them as prisoners. Your white brother was not among them, so he is safe. Yet I agree it is a bad sign, for I feel great grief. Someone's heart is very heavy. Bear Paw says the woman was heavy with child, and they were far from any town or settlement. We will send a runner and let him pose as one of the reservation Indians. He will find out what happened to Tom Prescott's wife."

Medicine Wolf closed her eyes, wondering when or how their troubles would ever end. If long-hair Custer was coming here, things were only going to get worse. For the moment, nothing mattered but the fact that Tom's poor wife and child had been attacked by the very people whom he had tried for years to help. "I wish to make a blood sacrifice," she told Black Buffalo, "here, over the holy flames. Then I will go into the hills to fast and pray. And I wish to give the runner one of the wolf's paws to give to Tom."

Both Bear Paw and Black Buffalo looked at her in surprise. "You cannot give one of the sacred paws to a white man," Bear Paw told her.

"It will give him power and lessen your own," Black Buffalo warned her.

"I do not care. I must tell him somehow of my sorrow, make him know we did not know his wife was among those attacked. If I send the wolf's paw, he will know its meaning. He will understand it was a great sacrifice for me."

"Then send him mine," Bear Paw said. "I am the one who attacked them."

Medicine Wolf's eyes widened in fear for him. "You know what happened the last time you were without the wolf's paw. With even more soldiers coming, you must not be without its protection."

Bear Paw rose. He wore only his breechcloth because of the hot day. He untied his medicine bag from the inside of his thigh and opened it, taking out the wolf's paw. "It should be my paw that is sent," he repeated. "It was all my doing. We will send it with the runner. He will give it to Tom. When he returns, he will tell us if Tom's wife lived. If she did, we will hold a special ceremony to thank *Maheo*, and you can give me another wolf's paw for protection. If for some reason she did not live, then I will not take another. Perhaps *Maheo* will continue to protect me simply because I sacrificed my most precious fetish as a sign of retribution for hurting the loved one of a blood brother."

Black Buffalo nodded. "I agree."

Medicine Wolf watched in near horror as Bear Paw handed the wolf's paw over to Black Buffalo. She could not forget what had happened to him the last time he was without it. He had nearly died, until she put it in his hand again. These were times of great danger. He should not be without the wolf's paw. She realized now just how much he truly loved her, for he was making a great sacrifice just because he might have brought great sorrow to someone about whom she cared very much.

"It is done," Bear Paw told her. "I go to be alone and make my own sacrifice. I, too, will fast and pray."

Medicine Wolf rose and faced him. "I do not like this."

Their eyes held in a gaze of love and sorrow. "It is my choosing. The spirits will keep me safe because of my sacrifice. And it is important that you keep the rest of the wolf's paws." He sucked in his breath almost as though he had been wounded, and Medicine Wolf knew how difficult it was for him to give up the sacred fetish that he felt had kept him strong and alive. He touched her cheek, then turned and went out.

Medicine Wolf looked at Black Buffalo, her throat aching. "I should never have made Tom Prescott my blood brother," she told the man. "It was wrong to care so much for a white man, for now white men are our worst enemy, worse than the Crow or the Pawnee or any of our old enemies ever were."

"You could not have known then, child," Black Buffalo told her. "Tom Prescott was a good white man, a man who understood the Indian heart."

Medicine Wolf stared at the flames. "But now he will be against us," she answered. *Tom,* she thought. *I am so sorry. I will pray for you and your family. Please know the meaning of the wolf's paw and know how sorry I am.*

Again came the dream of many soldiers and their bloody faces. They cried out, but their cries were not human. They howled like wolves. Their eyes were evil, and Indian men, all looking like Bear Paw, killed each one, putting an end to their howling. The Indian men cheered and held up scalps.

Then there came a great light from the heavens. A white wolf walked down a shaft of light to speak to the Indians, telling them they must quickly leave and must not violate the dead *ve-ho-e* bodies; but the People were too excited, felt too victorious. They told the wolf that he worried like an old woman. They took more scalps and began stripping and mutilating the bodies so that the evil white ones would be humiliated and so that when they went to the afterworld, they would forever be without limbs.

It had been a good day. Once the other *ve-ho-e* saw this, they would be sorely afraid and they would all leave the sacred lands and never return. The wolf kept telling them to stop, but they did not listen. They took their bounty and mounted their horses to leave, but suddenly the severed limbs and open wounds of the *ve-ho-e* started to heal. The dead men began moving arms and legs. Although most of their clothing was gone, they rose, and they all wore weapons. Their skin turned blue, and great steeds rose up from the ground beneath them so that they were mounted.

The Indians watched in shock and amazement, so surprised that they were unable to move. As if by magic the two hundred or so *ve-ho-e* they had killed began to separate and multiply. They became four hundred, six hundred, a thousand! They swarmed over the Indians, easily killing them all. Some attacked the wolf and stabbed him many times.

Medicine Wolf cried out and sat up, drenched in sweat, yet shivering. Bear Paw sat up beside her, touching her hair. "What is it?"

She looked at him as though he had returned from the dead, then turned and hugged him tightly. "Many soldiers will come," she told him. She did not need Black Buffalo to interpret her dream this time. "If this happens, Bear Paw, and if our people should kill them all, you must not desecrate the bodies! You must not! If you do . . ." He could feel her shaking and kept his strong, reassuring arms around her. "If you do," she repeated, "they will only multiply. Many, many more will come! So many that they will swarm over us like bees and sting us to death."

"It is just a bad dream because of your worry over Tom Prescott's wife."

"No." She drew back. The cuts on her arms, where she had shed blood in sorrow, were healing now. She and Bear Paw were both thinner from several days of prayer and fasting. Her eyes teared. "You know my dreams always have meaning, Bear Paw. Please listen to me. If there should be such a battle, where many soldiers are killed, a hundred, two hundred, you must not violate the bodies in any way.''

He frowned, touching her face. ''I will do what you say, but you know I cannot speak for every man. If such a thing were to happen, if we should defeat such a great force of soldiers and kill them all, it would be a great victory, greater than any battle ever won. Our joy and vengeance could not be controled. Surely such a victory would mean all whites would finally leave the Black Hills. To desecrate the bodies would only make them more afraid.''

''Don't do it, Bear Paw,'' she pleaded.

He searched her eyes, then grinned lightly. ''There are no soldiers here, Medicine Wolf. Only us. I cannot imagine that so many soldiers would come after us, or that we would be able to defeat such a force so badly that we killed every one of them. But if such an unlikely thing would happen, I will not take a scalp or violate any of them in any way. This is my promise.''

''We must hold a council with the Dog Soldiers so that I can warn all of them.''

He sighed deeply. ''You can try, but they may not all listen, especially those who listen only to the spirits in the firewater. And it is not likely we would face such a number of soldiers alone. Now we fight beside the Sioux. But we cannot tell our Oglala and Hunkpapa brothers what to do. They fight their own battles in their own way. Your magic and your dreams do not apply to them. We cannot stop the Sioux from doing what they will with their victims. It is the way of the warrior, each man for himself.''

She watched his eyes as he spoke. How could she explain this feeling she had? How could she tell him they would never go back to that special place in the hills where they could pretend all was well, where they had made love many times over and felt young again, where they could pretend all was peaceful and the Cheyenne still rode free? Her throat felt tight, and her chest ached with a need to weep openly, but she only lay her head against his chest.

"Remember that I love you, Bear Paw. I think I have loved you my whole life."

He frowned, petting her hair. "And I have loved you since I found you in the mountains." He laid her back. Both were naked because of the warm night. Both knew what they needed to assure each other that they were alive for the moment and that all was peaceful in the village. He entered her gently, and she breathed deeply, wanting to savor every movement, wanting to remember the feel of him, the smell of him, the aura of power about him.

Smiling Girl, awakened by their conversation, turned over to breastfeed her new baby boy, who was beginning to fuss. He had been born three months before, and he was called Prairie Owl, another son for Bear Paw.

Tom took the wolf's paw from the young Indian man who stood before him. A reservation Indian who could speak English had told him to come away from the fort, that an Indian from the sacred woman's clan had come to speak with him and to give him the wolf's paw.

His eyes hollow, his body thin from being unable to eat because of his sorrow, Tom studied the sacred fetish. He knew all too well what a sacrifice it was for Medicine Wolf to let go of it, how difficult it had to be for her to give it to a white man. He was surprised then when the reservation Indian interpreted the words of the runner who had brought the gift.

"He says to tell you it was Bear Paw's own sacred wolf paw. Medicine Wolf wanted to give you a wolf's paw from her own medicine bag, but Bear Paw said it should be the one she gave him many years ago. It had great magic for him. It kept him alive through many battles. It is a great sacrifice for him to give it away, but he did it as a sign of truth for you. It is his way of telling you that he did not know your wife was among those he attacked. When he realized who she was, he did not harm her or your daughter. He is worried because your wife was with child. He wishes to know if your woman is all right."

Tom's eyes teared. He closed the wolf paw in his hand, his emotions torn. He should hate Bear Paw, but he knew the significance of giving up the fetish. He realized Bear Paw and Medicine Wolf must have talked a long time about this, and he knew Medicine Wolf would never have wanted anything to happen to Elena. How strangely fate could twist lives and emotions.

"My wife died having the baby before anyone found them," he answered, his voice gruff. "The baby died too. Only my daughter lived. She hardly ever sleeps because of nightmares about the attack and her mother's slow death." He met the Indian's eyes, his own bloodshot. "Tell him that. But tell him that I do not blame Medicine Wolf or even Bear Paw. Tell him that I blame myself, and I blame my government for causing all the misunderstanding. At first I hated the Cheyenne. I felt they had turned on me." He looked at the wolf's paw again. He could have it sent back, but he knew Bear Paw would not want that. He would consider it an insult. "But I have had time to think. I know Bear Paw would not have deliberately brought harm to my wife. And tell Medicine Wolf I will be riding with the soldiers now, not to bring harm to the Cheyenne, but to do what I can to bring peace. Without my wife here, I must do something to stay busy or lose my mind. And until this is finally settled, until I know what will happen to Medicine Wolf and the others, I cannot go back to my home in the East. This land has become my home, as much home to me as it is to Medicine Wolf and her people. She will understand."

The reservation Indian explained to the messenger, and the messenger nodded. He mounted his horse and rode off, and Tom squeezed his hand tightly around the wolf's paw. "How did it come to this," he lamented. He put the paw into his breast pocket and headed for the supply house. He would pick out a uniform today.

White Horse, who had been watching the conversation from a distance, called over the reservation Indian, offering him whiskey to tell him what the runner had told Tom Prescott. He knew no Cheyenne would have a message for the man unless he was from Medicine Wolf's village. The reservation Indian very willingly told White Horse all that he knew, and White Horse took him to his cabin and gave him a flask of whiskey for the information. Then he headed straight for the commander's headquarters.

He grinned as he walked, thinking how foolish Medicine Wolf had been to send the wolf's paw. Bear Paw was a wanted man now, a murderous Cheyenne leader who had readily admitted he was responsible for the death of all those soldiers and civilians with that stagecoach and responsible for Elena Prescott's death! If the commander moved quickly, he could get some troops together and follow the messenger, who could lead them straight to Medicine Wolf's village, where they would surely find Bear Paw! No treaty would protect him now. If he could be caught, he would be hanged. White Horse could think of no sight more pleasant, and he would get credit for being the scout who had helped the army capture him! He would make sure that Medicine Wolf was captured right along with her "beloved." The thought of having both of them at his mercy was indeed sweet!

Medicine Wolf lay staring at the morning sky through the smoke hole of the tipi. She wondered if she would ever be able to sleep soundly again, for her nights were constantly disturbed by memories and sorrow and worry. Her memories were of better days, when her people roamed freely from far to the south all the way to the country of the Queen Mother. Never again would they know such peace and freedom.

Her sorrow was over the news the messenger had brought several days before. Tom's wife had died before help came. Her people had inadvertently brought great sorrow to her good friend, and now Tom would ride with the soldiers. His little girl was left with no mother, and her nights were filled with bad dreams. All the hatred and broken promises had led to the spoiling of a sacred friendship, for she knew that if she ever saw Tom again, his feelings for her and Bear Paw could never be the same. What they had shared was now destroyed, and she felt a terrible vacancy in her heart.

Her worry was over her prophetic dream about the killing of many soldiers. Always she wondered if this could be the day her haunting dream would be realized. She rose and dressed, then went outside. The village was barely lit by a sun trying to come over the eastern horizon but having not quite made it yet. She turned then and saw something on the southern horizon, something moving very fast toward the village. Soldiers!

She ducked back inside. "Get up! Get up," she screamed to Smiling Girl and Bear Paw. "Soldiers come! *Hopo! Hopo!*" Was this it? Were these the soldiers of her dream?

In an instant Bear Paw was on his feet and grabbing his weapons. Medicine Wolf was already outside running through the village, yelling for everyone to get up and flee, telling the warriors to be ready. Two Moons and Stands Tall were already outside, rifles in hand. Stands Tall ordered Summer Moon to hurry and get the horses together. Bear Paw's widowed father had taken Summer Moon for a wife and was now the one responsible for her and her children.

"Flee into the hills," men were telling their women. "Quickly! Quickly!"

They were camped in the first stand of trees at the edge of the vast Black Hills forests, open country stretched out before them to the east and south. They were not full strength, for this was a village of women who had stayed behind to clean some buffalo hides after the men had come across another herd. Most of the men had gone on, following the herd farther north. Only a few warriors had stayed with the women to protect them, for in this area there were no miners, and up until now no soldiers had been sent out to force them onto reservations, although they knew that could happen anytime. These warriors and the women were to leave tomorrow to follow the rest of the men.

Medicine Wolf hurried back to help Smiling Girl. They quickly knocked down the tipi and threw the skins and poles onto a travois that had been left tied to Thunder the night before. Standing Bear gathered the rest of his father's horses while Bear Paw and the rest of the men took positions behind trees and rocks, ready for the soldiers. There was no time to grab up the precious meat that was still not properly dried or smoked, no time to grab all belongings or herd together all horses. Women and children had to save themselves.

Smiling Girl held little Prairie Owl and grabbed the reins to Thunder, who carried Little Flower and Big Hands. Standing Bear, who was thirteen now and knew how to use a rifle, would stay and fight beside his father and his great-uncle, Two Moons, who had taught him the warrior ways. Summer Moon joined Smiling Girl in flight, leading two horses that carried her two half-blood children and her daughter and young full-blood son. Eighteen-year-old Crow Dog, who had adapted to the ways of his People, and was now as proudly Cheyenne as any of the others, would also stay behind and fight. The previous summer he had suffered the Sun Dance and was now a full-fledged Dog Soldier.

The women and children were barely into the trees before the soldiers came within rifle range. Bear Paw ran and grabbed one of his war ponies, riding it bareback and using only his heels and the horse's mane to guide it. He rode boldly in front of the soldiers to distract them, yelping and whooping, daring some of them to chase him. He diverted their attention long enough for the others to shoot down several of the soldiers, but a few got past the Indian men and headed into the trees.

Bear Paw followed some, while the rest of the men continued shooting at soldiers who remained behind, some getting into hand-to-hand combat. The attack had been so sudden and unplanned that it was each man for himself. Indians and soldiers alike were scattered.

Farther up in the trees Medicine Wolf took Prairie Owl from Smiling Girl so that she could run faster, for they were climbing, and Smiling Girl was already getting winded. Nearby the heavyset Summer Moon was having an even harder time of it.

"Mother," Summer Moon's half-blood son yelled, terrible fear in his voice. "White Horse!"

Both women turned to see the hated Cheyenne traitor bearing down on them, riding a huge roan gelding, his eyes looking wild, the ugly bald spot showing on his head.

"Take him," Medicine Wolf screamed to Smiling Girl,

handing Prairie Owl back to her. "Run! Run! Do not stop for anything, no matter what happens!" She pulled a knife and ran toward White Horse to keep his attention from Summer Moon. She knew that White Horse had led the soldiers here, probably tracking the messenger she had sent to Tom. She also knew that White Horse must want to kill Summer Moon and her half-blood children for spite. But there would be something he would much rather get his hands on, someone more important to him than his "unfaithful" wife.

She watched him turn, saw the wicked smile on his face. She waved her knife, and he rode toward her, letting out a war whoop. Two other soldiers followed him. In seconds White Horse was close. Little Wolf crouched, ready to leap upon White Horse and sink his fangs into the man's throat to protect Medicine Wolf.

Medicine Wolf heard a shot, but her eyes were on White Horse, and she could not look to see who had been shot. White Horse leapt from his horse and tackled Medicine Wolf to the ground. She managed to ram her knife into his side, but not hard enough. They tumbled together downhill, and Medicine Wolf landed with a jolt against a boulder, pine needles stuck in her hair and on her tunic. Somehow she had lost her knife. Quickly White Horse landed a fist into her face, and she felt him tugging at her medicine bag.

"Now they are mine," she heard him growl, "and *you* are mine!" She heard him say "Take this" to someone. "Hold it for me! We will each take our turn!"

Medicine Wolf felt her tunic being cut away. "My God," someone muttered. "Hurry up, White Horse. I want my turn."

Someone laughed.

Medicine Wolf felt a rock in her hand. She swung it wildly, managing to land a hard enough blow against the side of White Horse's head to knock him sideways, but for only a moment. She felt a sharp pain across her breasts then, and she knew White Horse had cut her.

"When I am through with you—" He did not finish.

"Let's get out of here," someone shouted.

Suddenly White Horse got up off her. She heard shooting close by, heard horses, heard men grunting and growling. She rolled to her knees, shaking her head, trying to see through blurred vision. She did not realize she was bleeding heavily from a gash that cut through her left breast and across her chest and stomach. She heard White Horse screaming, ''No! No!''

Her vision finally cleared, and she saw a dead soldier lying near her, a bullet hole in the middle of his face. Not far away Bear Paw was slashing at White Horse like a crazy man. White Horse was a mass of blood and was begging for his life. Bear Paw rammed his big knife into the man's lower stomach, then ripped it upward nearly to his throat. He yanked out the knife, and for a moment White Horse just stood staring at him. Finally he slumped to the ground.

Bear Paw stood over him a moment, panting, blood dripping from his knife. He wiped the blade on White Horse's blue uniform, then turned to face Medicine Wolf. His eyes widened when he saw how she was bleeding. He shoved his knife into its sheath. He was himself covered with blood, but this time it was not his own. He hurried over to her, picking up her tunic and wrapping it around her nakedness.

''Come! The rest of the soldiers have fled, but we must leave here quickly before more come! We must get you some help, Medicine Wolf!''

''The wolf paws! The wolf paws,'' she screamed. ''We must find them! White Horse cut away my medicine bag! He gave it to someone!''

She was in hysterics. This was the worst thing that could have happened! Without the wolf paws she was certain neither she nor Bear Paw nor her People could survive. She pulled away from him, throwing off the tunic and scrambling around on the ground trying to find the medicine bag. Blood poured from her wound as she stumbled over to the dead soldier to search him.

''Medicine Wolf, there is not time!''

''We must find them! We must,'' she screamed, tears streaming down her face, mixing with dirt. She frantically searched every pocket of the dead soldier, and Bear Paw quickly scanned the ground around them. He saw no sign of the medicine bag. He searched White Horse's body, but it was not there. He hurried back over to Medicine Wolf, who was scratching at the earth like a wild animal, throwing aside leaves and pine needles. He grasped her close, holding her arms.

"It is *gone*, Medicine Wolf! Another soldier with them got away. He probably has it. We must go and get you help or you will *die*!"

"It does not matter now," she sobbed. "It does not matter! I must have the wolf paws, for you, for the People! I will lose my magic! I will not be able to protect you!"

"We will be all right. We have no choice for now, Medicine Wolf! More soldiers will come! We have to go!"

"No! No!" She broke away and fought him until he had no choice but to backhand her, landing a blow to her already-bruised face. It startled her enough that she stiffened and quieted for a moment. Bear Paw jerked her close. "We have to *go*, Medicine Wolf! You know that I am right!"

Their eyes held, and she felt she was looking at a dead man, that all her People would now die. "Do not . . . let go of me," she whispered.

"I will never let go of you. For now we must save ourselves. Then we will talk to Black Buffalo about the wolf's paws."

"It's a bad, bad sign, Bear Paw," she sobbed. "It is the end."

He leaned down to again pick up her tunic and wrap it around her shoulders. "Stay still," he told her. He quickly walked over to the dead soldier and cut off his army shirt. He brought it over and pressed it against her bleeding breast. "Hold this against yourself to slow the bleeding." He was so full of fury at what White Horse had done that his head ached. He wished he could kill him many times over, torture him for days. If they were not in a position where they had to flee, he would have kept him alive for just such torture! All the Cheyenne would have enjoyed having a part in bringing pain to the man who had so cruelly betrayed them and had caused the holy woman to lose the wolf's paws. Worse than that, his beautiful, flawless Medicine Wolf now would carry a scar.

He led her to the dead soldier's horse, then took a blanket from the horse's gear and put it over the leather saddle so that her nakedess beneath the tunic would not rub against the leather. He helped her climb onto the horse, noticing that she was quieter now, looking dazed and confused. He could only hope she would not pass out before he could get her some help.

He led the horse over to the Appaloosa that he had used to distract the soldiers. He mounted up, and they headed uphill, Medicine Wolf hanging her head and sobbing. Suddenly she gasped, crying "*Hena-haanehe! Hena-haanehe!* It is ended! It is ended!" He looked to see Little Wolf lying dead, his white fur covered with blood near the neck where he had been shot.

Bear Paw climbed down and gently lifted the animal. He laid it across Medicine Wolf's lap. "We will bury him when we get to safety," he told her. His heart ached as though he had lost a child. He mounted up again, and they disappeared into the thicker pines higher in the hills.

In the valley below, those soldiers who had survived snuck back to burn what was left behind by the Cheyenne. One man joined them, laughing and holding something high. "I've got it," he bragged. "It's the medicine bag of that Cheyenne sacred woman! I'm holding out for the highest bidder!" He laughed again, shoving the little leather bag into his shirt.

Chapter Twenty-seven

Bear Paw climbed the last few feet of the ridge, then hesitated, still not sure he should be there. Medicine Wolf sat quietly alone, high above the village. Bear Paw thought how she always seemed to be attracted to high places when she needed to pray, high and wild and free, like the eagle and the wolf. She was in her own realm now. Wolves quietly lolled all around her, most of them raising their heads and perking up their ears at the sight of Bear Paw. None made a threatening move, and Bear Paw thought it must be a good sign that even though Medicine Wolf had lost Little Wolf and the sacred wolf paws, the wolves still had come to protect and comfort her in her hour of torment.

He knew he was expected to stay away, but he was worried about his beloved. When he first brought Medicine Wolf to safety after the attack, she was sick and distraught. The Shaman had dressed her wound, and Bear Paw had sat with her through several days of dilerium as her body fought a life-threatening infection. Never had Bear Paw been so aware of how empty life would be without his Medicine Wolf. Because she had lost the wolf's paws, he had feared she would not live; but to his great relief she seemed to have survived the worst. Still, she had hardly spoken since the infection left her, and the Shaman said she could still die, not from her wound, but from the sickness that burned inside her because she had lost the wolf's paws. "It is her spirit that is dying," he told Bear Paw.

As soon as she was well enough she had come to this high place to pray and be alone. The whole tribe had moved much higher into the Black Hills, joining a stronger force of Cheyenne. Many in the tribe felt the loss of the wolf's paws and wondered how it would affect them in their struggle against the *ve-ho-e*. They waited now for their sacred woman to come back to them. For three days Bear Paw had himself waited and worried. In the night all could hear Medicine Wolf's cries mingled with the howling of the wolves. Losing the wolf's paws seemed to be destroying her, and Bear Paw did not know how to help her. He had dared to come here to try to talk to her.

His Appaloosa was tied farther below, and he had climbed the rest of the way on foot. He approached slowly to where Medicine Wolf sat on a rock at the very top of the ridge. Bear Paw watched the wolves warily, but still they made no aggressive moves. Did they understand that he felt the sacred woman's pain and heartache? She had lost her most sacred fetish, the symbol of her mystic powers.

Now Bear Paw feared that he had himself lost Medicine Wolf, lost her to the animal spirit that guided and controlled her. Would she ever be his Medicine Wolf again? His moccasined feet made hardly any sound against the soft pine needles as he came closer. Some of the wolves rose to their feet, but he remained unafraid.

As though her mind and instincts were in tune with the wolves, Medicine Wolf suddenly turned to look at him. She rose, looking almost ghostly. Her eyes bore dark circles, and she was terribly thin. Her hair was tangled, and she showed no particular expression. The sun was beginning to set behind the ridge. Bear Paw walked even closer, trusting Medicine Wolf not to let the wolves harm him. Some simply remained lying on their bellies, their feet tucked under them. A few paced, and two sat on their haunches at Medicine Wolf's side.

Medicine Wolf stood with her back to the sun. She said nothing at first, looking down at the wolves as Bear Paw moved behind her. For the moment he felt too humble to face her, for she seemed almost inhuman, something powerful and magical. "Come back to us, Medicine Wolf," he finally pleaded. "I cannot go on without you."

Medicine Wolf stood still a moment while a gentle west wind teased her hair. She remained very quiet, then turned to face Bear Paw. The same wind blew the hair back from her face, and an odd radiance came into her eyes. She gazed at him as though he were an apparition, her eyes squinting then at the bright sunlight that glared behind him. A cloud moved across the center of the sun so that its rays spread out behind it in a glorious arc, becoming even more piercing and brilliant.

"Bear Paw," she said in a near whisper. "I have found my peace! The weight of my powers is lifted from me, and I have seen my last vision fulfilled!" The look in her eyes changed from desolation and sorrow to a look of wonderful peace and great joy.

Bear Paw frowned. "I do not understand."

"All my life I have waited for this! I was but a child when I dreamed that you and I stood high on a ridge, with wolves all about us. You stood behind me, and the sun's rays were spread out behind you. It is my vision! It is what I have waited for all my life!"

He said nothing, afraid he would break the spell of the moment. She came closer, touching his face. "Now I know the meaning of the vision," she said, searching his eyes. "The wolf spirit has given us this time, these last days we will spend on earth, time for each other. He has released me of my burden, made me simply a woman . . . your woman. I belong only to you now."

The wind moaned softly through nearby pines, and Bear Paw drew her closer. She rested her head against his chest. The wolves all watched, then one by one they trotted away until all were gone. Bear Paw circled his arms around her. "What did you mean when you said 'these last days we will spend on earth'?" he asked.

She kissed his chest, breathed deeply of his scent, feeling amazingly calm and at peace. "More soldiers will come. There will be victories, but they will be short-lived. You and I could never live on a reservation. We would both rather die." She raised her eyes to meet his. "And perhaps we *will* die. But we will die happy, Bear Paw, and we will be together. Nothing will ever part us, not even death. It would not be so bad if we did not grow old together. Growing old on the reservation is for others, but not for us . . . not for us."

He leaned down and touched her cheek. "I would rather have you this way, in my arms, belonging to me for just one day, than to lose you to the Wolf Spirit and grow old without you."

"I was always yours, Bear Paw. The Wolf Spirit understood that. Now he has released me. He has given me to you by taking away the wolf's paws."

"Na-htse-eme." He picked her up in his arms. "There is a cave not far from here. We will go there to be alone." He touched her cheek. *"Ne-mehotatse."*

He carried her down to where his horse was tied and put her on the animal's back. He was not certain what had just happened. He was only glad that it had, that she was his again. He led the horse away, and the wind continued to whistle through the pines while from a thick grove of underbrush several pairs of eyes watched them leave. One of the wolves whined. The beloved sacred woman was leaving them, going back to her human world.

Tom rode into camp with the relief company of cavalry. He turned up the collar of his winter jacket against the cold, hoping Rebecca was safe and warm back at Fort Laramie, where she was living with the wife and daughter of a Lieutenant Pierce. It was Pierce's men with whom Tom rode now, deep into the Black Hills.

For months Tom had served with other troops before going back to Laramie to see Rebecca. Although he was

tired and the weather was cruel, he had left again with
Pierce, his need for revenge now turned to concern for
what could happen next. He wanted to be a part of all of
it, thinking that somehow perhaps he could be more help
in the field than at the fort.

Army troops had been assigned to various areas of
Sioux country to search for Indians and warn them they
must come in to the reservation. The entire operation was
being commanded by General George Crook. Crook was
experienced in hunting and fighting Indians, but Tom
was convinced the man had been as fair as possible about
it. He did not seem quite so vindictive and thirsty for
blood as some of his cohorts, or as Sheridan himself
seemed to be; nor did he seem to be out for glory, like
George Custer.

It was well known among the troops that Sheridan and
Crook did not get along. Crook was under Sheridan's over-
all command, but Tom and the lower-ranking men with
whom he rode day after day were all aware of the discord
between the men who had been given the responsibility of
corraling the Sioux and Northern Cheyenne. To make matters even more confusing and unorganized, neither Crook
nor Sheridan had much respect for George Custer, who
they considered brash and careless. Most of the men
agreed among themselves about Custer, whom most had
met or served under at one time or another during this
campaign. He was a man who had little regard for proto-
col and who seldom thought out his strategy rationally or
consulted his fellow officers. Crook's and Sheridan's dis-
satisfaction with the man had created a situation of poor
communication, and even though Tom was not enlisted in
this army, he could see that the situation could lead to
disaster.

Tom had met Custer more than once, and he suspected
the man simply did not want to share the glory should he
realize any distinctive victories or captures. Because of
this he did not always obey orders to the letter, and he
was often left to handle a situation however he thought
best. Tom had never been part of the Seventh Cavalry, and
he was glad of it, for he knew that if he had been assigned
to work under the man whose reports of gold in the Black

Hills had started all this trouble, he might have been tempted to shoot him. He had come to blame Custer more for Elena's death than the Cheyenne. His hatred for the Cheyenne had vanished after receiving the wolf's paw from Bear Paw. Now his grief had subsided to a kind of numbness, and he continued to ride with the soldiers mostly to do what little he could to bring in the Cheyenne. He thought that if he could find Medicine Wolf, talk to her, maybe more bloodshed could be avoided. In so doing, perhaps being a part of helping bring the peace would help him deal with the loss of his wife.

He knew Rebecca still did not quite understand how he could so readily forgive and forget. He had tried to explain that he did not condone the horrible thing Bear Paw and his warriors had done, but that he understood the reason behind it. And until she was older, Rebecca would not be able to understand his feelings for Medicine Wolf. Maybe she would never understand. He didn't understand it fully himself, especially now that Elena was dead because of Medicine Wolf's People. He simply could not hate her, and he could not help this desire to help the Cheyenne if the opportunity arose. He still felt that all of this could have been avoided if the Indians had been dealt with honestly from the beginning. Now he could not bear the thought of Medicine Wolf being dragged to a reservation, perhaps being abused by soldiers. He was here in hopes of preventing such a horror.

A cold wind stung his face as he dismounted, and his bones ached from a long day's ride. He was not really a full-fledged army enlistee, but rather still rode with these men as a civilian. He was expected to follow orders, but he was also free to leave whenever he chose. He simply had been unable to go back to Laramie to stay. He had ridden with Pierce's men more deeply into Indian country than he had ever been before, and he could see why the Sioux and Cheyenne fought for this country, for it was some of the most beautiful he had ever seen, and it truly did seem to have a mystic quality about it.

He walked over to a fire to warm his hands while Pierce went to talk to the commander of the company they were replacing. Several men sat around the fire, some of them playing cards. The new arrivals began putting up tents. Tom listened to the conversation of the men already there, discovering they had seen no Indians. Various men delivered several descriptive terms for the elusive Sioux and Cheyenne under Sitting Bull and Crazy Horse, and not all words were complimentary.

"This is going to take one hell of a long time," one man put in. "It's going to be a long, cold winter. Crook was crazy to try to go after those bastards this time of year."

"He's got his orders from higher up," another grumbled.

"Yeah . . . Sheridan. He's even crazier. Besides, he doesn't have to be out here in the hills with his toes froze half off, wondering if Indians will come along in the night and hack them off for him."

"They'd hack off more than your toes," another man replied.

Light laughter circled the campfire. Tom looked over at the men playing cards. They were seated around a barrel, and one looked upset. "I don't have anything else to bet," he grumped.

"Put up or get out," another told him.

"I wish I had some whiskey," someone else complained.

"I wish *I* had me a squaw waitin' for me in my tent," another answered, his remark followed by more laughter.

"I've got somethin' on me that's worth a lot," the betting man said then.

"We only take cash," one of the others told him.

"This is as good as cash," the man answered. "It will be worth a lot someday to some idiot who collects Indian paraphernalia. A scout took it off a Cheyenne woman and gave it to me before he got killed by her husband. She was some kind of holy woman."

Tom quickly forgot how cold he was. *Holy woman!* Medicine Wolf? He moved a little closer as the man who had made the remark took a leather pouch out of the inside of his jacket. He plunked it onto the barrel, and Tom's eyes widened in horror. Medicine Wolf's medicine bag! There was no mistaking it. He could even see the scorch marks from when his mother had thrown it into the wood-burning stove. One of the other men picked it up and opened it, dumping out three wolf paws and two eagle feathers, along with what looked like simple trade beads.

A chill moved down Tom's back, and he swore he could hear drumming and rattles and a distant chanting. He rose, standing behind the man who had opened the medicine bag.

"What the hell am I going to do with a couple of dried-up paws and feathers," he laughed. "Sell them to an Indian Shaman for a buffalo robe? Maybe some squaw would lift her tunic for these damn beads." There came light laughter. "How stupid do you think I am, Gregson?"

"I'll give you fifty dollars for it," Tom said to the one called Gregson. All the men turned to look at him in surprise. "You can use the money to keep gambling. I'll throw in another ten if you'll tell me the circumstances surrounding how you got it. I want to know what happened to the woman it belonged to."

Gregson frowned. "Why do you want it so bad? Is it really worth more than that?"

Tom smiled sadly and shook his head. "No. It is worth that much only to me. It's personal."

"Say, aren't you the one who knew that Cheyenne woman called Medicine Wolf?" another asked. "I've seen you around Fort Laramie."

"Yes, I knew the holy woman."

"What the hell was between you two?"

Tom felt the ache in his heart. "She lived with my family for two years, back from 'fifty-one to 'fifty-three. She was just a young girl then, but we became good friends. That was before all this trouble started, back when there was not so much bloodshed." He turned pleading eyes to Gregson. "At any rate, I recognize that pouch as her medicine bag. It means very much to her. Please, let me buy it."

Gregson shrugged. "If you want to pay that much for it, you can have it. I swear I've had nothing but bad luck since I took the damn thing anyway. Maybe now the curse will be on you instead of me."

"And you were going to make *me* take it," the man

betting against him snipped. "Thanks a lot." He gathered up the paws and feathers and stuffed them into the bag, handing it to Tom. "Here. Give the man his fifty dollars so I can win it off him."

"Sixty dollars," Gregson reminded him. He looked up at Tom. "She was with a small village my company attacked a few months ago. A scout called White Horse led us to it. He went charging after the women and children, after some wife of his who had deserted him and after the medicine woman, or whatever she's called. He spotted the medicine woman and tackled her down. Him and me and another private, Bill Merrick . . . we were all fixin' to have us a good time with her. She tried to stab White Horse, but she didn't do him much harm, and he wrestled the knife out of her hand. He took his own knife then and cut off the medicine bag and threw it to me. Told me to keep it till he was finished with her." He shook his head. "I'll tell you, she was a looker, that one. God don't make them much better than that."

They all laughed, and Tom felt his anger rising. He closed his fist around the medicine bag, feeling closer to Medicine Wolf.

"Well, she put up one hell of a fight," Gregson continued. "White Horse cut her a good one across one of them pretty breasts and was just about to enjoy himself when here comes this Cheyenne warrior charging at us— meanest-looking buck I ever saw in my life. He shot Merrick right through the head. I lit out of there like a rabbit—still had the medicine bag. I could hear White Horse's screams, but I didn't look back to see what that buck was doing to him. The woman must have belonged to him. Me and the rest of the men left. After a while we went back to burn all their tipis and supplies. We were afraid they'd come back with ten times more warriors, so we waited a couple more days to go back to bury our dead. Apparently that buck and a few of his friends *had* gone back once they got their women to safety and made sure we were gone. They had picked up their own dead, and apparently they were as afraid of us as we were of them, because they didn't stay around long enough to mutilate the soldiers' bodies like they usually do, all except White

Horse." The man shook his head. "I don't think there was a joint in his body that hadn't been severed. Found his privates stuffed in his mouth."

"Jesus," someone muttered.

Tom kept hold of the medicine bag. He could just imagine Bear Paw doing something like that to White Horse for wounding Medicine Wolf that way and stealing her precious fetishes. How had it affected her? He knew how terrible it must be for her. The medicine bag was her life.

Now he knew he had to stay out here with the soldiers. He had a much better chance of finding her this way; and after hearing how Gregson talked, he knew she would need his protection if she was taken alive. If he was lucky enough to be among those who found her, he could give her back her wolf's paws. It would mean so much to her.

He wanted to kill Gregson for his attitude, but it would be pointless. Half the men in camp felt as he did. "I'll get the money from my gear," he told the man. "I'll be pretty much broke, but I'll get by." He turned and walked toward his horse, now knowing the answer to why he had deliberated over how much money he should keep with him when he rode out. The army provided all his needs, so it was not necessary to have a lot of cash on hand. In fact, he had been told not to take too much because the other men could not always be trusted. Yet he had stuffed a hundred dollars into his gear, money it had taken him many months to save. Something seemed to have made him bring it with him, and now he knew what it was. It was Medicine Wolf's magic. Her power to influence him was still strong.

He smiled sadly, pressing the medicine bag to his heart, then shoving it into a pocket on the inside of his jacket, where it would always be safe and close to him. Somehow, someday, perhaps he could give it back to its rightful owner. *Where are you, Medicine Wolf,* he thought, looking up at higher country. His only reply was the moaning of the cold winter wind.

·   ·   ·

Throughout the winter of 1875-76, Bear Paw and Medicine Wolf and all Northern Cheyenne, along with the Sioux, ignored the call to come in to the reservations. Troops commanded by Brigadier General George Crook, called "Three Stars," by the Indians, moved in various formations and from various directions through the Black Hills, forcing the Indians north and west until they were moving into Powder River country, the very country from which they had chased soldiers and whites ten years earlier.

What the soldiers seemed to fail to realize was that they were only herding many tribes closer together, Indians who were becoming more and more angry at the forced takeover of land promised to them under the treaty. Northern Cheyenne and Arapaho joined the many tribes of Sioux, the Oglala, Hunkpapa, Miniconjou, Blackfoot, and Sand Arc. Adding to these were many reservation Indians who fled the reservations because of the terrible living conditions, peaceful Indians who had decided the *ve-ho-e* had betrayed them, and who longed for the freedom they had once known.

When their own village was brutally attacked by a battalion of men under a Colonel Reynolds, Bear Paw took his family closer to the rest of the growing numbers of Indians who were coming together at the Rosebud River. Here Summer Moon cut her hair and shed blood in mourning for her half-blood son, and for twelve-year-old Red Beaver, who had both been killed.

It was a time of great sorrow, yet a time of hope, for the Sioux and Cheyenne together held a Sun Dance early in the spring of '76 along the Rosebud. All knew a major confrontation could not be avoided. Men wanted to make new sacrifices to strengthen themselves for war. Budding young warriors wanted to prove their devotion and seek visions. Bear Paw renewed his own commitment to dying rather than going to the reservation. He had lost his wolf's paw. He needed the power of *Maheo* with him, needed to renew his sacred vows and find protection from other sources.

Medicine Wolf was especially proud because Bear

Paw's oldest son, fourteen-year-old Standing Bear, also took part in the ceremony, as did White Horse's nineteen-year-old son, Crow Dog, for the second time. Watching Crow Dog rededicate himself to his people helped comfort Summer Moon.

As Medicine Wolf watched her husband dance around the the sacred pole, deliberately leaning back to allow the skewers piercing his breasts to pull at the skin, she felt pride. She wanted to exemplify her own devotion to her People, to prove to them that the loss of the wolf paws did not have to mean there was no hope. In her heart she knew only death lay ahead for many, but perhaps not for all; and if they would remember these things, if the children would remember this ceremony and understand its significance, perhaps they would remember . . . remember. They must remember, above all else, so that if the day came when they were no longer free to do these things, they would keep them alive in their hearts.

She rose, walking to Black Buffalo and holding out her arms. "I wish to make my own sacrifice, my father," she told him.

The old man slowly rose. The huge Sun Dance lodge was filled with so much drumming and singing that one had to speak louder than normal to be heard. Black Buffalo leaned closer to her. "You have already sacrificed most of your life to the People," he told her.

"I have lost the wolf's paws. I want them to know I do not feel defeated, to know that we can still fight and be strong even without my powers of blessing. They should know that I believe each person's sacrifice is all that is necessary."

"You shed blood when you saved Summer Moon and her children from White Horse's wrath the day he attacked you. You nearly died."

"But I did not, even though I did not have the wolf's paws. I feel I must do this for the People. Help me."

The old man looked very sad, but he knew it was important to her. He had long ago learned to love Medicine Wolf like his own daughter, for it was to him she had come so many times for help in interpreting her dreams or in making other decisions. Was it really so long ago the six-year-old child met his challenge and refused to give him the wolf paws?

She held out her arms, and he nodded. He turned to take up his knife, holding it over the flames of a holy fire first, then turning to carve several pieces of flesh off her arms. Medicine Wolf barely flinched. She turned then, moving beside Bear Paw, who was lost in pain and visions. He danced in the circle, blowing on his bone whistle, and Medicine Wolf danced beside him, moving with him, letting the blood flow from her arms. She was a woman of near perfection, except for the scar White Horse had left across her breast. Now her arms would bear scars from her own deliberate sacrifice.

The others watched their holy woman, and it was good. They were many now, strong. The bluecoats had pushed them this far, but Sitting Bull, who was himself making the flesh sacrifice in a Sioux Sun Dance lodge, had given fair warning. The soldiers had been told by runners that if they came as far as the Rosebud, they would "cross the river at their own peril."

The village came alive with celebrating as Cheyenne warriors rode among the tipis shouting their victory. Medicine Wolf breathed a sigh of relief that Bear Paw was among them, for she knew of the fighting that had been taking place against Three Stars Crook at the Rosebud.

"They are retreating! They are retreating," the warriors shouted, their horses thundering through camp. "We have beaten Crook and he runs from us!"

Some women broke out in chanting. Dogs barked and children ran alongside their fathers. Standing Bear rode in behind his father, holding up a soldier's rifle he had taken and looking the proud warrior. Medicine Wolf's heart was touched, for in that moment she saw a young Bear Paw. The boy looked so much like his father, and he was the same age Bear Paw had been when he had found her in the mountains with the wolves.

Thirty summers had gone by since then! She had counted the seasons by adding a bead each summer to her medicine bag. She remembered that when she had lost it last summer there had been twenty-nine beads in the bag. She put a hand to her face. She was thirty-six now. Was Bear Paw just trying to spare her when he told her she still looked like a young girl? She had been blessed with a rare beauty, but lately, when she used the looking glass, she had seen little lines in her face. Had Bear Paw noticed them? Perhaps the wolf paws had had something to do with keeping her young. Now that she had lost them, perhaps she would grow old more quickly.

Bear Paw rode back through camp, yipping and celebrating, still strong and lean for his forty-four summers. He had survived so much. Both of them had. She was sure that it was their love that had pulled them through so many things. She was equally sure that no matter what happened now, nothing would ever change that love.

Smiling Girl called out a shrill cry of celebration. Medicine Wolf glanced at her, thinking what a faithful, abiding sister she had been. Smiling Girl had always accepted the love she and Bear Paw shared, had never seemed to mind taking second place. Her happiness was her children, her now-warrior son Standing Bear; her son Big Hands, now eleven; eight-year-old Little Flower, and the "baby" Prairie Owl, now a one-year-old boy, who was walking on sturdy legs and causing Smiling Girl to forever be chasing after him.

Bear Paw rode up to them. "We break camp," he said, smiling as he dismounted. "We move farther up near the Greasy Grass, where many Sioux are camped! It is good that we have decided to stand together. Sitting Bull says that we must fight the soldiers together, for separately they will kill us. Today proves that he was right! Crazy Horse led us well! Crook and his men are leaving the Rosebud!" He pulled her, laughing, inside the tipi. "It was a good battle. When we knew we had them going, we laughed at them! We even turned around and pulled down our leggings and breechcloths to give them targets, showing our contempt for them."

"Bear Paw!" Medicine Wolf covered her mouth and laughed as he pulled her down to a blanket. She was glad she had stayed away from the battle. Since losing the wolf's paws, she had not joined him as she had done before over the years. This was Bear Paw's time of glory. For this time of rare victories and combined strength she would just be his woman.

He rolled her onto her back. "You said once that our days were numbered," he said, sobering. "But perhaps there are more left than you thought. We are in the right, Medicine Wolf. The white man's government knows it. We can win this!"

She searched his dark eyes. "Only if we are careful," she warned him. "Remember my dream about many soldiers. If such a battle should take place, you must not violate the bodies or take anything from them."

He only grinned again, as though to say she worried too much. "I do not want to think of these things," he told her. "Today we were victorious, and winning makes me feel strong and good! It makes me want my woman!" He turned and shouted to Smiling Girl to close the flap of the tipi. Medicine Wolf heard a giggle outside, and the tipi became darker. "We move on soon," Bear Paw told Medicine Wolf. "But not before I know another victory."

Medicine Wolf smiled. "Do you consider me an enemy?"

He smiled the handsome smile she loved so dearly. He moved a big hand along her leg to push up her tunic. "No. You are just a woman who could tell me no. If you did, I would have to leave you, and it would be very painful for me."

She opened her legs, leaning up to lick his lips, tasting the salt of his perspiration, but loving the smell of him even when he was heated from a hard ride. "I would never want to bring you pain," she answered. "Let me take the pain away, my husband."

She breathed deeply as he entered her. How she loved to take her man after a heady victory, and how he loved to celebrate by relishing the delicious fruits of being the victor. Outside, the celebrating continued, while inside, Bear Paw made love to his woman with as much energy and passion as he had used to fight George Crook and his troops. It had been a very good day!

Later they would take down their tipis. It was time to join Sitting Bull and Crazy Horse and the other thousands of Sioux at the Greasy Grass, the river the *ve-ho-e* called the Little Bighorn.

Chapter Twenty-eight

The valley of the Greasy Grass was alive with excitement. Soldiers were coming, many soldiers! Some of the warriors who galloped through village after village shouted that they even thought Custer himself was coming! For as far as Medicine Wolf could see and hear, women trilled their own war cries to support their warrior husbands and sons who prepared to go out and meet the soldiers.

Sioux and Cheyenne were camped in such great numbers that their circles of tipis stretched for nearly three miles up and down the river. Now those camps were a beehive of excitement. Warriors from many tribes quickly smeared on their war paint and took up weapons. Scouts were riding through the villages, shouting that one battalion of soldiers had already been nearly annihilated at the southern end of the river and the survivors had retreated, meeting up with another battalion that was being held down by many Sioux.

"Many more come," the crier shouted throughout the

village. "Many soldiers! Many soldiers! Across the river to the east they come, heading north toward us! Make ready to fight! It is a good day to die!"

"*Hoka hey,*" Sioux criers shouted in their own villages. "It is a good day to die!"

There was no time for good-byes. Medicine Wolf hastily helped Bear Paw make ready. In minutes he was on his best Appaloosa, Standing Bear riding up to join his father. Bear Paw held up his lance, giving out a war cry.

"Do not forget the dream," Medicine Wolf warned him. He did not seem to even hear her. She felt a strange apprehension. *Many soldiers* the crier had said. *Many soldiers!*

Medicine Wolf ran to the edge of the river. As far as she could see, warriors gathered. So many! She saw Crazy Horse then. He came bounding across the river, water splashing and foaming. On through camp they came, hundreds of warriors following Crazy Horse. Medicine Wolf heard someone say something about moving around to the rear of the soldiers.

"Chief Gall will hold them until we get behind them," one warrior said excitedly when he stopped to wait for another to adjust his horse's bridle.

"How many are there?" Medicine Wolf shouted to him.

"I do not know. Perhaps two hundred bluecoats," the warrior replied.

The men rode off. "Two hundred," Medicine Wolf repeated in astonishment. Two hundred soldiers were a great force, indeed, under normal circumstances. But never had so many Indians been gathered together in one force. The two hundred soldiers were going up against perhaps two *thousand* Indians! Where were the soldiers' scouts? Did they not know how many Indians were camped here? Were they crazy men? "Long-hair," she muttered. Only the careless and arrogant Custer would be foolish enough to ride directly into an area where he had to know most of the Indians had been driven. What other explanation could there be? Three Stars Crook would not do anything so ridiculous, nor would any of the other soldier leaders about whom Bear Paw had spoken.

She hoped it *was* Custer, for he was the one who had slain so many Cheyenne at the Washita. He had no pity for any Indian, and it was his foolish talk of gold that had brought so many white men to the Black Hills. She went to the tipi and took a rope bridle from where it hung on a pole near the tipi entrance. "I must see this for myself," she told Smiling Girl. "Gather the children. Have Little Flower help you take down the tipi. Be prepared to flee if it is necessary. I am going to follow the warriors."

"Be careful, Medicine Wolf," her sister told her with concern.

Medicine Wolf only smiled wryly. "This is not a day to worry about our own People. It is a day for those blue-coats to worry!" She hurried to where the horses were kept and picked out a fine, strong Pinto that Bear Paw had stolen from a Crow scout after the battle at the Rosebud. She quickly fixed the bridle and climbed onto the animal's bare back, then rode off to follow the warriors, as a few other women were doing.

It felt good to ride this way again, to run the horse hard, feel the wind in her face! She had always loved riding with Bear Paw, helping with raids, sometimes leading the Dog Soldiers. Those days were over now, but no one could stop her from observing. This was going to be a battle to remember! She turned her horse to splash through the north end of the river, following Crazy Horse and Bear Paw on a ride that took several minutes.

Now she could hear the crack of rifles! A battle was already taking place! It must be Chief Gall, who was to turn the attention of the soldiers while Crazy Horse came at them from behind. War cries increased to a deafening frenzy, now and then muffled when warriors rode down into a gully, only to reappear again. The land here was a maze of rolling hills, the ground rising and dropping again so that anyone in the gullies could not easily be seen or heard. She realized that must be why the soldiers had apparently not been aware of just how many Indians were camped here. A man could sit on a rise and look out and not even notice others camped below a swell in the distance. And such rolling land muffled the sound of voices, even gunfire.

She and other women came upon another rise then, and Medicine Wolf's eyes widened in fascination. Farther down the hill of yellow grass a huge battalion of soldiers stood their ground against Gall and his hundreds of warriors, while behind them came Crazy Horse and Bear Paw and a thousand more! The soldiers had formed a circle, most of them dismounted, a few of them still riding in circles, shooting frantically, their eyes wide with fear. Some of their horses lay dead, as well as many men. Many Indians also lay wounded or dead.

Now the mass of swarming Sioux and Cheyenne converged in a battle that was obviously hopeless for the soldiers. Medicine Wolf could not help feeling pity for some of them, for surely they were only doing what they had been ordered to do by some crazed leader who had foolishly thought that whatever Indians they came across could be defeated. Someone had made a very bad decision, and the Indians they encountered were no longer Indians who were ready to talk peace. They were angry over broken promises, angry over appalling living conditions on the reservations, angry that the army had allowed white miners to invade their sacred lands, angry at a government that continually lied to them. Most of all they were angry at the frustration they felt over losing all that was dear to them; losing their land, the buffalo, their lives to white man's diseases; losing their very pride.

She could see now that the soldiers below had become to the Sioux and Cheyenne nothing more than representatives of all that they hated, all that had brought them nothing but loss and sorrow. For so long the warriors had needed a great victory, and now they would have it! When one is so carried away by hatred and fear and frustration, he thinks of nothing but wreaking the worst havoc possible. No soldier down there would be left alive.

She watched with mixed emotions, realizing how important this was to Bear Paw, but also realizing that to kill so many soldiers was to invite many, many more to come. This time it was the white man's government who would be angry. There would be no more bartering, no more peace offerings. The warriors would win this battle, but in the end they would be defeated by it. Still, for the moment she could not help the wonderful feeling of satisfaction at the victory they would realize today. No matter what happened after this, they would long remember this sweet taste of vengeance!

For several hours the warriors circled the dying soldiers, who hung on with more bravery than Medicine Wolf thought they possessed. Finally hundreds of warriors descended on a few remaining men, shooting, stabbing, ending the last resistance. A great cry went up. Lances were raised. Drunk with victory, warriors began stripping bodies, taking weapons. Some of the women with Medicine Wolf rode down to join in the looting.

"No! Wait," Medicine Wolf called out to them. "It is bad medicine!"

They did not listen. Only last night runners had come to tell them that Sitting Bull had had a vision that there would soon be a great battle with soldiers, but that his People must not take their guns or horses, or a curse would be upon them. It pained her heart to see how the warriors, too elated to think about warnings from one man who had not been present to see the battle, ignored the vision. Now she could see Summer Moon. Even she joined in the looting, for she carried a great hatred in her heart for white men, who had used her so vilely when she lived with White Horse.

This was their victory, and her People would enjoy its spoils. What was left of Medicine Wolf's joy faded when she noticed Bear Paw take a pistol from one of the soldiers, a pair of boots from another. Even he had forgotten her warning. The women, some of them beginning to moan over the loss of a son or a husband, searched through the dead bodies of the Indians who had been killed, looking for a familiar face. In their grief, they began slashing at the soldiers' bodies, wanting to be sure they suffered in the afterlife.

It was done. A battle had been won, but, Medicine Wolf knew, because her People and the Sioux had not heeded the warnings of the spirits, the real war had just begun. The looting and celebrating went on well into sunset. Finally the warriors left, taking their loot and the dead bodies of their friends and relatives with them.

Tonight the drums would beat loudly. The night air would be filled with victory songs. There would be much dancing. Medicine Wolf saw Standing Bear then and knew that he, too, was all right. She turned her horse and headed back to the village. This time she would not join in the victory celebration.

It had been a hot day, but Medicine Wolf felt a chill in the air.

A freezing wind whipped at the tipi, and Medicine Wolf huddled around the central fire with Smiling Girl and the children while the men were again out searching for game. Since the battle at the Greasy Grass River, bellies had gone hungry, for seldom were they allowed to camp in any one place long enough to hunt. The men had been kept busy fending off soldiers, who crawled through the Bighorn Mountains and foothills like ants. It seemed everywhere they turned, soldiers were again on their trail.

Medicine Wolf was not surprised. This was what she had feared all along, for the Cheyenne had ignored her warning not to desecrate the bodies of the soldiers they had killed that fateful day along the Greasy Grass. There had been much celebrating afterward, and many warriors got so drunk that they passed out. When runners told them a few weeks later that Custer had indeed been the leader of the soldiers that day, another celebration was in order. Custer had cut his hair short just before his campaign, and the Indians, few of whom truly knew the man's looks up close, had not been sure just who had led the soldiers.

Now more soldiers had come, many more. To keep them confused, and to avoid being surrounded in one place, the Indians had split up. The Sioux had scattered in many directions, as had the Northern Cheyenne. Bear Paw and Medicine Wolf and their clan had followed Cheyenne leaders Dull Knife and Little Wolf here to this canyon in the mountains, where they hoped to hole up for the winter. In warm weather it was fairly easy to avoid the soldiers and stay on the move. But in winter little children had to be kept inside. There was always more sickness, less grass for the horses, less food for strength.

Suddenly they heard shots, not one or two like that of hunters who had found game, but many firings, like men shooting at each other. Instantly Medicine Wolf and Smiling Girl were on their feet gathering things together. This was a terrible time to have to flee, for it was bitterly cold outside, and there was much snow. Both women and all the children were already dressed in winter moccasins and clothing, always ready to run again.

Medicine Wolf doused the fire and helped gather their things together. Quickly she and Smiling Girl took down the tipi, a cold wind howling around them and stinging their faces. "Get the roan mare," Smiling Girl shouted to Big Hands above the howling of the cruel wind.

Running had become routine now. Everyone knew what to do. Medicine Wolf wondered how much longer they would be punished for ignoring the warning in her vision. If only she still had the wolf paws. Quickly, along with the others in the village, they loaded belongings onto horses and travois, which were always kept ready near the tipis now. Already Medicine Wolf was having trouble feeling her fingers. The gunfire continued farther up in the canyon, and when she looked up she could see, soldiers moving along a ledge.

"Bear Paw," she whispered. He was up there somewhere, and so was Standing Bear.

Summer Moon soon joined them, and the women and children and old ones made their way up the opposite side of the canyon, a long, slow climb, the freezing wind scraping at them, heavy, wet snow pelting them all the way. Some had not had time to take up their tipis or pick up all their belongings. It seemed to take hours to reach the top, and when they did, Medicine Wolf turned to see what was left of the tipis were on fire. Horses left behind were being deliberately shot down by the soldiers so that they would have even less means of fleeing. The horses . . . once a proud Bear Paw had owned so many. Now he was down to four. Even her beloved Appaloosa, Thunder, had been lost.

Medicine Wolf realized that the bluecoats did not have to come and shoot them to capture them. They were already slowly starving or freezing to death, slowly being forced to surrender out of a sheer need to survive. She turned to Smiling Girl with tear-filled eyes.

"Do not be afraid to go with them if it is necessary to save the children," she told her. "I will never surrender, nor will Bear Paw, but we do not want the children to die. If and when you must surrender to save them, then do it with pride. Never let the children forget, Smiling Girl. Promise me. They must never forget the Cheyenne way."

Tears trickled down Smiling Girl's face and froze on her cheeks. "I will not let them forget." Their eyes held. "I love you very much, Medicine Wolf. I have been proud to call you my sister."

Medicine Wolf embraced her. "And I have been proud to call you mine, and to let you be the mother to Bear Paw's children."

Darkness was coming. They moved to a place where they found a little shelter and stayed there for the night, little Prairie Owl sleeping between the two women for warmth, Big Hands and Little Flower sleeping together with Summer Moon's seventeen-year-old daughter, Little Beaver, and with her twelve-year-old half-blood daughter, Sun. Summer Moon, suffering from a painful chest cold, and having lost considerable weight because of her sickness, curled up alone, afraid of giving her "coughing curse" to one of the children. Her once-hefty body had shriveled alarmingly.

All night they lay trying to keep warm, what little sleep they did realize constantly interrupted by Summer Moon's coughing. Finally, toward morning, the coughing ceased. Medicine Wolf was glad her good friend had realized some relief, but when the morning sunlight told them it was time to again move on, she discovered with horror the real reason Summer Moon had stopped coughing. Sometime during the night she had died.

There was not even time for Medicine Wolf or the children to express their grief. Grief had become so constant to them that they were beginning to feel numb to it. Several women, including Medicine Wolf's aunt, Shining Woman, gathered together to lay Summer Moon's body on a ledge and cover it. Today the wind was not so strong, but the temperature was unbearably cold. The ground was too hard to try to bury the body, and there was no time to build a scaffold for it. Medicine Wolf touched Summer Moon's cheek, thinking what a sad life she had led because of her love for White Horse. She wished she could herself kill White Horse many times over. How she wanted and needed to weep, but she dared not, for fear she would never be able to stop.

They left the body and traveled on, always running and hiding, never sure when the soldiers would strike next; and for now, they were not even sure what had happened to Bear Paw and Standing Bear; or to Two Moons, or Bear Paw's father, Stands Tall. Stands Tall would be greatly grieved over Summer Moon's death, for he had taken her into his tipi and cared for her ever since she rejoined the Cheyenne almost nine winters past. Summer Moon's children wept openly as they ran, tears freezing on their cheeks.

It was three days before the men finally found them. Two Moons was not with them. "He was killed," Standing Bear told Shining Woman, who was herself old now, the lines of her face showing all the agony and suffering of the years. She sank to her knees and began wailing in grief over the loss of her husband. Medicine Wolf looked up at Bear Paw, only then realizing the pale look to him.

"You have been hurt!"

"We must keep going," he told her, grasping his stomach area. The fur at the front of his buffalo robe showed bloodstains, and Medicine Wolf knew the wound was very bad. She suspected then that he had forced himself to come this far only to see her once more.

The world around her became suddenly silent. There was no wind, no cold. There was no Smiling Girl, no wailing Shining Woman, no children. There was only Bear Paw, sitting so proudly on his Appaloosa, valiantly trying to stay alive long enough to get his woman to safety. She did not have to see the wound to know it was grave. How strangely cruel to have his life end this way, so quietly and slowly. A man like Bear Paw should die in the midst of a savage battle.

Medicine Wolf said nothing. When she moved, she felt as though she were only watching herself from some far-

off place. Someone managed to make Shining Woman get
up and walk. They continued on, hoping to lose the soldiers. With every step Bear Paw's Appaloosa took, blood
dripped into the snow as the life drained from its rider.

Tom trudged through the snow, giving his horse a rest
from his weight. *So,* he thought, *this is war.* He wanted
to hate the Indians as much as the other soldiers did for
what had happened to Custer and his men at the Little
Bighorn; but he had little doubt that Custer had ridden into
that disaster with all the pomp and daring of a man hell-
bent on realizing another glorious "victory." He had been
a man thirsty for glory and recognition; a man who, it was
rumored, had intended to run for president someday.

It would be a long time before anyone discovered what
had gone wrong that day. Maybe it would never be decided. Why had Custer split up his battalions and sent
Reno one way and Benteen another? And what had been
Crook's orders? Had there been any kind of communication between commanders?

There would be an investigation, inquiries. If and when
all the Indians involved could be gathered and brought to
the reservations, perhaps some of them could shed some
light on what had happened. But managing to find the
Sioux and Cheyenne had not been easy. They had been at
this for months now. He and the other men were tired,
and at the moment colder than they had ever been in their
lives.

Tom was eager to get back to Rebecca, hoping his poor
daughter would remember him, for he had been away many
months. This was the end of it. If he didn't discover what
had happened to Medicine Wolf by the time they reached
Canada, he would go back to Laramie and give it up. It
was obvious that Canada was where Sitting Bull and Crazy
Horse and the others were headed, but to do so in the dead
of winter was near suicide. They had found more bodies
dead from freezing than from the minor battles they fought
here and there.

He had more determination now, since finding the
Cheyenne woman stretched out on that ledge a ways back.

He was almost certain it had been Summer Moon, the wife of White Horse who had left with Medicine Wolf and her clan back in '68. She was thinner, but it was her face. He remembered it had pock marks on it, apparently from having measles or smallpox as a child, and he remembered she had had a little white scar on her chin from a beating White Horse had given her once.

He hoped that Medicine Wolf would be among those they hunted. The scouts were sure these were Cheyenne. The sad part was that they had to be suffering terribly from the cold, and there were little children with them. He had not enjoyed helping burn the tipis and supplies the Indians had left behind. One of the scouts had been bragging that he was sure he had shot the infamous Bear Paw himself. He claimed that although the famed warrior escaped, he surely was mortally wounded and could not last long, for he had shot him in the belly, just after Bear Paw had slain two other scouts and a soldier. "Nobody survives bein' gut-shot," the man had bragged.

Was it true? How awful for Medicine Wolf if it was! In spite of his months of searching, he almost hoped he never found either Medicine Wolf or her husband, for if they were not found, he would know that Bear Paw had lived and they had both escaped. This expedition, which originally had been a way for him to relieve his own grief and find some answers to the hatred and woe, had turned into a quest to save and help Medicine Wolf.

How sad that it should all come to this. In spite of the things her People had done to his own, it did not seem right that they should have to suffer so now. After all, they had merely been trying to hang on to what land and freedom was left to them. He felt sick inside that such a proud People should have to constantly run and hide now, that they should have to watch their own die such slow, cruel deaths from exposure and hunger. This was not the way it should be, not for men like Bear Paw, and not for such a beautiful, gentle, gifted woman as Medicine Wolf. He could only pray he would reach her before something terrible happened to her.

He put a hand to his chest to feel for her medicine bag.

Yes, it was still there. Somehow he would see that she got it back. Surely it would bring her great hope and joy.

Medicine Wolf was glad that the day had warmed slightly. She sat inside the tipi next to Bear Paw, who lay on a mat near the fire, pale from loss of blood, weak, hardly able to move. He had ridden as far as he could, until he fell from his horse. In spite of knowing the soldiers were still coming, they had made camp, Smiling Girl, fourteen-year-old Standing Bear, Big Hands, Little Flower, and little Prairie Owl. The others had gone on, surviving warriors helping old Shining Woman, as well as taking Summer Moon's children with them. Stands Tall, Bear Paw's father, stayed behind to help fight if soldiers came before his son died.

Bear Paw's breathing had grown shallow, and he could eat nothing. Everyone sat around inside the tipi, all quiet, even little Prairie Owl, who seemed to sense that something bad was happening to the man he called Father. Medicine Wolf had done all she could for Bear Paw's wound. She knew that she had been right that day they stood together high on the ridge with wolves all around them. Their days truly were numbered from then on. But they had lived as they chose to live, and they had kept their promise to live free or die in the effort.

Bear Paw opened his eyes, staring at her a moment, moving his lips as though to speak. She leaned closer, struggling against the urge to scream and weep. "They must go," he whispered. "Leave me. My time . . . is done. Save the children . . . my wife. Save my . . . sons."

She rose up slightly to meet his eyes, her own misty with tears, her throat aching fiercely. "I will tell them to go on," she whispered. "But I will stay here with you, my beloved. I will not leave you here alone." She touched his face; so many scars, yet so handsome. "I will pray and sing over you. If the soldiers come, let them. I am ready for them, for all I want now is to be with you, forever."

She looked at Stands Tall. "He says you must all go and save yourselves. You know that he is right."

"I will not leave him," Standing Bear said firmly.

Medicine Wolf watched him, thinking how very much like his father he was. Oh, yes, Bear Paw had had fine sons! This one would do his name proud.

"If you truly love him," she told the young man, "you will save yourself, and you will help save your brothers and sister. How many times have we told you that the children are the most important thing? What your father has suffered would all be for nothing if his children should die. If you can get over the next mountain, my son, you might catch up with Sitting Bull and make it to the land of the Queen Mother, where the soldiers cannot come after you. If you could do this, your father's heart would sing with joy. He will know, Standing Bear. He will know."

The young man stood shivering, tears on his cheeks. Oh, how she loved him, as much as if he had come from her own womb! How she loved all of them! How she hated the thought of never seeing them get any older, for she knew in her heart that once they left, she would not see them again. Her place was with Bear Paw.

She moved her eyes to Smiling Girl. "You gave yourself to Bear Paw in order to give him sons. Now it is your duty to save them. You must do as your husband says and leave, Smiling Girl. Bear Paw knows that your love will always be with him." She looked at a sniffling Big Hands and Little Flower. "You will bring joy to your father's heart if you go on to the land of the Queen Mother. If after a time you must come back and live on the reservation, you must always remember the Cheyenne way. You must make others remember your father's name and the pride and honor it carried. He was one of our People's greatest warriors, and my own joy has come from being his first wife. That meant more to me than being the holy woman and owning the wolf's paws. We have had many years of happiness, so do not be sad for us. We both knew long ago that it must be this way."

She moved her eyes to Standing Bear, wondering where she got the strength to speak, praying she could keep from breaking down before she said what must be said. She swallowed at the lump in her throat. "Your father could never live on a reservation, but you, my son, are young. It is possible you will have to learn a new way in order to survive, but it does not mean you must forget all that is Cheyenne about you."

"I will *never* live that way," Standing Bear retorted, tears now streaming down his face against his will.

"You will if it is the only way to save the children," Medicine Wolf told him sternly. "Once I spoke the same as you. I and my elders tried not to let it happen, Standing Bear. We tried to keep to the old ways, tried to keep our freedom. This is what happened for our efforts. We were wrong to think we could forever hang on to a way of life that was being stolen from us by a people who have greater numbers and mightier weapons and are superior to us in many ways. Just remember that they are not superior in wisdom, Standing Bear. They are not superior in spirit. They are a lost people, and one day it is *they* who will learn from *us*. We must save ourselves so that one day we can teach them, and save Grandmother Earth and the wild things that the white man so easily destroys. Do this one last great thing for your father, Standing Bear, for you will only show yourself to be a man of great wisdom and courage. Go and find Sitting Bull. Stay with him. He will help you. He will know when the time is right to come back to the sacred land. You will live on reservations, but Sitting Bull and the young men like yourself can *use* the white men's laws to protect the sacred hills. Sitting Bull will never sell one more inch of land to the government, and neither should you or any of the descendents of the Sioux or Cheyenne. The heart of Grandmother Earth beats there. Her blood runs in its streams. And when you hear the wolves singing to each other at night, you will know that your father and I are with you."

For several long seconds Standing Bear only stood shaking, his eyes fixed on his mother. He knelt beside his father then, leaning over to touch his cheek. "I will make you proud, Father."

Bear Paw managed to move his hand to touch his son's hair. "You have . . . already made me proud. Protect your . . . brothers and sister now. Take them north, my son. If you must come back . . . to the reservation life . . . one day . . . look for the . . . white man called . . . Tom Prescott. He will . . . help you.''

Standing Bear took his hand and squeezed it. He rubbed it against his tears. *''Ne-mehotatse, Ne-ho-eehe,''* he groaned. He rose and went out to prepare to leave.

All night the wind howled. Medicine Wolf lay beside her husband of twenty years, remembering those first few days after their wedding, both of them young and strong, so much in love. She remembered how she thought then that the world would always be as it was, beautiful and peaceful. She remembered how it felt to ride free, to lie beneath her husband and take him inside herself. She could almost smell the wildflowers, feel the wind in her face, shiver at the feel of the cold stream water when they would bathe and splash together. She thought of all the times he had made love to her after a victory over enemy Indians or soldiers.

They had had their time of greatness. She had been the holy woman of the Cheyenne, the Soldier Girl. She had been the chosen wife of Bear Paw, who had known many victories and had survived many wounds. Their love had brought them through many trials and triumphs. This was the last great test. She would not leave him, even if the soldiers came before he died.

He moved an arm around her, and she pulled the buffalo robe closer over them, breathing deeply of his scent, wanting to always remember it. She stroked his hair, moved her hand along his arm, still firm and muscled.

''I . . . see them,'' he said.

''What do you see, my love?'' she asked.

''I see my children. They . . . will live.''

''Ai. They will survive. One day they will get over their grief, but always they will speak of the great warrior Bear Paw, who was their father.''

''I know they will live,'' he whispered, ''because there are wolves . . . all around them . . . following . . . protecting.''

''Yes,'' she assured him. ''The Wolf Spirit will protect your children.''

He moved to look into her eyes. He touched her face. *"Ne-mehotatse, Na-htse-eme. Hena-haanehe."* "I love you, my wife," he had said. "It is ended."

He smiled and laid his head back down. His eyes closed, and his hand became heavy against her face.

Medicine Wolf could not move at first. How could she leave his side? To do so would mean she would never lie next to him again. To do so would mean she had to face the fact that the life had slipped away from him. She lay against his shoulder, leaving his hand at her face. "Sleep well, my love," she whispered.

Chapter Twenty-nine

"There goes one," a soldier said excitedly. He raised his rifle.

"Wait," Tom yelled. "It looks like a woman!"

"Who gives a damn? Them bastards all deserve to die, man, woman, child, whatever."

In desperation Tom charged into the soldier, knocking the rifle upward. A shot went off, cracking through the cold air. The soldier, furious, turned and landed the butt of the rifle into Tom's gut, and Tom grunted, falling backward into the snow. Tom heard another shot. Someone else was shooting at the fleeing figure.

"I think I got her," the man said excitedly. "She stumbled!"

Tom wanted to vomit at the words. Could it have been Medicine Wolf?

"She disappeared around behind those boulders up there," the man shouted.

"You men stay in order and fire when I tell you!" the

lieutenant in charge of the troops ordered. He walked up to Tom, helping him up. "You all right, Prescott?"

Tom rubbed his stomach, a searing pain stabbing at his side. "I might have a broken rib," he grunted.

"All right, everyone to your posts," the lieutenant told the others. He led Tom to his tent. "Sit down and take off your coat and shirt. I'll wrap your ribs," he told him. "That was a pretty stupid thing to do, you know. Not only is there nothing wrong with shooting at Indians, but you could have caused one of our own men to get hurt."

"I know. I'm sorry. I just can't help feeling sorry for them, Lieutenant." He enjoyed the warmth of the tent, which had no fire but was at least out of the wind, which made it seem warm compared to the cold outside. "Why don't we just give up and let them go? What the hell harm are they now? They're a broken, starving people. In time they'll come back to the Black Hills because they can't stay away. It's their home, their life's blood."

"I know. But I have my orders, Prescott, and having someone like you along doesn't make my job very easy. You're the one who should give up and go home—go home to your little girl. You don't belong here and you know it."

Tom winced as he removed his clothing. He managed to raise his arms enough to let the lieutenant wrap white strips of cloth around his middle. "You're already getting a hell of a bruise," he grumbled. The man tied off the cloth and met Tom's eyes. "Give it up, Prescott. Do you think the other men and I don't know the real reason you're here? There's no way of knowing if that medicine woman is with the ones we're chasing. She could be dead, for all you know, or already back at the reservation, where she belongs, if she has any sense at all."

Tom pulled his shirt back on, realizing it was colder in the tent than he first realized. "No," he answered. "She would never go to a reservation. Neither would Bear Paw, and she would never leave his side—never." He grimaced as he pulled on his coat.

"Well, from what I'm seeing through my telescope, I think the bulk of what was left of them got away. We'll go to the top of this damn ridge, and no farther. If we go on, by the time we reach the top of the next mountain it will be too late anyway. By then the rest of them will be in Canada, and there's nothing we can do about getting our hands on them then. We'll just have to wait until they come back, and they will." The lieutenant pulled his gloves back on. "One thing about these Indians, they can't stay away from their homeland for long. Something keeps drawing them back. Sitting Bull will come back, and the others will follow. Besides, the Canadian government has enough problems with their own Indians. They won't do anything to help the ones who go there from our country. Hunger will bring them back here quicker than anything, and they'll get hungry up there. They'll start thinking how if they come home, the government here will see that they get fed. The Indians can tolerate a lot of suffering and privation, but one thing they can't stand is to watch their children go hungry."

Tom wondered how the man could speak so matter-of-factly about the issue, as though they were tracking a herd of deer.

"Let's go," the man said.

Tom rose and followed him out, and the lieutenant directed that the tent be knocked down and packed. The morning sun had risen bright. There would be no snow today, and there was hardly any wind, but it would still be very cold.

Tom took hold of his horse's bridle, trying to forget the pain in his side. He was more concerned with who the fleeing Indian woman might have been. He cast a look of contempt at the soldier who had fired the second shot. The man wore the look of a hunter who had just bagged a big buck. The nausea returned to Tom's gut, and he grasped at it as he started out again with the others, wondering if he would ever again be able to feel his toes.

Medicine Wolf struggled as far as she could go. In her confused state, she had the urgent feeling that she must reach the top of the ridge. Just reach the top. She held her side and could feel the blood running down under her tunic over her back and bottom and the back of her right leg. The soldier's bullet from his long rifle had hit her from behind and exploded somewhere inside her, between her back and her belly. It was still in there, she could tell.

At least Bear Paw's body was lying high on this mountain, close to *Heammawihio*, God of the Sky. She had not been able to sing and wail over him as she so needed to do, for the soldiers would hear her and they might find and desecrate his body. She had laid his weapons all around him, and she had softly sung her prayer song. She had left beside him what little food she had, and what blankets she had, so that he would go to the great beyond with something to eat and something to keep him warm. He wore his winter moccasins, and he had his weapons if he needed them. She was glad he had died high on a mountain. It seemed fitting, for it was in the mountains that he had first found her. Now she would also die here, but not without a good fight. She had deliberately let herself be seen by the soldiers. She wanted to die this way, the same way Bear Paw had died, holding out against the enemy to the end, and she wanted to steer them away from Bear Paw's body.

There it was, the top of the ridge! From there she could see the next mountain, over which Smiling Girl and Bear Paw's children would now be traveling on their journey to freedom. Perhaps she could even see them! Why did she already feel so weak? She had to get to the top first! She climbed and stumbled, felt a terrible hot burning at her insides. Blood began to squish inside her right moccasin. She fell but managed to rise again. She climbed more, grasping at rocks, her hands beginning to bleed.

It was then she saw her, Old Grandmother! She was standing near a cave, beckoning her to come there, where she could rest. She smiled. Old Grandmother had returned from the dead to help her! She managed to climb over more rocks, slipping on wet snow, climbing again. She reached the cave, but Old Grandmother was not there now. She looked all around for her, then felt a terrible dizziness. She lay down to rest . . . just for a moment.

In no time sleep overcame her. She had no idea how long she had rested when she awoke again to realize to her amazement that it was no longer cold! A lovely warm breeze entered the cave from a sunny warmth outside. She rose, realizing that the pain and burning at her insides was gone! She felt wonderful! She moved toward the front of the cave, and there before her eyes was Old Grandmother again, two wolves standing at either side of her—Wolf and Little Wolf, but alive!

She smiled, walking to Old Grandmother and hugging her. The woman did not speak; she only held Medicine Wolf for a moment. Medicine Wolf knelt then to hug the wolves, her precious, precious wolves! When she rose she saw more people standing in the cave, her brother, Swift Fox; her mother and father, Star Woman and Arrow Maker. This was too wonderful! Surely the spirits had saved them all! Her ancestors were returning to reclaim the land! She embraced her brother, her parents, and her joy knew no bounds.

They all turned then, walking through the walls of the cave. Medicine Wolf was astonished and confused. She walked up and touched the walls, but they were hard, and she could not go through.

"You must give it up and come with me if you want to see them again," came a voice.

She turned to see Bear Paw standing at the cave entrance, his arm stretched out. He looked magnificent! He was young again, so handsome! He did not even have any scars! He wore his finest white buckskins and many eagle feathers. He looked as he had looked the day she became his wife. He was smiling that wonderful warm smile that made her want to laugh and sing.

She looked down at herself to see that she wore the white tunic she had worn on her wedding day. She studied her hands, which were young and velvety, showing no age lines, no sign of years of hard work. She looked back at Bear Paw, then turned to see her own body still lying on the floor of the cave. The woman there was older, but beautiful. She looked back at Bear Paw and he nodded.

"Death is not so bad," he told her. "You once said nothing could part us, not even death. You were right, Medicine Wolf. Come with me. Many await your presence, all your friends and loved ones who have been waiting for you to come to them."

She smiled, walking to the ledge of the cave. More wolves came then, surrounding them, protecting them. Bear Paw moved his arms around her from behind and held her close, and the sun shone brightly behind them. They stood there, high on the mountain, and again her vision was realized. But this time their days were not numbered. This time they were together forever, in a land where no white man walked, a land that was pure and green. She looked below to see a great herd of buffalo roaming freely. This was a good place, a place where now they could know the peace and beauty for which they had searched their whole lives.

"Come, my beloved," Bear Paw told her. He led her off the ledge and they walked on the air to two grand Appaloosas. They mounted the horses and rode toward a sun-filled Indian village that was spread out as far as the eye could see in the grasslands below, the buffalo ranging peacefully next to it.

In spite of his pain, Tom was determined to keep up with the others, who had found a tipi high on the ridge. "There's a body inside," one of the men shouted. "I think it's that one called Bear Paw, the one with all the scars!"

Tom pushed his way past them to find a soldier inside the tipi picking up one of Bear Paw's weapons. The buffalo robe that had covered his face was pulled away, and Tom's heart ached at the sight. It *was* Bear Paw! That could mean only that the fleeing woman they had seen earlier was Medicine Wolf!

He pulled his pistol. "Put that weapon back," he ordered the soldier. "Put it back, or so help me God I'll blow your guts away!"

The soldier looked at him in astonishment. "What the hell—"

"The man is dead! He was a great warrior! Have some respect for the dead, you bastard! Can't you see this was meant as his burial platform? Whoever left him here meant for all those things to be left *with* him! Now put the knife back!"

The lieutenant ducked inside to see Tom and the soldier facing off. He frowned, ordering the soldier to put the knife back. The soldier threw it down and stormed out of the tipi. Tom turned his eyes to the lieutenant. "You think that time and the cold have made me crazy, but I know exactly what I'm doing," he growled. "This is Bear Paw! I *knew* him! He was as great and important as Sitting Bull or Crazy Horse, or as General Crook or Custer or any other great leader! Don't let those men desecrate his grave! Please, Lieutenant, get them away from here! Just keep going!"

The lieutenant saw the tears in his eyes. He nodded. "I'm sick of this whole mess myself, Prescott. Put the gun away. No one is going to bother him."

The man left and Tom slowly put the gun back in its holster. He knelt down then, drawing the buffalo robe back over Bear Paw's face. He carefully put the knife back under the robe at his side. "You did yourself proud, Bear Paw," he managed to choke out. "Now I give you one more thing to take with you to the Great Beyond."

From his pocket he took the single wolf's paw Bear Paw had given him all those months before in retribution for attacking Elena's coach. He lifted the blanket to find Bear Paw's hand and he pressed the wolf's paw into the man's palm. "Take it back, Bear Paw. You should never have given it to me, but I understood why you did. Now it is yours again."

He wrapped his hand around Bear Paw's cold, stiff fingers and quietly prayed over him. He rose and went outside, where the rest of the men had been ordered to continue on. They were filing past the tipi, some of them glowering at Tom. He didn't care how much they talked or if they chose to beat him. He knew the last thing Medicine Wolf would want was for her husband's grave to be ransacked. He took hold of the reins of his own horse and followed the others.

A light wind whipped at the tipi. He wondered how long it would remain standing. It gave him a terribly lonely feeling to leave it, for he knew that Medicine Wolf must have stayed there with her husband until he died. What a painful thing it must have been for her.

The little procession climbed higher, until one man

spotted bloodstains in the snow. "Look here! Must be where she was when she was shot," he exclaimed.

The lieutenant examined the stains, then looked higher. He turned to Tom. "I'm going to let you follow the blood," he told the man. "My men and I will wait for you. If she's still alive, fire twice, and we'll come and see what we can do for her. If she's dead, fire once. We'll wait here until you pray over her and see that she's properly wrapped. There's not much else you can do. In this cold she can't be buried."

Tom's eyes teared. "Thank you, Lieutenant." He turned and took a blanket from his gear, then hurried past the others, who watched dumbfounded, angry that the lieutenant was leaving them out of the exciting moment. The lieutenant turned to his men. "The first man who tries to go up there, or who goes back down and tries to steal anything from that tipi, will be shot. Understood?"

"Yes, sir," they mumbled at different intervals.

"We'll camp here and wait for Prescott."

Tom made his way up the ridge, ignoring his pain. His feelings were mixed over what he would probably find. Medicine Wolf would want to die up here on this mountain where her husband was buried. She had probably deliberately let herself be seen so that the soldiers would shoot her. From all the blood he found, he was amazed she had gotten this far.

He struggled through snow and over slippery rocks, finally leaving his horse and going on up without it. His rib screamed with pain as he grasped boulders and shimmied higher, astounded that Medicine Wolf had chosen such a steep, difficult path. He finally reached a flat area where he could stand up. His eyes followed the bloodstains up a gentler slope and saw that they led to a cave. There in front of the cave was a pack of wolves, all watching him.

"So, even in death you protect her," he muttered. His eyes teared anew. He knew without looking that she was in that cave and probably dead. Wolves or not, he had to get to her. If it meant his life, he had to give back the medicine bag and its wolf's paws. He struggled up the path, keeping his eyes on the wolves. They made no ag-

ressive moves. As he got closer, he stood still a moment.
"I am blood brother to Medicine Wolf," he told them,
wondering if he was crazy to talk to the animals as though
they were human. "I mean her no harm."

They stood still, a couple of them wagging their tails.
Tom swallowed and moved forward, walking very slowly.
He reached the cave entrance, and still the wolves did not
advance. One simply lay down, another walked closer and
sniffed at him, then wandered away. Tom ducked inside.
As soon as his eyes adjusted to the darkness, he saw her
lying on the floor of the cave.

"Medicine Wolf," he groaned, walking closer. He
knelt beside her and knew without touching her that she
was dead.

So beautiful she still was! Strangely, she looked
younger, almost like a young girl!

"My darling Medicine Wolf," he sobbed. For several
minutes he could do nothing but weep, not just for how
this beautiful, intelligent woman who could have done so
much for her People had died alone on this mountaintop,
far from her homeland; but for all the Cheyenne, and the
Sioux and the Navaho and the Cherokee and Apache and
all the others. What had happened was as unstoppable as
breathing itself; yet he could not help wondering what kind
of curse his own people would one day suffer for what
they had done to these People who had once lived so free
and happy, so innocent of the greed and lust for wealth
and power that had finished them.

He took the medicine bag from inside his jacket. He
leaned over to gently put the cord that held it over her
head and positioned it against her heart. "I saved them
for you," he told her. "Darn near went broke getting these
back for you." He smiled through tears. "I gave Bear Paw
his wolf's paw. Now I give the rest back to you, Medicine
Wolf, with the beads and the eagle feathers. They're yours
again."

He hoped there truly was a special place where her
People went after death. He prayed she was there with Old
Grandmother and Bear Paw and all the others. He took
the blanket he had brought with him and carefully covered

her, taking one last look at her beautiful face before pulling the blanket over it.

He rose then, standing there a moment longer, letting the tears come. He had done what needed doing. She had her medicine bag. He turned to go out, and it was then he noticed the footprints, small and large moccasins, a man and a woman. He frowned, looking around the cave. There was only Medicine Wolf. He followed the footprints outside to a ledge that led to nowhere. If you were to walk off it, you would fall several hundred feet, yet the footprints led right to that ledge! He looked all around, leaned over to look below. There was nothing, no sign of any other footprints, no possible way a man and a woman could have walked off that ledge. . . .

Suddenly a wind hit his face. It was unbelievably warm, and he was sure he heard drumming and singing. He smiled. "So, you *do* still live," he whispered. "I love you, Medicine Wolf." He pulled out his pistol to fire one shot, then headed back down to the waiting soldiers.

The wolves gathered protectively around the cave entrance again. That night their mournful howling could be heard throughout the Bighorn mountains. The sacred woman of the Cheyenne was gone from the land . . . but only in body. Her spirit would forever live in Grandmother Earth, in the sweet summer winds, and in the heart of the great white wolf. . . .

"What is life? It is the flash of a firefly in the night. It is the breath of a buffalo in the winter time. It is the little shadow which runs across the grass and loses itself in the Sunset. . . ."

The dying words of Crowfoot, a Blackfoot Indian, as taken from *Touch the Earth*, by T. C. McLuhan (New York: Promontory Press, 1971)

From the author . . .

I hope you have enjoyed my story. Please feel free to write me at 6013 North Coloma Road, Coloma, Michigan 49038-9309. Send a #10, self-addressed, stamped envelope, and I will send you a bookmark and a newsletter telling you about other books I have written. Thank you so much!

Bibliography
of Resource Material

Berthrong, Donald. *The Southern Cheyennes*. Norman, Oklahoma: University of Oklahoma Press, 1963.

Burt, Struthers. *Powder River*. New York: Farrar & Rinehart, 1979.

Frazer, Robert. *Forts of the West*. Norman, Oklahoma: University of Oklahoma Press, 1965.

Graham, W. A. *The Custer Myth*. Norman, Oklahoma: University of Oklahoma Press, 1986.

Grinnell, George Bird. *The Fighting Cheyennes*. Norman, Oklahoma: University of Oklahoma Press, 1956.

Hungry Wolf, Adolf and Beverly. *Shadows of the Buffalo*. New York: William Morrow & Co., Inc., 1983.

Marshall, S.L.A. *Crimsoned Prairie: The Indian Wars*. New York: DeCapo Press, Inc., 1972.

Mech, L. David. *The Wolf*. Minneapolis, Minnesota: University of Minnesota Press, 1970.

Schultz, Duane. *Month of the Freezing Moon: The Sand Creek Massacre.* New York: St. Martin's Press, 1990.

Standing Bear, Luther. *My People, the Sioux.* Lincoln, Nebraska: University of Nebraska Press, 1975.

Stands In Timber, John. *Cheyenne Memories.* Lincoln, Nebraska: University of Nebraska Press, 1967.

Storm, Hyemeyohsts. *Seven Arrows.* New York: Ballantine Books, 1972.

Time-Life Books "Old West" series. *The Great Chiefs.* Text by Benjamin Capps. Alexandria, Virginia, 1975.

Utley, Robert M. *The Indian Frontier of the American West, 1846–1890.* Albuquerque, New Mexico: University of New Mexico Press, 1984.

Wellman, Paul I. *Death on the Prairie.* Lincoln, Nebraska: University of Nebraska Press, 1987.

FANFARE

Now On Sale
New York Times Bestseller
TEXAS! SAGE
☐ (29500-4) $4.99/5.99 in Canada
by Sandra Brown

*The third and final book in Sandra Brown's beloved TEXAS! trilogy.
Sage Tyler always thought she wanted a predictable, safe man-. . . until a
lean, blue-eyed drifter takes her breath, and then her heart away.*

SONG OF THE WOLF
☐ (29014-2) $4.99/5.99 in Canada
by Rosanne Bittner

*Young, proud, and beautiful, Medicine Wolf possesses extraordinary
healing powers and a unique sensitivity that leads her on an unforgettable
odyssey into a primeval world of wildness, mystery, and passion.*

LATE NIGHT DANCING
☐ (29557-8) $5.99/6.99 in Canada
by Diana Silber

*A compelling novel of three friends -- sophisticated Los Angeles women with
busy, purposeful lives, who also live on the fast track of romance and sex,
because, like lonely women everywhere, they hunger for a man to love.*

SUMMER'S KNIGHT
☐ (29549-7) $4.50/5.50 in Canada
by Virginia Lynn

*Heiress Summer St. Clair is stranded penniless on the streets of London,
but her terrifying ordeal soon turns to adventure when she captures the
glittering eyes of the daring Highland rogue, Jamie Cameron.*

FANFARE

On Sale in March

THE GOLDEN BARBARIAN

☐ (29604-3) $4.99/5.99 in Canada
by Iris Johansen

*is Johansen has penned an exciting tale. . . . The sizzling tension . . . is
e stuff which leaves an indelible mark on the heart." --Romantic Times*
"It's a remarkable tale you won't want to miss." --Rendezvous

MOTHERS

☐ (29565-9) $5.99/6.99 in Canada
by Gloria Goldreich

*he compelling story of two women with deep maternal affection for and
claim to the same child, and of the man who fathered that infant. An
honest exploration of the passion for parenthood.*

LUCKY'S LADY

☐ (29534-9) $4.99/5.99 in Canada
by Tami Hoag

*Brimming with dangerous intrigue and forbidden passion, this sultry tale
love . . . generates enough steam heat to fog up any reader's glasses."
--Romantic Times*

TOUCHED BY THORNS

☐ (29812-7) $4.99/5.99 in Canada
by Susan Bowden

*wonderfully crafted, panoramic tale sweeping from Yorkshire to Iceland
. . to . . .London. An imaginative tale that combines authenticity with a
rich backdrop and a strong romance." -- Romantic Times*

THE SYMBOL OF GREAT WOMEN'S
FICTION FROM BANTAM

Ask for these books at your local bookstore or use this page to order.

FN28 - 3/92